MURDER IN THE VINEYARD

BOOK 12 OF THE MAGGIE NEWBERRY MYSTERIES

SUSAN KIERNAN-LEWIS

SAN MARCO PRESS

Murder in the Vineyard. Copyright © 2018 by Susan Kiernan-Lewis. All rights reserved.

Life in Provence was just settling down for American ex-pat Maggie Newberry when a dead body shows up in her vineyard...with a knife in its back. Curious to learn about who the victim is, Maggie's motivation skyrockets when her husband Laurent is arrested for the murder.

With the evidence piling up against Laurent and witness after witness coming forward to swear he is the killer, can Maggie find the real murderer and will she find the cabal behind the campaign to send Laurent to prison for life? And can she do it before her life and those of her dear ones come crashing down around her?

Books by Susan Kiernan-Lewis

The Maggie Newberry Mysteries
Murder in the South of France
Murder à la Carte
Murder in Provence
Murder in Paris
Murder in Aix
Murder in Nice
Murder in the Latin Quarter
Murder in the Abbey
Murder in the Bistro
Murder in Cannes
Murder in Grenoble
Murder in the Vineyard
Murder in Arles
Murder in Marseille
Murder in St-Rémy
Murder à la Mode
Murder in Avignon
Murder in the Lavender
Murder in Mont St-Michel
Murder in the Village
Murder in St-Tropez
Murder in Grasse
Murder in Monaco
Murder in Montmartre

Murder in the Villa
A Provençal Christmas: A Short Story
A Thanksgiving in Provence
Laurent's Kitchen

The Claire Baskerville Mysteries
Déjà Dead
Death by Cliché
Dying to be French
Ménage à Murder
Killing it in Paris
Murder Flambé
Deadly Faux Pas
Toujours Dead
Murder in the Christmas Market
Deadly Adieu
Murdering Madeleine
Murder Carte Blanche
Death à la Drumstick
Murder Mon Amour

The Savannah Time Travel Mysteries
Killing Time in Georgia
Scarlett Must Die

The Stranded in Provence Mysteries
Parlez-Vous Murder?
Crime and Croissants
Accent on Murder
A Bad Éclair Day
Croak, Monsieur!
Death du Jour
Murder Très Gauche
Wined and Died
Murder, Voila!
A French Country Christmas
Fromage to Eternity

The Irish End Games
Free Falling

Going Gone
Heading Home
Blind Sided
Rising Tides
Cold Comfort
Never Never
Wit's End
Dead On
White Out
Black Out
End Game

The Mia Kazmaroff Mysteries
Reckless
Shameless
Breathless
Heartless
Clueless
Ruthless

Ella Out of Time
Swept Away
Carried Away
Stolen Away

1

PARENTAL OBLIGATIONS

Maggie narrowed her eyes as she regarded the ancient elevator in the stairwell.

It looked like some kind of medieval torture chamber—not something you'd willingly put yourself inside of with any hope of it taking you anywhere except maybe to an early grave.

She sighed and turned back to the late eighteenth century building where her parents' apartment was.

She'd made a vow that she wouldn't ask her mother how it was her father had gotten trapped in the elevator in the first place. Elspeth had enough on her plate without the burden of guilt at having allowed her beloved—albeit confused—husband to get into an ancient elevator where he promptly panicked once the wrought iron gate automatically closed on him. His hysterical screams had brought Maggie's mother running but not before he'd broken his wrist trying to free himself.

Maggie stepped back into the apartment and instantly felt a wave of exhaustion.

Her mother was sitting at a small breakfast table next to the palladium window that overlooked rue Granet, a cooling cup of coffee in front of her.

As soon as they'd gotten back from the hospital John Newberry and his new cast had retired to take a nap as if nothing had happened. As if his wife hadn't lost ten years of her life when she saw him clawing at the interior of the elevator cage, his eyes wide with terror. As if his daughter hadn't raced from her home twenty miles to the southwest—breaking every imaginable speed limit in the process—envisioning horrors beyond reckoning once she arrived in Aix.

Maggie glanced around the apartment. After much coaxing, her parents had finally agreed the summer before to rent a two bedroom apartment in the square off the *Place de l'Hôtel de Ville*. Maggie's father's Alzheimer's seemed to be worsening by the month and her mother could no longer handle him or his daily litany of crises on her own. Maggie had done everything she could to make their move from Atlanta to France as easy as possible.

So far it had been a weekly disaster that had Maggie racing back and forth to Aix—all the while waiting for the other deadly shoe to drop.

Elspeth was herself debilitating before Maggie's eyes. Her French was rudimentary at best which made even simple matters like shopping or dealing with the electric company insurmountable. Added to the fact that John was so needy and unpredictable, it was no wonder Maggie's mother looked like she was coming apart at the seams.

"You okay?" Maggie asked as she shut the door quietly behind her.

"No," Elspeth said, looking into her coffee cup. "I don't know how much more of this I can take."

Maggie sat down with her. "Do you want me to stay?"

She'd been with them since early that morning. Laurent had to take the children to school and pick them up and while he hadn't complained, Maggie knew it hadn't been convenient. He had no fewer than two hundred hectares of vineyard to manage now and twenty workers to oversee. Plus, he was in the process of building a series of small single-family dwellings on their property and was working with platoons of area subcontractors and builders on an hourly basis.

On top of that Maggie had her own work. The newsletter she'd begun three years ago had grown to nearly twenty thousand subscribers. Maggie loved the work and she was proud that it brought in money—which it wouldn't continue to do if she didn't constantly create original content. She could hardly do that at the rate she was burning up the asphalt between St-Buvard and Aix.

"No, darling," Elspeth said with a sigh. "You have your own life. I feel terrible calling you all the time."

"That's what I'm here for, Mom."

"I just keep thinking it will get better."

"I know."

Elspeth took in a long breath and smiled bravely at her daughter. "I'm fine," she said. "We're fine."

"If you're sure. Then I think I'll head home."

"Yes, please, darling. Go. My love to Laurent and the children."

"Make sure Dad takes his pain meds for his wrist."

"I will."

"And I saw an ad on the bulletin board downstairs about a French conversation group that meets at the Uni Cafe. Did you see it?"

Elspeth looked at her in confusion and Maggie was instantly sorry she'd mentioned it. Her mother couldn't leave her father to go to some French language meet-up—not even if learning the language better and meeting people would do Elspeth a world of good. It just wasn't manageable.

"Never mind," Maggie said, leaning over and kissing her mother. "Call me if you need me. Okay? Promise?"

"I promise, darling," her mother said, her smile tremulous and unsure.

2

FLAG ON THE PLAY

Laurent watched the young people weave through the tight rows of vineyard. The wind was blowing in sharp angry gusts that flapped the young girls' head scarves like colorful flags. The sun was fading and the temperature had fallen rapidly. It was edging toward late afternoon.

There was little to do at this time of year. The harvest was done and it was too early for the pruning and general field maintenance that would busy him and his crew as winter ended and they got closer to spring. In spite of that, Laurent liked to have the young people from *l'Abbaye de Sainte-Trinité* monastery come over even if it was just to walk the fields.

Loving the land—the *terroir*—and the treasures it produced came from knowing it in all seasons and all kinds of weather. It made the workers more in tune with the planting and growing, not just the harvest. They may not own this land but Laurent's intention was to make sure they felt as if they belonged to it. Only then would they learn to love the work. Only then would they get the best possible product in the end. And only then would they truly know their new life's work *in their bones*.

Laurent enjoyed hearing their laughter and sounds of general merriment as the group walked the field. Most of the young people from *l'Abbaye de Sainte-Trinité* had lived as homeless refugees for months before coming to Frère Jean's monastery and before Laurent hired them to work his fields. With few exceptions they had eagerly embraced farming and wine-making as vocations. The older refugees at the monastery—the unemployed artisans and day laborers—typically worked the monastery garden or hired out as contract workers to the surrounding villages.

It was the young people who were the future of wine-growing in Provence, Laurent thought as he watched them amble through the manicured rows of *Bourboulence* and *Grenache blanc,* their voices rising and falling over the tidy, manicured rows.

"*Tais toi!*" a harsh voice suddenly barked out from deep in the vineyard.

Frowning, Laurent turned in the direction the voice had come from. He had already strongly suggested on more than one occasion that Henri Dupree—the owner of the voice—should no longer accompany the young people to the vineyard, although Laurent had yet to absolutely ban him.

At fifty, the man was too old and too soft to endure the rigors of harvest time in the summer and he was too intractable to learn from Laurent the rest of the year.

Labor in the vineyard was hard work. Hours spent bent over picking grapes for hours on end—usually in the punishing heat—made the work a better fit for the young with their abundance of exuberance and energy and their ability to recover from a grueling day's work.

As Laurent walked through the vineyard, he heard two of the younger men—teenagers really—yell out in dismay. Laurent quickened his pace.

This part of the vineyard—the original hectares he'd inherited from his uncle—was divided by a wide tractor road. It was furthest from the monastery but abutted Domaine St-Buvard,

Laurent's imposing country *mas* that fronted the village road. This section wasn't large and one could usually see down each row in just a few minutes.

Laurent narrowed his eyes as he walked through the staked, depleted stalks and vines until he saw the heads of the young men and women gathered around the scuffle. Turning down the last corner of neatly staked vines, Laurent saw the man at the far end of the row.

Herni Dupree was barrel-chested with a crooked nose and a powerful jaw shaded by several days' growth of beard. He stood now holding his fists over a young boy who sat on the ground with a bloody nose.

Instantly Laurent felt heat flushing through his body as he strode purposefully to the man.

This wasn't the first time Dupree had picked on one of the littlest in the group.

But by God it would be the last.

3

BEST LAID PLANS

As Maggie left her parents' apartment, she couldn't stop thinking about her mother. She did not know when she'd seen her mother so vulnerable. Elspeth Newberry was hard as rocks. She was tough. She was the grand dame of Buckhead, all Southern lace and magnolia leaves on the outside and Stone Mountain granite inside through and through.

Except that was not who Elspeth had been these last few months.

Living with Maggie's father as he descended bit by bit into dementia had taken its toll on Elspeth. She looked haunted and wary as if waiting for bad news to come any minute.

After walking down rue Aude and then rue Nazareth past the tourist shops and expensive shoe shops of Aix-en-Provence, Maggie emerged onto Cours Mirabeau. She hesitated for a moment and checked the time on her phone before crossing the street and taking her place in the line snaking slowly into Bechard's *patisserie* off the main drag.

There were few things that could take the annoyance out of Maggie having to pull Laurent away from his vineyard, but a bag of glazed *canelés* from Bechard's was definitely one of them.

Maggie didn't know what Laurent was making for dinner tonight but it was a reasonable assumption that *canelés* would finish up any meal, any time.

Now that the village of St-Buvard had its own *boulangerie* again—after nine years of not—Maggie didn't waste time thinking about bringing home a baguette for dinner. As good as the new St-Buvard bakery was, there was only one Bechard's, she thought as she approached the display case with its dazzling array of pastries and other delectable baked treats.

A few moments later, carrying a shopping bag full of amazing aromas—she couldn't pass up the *éclairs* or the *chouquettes*, could she?—Maggie hurried down the street to where she'd parked the car. As she walked, her phone rang and she saw it was Grace.

Her best friend Grace Van Sant had moved to St-Buvard six months earlier with her twelve year old daughter Zouzou to run the *gîte* that Laurent had created when he bought Danielle and Eduard's old *mas*. Most of the spring and a good deal of the summer had been taken up with renovations on the house and garden and Grace had only just now begun to have guests in the bed and breakfast she'd named *Dormir*.

"Hey," Maggie said, balancing the phone between her shoulder and ear as she used the keyless entry on her key fob to unlock the car. "I was just thinking of you."

"That must be because you're at a bakery, am I right?" Grace said.

"Bechard's."

"Oh, my God, I hate you. What are you doing in Aix? Your parents?"

"Yeah, my Dad got trapped in the apartment elevator and broke his wrist."

"Oh, darling, that's terrible. Is he okay?"

"As he'll ever be. How about you?"

"Losing my mind is all. Danielle and Jean-Luc are here scrubbing and running around like mad. Jean-Luc is working with

Gabriel to fix the garden gate. I just know someone is going to fall through it and sue me."

"Oh, that's right, you've got a group of Americans coming this week, don't you?"

"Exactly. It's impossible to get Gabriel to work at the best of times but he's positively somnolent this week. I'm truly losing my mind."

"It'll all be fine, Grace," Maggie said as she got in her car and maneuvered down the street crowded with pedestrians and onto the roundabout encircling the famous Dolphins fountain. "Can I do anything to help?"

"As if you don't have your own hands full. No, I just needed a break from all the mayhem to hear about someone else's life. How's Laurent doing with the houses? Any ready for flush toilets yet?"

Maggie laughed as she turned onto the route heading toward the A7 and home.

Laurent's ongoing project to create housing for the people who worked his vineyard was a passion for him that Maggie had rarely seen in her husband.

"He's actually got a few done," Maggie said. "They're so tiny, Grace. They look like playhouses. Mila keeps begging to have one for her very own. But they're fully equipped with kitchens, showers, toilets, the works."

"Where are they exactly?"

"They're pretty close to you. On the back twenty hectares of Eduard and Danielle's old property."

When Danielle had been married to Eduard she'd lived in the old mansion, which was falling down even then, and she rarely came into the village. Since Eduard's incarceration and the subsequent divorce followed by her marriage to Jean-Luc, Danielle had blossomed.

Although she had not kept in touch with Eduard during his

imprisonment, he had left the house and vineyard to her when he died last spring.

Laurent bought the house and property from Danielle with the intention of turning the land—long gone to seed—into a viable vineyard once more and the house into a working bed and breakfast.

Grace needed the work and both she and Zouzou needed to come back to France. While Laurent was the owner of the *gîte*, Grace ran it and through it was able to support herself and Zouzou.

"When I have five minutes to breathe you can take me out to look at them," Grace said. "Gotta go now. Danielle is holding up something that looks like a dripping pipe. Oh, God. I hope not."

"Good luck," Maggie said with a laugh and then disconnected.

She put music on in the car and let the miles and the tension of the day—her parents, the emergency room—all just roll away.

It was late October and the landscape was bleak and barren, the temperature downright cold. It was of course already dark even though it was only a little after six in the evening.

When she was five miles from the exit that would take her home, she called Laurent. He picked up immediately. She could hear the noise of a TV on and children's laughter in the background and her heart soared. It sounded so warm and cheery there.

"Where are you?" he asked. She'd given him an app for his phone to enable him to track her but Laurent was seriously anti-tech and he never used it.

"Five miles from St-Buvard then another two after that," she said. "I got *chouquettes*."

"From Bechard's?"

She could hear the happy surprise in his voice.

"Where else?" she said, feeling very proud of herself.

"It was a hard day with your parents?"

"Let's just say I'll be glad to be home."

"And when you are home I will tell you great news about the co-op asking to buy wine from the monastery."

"I think you just did."

Almost all the grapes grown on Domaine St-Buvard—now enlarged by the additional one hundred and sixty hectares—were fermented and aged in the cellars of *l'Abbaye de Sainte-Trinité* which had a medieval wine cellar. Laurent had invested in stainless steel fermentation vessels and oak barrels for the monastery and had hired several of the formerly homeless refugees living there to learn the art and skill of making wine. Getting the co-op to buy the wine was very good news for the credibility of Laurent's label—and for the future employment prospects of the people now living at the monastery.

"*Maman* is nearly home," he said to one of the children. "Go set the table."

"What's for dinner?" Maggie asked as she saw the exit off the A7.

"*Sole Meunière*," Laurent said.

"That sounds amazing."

"And for you, *ma chérie*, a foot massage and a glass of champagne after your very difficult day."

"I love you, Laurent." Maggie felt a lightness in her limbs as she said the words. Sometimes it was hard for her to believe that she'd met this mysterious, sexy man in the middle of a long con he was pulling in the south of France where she had gone to try to find her missing sister. That was ten years ago and amazingly the experience had turned into the greatest love of her life.

Not to mention two darling children.

Her phone buzzed indicating another call was coming in and instantly her stomach began to churn.

"Let me call you back, Laurent," she said. "My mother's calling."

"*Bon.* See you in a few moments."

Maggie disconnected and then took the call. "Mom?"

"Maggie, I need you to come back," her mother said breathlessly.

Maggie instinctively slowed the car even though there was no exit for at least another mile.

"What's happened?" Maggie said her shoulders tight with mounting fear.

"Your father is having trouble breathing," her mother said shrilly. "And I can't get him to wake up!"

"Hang up, Mom and call 999," Maggie said.

"I can't!" her mother wailed. "I can't speak French!"

"Okay. Just stay calm. I'll call them and meet you at the hospital."

"Yes, yes, thank you, thank you," Elspeth said, relief filling her voice.

Maggie disconnected and quickly called the emergency number, giving the problem and her parents' address. When her exit came, she took the off ramp and immediately turned and climbed onto the return ramp heading back to Aix.

4

READY OR NOT

The sun was sinking low behind Cézanne's Mountain—its light filtering through the leafy canopy of the plane trees to cast a dappled shade on the cobblestones in front of the main chapel of the monastery where Guy sat with Noelle.

A handsome young man with prominent cheekbones and a wide mouth with full lips, Guy was used to girls being open to his offers—pretty much any of his offers. The fact that Noelle Dupree was without argument the most exquisite creature on the face of the earth and somehow immune to his charms made her all the more irresistible to him.

He sat next to her now as they waited for the monastery bell that would announce dinner and wondered how she would react if he were to take her hand.

Guy had come to the monastery from Spain three months ago where he'd gotten day work until it ran out. Noelle had arrived at about the same time.

From the moment Guy had laid eyes on her, he knew she was the one—his *amie de coeur*.

Now if he could just convince *Noelle* of that.

A classic beauty, Noelle had smooth alabaster skin to set off the most luminous blue eyes. Her dark hair was long and draped around her shoulders like silk. When Guy knew she wasn't aware of him, he loved to watch her walk across the monastery grounds or in the gardens—her hair swinging like a hypnotizing metronome.

"Will you sit with me at dinner?" he asked her as he had nearly every evening since she'd arrived at the monastery.

She giggled and stretched out her long legs in front of her.

"You always ask me that," she said. "I like to eat with my friends."

The monastery had given refuge to a family with two daughters near Noelle's age. Guy had often seen them walk together to the vineyards. He couldn't imagine her friends enjoyed being compared to Noelle. She was so beautiful she would make the Madonna look plain.

"Am I not your friend?" he asked hopefully.

"You are welcome to join us," she said teasingly, knowing full well that dinner with three giggling girls would not be an offer most men would accept. Especially not someone as moonstruck as Guy. He didn't trust Noelle's friends not to tease him right to his face.

He felt a stab of humiliation as he remembered Noelle's father who had done exactly that the morning before. Guy had been caught staring at Noelle as she and the other girls gathered their baskets to go to the garden when the old bastard jumped out of nowhere.

"See something you like?" Monsieur Dupree had sneered. And when Guy had answered with a fierce and crimson blush, it only made it worse.

"Keep away from her," Dupree had snarled. "Or I'll tell Frère Jean you've been buggering the goats."

Guy had been so appalled by the threat—which he had every reason to believe Dupree would make good on—that he'd stalked off to the sounds of the old bastard's raucous laughter behind him.

Even now as he and Noelle sat on the stone bench—*perfectly innocently!*—he kept a sharp eye peeled for her father.

"Maybe a walk after dinner then," he said, knowing the dinner bell would ring at any moment and his time with Noelle would be finished for the day if he didn't do something quickly.

"Did you forget I'm moving into one of the *petites maisons*?" she asked, her face flushed with pleasure and anticipation.

He had forgotten. Or he hadn't wanted to remember. Laurent Dernier was building small huts to house the workers for his vineyard. Guy knew that the imposing *vigneron* was working with Frère Jean to ensure that families had enough room at the monastery and that meant the young people were going to live in the small hostel-like homes on the man's property.

When Guy had been asked if he would like to move into one of the small houses he'd immediately declined because Noelle was at the monastery.

It hadn't occurred to him that when *she* was asked the same thing she would jump at the chance.

But why wouldn't she? Her father wasn't just a bastard to every living thing around him, he was also a wretch to his own daughter. Of course she would leave when the chance came.

Tonight would be Noelle's first night in her little cottage, nearly two miles from the monastery. Much too far for any after-dinner walks.

"It is so beautiful," Noelle gushed happily. "It is small but there are three beds and a tiny *cuisine* and a bathroom, too."

"Sounds like it will be very crowded with two other people," Guy grumbled.

Noelle laughed, the sound like silver bells on the breeze. "It will be exactly perfect for me," she said happily.

Before Guy could think of any other reason that she might

stay after dinner, the monastery meal bell rang—muffled but insistent.

Noelle jumped to her feet at the same time that Guy—not knowing he was going to do it—grabbed her hand. She twisted around to look at him, a suddenly annoyed look on her face.

"Stop it, Guy," she said firmly.

He dropped her hand.

Her face cleared then and she turned to hurry toward the refectory.

"Better hurry or all the wine will be gone," she called out to him over her shoulder.

He watched her go, his lips pressed tightly together as he fought the twin emotions of disappointment and longing.

5

A WING AND A PRAYER

Winter in Provence arrived early wearing spikes and Brillo pads, Maggie thought as she used her shoulder to shove open the heavy wooden door to her parents' apartment. As cold as it had felt at eight o'clock last night when she'd arrived at the hospital, it felt much worse at two a.m. arriving back at the apartment without her father.

She felt her mother's presence, stiff and numb behind her.

The moment Maggie had arrived at the hospital her mother had immediately handed over all responsibility for her father's care to her. Elspeth sat mute and childlike while Maggie spoke with the doctors and maneuvered the sometimes complicated pathways of the French health care system.

Her father had rallied long enough to snarl at any and all who were attempting to make him more comfortable and in spite of the overall stress of the event, Maggie found herself swearing on everything she held dear that she would never devolve into the kind of cantankerous curmudgeon she was witnessing today.

Her father—the man she loved who was buried deep under the layers of confusion and disorientation of the disease that gripped him—would never have behaved like this. Maggie knew how horrified John Newberry would be if he ever found out he'd treated these kind and well-meaning nurses and aides as he had.

But of course he would never find out. Because even after he was released home from the hospital he was never really coming back to them.

Maggie punched the button for the lift and turned to her mother.

"Do you feel like a cup of tea?" she asked.

"I just feel so helpless," Elspeth said quietly.

Maggie knew that was her fault. She'd insisted her parents come to France if they wanted to be near her—which of course meant them having to navigate the French health care system with this debilitating soul-sucking, heart-breaking disease without even knowing the language.

Maggie had taken her mother's helplessness over her father's illness and magnified it a thousand fold by making her come to France to deal with it.

They rode the antique elevator in silence. Maggie unlocked the apartment door, noting that even this task Elspeth had relegated to her. The burden not only of watching her dear Southern gentleman papa disintegrate into an ill-mannered churl and someone she didn't know steamrolled Maggie and was joined by the pressure of the job she'd signed on for—taking care of *both* her father and her mother during the most stressful time in their lives.

Once inside the apartment Maggie checked her phone to see if there were any more texts from Domaine St-Buvard but she knew everyone was long asleep.

Her father—the cause of their dreadful day—was being kept overnight for observation and now slept soundly and at peace in his hospital bed.

Maggie dropped the apartment keys on the kitchen table and went to turn on the electric kettle. She knew she should at least try to get some sleep or she would be useless tomorrow. But she also knew if she tried she would just lie in bed wide awake staring at the ceiling.

She went to the refrigerator and pulled out a large wedge of Comté cheese that she'd bought the week before. She'd encouraged her mother to visit the local bakery for her daily bread but Elspeth never ventured out so Maggie had taken to hiring one of the neighbors to drop off a fresh baguette each day. She found it now—untouched and hard as a stone—still on the kitchen counter and wondered not for the first time if her parents were eating properly.

Quickly preparing a plate for her and her mother, she decided to eschew the hot tea after all in favor of a glass of wine. She set out the cheese and some crackers on the table and poured two glasses of the local Côtes du Rhône.

"He'll be okay," Maggie said as she placed a chunk of cheese with a dollop of tapenade and realized as she poised it in front of her mouth that she was suddenly starving.

Elspeth smiled and reached for her wine. It was a sad smile, a smile that signaled an appreciation of Maggie's attempts to console her.

"Have you heard from Ben?" Maggie asked. Her brother had had some legal troubles in the past year and he'd lost his job at the Atlanta law firm he'd belonged to since he graduated from law school. But Maggie knew him to be a loving son—that is, when he remembered he had parents.

"He has his own problems," Elspeth said.

Yeah, don't we all? Maggie thought sourly. *That doesn't mean you don't rise up when your loved ones need you.* She banished the ungenerous thought and leaned back into her chair to savor her wine.

"I know you're annoyed with your brother," Elspeth said. "But not everything is what it seems."

"What do you mean?" Maggie said, narrowing her eyes. "Is something going on with Ben that I don't know about?"

"You can't know everything," Elspeth said cryptically.

"Are you keeping something from me?"

"No, I mean *one* can't know everything. Just because something looks a certain way, doesn't mean it is."

"If you say so." Maggie got up to retrieve the bag of *chouquettes* she'd bought earlier at Bechard's and brought the bag to the table.

"When you were a girl," Elspeth said, extricating a *croustade* from the bag and slowly licking her fingers of the sugar flakes that scattered across the table top, "you were always impatient to size something up and move on."

Maggie wasn't surprised to hear her mother say this. Even Laurent had mentioned more than once that Maggie tended to judge a book without bothering to read its title first.

"Whenever you would take standardized tests in school," Elspeth went on, "you did well on every part except the listening part. Did you know that?"

Maggie shook her head.

"Your teacher said that like many smart children, you had a habit of scanning the instructions and immediately jumping to an assumption before answering the question—basically without reading the instructions."

Maggie had to admit it did sound like something she'd do.

"You're always in such a hurry, darling."

"Maybe so, Mom, but you know what? I've learned that nine out of ten times if something looks like a duck and sounds like a duck, it's almost always a duck."

"And that's fine," Elspeth said, smiling sadly at her daughter, "unless you've gambled something valuable on that tenth time."

6

HELL TO PAY

The monk frowned as he looked at the paper in his hand. A Benedictine monk and head of the order at *l'Abbaye de Sainte-Trinité*, Frère Jean was slight, of less than medium stature, with a thick head of prematurely white hair.

The young man standing in front of his desk in the rectory was large for his age—if the note the boy had handed him was to be believed—only seventeen. His hair was plaited in dreadlocks to his shoulders, his complexion olive and his eyes so dark they looked as if they had no pupils. Not attempting to hide his dubious heritage—even if he could—the idiot boy seemed intent in reveling in it.

A good-looking boy, Frère Jean admitted, but there was something unsettling about him. The monk looked at the paper again. The handwriting was nearly illegible. Frère Jean could barely make out the words—most of which were actually misspelled.

"You say this came from your last employer?" Frère Jean said.

"Yes, *mon frère*," the boy Pierre said with a smirk.

Frère Jean looked up from the paper.

Would he openly mock me? Frère Jean wondered. While it was true the core of his mission did not require referrals—*all of course are welcome*—even Frère Jean knew that some were a little more welcome than others.

The boy was of Romani descent and while the monastery's population of homeless was composed of refugees from all over —Spain, Morocco, Syria, as well as other areas of France—this boy would be discriminated against by all. About that Frère Jean had no doubt.

And for better or worse—and Frère Jean would bet on worse —the boy didn't look to be the kind who would take those insults well.

"All must work here," Frère Jean said.

"I am not afraid of work."

Frère Jean tapped the soiled scrap of paper with a pen as if in thought.

"There is no fraternization among unmarried people while you are with us," Frère Jean said. "You may not leave the monastery without permission and that will not be given after seven in the evening. You will be required to attend mass. You will be required to help in any way you are asked—even if it is not your assigned job."

"Suits me," Pierre said with a shrug.

Frère Jean did not like him. The very thought prompted a spasm of guilt when the realization came to him. A foreboding sensation settled across his shoulders and he had to fight not to visibly shiver. In the two years since the monastery had opened its doors to the homeless and the refugees from the world's wars and strife, there had been remarkably few altercations and even less of the kind of gut reaction he was picking up now from this boy.

Evil.

Suddenly loathe to touch it again. he pushed the scrap of paper away using his pencil.

Pierre snorted and Frère Jean looked at him. The boy was clearly ridiculing his discomfort.

"You will keep yourself clean here," the monk said. He could smell the boy in wafts of rank odor from where he stood. "Frère Alponse will show you where to bathe."

"Is that it?" Pierre asked, his lips turned up in a cruel, mocking sneer.

"You will work in the stables," Frère Jean said. "Do you know anything about livestock?"

"How much do I need to know to shovel shit?" Pierre said before turning and walking out of the room.

Frère Jean heard the door to the rectory slam shut and he felt a swell of relief. As he glanced up at a religious relic on the mantle over his small fireplace, he felt the warmth and peace that he normally enjoyed in this room come rushing back to him.

It made him realize with a small shock that that peace had been palpably missing for the whole time that the Devil had stood in the room with him.

7

BELOW THE BELT

The next afternoon Maggie finally arrived home from Aix, tired and achy. She'd ended up sleeping until late morning at her parents' apartment and then went to bring her father home from the hospital. Because her father had gone straight to bed when he got home, Elspeth insisted Maggie go home to her family.

After making sure there was enough food in the apartment to last her parents until she returned in a couple of days, Maggie made the hour-long drive back to Domaine St-Buvard. Unlike the last time, she did not put music on. If it weren't for the fact that she was afraid to be out of touch with Laurent in case something happened to one of the kids, she would have turned her phone off, so suffused with dread was she that her mother would call her again.

She pulled into the long gravel drive of Domaine St-Buvard, the *mas* she shared with Laurent. There were few times when she came home that she didn't remember the first time she'd seen the large farmhouse.

A two hundred year old country manor home, Domaine St-

Buvard was built with materials from the rough landscape with stones of varying sizes stacked into sloping knee walls, corralling thick hedges of lavender and junipers.

Cherry-colored roof tiles covered the entire roof and the bright blue shutters, handmade in the village over a hundred years ago, were latched with ironware forged in the seventeen hundreds. A black wrought-iron railing framed a second-story Juliette balcony jutting out over the front door.

Maggie parked the car and hurried into the house. The afternoon sun had dropped and she shivered until she reached the house.

She stepped into the foyer—almost severe in its simplicity except for the intricate Moroccan mosaic tiling underfoot. The living room directly off the foyer was covered almost the entire ground level of the farmhouse. It was anchored at one end by a massive fireplace. French doors at the other end led to the garden.

This afternoon a fire was in the hearth and a single glass of wine sat on the heavy hand-carved coffee table in front of the couch.

"*Maman!*" a little girl's voice called out and Maggie turned to see her six year old daughter scampering toward her from the kitchen.

Maggie knelt on one knee and scooped the running child into her arms.

"I missed you, *Maman!*" Mila said kissing Maggie's cheek.

"I missed you too, angel," Maggie said, standing up as Laurent came into the room, a dishtowel over one broad shoulder.

"*Ça va?*" he asked as she released Mila and moved to him. She slipped into his arms and instantly felt his strength like an infusion of courage and stability into her.

"*Now* it is," she said. "Where's Jemmy?"

"I am here, *Maman!*" the little boy called out from the kitchen. "Helping Papa make you a special dinner!"

Laurent gave her arm a squeeze and nodded toward the stairs. "Go take your bath," he said. "I will bring your wine up to you."

"Where's Petit?" Maggie said, looking around. She'd had the little dog for the entire time she'd lived in France and there hadn't been a day the dog hadn't greeted her at the door.

"She is napping," Laurent said. "I will bring her to you when you come down to the fire."

An hour and a half later, Maggie was curled up in front of the fire, a glass of wine in her hand and her little dog Petit-Four in her lap. As Maggie combed her fingers through the dog's curls, she felt her heart catch. Petit-Four was growing more frail by the day and tonight Laurent admitted she could not be enticed into eating her dinner.

Don't leave me, Petit. Maggie thought as she cupped the dog's chin and looked into her sleepy dark brown eyes. *Now of all times, I can't bear it.*

Jemmy and Mila were playing with the two new puppies on the rug in front of the fireplace. Laurent had gotten the dogs—standard poodle mixes—the summer before but they didn't show any sign of maturing or responding to training yet. Intended as guard dogs, they still slept in their crates in the alcove off the back of the living room where the south-facing French doors that led to the garden and the vineyard were.

Laurent came in and sat down next to her.

"Dinner was amazing," Maggie said. She saw Jemmy turn his head to smile at her. "You're getting to be as good in the kitchen as your Papa," she said to him. She watched him beam before turning back to the dogs.

"How is your father?" Laurent asked as he leaned back into the couch.

She'd kept him abreast while she was in Aix so she knew he

was interested in hearing the deeper tones of his father-in-law's condition.

"I don't know who I'm more concerned about," Maggie said with a sigh, "him or my mother. I've never seen her act so helpless before."

"It is time to move them to Domaine St-Buvard."

"Mom doesn't want to be so far from the hospitals."

"It is time for you to tell her what she needs."

They were silent for a moment listening to the crackle and snapping of the fire and the murmurs and laughter of the two children with their puppies. Then with a sigh, Laurent tousled Petit-Four's grey top-not and kissed Maggie.

"Bath time," he said loudly to the two children.

The children knew better than to argue with their father but Maggie saw them cling to the puppies, reluctant to bring the evening to a close.

"I'll do it," Maggie said to Laurent as she moved Petit-Four to a spot next to her on the couch.

"You are sure?" Laurent said. "I am hoping you will catch your breath from your ordeal."

Maggie laughed and leaned over to give him a kiss. "I'm fully recovered. Come on, Mila and Jemmy. Upstairs."

Both children began to complain until Laurent cleared his throat at which point they both jumped to their feet.

How does he do it? Maggie marveled as she followed the children upstairs. She knew for a fact he didn't smack them. She shook her head in wonderment. Some people where just born to lead.

"Are you putting the dogs in their crates?" she asked over her shoulder.

"Not yet," Laurent said. "They need a quick run around the vineyard first."

As she watched him release the dogs and disappear through

the French doors into the garden Maggie felt her heart fill with joy. Through the good and the bad, the high and the low, and whatever it was she could sense was coming down the road with her parents, Maggie thanked God every day that she had Laurent by her side.

8

A TIME TO DIE

Even with a fire blazing in the central fireplace in the stone-lined refectory, Pierre could still feel the wind invading the cavernous dining room through the many cracks in the stone.

A high arched ceiling of rock hung over the slate floors and made him shiver just to look up at it. He spotted the monk who'd interviewed him earlier today standing at the head of the line at the far end of the hall handing out food to all the pathetic people lined up to receive it. It was all Pierre could do not to snort in disgust.

He stepped into the back of the line, hunching his shoulders against the chill in the hall. He felt uncomfortable in this place but didn't bother wondering if it was due to its religiousness. He was a *gitane*. He would always be happier out of doors.

Children ran laughing and screeching across the stone floor. The dining tables—crude metal folding affairs that jarred with the image of the ancient abbey—lined the center of the long hall. Groups of men and women sat at the tables with bowls of steaming soup before them. Everyone seemed to know everyone. The laughter teemed in the hall, the noise of it echoing and re-doubling in volume as it reverberated off the stone walls.

As Pierre made his way up the line to the front of the room where the white-headed monk and a few old ladies were ladling out soup, he watched as the heads of the seated diners turned as he passed and their conversations ground to a halt.

One old bitch glowered at him as she held her soupspoon in a fisted hand like she might fling it at him any moment. He winked at her as he passed and was rewarded by a startled gasp as her mouth fell open. He kept his smile in place and told himself that when the time was right her room would be the first one he'd hit.

Pierre caught a snatch of guttural French, "...so they will now just let anyone in here? Disgusting!"

His smile never wavered. Not a single person in this room wanted him here. Even the children had picked up on the tension from their parents and their giggling and playful shrieks had muted.

And then he saw her.

She had long black hair like an Indian princess but her eyes were as blue as a Cyprus sky. Pierre nearly stopped walking when he saw her, so incredibly beautiful was she.

Like the others, she stared at him but with curiosity, not revulsion.

Or at least that was what Pierre told himself.

He didn't know what made him look at the table behind where she sat. Perhaps there was something to the idea that if someone stared at you with enough hatred, you could feel it in your bones.

Or between your shoulder blades.

A man was sitting at the table looking fixedly at Pierre. He was about Pierre's own age, handsome but soft where he should be angular. The man was staring at him with an intensity that felt different from the usual racial hostility. Pierre looked again at the girl and then back at the man.

So that's your girl?

Pierre turned away, a smile on his face, and continued his way up the soup line.

Well, we'll just see, won't we?

Noelle had heard about the *gitane* before she saw him of course.

He was the only thing she and her friends had talked about ever since Marie-France revealed that she saw Frère Alphonse showing the hot gypsy boy where he would sleep.

Of course the adults were all very cross about it. Noelle heard that her friend Francoise's mother even went to Frère Jean to complain but she should have saved her breath. Frère Jean was an angel on earth who would always do what was right. Even tonight, he was serving them with only the help of a few of the widows because the rest of the monks had gone to a retreat in Dijon.

Only Frère Jean would insist that his Brothers go while he did their work in their absence.

Noelle idly stirred her soup and nonchalantly gazed around the room, affecting to be looking for a friend. She continued the charade even after she'd located the gypsy boy. He sat alone of course. When she turned back to her friends Noelle could feel his eyes burning through her.

That made her feel good but in the end it didn't matter. Just as she'd told Guy before dinner the only thing she cared about was moving to her new cottage with Marie-France. It would be so wonderful to be away from her father, away from the nosy, relentless judgments of the women in the monastery with nothing better to do than gossip and create drama, away from the tiresome expressions of Guy's oppressive infatuation.

Her father hadn't showed up for dinner tonight which wasn't unusual but Noelle had heard there had been an incident at the vineyard with Laurent Dernier. Just thinking of her father making a fool of himself like that—she was sure he had been at fault —made Noelle want to slam a door or punch something.

Monsieur Dernier—Laurent—was so handsome and so masterful. There wasn't a woman in the monastery who didn't fall asleep at night imagining those strong arms holding her. Noelle blushed.

At least if they were anything like Noelle and her friends.

For her father to have embarrassed her by provoking Laurent was just too embarrassing to be borne. If she weren't in such a hurry to pack up and move into her new little house—the one Laurent had built for her—she would track her father down and let him know how seriously he had disappointed her.

"Noelle?" Marie-France said. "Are you ready to go?" she leaned in and whispered. "Or do you want to follow the new boy back to his stable?"

Rumor had it the brothers had given the gypsy a stall with hay as a bed for the night.

Nicole and Marie-France giggled but after thoughts of Laurent, Noelle wasn't in the mood to join in.

"I am ready," she said coolly.

Making an effort not to glance around the dining hall to see if the gypsy was still watching her, Noelle picked up her soup bowl and followed her friends to the back of the refectory where they deposited them in a large rubber kitchen bin. Everyone in the monastery took turns washing the dishes but this week was not Noelle's week for such menial work.

This week was the beginning of the rest of her life, Noelle thought with a lightness in her chest as she and Marie-France looped arms and walked together down the long hall to the double wooden doors that led to the parking lot.

The moment they pushed open the door Noelle's mood dipped. She could see her father coming from the direction of the village. He stumbled and wove like the drunkard she had no doubt he presently was. Her stomach clenched as she watched him.

"Is that your father, Noelle?" Marie-France said, squinting in the gloom.

Noelle released her arm. "You go on," she said. "I'll follow later."

"Are you sure?" But Marie-France was already hurrying in the direction of the car park. The new little house was at least two miles from the monastery and the light was already fading.

Noelle waited on the gravel half-circle drive in front of the main monastery building that housed the refectory until she was sure her father saw her. He stopped abruptly and then lumbered uncertainly in her direction.

Why had he done this?

But she knew why.

"Papa," she said when he came closer. "What happened to you?"

She hadn't meant it to come out so accusatory but the closer he got, the more clearly she could see his swollen lip reminding her of his run-in this afternoon with Laurent Dernier.

He staggered over to her but stopped short of putting a hand on her shoulder to steady himself. He reeked of wine.

"Do not address me in that...that tone," he hiccoughed, his eyes glittering with hurt.

His blatant lack of contrition inflamed the vexation Noelle had been trying to hide. Suddenly she saw her father as the reason for all their problems, all their heartaches, their homelessness, their poverty. She wanted to smash his drunken, unrepentant face with both fists.

"How dare you offend Monsieur Dernier today?" she blurted out. "He is our benefactor! What is wrong with you?"

He narrowed his eyes at her as he worked to understand what she was saying.

"That bastard...!" he said indignantly. "He attacked me!"

"He pulled you off a little boy is what I heard," Noelle said angrily. "Which child was it this time? Which child today didn't have the right to live because Fabrice and Marcel cannot?"

She hadn't even realized the thought was in her head until she formed them into words and spat them out at her father, because of course that's why he'd done it. That's why he'd always done it.

He slapped a ten-year old boy just last week. And a month ago he'd been caught shaking a seven-year old. He'd been threatened by Frère Jean with immediate expulsion should there be another incident.

Did he think it was safe to hurt children as long as it was not at the monastery?

Noelle's anger built up inside her but it was tempered by the squeeze of the terrible, bottomless agony of their shared loss.

Fabrice and Marcel would never be in their lives again.

As with Noelle's mother, they were lost to them forever.

But attacking all little boys lucky enough to still be alive wouldn't bring them back.

"We are homeless because of that bastard!" her father sputtered nonsensically.

"You are drunk," Noelle said in disgust. Behind her she could hear the sounds of people coming out of the refectory. Dinnertime was ending. There would soon be a crowd gathered to witness the humiliating scene with her drunk father who wore the evidence on his face of this afternoon's cowardice.

Her father grabbed at her arm causing her to drop her purse on the ground.

"You...you can't speak to me like that," he slurred.

Noelle jerked her arm out of his grip and turned to pick up her bag. There were at least half a dozen people standing outside the refectory door now staring and listening to her and her father. Torn between the desire to run away and tell them all off,

Noelle took a long breath as she angrily searched the ground for her purse before realizing it wasn't on the ground.

It was in the hand of the gypsy boy who stood before her now, a smile curling on his handsome lips, and a malicious gleam of delight at her discomfort in his eyes.

"Drop something, Mademoiselle?" he said, holding out the purse.

Noelle snatched the purse from him but before she could turn to leave with some vestige of dignity, her father pushed past her and jabbed his finger at the young man.

"You stay away from her, do you hear?!" her father snarled. "Gypsy scum!"

The sounds of snickering from the group of onlookers filled Noelle's ears. Mortified, she turned and ran in the growing gloom to the dormitory behind the refectory.

Pierre watched the girl run away and he felt his heart constrict as he did. She was even more beautiful up close. When he redirected his attention back to the old bastard who'd insulted him he saw that the crowd had parted and the man was making his way to the dining hall.

He felt a hard jab of fury at the man's words but forced it down as he turned toward the stables where he'd been assigned to sleep. Suddenly a figure separated from the assembled group and approached him.

It was the girl's boyfriend.

It had been a long and humiliating day. Right now Pierre would love nothing more than a reason to smash this bastard's teeth down his throat.

"Whatever you're thinking of," the boyfriend said to him, his jaw muscles clenching and twitching as he spoke, "you can forget it."

"Oh?" Pierre said. "Why is that? Because she belongs to you?"

The boy flushed with embarrassment and outrage.

"No, because her father will never let Noelle be with a *gitane*."

"Noelle? Thanks. I didn't know her name until now. But I think I'll let her decide."

The boy facing him held himself rigidly, his neck corded with tension.

"Noelle would never do anything against her father's wishes," the boy said. "And Monsieur Dupree would rather die than see her with someone like you."

Pierre watched him leave and tried to recapture the amusement he'd felt only moments before—instead of the steadily building anger and hate writhing in his chest.

"I might be able to arrange that," he said under his breath.

9

IN THE WEE HOURS

After supervising the children's baths and reading two long stories to both Mila and Jemmy separately, Maggie collected Petit-Four from the couch and tucked her away in her dog bed in Maggie's bedroom. It had been months since the little dog had managed the tall staircase on her own.

Maggie brushed her teeth and slipped on a flannel nightgown before climbing into bed with a book, surprised that Laurent still wasn't back yet. If she'd read his signals correctly—and she had no doubt she had—she expected him to join her in the bedroom as soon as physically possible. She glanced at the clock and noted with surprise that nearly an hour had passed since he'd gone out with the dogs.

The rain had begun lightly tapping on the bedroom windows while she was reading to the children and now it was coming across the panes in waves. She shivered under her covers more at the idea of the bad weather than any actual discomfort. It was really storming outside. Maggie felt a flash of concern that Laurent still hadn't come back.

She tried to focus on her book again and just as she was

feeling her eyes beginning to grow heavy, she heard the downstairs doors open and the sound of the dogs as they scurried over to their crates.

Only Laurent could make that happen without uttering a word, she thought marveling.

She listened as he moved into the kitchen—no doubt doing some last-minute clean up downstairs—and then she heard his footsteps go to the front door as he checked that it was locked. By the time he made his way upstairs—pausing at each of the children's bedroom doors—Maggie was wide awake.

"What took you so long?" she asked, scooting over to make room for him in the bed.

"One of the dogs got away," Laurent said as he stripped off his sodden wool pullover and the Henley tee underneath in one movement. "I had to find her and then I had to catch her."

"You're taking a shower?" Maggie asked with surprise.

"I will only be a few minutes," he said before disappearing into the bathroom.

Laurent was true to his word. His hair was still damp when he slid into bed with Maggie and immediately took her into his arms. And even after all the lovely things that had happened tonight that had aided her in shaking off the stress of her two days in Aix and her parents' situation —the amazing *bourride* she loved so much, thick with redolent garlicky aïoli and crusts of French bread, the happy, laughing children and the quiet evening safe and cozy in front of the fire—it wasn't until this moment when she was securely in Laurent's arms that Maggie truly felt the strain of the day disappear.

Later, Laurent got up to check on the children again—unnecessary since both Mila and Jemmy slept soundly and rarely woke —but a routine that Maggie and Laurent had gotten into the habit of.

She teased him when he came back to bed.

"You know it's going to be very weird for them when they're away at college when we check on them to make sure they're safely in bed."

"I am sure they will be used to it by then."

Maggie laughed and snuggled close to Laurent's chest, resting her cheek against his bare skin. He wrapped one arm around her.

"You will need to bring your parents here, *chérie*," Laurent said. "It is time."

"I can't convince my mom."

"*Convincing* is over rated."

"Glad to hear you finally admit it," Maggie said with a laugh. "I've long suspected it about you."

"Besides," Laurent said as he toyed with a long strand of Maggie's hair, "the house will be even more full soon and two more won't even be noticed."

Maggie froze and then sat up straight, looking at Laurent and leaning on one elbow.

"I'll be damned," she said, her mouth falling open in astonishment.

"Surely you did not think to keep it a secret from me?" Laurent said, his eyes twinkling.

"How did you know? *I* barely even know!"

She had been waiting for the right time to tell him that the pregnancy test she'd taken last weekend had shown positive.

"You are different when you are with child," Laurent said with a slow smile as his hand dropped to her hip.

He means in bed, Maggie thought and she blushed.

"I don't want to hear how," she said firmly. "I just can't believe you knew!"

But this was Laurent. Of course he knew. When had she ever been able to keep anything from him? Well, there was that one time in the very, very beginning but even now Maggie didn't like to remember that.

"And you're okay with it?" Maggie said. "Three kids is a lot."

"I am...*très ravi*," Laurent said, leaning over and kissing her. *Over the moon.*

Smiling, Maggie turned to snuggle down next to him again. Just as she was beginning to feel sleep claim her, she felt him move away and then leave the bed. She struggled to wake up.

"Laurent?" she said.

"Go back to sleep, *chérie*," he said. "The dogs are whining. I will be right back."

Maggie turned over and fell back to sleep. She had no idea how long she'd slept before she felt Laurent—this time standing by her side of the bed—his hand on her shoulder and gently shaking her awake.

"*Mon chére*," he said. "You must wake up."

Maggie sat up instantly, her hair flying around her as she fought to come fully awake.

"What's happening?" she said, her heart jumping in her throat. She swung her legs out of bed and was halfway out of the room toward the hallway when Laurent captured her and pulled her back.

"*Non, chérie*. The children are safe. But you must get dressed."

As Maggie stood in the middle of her bedroom, the lightning outside sharply illuminated the vineyard below in startling spasms of light. She felt Laurent's hand, warm and firm, on the small of her back as he guided her toward the dresser.

"Get dressed, *chérie*," he said firmly. "The police will be here in moments."

Maggie swung around to stare at him in the half gloom of the room, his face jumping into sharp relief with each flash of lightning.

"The police?" she said, her heartbeat suddenly racing. "Laurent, tell me what's happening right *now!*"

His face was a mask of resignation. He sighed heavily and his eyes went to the window where he could see the vineyard beyond being lit up by the storm.

"One of the refugees from the monastery is in our vineyard," he said.

"What in the world is he doing out there this time of night?" Maggie said. "And in this weather?"

"He is doing nothing, *chérie*," Laurent said. "He is dead."

10

LIKE FALLING OFF A LOG

Even at three in the morning Laurent's kitchen seemed to radiate a feeling of sunshine and geniality. Painted in a pale ochre yellow and persimmon and lined with the open shelving that Laurent preferred, it produced a warm but all-business effect—again, the way Laurent preferred.

Maggie sat at the kitchen counter, an untouched mug of fresh coffee in front of her while Laurent and Roger Bedard—the Aix-en-Provence area's *Commandant de Police* spoke in low tones in the living room.

Through the wide window over the sink Maggie could see the flashing lights of the police cars parked on the front driveway and hear the low thrum of the coroner's wagon when it arrived.

She still wasn't exactly sure what had happened. The dogs had heard a sound around midnight and when Laurent got up to let them out, they took off, presumably in search of whatever they'd heard. In the process of catching them, Laurent found a body face down in the vineyard quadrant nearest to the village road.

Maggie shivered and rubbed her arms. She glanced at the two men standing in the living room, their heads close together as they talked. Laurent, easily six inches taller than Bedard, stood now with his hands on his hips and nodded from time to time.

Bedard was a handsome man with chiseled features and a strong jaw. His lively gray eyes were always easy to read whereas Laurent's brown eyes were dark and opaque. Much like Laurent himself.

It had been seven months since Maggie had last seen Roger Bedard and that had not been under the best of circumstances since at the time she was being pulled out of a demolished ski chalet that had just been buried by an avalanche.

Roger kept very busy at his job overseeing the major crimes in their part of Provence. But she knew he worked just as hard to stay away from her.

She'd met Roger during her first year of marriage—a difficult first year of attempting to adjust to being an ex-pat and married to a Frenchman too. While she didn't betray her wedding vows, as unhappy as she'd been that first year, she'd come close. In the end she'd racked up a lesson hard-learned for herself and her marriage going forward with Laurent. But she'd also left battered in her careless wake a good man who'd fallen in love with her with no signs of quitting—even after two children and every rebuff that Maggie had since delivered.

The fact that Roger and Laurent had somehow become friends was a constant source of amazement to Maggie. As she watched them now, she thought how different they were. Roger, the career policeman, provincial and solid. And Laurent, an ex-con-artist from Paris now a wealthy *vignernon* and landowner.

The set of French doors that opened to the back terrace swung open, surprising Maggie, and two detectives joined Laurent and Bedard in the living room. Maggie could see through the open back doors that it was still raining hard. The terrace slate tiles glistened like mirrors with the police lights that had been erected there.

She went into the living room and Laurent held out an arm to her. She slipped her arm around his waist and he pulled her close as the detectives made their report.

"The doctor said we may remove the body now," one of them, a horse-faced young man who was not wearing a uniform said. He glanced at Laurent as he spoke in clear annoyance that Bedard was allowing Laurent and Maggie to hear what he had to say.

"It's a mess out there," the uniformed policemen said, shaking his cap and sprinkling water onto the carpet in Maggie's living room. She felt a flash of pique.

"*D'accord*," Bedard said, running his hand through his close cropped hair. He snapped his fingers in the direction of the door and the uniformed policeman turned and shut it against the weather.

Bedard addressed Laurent. "So we'll finish this in Aix?"

"Finish what?" Maggie said, looking at Laurent. "Surely you don't mean *tonight*?" she said turning back to Bedard.

"It is fine, *chérie*," Laurent said. "I will not be long."

"I'll leave a man at the crime scene—" Bedard said, nodding at his detective.

"What?" Maggie blurted out. "What do you mean *crime scene*? I thought the man had a heart attack. Are you thinking it *wasn't* an accident? Laurent?"

"Nobody knows, *chérie*," Laurent said, his face tense. "Just let the police do their job."

"I have no intention of interfering with them," Maggie said, feeling the anxiety beginning to build in her chest. "I just want to know what's going on."

"As do we, Madame," Bedard said formally, giving her a barely perceptible bow and turning to lead his men outside into the pouring rain.

"Laurent?" Maggie said turning to her husband. "Why can't you answer his questions here? Why does he need you to go to Aix?"

"*Chérie*, I found the body. You know how these things go."

That was exactly her concern. She *did* know how these things went *especially* with the person who found the body and she was hesitant to make it easier on the police to make a foolish mistake.

In her experience the police were always attracted to low hanging fruit.

As a renowned former con artist, her husband was the lowest hanging fruit imaginable.

After Bedard and Laurent left, the rest of the early morning dragged slowly for Maggie. She went upstairs to check that the children were still sleeping and decided to work in the den downstairs on her newsletter.

She wrote an ex-pat blog of her life in Provence that had become popular with other ex-pats in France as well as over twenty thousand Francophiles in the US and the UK. She'd been able to monetize the blog when she added ads for local artisans and specialty farmers in Arles and Marseille. Normally, the blog posts wrote themselves when describing the delights of living in the south of France. But this morning she struggled to write any sort of light-hearted piece on the joys of late autumn in Provence and concentrated instead on creating a list of places to visit for the first-time visitor to the area.

Unfortunately, the work wasn't engaging enough to keep her from checking the time on her phone every few minutes.

She should have known! *Why* had Roger insisted Laurent come with him? And had she mistaken it or had Roger refused to get eye contact with her? What was he up to?

Giving up and closing her laptop with a loud click, she grabbed her cellphone and called Laurent. Instantly it went to voicemail. She had a bad feeling about this.

Quickly Maggie jumped up and went to the kitchen. The

kitchen was Laurent's domain. He spent nearly as much time there as he did in the vineyard—or at least he had before he'd started building his mini-cottages to help house the refugee families staying at the nearby monastery.

She jerked open the first kitchen drawer she came to and sure enough, there was his phone.

She felt a flash of anger. She'd told him a thousand times to please carry his phone and *now? of all times? when he's been hauled off to the police station, he forgets to bring it?*

Frustrated knowing she couldn't call him, she put a call in to Bedard. She listened to it ring before it too finally went to voice mail. She tried to remember what it meant when that happened. Did it mean Bedard had screened her call?

Now that the French government had stopped mandatory school attendance on Saturdays Maggie didn't need to drive to Aix this morning. But given the fact that nobody was answering their damn phones, she decided to get the kids up and go into town anyway. As she was hurrying up the stairs, her phone rang. Excitedly she pulled it out of her pocket and saw that it was her mother.

She hesitated but her heart rate began to accelerate.

"Hey, Mom," she said into the phone. "Is everything okay?"

"Well..." Elspeth said slowly. "You did say I should call if I needed anything."

"Yes, of course," Maggie said, tapping her foot. "What do you need?"

"Can you possibly come by this morning? Just a few things. I still can't figure out how to operate this French stove and your father wants soup."

For breakfast? Maggie felt a growing wave of frustration.

"Yep. No problem," Maggie said as she paused outside Mila's room. The little girl was sound asleep. Maggie tiptoed away without waking her. "I'll be there in a few hours. Is that okay? Can you give him something else in the meantime?"

"Well, you know your father these days," Elspeth said. "If you could hurry, that would be a big help."

"Sure," Maggie said. "I'll hurry."

With a headache beginning to form behind her eyes, Maggie stood in the doorway of Jemmy's room and saw that he was also deeply asleep. She could hear the sounds of his little-boy snores from where she stood. She quietly shut his door.

It went against every molecule in her maternal body to wake them. Standing in the hallway trying to decide how to manage her morning, her eyes strayed to her own open bedroom door when the thought came to her that she hadn't heard a sound from Petit-Four all morning.

A splinter of ice embedded in her heart at the thought.

That wasn't like Petit-four. Not with all the activity of the police downstairs in the early hours of the morning. The two other dogs—now sleeping safely in their crates—had yipped and barked steadily the whole time until the police left.

Maggie took a slow hesitant step into her bedroom. The dog bed next to Maggie's side of the bed was quiet. A tumble of grey curls was visible.

"Petit?" Maggie said softly, her heart breaking as she spoke her dog's name.

There was no response from the dog bed. Nor would there ever be again.

11

LETTING GO

Maggie was glad the kids weren't awake. She imagined it would be disturbing for them to see their mother break down in gut wrenching sobs on the floor while rocking her beloved dog in her arms.

Petit-Four must have died some time during the night because there was no warmth to her now and it broke Maggie's heart to think of how she hadn't been there for her at the end.

With tears streaming down her face, Maggie kissed the little dog. Petit-Four had been with her since the very beginning of her life in France. She'd been given to her as a puppy and had sailed through the ensuing years of marriage and children close by Maggie's side.

Maggie had never had a better pet, a better *petite amie*, in her life.

Carefully, she cradled the little dog in her flannel dog blanket —one of Mila's old baby blankets—and carried her downstairs. She laid her on the couch and fished out her phone and without checking the time called Grace.

Grace picked up immediately.

"Hey, sweetie," Grace said. "What's up? You thinking about

coming over here to give me a hand? You know my Americans are coming today, right? Gabriel, no!" Grace barked out to her handyman. "I told you I need the small couch moved next to the fireplace!"

Maggie took in a long breath, her hand resting on her little dog. In many ways it helped just to hear Grace's voice. Grace had been given a puppy from the same litter as Petit-Four but had given the dog away when she and Windsor moved back to the States.

"I forgot about your Americans coming this morning," Maggie said.

Grace had been particularly nervous about this group of guests. While they weren't her first at the *gite*, they would be without doubt the most profitable. But Grace had mentioned there had been issues even in the booking process. The woman who was in contact with Grace for the group had sounded extremely picky and not at all friendly.

Grace had enough to deal with this morning.

"Yes, well, I'm about to go out of my mind," Grace said. "So unless you're on your way over here with a wet vac or a carpet shampooer, can we catch up later?"

"Sure," Maggie said. "Good luck. Oh, listen, is Danielle there?"

"Of course. I'd be lost with out her. Why? Do you need her?"

"No. Just wondered. I'll talk to you later."

She disconnected and touched the dog again sadly. Before the tears could fall again, Maggie called Danielle and Jean-Luc's house next door and was relieved when Jean-Luc picked up almost immediately.

"*Bonjour*, Jean-Luc," Maggie said. She thought of how Laurent always chided her for not spending enough time with the social pleasantries before blurting out the purpose of her call. She knew she should ask about Jean-Luc's health and maybe comment on the weather but she just couldn't help herself.

"Can you watch the kids for me today?" she asked.

Jean-Luc and Danielle were the children's faux-grandparents. They'd stepped in when the children were born because Laurent had no living parents of his own for the role and Maggie's were too far away. It was a job that Jean-Luc took very seriously and not surprisingly both children adored him.

"Of course. I will be right there."

By the time Jean-Luc arrived, Maggie had taken the two dogs out on leashes, fed them and tucked them back in their crates, made a fresh pot of coffee and pulled out the children's favorite cereal boxes and bowls. She splashed water on her face and ran a comb through her hair. As she crossed the living room to open the door for him, she could see the rain had eased up a little and the police lights were no longer on. She caught a glimpse of a man in uniform standing at the edge of the terrace.

"What has happened?" Jean-Luc said immediately and Maggie knew he meant the policeman although how he'd seen him as he came from the front she had no idea.

"You're not going to believe this," Maggie said leading him to the kitchen. "Some guy dropped dead in the vineyard last night."

"*Vraiment*?" Jean-Luc said in astonishment. The old farmer's face was weatherworn and reddened from years in the Provençal sun. As usual, he wore clean dark trousers, a white shirt, a dark blue tie and a cloth cap covering a thick head of white hair.

"Yes, really. And Laurent went off with the cops to fill in the blanks for them."

Jean-Luc frowned which in Maggie's mind seemed to underscore what she already knew—that it was a bad sign for Laurent to have gone down to the police station.

"Thank you so much for doing this, Jean-Luc," she said, dropping her phone in her purse and looking around to make sure she had everything. "I have to run to Aix to help my parents sort something out."

"*Pas du tout*," Jean-Luc said. "I am happy to do it." And then he frowned. "But there is more?"

Maggie froze when he said that. For Jean-Luc to pick up on her underlying sadness touched her. Jean-Luc was a tough old farmer. In his late seventies, he vividly remembered the war and a long hard life since then. But regardless of how rough or bristly he could come off, Maggie knew he felt and cared deeply.

Especially when it came to dogs.

Without saying a word Maggie led him to the couch where Petit-Four lay.

Jean-Luc clapped his hands once and looked at the little bundle with dismay. Then he looked at Maggie with such sad understanding that she burst into tears. He put his arm around her and patted her on the back.

"I knew she was sick," Maggie said through her sobs. "I just didn't know she was *dying*."

He tut-tutted her and sat down on the couch next to the dog.

"I am so sorry, *chérie*," he said putting a large weathered hand on the animal. "She was a good dog. A good friend."

"I loved her so much," Maggie said, wiping her tears with her fingers.

"I know."

And he did know too, Maggie thought. After all it was his niece Marie-France who'd given Petit-Four to Maggie ten years ago.

"I remember the day you brought her home," he said.

"I just can't believe it's her time already," Maggie said. "So much has happened in the last ten years."

"Mostly good things," Jean-Luc reminded her, patting her hand.

"True."

"I would be honored to help you bury Petit-Four," he said, but Maggie shook her head.

"Thank you, Jean-Luc," she said. "But we'll do it when Laurent comes home. The kids will want to be there too."

"Of course."

Together they wrapped the dog in her blanket and Jean-Luc carried her downstairs and put her on a bench in the cold basement next to the stacks of wooden wine bottle crates.

When he came back upstairs Maggie felt her heart go out to him. She and Jean-Luc had had their moments and in the beginning none of those had been good. But over the years she'd learned forgiveness and she'd learned to love him. If for no other reason because she knew how her children adored him but probably even more than that because of Laurent.

Laurent's family history was complex and his childhood an unhappy one. He had nothing good to say about any of his relatives, least of all his father. While Laurent would never admit it, Maggie knew he loved Jean-Luc in the way a son loves a father.

And because until the last seven years, Jean Luc had never married or had a family, his relationship with Laurent was not just a gift to Jean-Luc but truly a miracle. And it was one that Maggie knew from conversations with Jean-Luc's wife Danielle that Jean Luc was grateful for every day of his life.

"Danielle is really enjoying helping Grace with the *gite*, isn't she?" Maggie said as she pulled on her raincoat.

"She loves doing it," Jean-Luc said. "But I admit I am a little jealous."

"Of Grace?"

"No, no. I am jealous because I would love to have work to do."

Maggie and Laurent had both noted that Jean-Luc's retirement from his vineyard which he'd sold to Laurent last spring had been gradual in coming but she could see how doing absolutely nothing the last six months was wearing on him.

"I know there's a ton of work to do at *Dormir*," Maggie said. "I'm sure Grace could find you something to do."

"Madame Van Sant has a young handyman for that."

Maggie happened to know that the *young handyman* was in his late forties.

She stood at the door, her purse over her shoulder and took in a deep breath. She was grateful for this man who loved her children and who could step in when she needed him. But she felt a burst of sadness too, with thoughts of her own father who would have loved to have played this role—Jean-Luc's role—for his grandchildren but who instead had trouble remembering Maggie or even his own wife on a daily basis.

"Thank you, Jean-Luc," Maggie said breathlessly, fighting her tears anew before turning to brave the rain outside.

The drive to Aix was a somber one. Maggie was sleep-deprived and feeling fragile at the loss of her beloved pet—all compounded by the insecurity of not being able to reach Laurent. As she drove into Aix and fought the weekend market crowds to find a parking spot not too far from her parents' apartment, it occurred to Maggie that she could go to Bedard's office in person and demand to see Laurent.

Comforted by this thought, Maggie hurried through the wet streets of Aix, using a broken child's umbrella she'd found in the back seat that was so beat up she would likely have to throw it away before she found her way back.

As she shook off the rain from her raincoat in the foyer of her parents' apartment building, she pulled out her phone and tried calling Bedard again.

Again it went to voicemail and Maggie felt her irritation beginning to swell. It was nearly ten in the morning! They'd been gone seven hours! What did Roger think Maggie was doing?

Making cookies and not caring if her husband was in police custody?

He must know I'm trying to reach him!

She took a deep breath to calm herself down and stepped into the ancient elevator. *If this is all no big deal and I make it a huge production,* she thought, *nobody will thank me, particularly not Laurent. I should probably just assume he knows what he's doing.*

When the elevator stopped on her parents' floor, she could see the door to their apartment was open. Inside she heard her father's argumentative voice and she felt her shoulders slump as she moved toward their apartment. Before she reached the door, her phone rang and thinking it might be Laurent she answered it without looking at the screen.

"Hello?" she said breathlessly.

"Madame Dernier?" a man's voice came over the line, reedy and thin.

"Yes? Who is this?"

"I am Frère Jean from the *l'Abbaye de Sainte-Trinité*."

"Oh, hello, *mon frère*," Maggie said, a spasm of disappointment throbbing through her.

Laurent worked with the monk at the monastery coordinating work details and helping to set up housing for the families. Because this was Laurent's personal project, Maggie had yet to visit the monastery or meet Frère Jean. "How can I help you?"

"I am trying to reach Laurent."

"He forgot his phone this morning. Can I give him a message?"

The man hesitated. "I am not sure. I needed to ask him about Monsieur Dupree. He is one of our refugees and he did not come home last night."

Maggie felt a sliver of apprehension.

"Why do you think Laurent might know where he is?" she asked, her heart beating quickly.

"I understand they had a...disagreement yesterday," Frère

Jean said. "I was afraid Monsieur Dupree might have attempted to confront Laurent again. His daughter is worried about him."

"Yes, well, I'll have Laurent call you when I see him," Maggie said.

"Oh!" Frère Jean said to someone on his end. "*Qui est la? Les police? Attends!* Goodbye, Madame."

When he disconnected Maggie stood holding her phone and staring at it.

There was a person missing from the monastery and Frère Jean just exclaimed to someone on his end of the phone that *the police had just arrived.*

Was the dead man in their vineyard one of the monastery's refugees?

12

UNDER A FALLING SKY

Frère Jean sat on the couch in his rectory, the sobbing girl in his arms. His mouth was dry and he felt an empty feeling in the pit of his stomach while his mind whirled in a million different directions.

The police arrived a little before lunch. *How could this have happened?* Frère Jean thought miserably, his stomach roiling. *And why?*

He absently patted Noelle's back in time with her heaving sobs. He wasn't as good with the personal ministries as some of the other brothers were. But they were all still in Dijon.

He looked up at the two detectives and the one female uniformed office.

On the other hand, the longer I can be of service to the poor child, the less likely the police will want to speak to me alone. He shivered at the very thought.

What could they possibly imagine I know about this terrible affair? he thought, his eyes darting manically around his own office as if looking for a way out.

"*Mon frère?*" one of the detectives said to him.

Frère Jean looked at him, startled, his eyes wide and panicky.

"Yes?" he squeaked.

"Madame L'Agent Levert here will take Mademoiselle Dupree to her room to take her statement. Will you answer a few questions?"

"I don't know anything," Frère Jean said hurriedly. "Absolutely nothing. I didn't see Henri last night."

"Was that unusual?"

"Unusual?" *What does he mean by that? What is he trying to imply?*

"I mean, *mon frère*," the detective said patiently, "did Monsieur Dupree often spend time with the others here? Was he social?"

"Not really," Frère Jean said, affecting to be thinking about it and hoping he didn't look like he was playacting.

"And so last night, you don't remember seeing Monsieur Dupree?"

"No. We have religious services at eight o'clock. But I can't remember who was there and who wasn't."

"Was everyone accounted for last night?" the detective pressed. "I understand you have a curfew and none are allowed to leave after eight o'clock?"

"Yes, yes, that's right. Everyone knows it is against the rules to leave without permission. There were a few girls who were moving into their new houses—the ones built by Monsieur Dernier on the Domaine St-Buvard property—but they would have left before eight o'clock."

"And the victim's daughter, Mademoiselle Dupree, was one of those, I understand?"

Frère Jean looked at him and for a moment felt totally frozen.

"*Mon frère?*" the detective prompted.

"I believe she was, yes," Frère Jean said woodenly.

"Can you remember the last time you saw Monsieur Dupree?"

Sweat popped out on Frère Jean's lip and he prayed it wasn't obvious to the detective.

"I don't remember," he said, his voice trembling.

"Are you all right, *mon frère?*" the detective said, frowning.

"Yes! Yes, of course," he said swallowing hard. "It is just a very upsetting time for all of us."

"Well, that's all I have for now. If you think of anything, please call us."

"I will, absolutely I will," Frère Jean said. *Were they going to search the monastery?*

Fighting a pain in the back of his throat, Frère Jean smiled woodenly at the detective who put away his notepad.

He began to pray.

Please don't let them search the monastery. And please not my quarters, I beg you.

The rain was lighter now, not the downward pummeling it had been last night. As Pierre stood in the entrance of the stable and watched the police walk back and forth from the rectory to the refectory, his stomach clenched in anticipation and dread.

He paced in the opening of the stable, opening and closing his fists.

Will she tell them?

His stomach churned as he watched a policewoman with her arm around Noelle walk to the refectory where they disappeared inside.

Why wouldn't she? What could possibly stop her?

Pierre imagined the female cop asking Noelle all her questions in order to lead directly to the desired answer.

"How long have you known the gypsy? Wasn't your father overheard telling him to stay away from you? What exactly happened last night, Noelle? What did the dirty *gitane* do last night, Noelle?"

Pierre felt a flush of panic invade his body, and he sat down abruptly on a nearby hay bale.

Of course she'll tell. Why wouldn't she?

Should he run? Should he talk to Noelle first to see if she could be *convinced* not to talk?

Running was bad.

He wiped a shaking hand across his perspiration-coated forehead.

Running meant the cops would know without a doubt it was him.

Guy watched the policewoman walking with Noelle and trying to comfort her. This was the part he'd failed to imagine last night—Noelle's heartbreak and grief. Not that he could have changed anything about what happened but he might have been a little more prepared.

His stomach twisted in agony. How he wished he could go to her and give her the comfort and support she needed now.

But why would she ever take that from him? After what he'd done?

After what she saw me do last night?

His tongue probed his split lip gingerly.

Still, her misery was so palpable. It stretched across the rain-soaked pavers and touched him like an adder's kiss. The pain she was feeling now, that was his fault. The agony she was struggling to endure? That was a gift directly from him.

He hung his head in shame.

13

HALLELUJAH

After sorting out the operational aspects of the perfectly basic French stove and getting the soup cooking—long after her father was in the mood to eat it—Maggie made her mother a cup of tea and took the new market basket she'd bought them down from the kitchen shelf. Then she walked out the front door of her parents' building and into the nearby Richelme market in full swing.

She would have preferred that Elspeth do the shopping. Her mother needed a break from the constant demands of her father, and Maggie couldn't help but think a morning walk through the famous and colorful weekend markets of Aix would do Elspeth a world of good. But Elspeth didn't want to try to speak French to make herself understood "just to buy a simple carton of milk."

It was pretty clear to Maggie that this move to France was not working out for her parents. Maggie didn't know whether to suggest they go back to Atlanta or press them to move to Domaine St-Buvard. From her perspective *nothing* seemed like it was going to help. Nothing except the inevitable passing of her beloved father. And just the thought of that—the relief combined with the heartbreak of losing him—made Maggie stop in the middle of the market and lean against one of the plane trees encased in cobblestones.

She'd read recently on the Internet that Alzheimer's patients can live for decades. She didn't know which was worse: thinking it would be better for everyone if her father died or him actually dying and losing him for good. She couldn't bear to wish to lose him. How could she? A world without her father in it? How would that world look? Losing him was the single biggest thing she dreaded.

She shook off her morbid thoughts and strolled the market aisles, loading up on eggplant and bright red tomatoes before heading back to her parents' apartment. Along the way she stopped at a *boulangerie* for a baguette and three chocolate éclairs. She couldn't remember the last time she saw her mother enjoy anything whether it was food or one of the grandchildren, but on the off chance that it might help, Maggie loaded up the bag with pastries.

When the chips were down Maggie was a firm believer in sugar therapy.

Within the hour Maggie unloaded the groceries, reviewed the kitchen stove instructions one more time with her mother, and was back in her parked car. She called Jean-Luc to confirm that he and the kids were fine. As she sat with her finger poised over Bedard's number to call him *yet again* she realized that every time she put a call in to him and he didn't answer she felt even angrier and more upset than she had before.

She sat in her car and took in a long breath and tried to block out the world while being mindful of how her body felt. She closed her eyes and tried to let the anxiety trail out her fingertips as she blocked out thoughts of her father, of Petit-Four, of Laurent and of that poor man face down in their vineyard.

At the thought of the dead man she opened her eyes.

So his name was Dupree.

And Laurent knew him? Frère Jean said he and Laurent had had some kind of run-in the day before.

Maggie gripped the steering wheel tightly as the thought came to her: *Would Frère Jean mention that to the police?*

She turned on the car and slowly navigated her way out of the parking space.

Trust the process, she said sternly to herself.

The cops are talking to everyone. They're turning over every stone. They're examining the body for clues.

Trust the process.

Except this is Roger we're talking about, she argued with herself. *A well-intentioned schlub who, when it comes to competent detective work, has never risen to the task.*

Ever.

He's got a suspect. And lo and behold it's the husband of the woman he professes to love.

Maggie felt a nauseating spasm clutch her stomach. She dropped her hand to her abdomen in an attempt to calm it.

Should she really trust the process?

No, she thought morosely. Not as long as Roger was in charge of it.

She shot free of the Aix perimeter road and set her phone on the dashboard, quickly clicking in the address of the village Ponte l'Abbe.

Screw the process.

If Roger won't call me back when I know for a fact he has a record of all the times I've called him today, then he has no one to blame but himself for my taking a look at this case on my own.

The phone screen reset to show a map to the village of Pont l'Abbe. Maggie could see the little icon that showed up as *l'Abbaye de Sainte-Trinité* next to the icon for the village.

As she drove toward the monastery, she reminded herself that the only thing she knew for sure was that the dead guy had lived at the monastery.

And for now that's all she needed to know.

Thirty minutes later the sight of a sharp Gothic spire on the horizon told Maggie she was getting close.

She drove through the medieval village of Ponte l'Abbe until all there was left to see was the looming presence of *l'Abbaye de Sainte-Trinité*— a sprawling complex of weathered ancient buildings built from the limestone of the surrounding area around the year 1100.

A small stone chapel, forlorn and no longer used due to its ruined roofline, sat next to the ancient rectory and beside a row of even older low-roofed buildings—the first clearly now being used as a stable.

Maggie knew from what she'd heard Laurent say that the monastery had a decent sized garden where they grew potatoes, corn and cabbages. The cellars were vast and cavernous and now being used to ferment and store the grapes harvested from Laurent's fields.

As soon as she saw the monastery, she also saw two police cars and two men—one in uniform and one not—standing at the entrance to the monastery.

So I was right. The dead man is from the monastery.

She pulled onto a gravel verge about two hundred yards from the massive front door of the monastery and buttoned her coat to her chin. As the afternoon drew older, it drew colder too.

The men watched her walk toward them.

It began to rain and Maggie quickened her pace. Her intention was to have a conversation with the monk who'd called her. Since he was clearly a friend of Laurent's, she had no reason to think he'd balk at speaking with her.

Maggie looked around. Driving over she'd thought she might see Roger here but quickly dismissed the idea. Roger had long since given up the practice of doing his own interviews which was just as well since he was useless at them anyway. But she could at least use his name to get inside.

She smiled at the men at the door, one of whom—the one dressed in plain clothes—she recognized as the horse-faced man who'd been in her living room this morning. He was obviously the detective assigned to the case. The other man, a uniformed policeman, stepped in front of the door making it clear she wouldn't be allowed inside.

"The monastery is closed today," he said.

"I'm here to see Chief Inspector Bedard," she said. "He is expecting me."

"Chief Inspector Bedard is not here," the horse-faced detective said.

Maggie eyed the young detective. "I see," she said. "My mistake. And Frère Jean? I spoke with him earlier."

"No one is to enter," the detective said almost menacingly.

Maggie couldn't help but wonder why he was behaving so coldly to her. Clearly he knew who she was so he also knew they were all on the same team. It was almost like he didn't trust her.

Frustrated but not knowing what else she could say to get entrance, Maggie turned away and headed around the crumbling stone wrap wall to the north where she'd seen the annex buildings and what looked like a stable. The policemen didn't stop her so she could only assume there was nothing to find in the direction she was walking.

Still, she'd gone out of her way to come to the monastery and it wouldn't hurt to take a look. Except for the now pouring rain that found its way down her collar like invading needles of ice, there was no real harm in having a look around.

As she walked she reviewed what she knew so far. It wasn't much.

A man whom Laurent had supposedly quarreled with had subsequently died in *their* vineyard.

This man lived at the monastery where presumably he was either a refugee or previously homeless. He had a daughter who'd been worried about his absence.

That was it.

Maggie knew that most of the families living at the monastery had been in transit to what they hoped would be a better way of life. All had either lost their jobs in other areas of France for various reasons or had come from as far off as Morocco and even Turkey escaping oppressive political regimes.

Once around the corner and out of sight of the police, Maggie found herself relaxing even though the rain was coming down harder. Forcing away images of hot tea and sticky *canelés* in front of her fireplace, she walked until she came to the stables.

Back in Atlanta, Maggie had ridden competitively as a teenager. Although she never owned her own horse her parents had happily paid five times the amount one would have cost to lease various mounts as her skill level grew into them. Even today Maggie often thought about finding a way to bring a horse to Domaine St-Buvard but Laurent was uncharacteristically against the idea. She hadn't heard the story of why that was but she had a feeling it was tragic and so she didn't push it.

She walked to the entrance of the stable and looked down the long center aisle. Two rows of five stalls faced each other. Instantly, the smell of a stable—lush and fetid with manure and sweet feed—transported her back to her girlhood, back to long happy afternoons riding along the Chattahoochee River with her girlfriends, of riding aimlessly alone across pastures or training in the dressage ring for hours at a time.

A pony's head thrust out over its stall rim as Maggie stepped inside. It nickered softly and Maggie wished she'd saved an apple from the market this morning.

Next to the stall was a combination storage and tack room. Maggie peeked inside to see harnesses hanging from big rusting hooks on the wall. Barrels of grain and feed lined the wall. She stepped over to the bins and opened one expecting to see the fine grain she'd always fed her horse back in Atlanta. She scooped up a handful. Big kernels of dried corn studded the cask-filled grain.

"What are you doing in here?" a harsh voice barked at her.

She turned to see a slim young man—looking at first glance to be no more than a teenager.

"You're not supposed to be here," the young man said.

"Why are *you* here?" Maggie countered, determined not to be run off so easily. Besides, it was really coming down outside and she was at least dry inside the stable.

"I work here!" he said belligerently.

Maggie noticed that there was quite a bit of horse manure on the ground. A pitchfork was propped up against one of the stalls. If he worked here, she thought dryly, he must be on his lunch break.

"Did you know the man who died last night?" she asked abruptly.

The young man's mouth fell open at her question and Maggie couldn't help but notice he had a mouth full of crooked or broken teeth. As he stepped out of the shadows she could also see what she hadn't noticed before—that he was obviously of gypsy descent with olive skin and matted black hair that fell into his dark eyes.

He picked up the pitchfork, his eyes now hooded and dangerous.

"I would risk the rain, Madame, if I were you," he said in a thick peasant's patois. "Before something bad happens."

In spite of his implied threat and before Maggie could react he turned and slunk into the depths of the darkened stable interior.

14

DIRTY LITTLE SECRET

Frère Jean shivered on the cold slate tiles where he was stretched out face down and naked. The police had left but he could not rid himself of the persistent feeling of dread and guilt.

He turned and lay his cheek against the freezing floor and watched the candles on the high mantle as they flickered and tossed spasmodic shadows across the wall of his bedroom. He would need to dress soon to get ready to serve dinner. A wave of dread washed over him and he groaned.

How was he to receive forgiveness for his crimes if the littlest thing that popped into his head was met with resistance and bad grace?

It didn't matter what he had done. It didn't matter what sin —what terrible, terrible sin—he'd committed. His flock needed to eat. And they needed him to feed them. As it was, this feeling of persecution was an indulgence he didn't deserve to feel.

The poor child, Henri's daughter...she needs my help.

Again, an intermingling flash of dread and resistance shot through him. Tears stung his eyes at the realization of how evil he must be if every act of kindness he intended was met by his body with an intrinsic reaction of repugnance.

Forgive me, Father, he murmured with his eyes closed, his tears splashing against the cold tile. *Although I don't deserve it.*

He suddenly heard the sound of his cell phone vibrating from where he'd put it in the pocket of his robe folded on the bed. The humming sound shot up his spine like an electric shock.

He pulled himself to his knees, feeling the instant relief from the agonizing cold and once more scolded himself for the pleasure that relief gave him. He walked to where his phone was insistently vibrating, his eyes going to the ancient eighteenth century wardrobe and his stomach clenched in fear and guilt.

Forcing himself to listen to the phone demanding he answer it—and yet not answering—was his penance. He so wanted to reach out and see if his worst fear was to be realized. He prayed it wasn't the police calling to say they would be getting a search warrant for his office, his room.

His wardrobe.

He delayed answering the phone because he didn't deserve to feel the relief of that hope. He deserved to feel exactly what he was feeling: gut churning fear that everything he had worked for was about to come crashing down around him.

The phone stopped vibrating and Frère Jean took in a long shaky breath.

He knew what he had done was enough to make him burn in hell but that wasn't the worst of it. The worst of it was that he couldn't yet say he'd have done anything differently.

So how can I expect God to understand and forgive? he thought forlornly.

He picked up the phone and looked at the screen. The number was not familiar to him and he felt anxiety gnaw harder at his stomach lining. The caller had left a voicemail.

Forcing himself not to look on his wall mantle with its statue of Saint Aderald because even a glance would signal that he was petitioning him for help and he didn't deserve any for what he'd done.

He pushed the play function and listened to the brief message as the Aix police department informed him that his continued cooperation was requested in further questioning.

A police car would come tomorrow morning first thing to bring him to the station in Aix-en-Provence.

Frère Jean disconnected and dropped the phone on the bed with a shaking hand. And then turned and vomited onto the cold floor.

15

GOING NOWHERE FAST

Maggie drove slowly away from the monastery knowing nothing more than she had before she'd gotten totally drenched and ruined her favorite pair of Balenciaga sneakers.

She checked her phone to see that nobody had tried to reach her. She put another call into Jean-Luc to check on him and the children. When he assured her that they were fine, she decided to detour long enough to hit the new *boulangerie* in St-Buvard before heading home.

The long day had worn on her and she found her nerves jangling with exhaustion and renewed pique at Roger's dodging her phone calls all day. She parked on the street in front of the St-Buvard *boulangerie* and waited until the rain lessened somewhat before climbing out of the car.

It always gave her a boost to see the new St-Buvard bakery open and full of villagers. It had been nearly ten years since St-Buvard had its own bakery. It had been a hardship for the village having to rely on bakery trucks or inconvenient out-of-the-way trips to neighboring villages.

Run by a man Laurent had met at the monastery last winter,

the new bakery was doing a brisk business this morning. The bell over the door rang when she entered and she saw Madame Pelletier look up from behind the pastry display counter. Because Laurent had bought the bakery last winter and hired Antoine—who had been jobless and homeless before then—to run it, Maggie always got a royal welcome when she visited the shop.

She'd had to insist early on that Antoine and his wife stop moving her to the front of the line because of the annoyed glares from the villagers who'd been waiting in line before her but she could do little about the fact that they refused to allow her to purchase a single bun or baton with her money.

It was embarrassing but in every way also very real. In the minds of the Pelletiers—and probably the village too who universally adored him—Laurent had lifted them from the muck of poverty and disgrace and therefore they were his devoted apostles forever more.

"*Bonjour*, Madame Dernier!" Madame Pelletier called out. She was busy wrapping up several *batons* for Madame Dulcie, the woman who ran the *charcuterie*, who in turn gave Maggie an arched eyebrow as way of greeting.

"Antoine!" Madame Pelletier called out and Maggie cringed thinking she was calling her husband to wait on Maggie before everyone else in line. She waved her hand at Madame Pelletier.

"*Non, Madame*," Maggie said. "I'll wait my turn."

But Antoine was emerging from the back, his eyes searching the small crowd until they landed on Maggie. He let out a low whoop that was a combination of surprise and pleasure and quickly untied his apron and came around the counter.

This was unusual. Never before had Antoine come to her from behind the counter and Maggie looked sheepishly at the women around her and smiled apologetically.

"Madame Dernier," Antoine said as they shook hands. "May we speak in the back?" He waved a hand to indicate a small alcove that led to the back room.

Surprised but relieved it didn't look like she was going to get special treatment, Maggie followed him to the back room.

"Is everything all right, Antoine?" she asked.

"For me, everything is wonderful," Antoine said seriously, his tone belying his words. "It is only for you and Laurent that I worry."

Maggie didn't know why she assumed nobody would know about what had happened. This was a small village. Of course everyone knew.

"What have you heard?" Maggie asked. Without thinking her hand moved to her abdomen as if to protect the baby from bad news.

"Everyone has heard about the body found in the vineyard this morning," Antoine said.

"I'm not surprised," Maggie said. "Do you know who he is?"

Antoine's eyebrows shot up into the bandana he kept wrapped around his large bald head.

"Yes, of course. It is Henri Dupree," he said. "He was a teacher in Dijon before losing his job last year."

"You knew him when you lived at the monastery?"

"*Oui.* Knew him but stayed clear of him," Antoine said with a grimace. "Not a nice man. A lovely daughter, to be sure. Beautiful girl. She often kept company with my own daughter Mireille."

"Okay," Maggie said, still not sure why Antoine was looking so worried. "Do you know how he died?"

He threw up his arms. "But of course. It was murder, Madame."

After what she'd overheard from Roger this morning, this didn't come as a total shock to Maggie but she still felt a little dizzy hearing it spoken so plainly now.

"Madame? You are wishing to sit down?"

"No, I'm fine. How did you hear about it? I mean, how do you know it's murder?"

"The police," Antoine said matter of factly. "They were here this morning. They think I have no ears to overhear with." He gave a disgusted expression at the mention of the police.

"And *they* said he was murdered?" Maggie asked.

Antoine nodded. "Stabbed in the back."

Now Maggie really did need to sit down and she blamed the little hitchhiker inside her for the reaction. Antoine swiftly pulled a stool out and helped Maggie onto it. She tried to remember the last time she'd eaten anything.

"You are not well, Madame?"

"I'm fine," Maggie said, feeling too warm all of a sudden. "I didn't know that part about the knife." She cleared her throat.

"But of course. And then Laurent being arrested for it? It is horrible! The whole village is up in arms over it."

"Oh, well, he's just answering a few questions for the police," Maggie said, beginning to fan herself with a folded up flyer she found in her purse. "He's just helping them to understand the timeline."

"*Mais non, Madame!*" Antoine said shaking his head. "The police who were in the *boulangerie* today? They were very emphatic about this!"

Maggie's head began to swim.

"What are you saying?" she said. "What did the policemen say?"

"They said that Laurent is their main suspect."

16

MISSION CRITICAL

Maggie drove the three miles from the *boulangerie* to Domaine St-Buvard in a trance. She didn't even register when Madame Pelletier handed her a free baguette, nor the scowls of the waiting, paying customers as she stumbled out the door unmindful of where she was.

Laurent is under arrest for murder.

That's why he hadn't called. *That's* why Roger hadn't returned any of her calls. Deep down, hadn't she known? Wasn't that the only explanation for why nobody had called her all day long?

She pulled into the driveway of Domaine St-Buvard and noted the light glowing in the kitchen window and the smoke coming out of the single chimney and she wanted to open her car door and vomit onto the gravel drive. Instead she took in long breaths to steady herself. She needed to act normal for the sake of the children. And Jean-Luc.

She couldn't flip out. She didn't have the luxury of breaking down.

Her phone vibrated from inside her purse and for a moment she didn't even register it. Then she grabbed her purse and dumped its contents out onto the passenger seat. Her phone screen was lit up with an *Unknown Caller.*

Hesitating, she picked it up and hit *Accept.*

"*Allo?*" she said breathlessly.

"*Chérie?*"

At the sound of Laurent's voice it was all Maggie could do not to burst into tears right there. Instead, since there was no room in the car to jump and dance, she opted for the ages old wives' method of expressing joy in a crisis.

"Why didn't you call me?" she demanded. "I've been worried sick all day! What is going on? Antoine said you've been arrested for murder!"

"*Chérie*, calm down," Laurent said soothingly. "I am sorry I have not called. I forgot my phone."

That's no excuse! Maggie wanted to say but she bit her lip.

"I am calling to say I will be here a little bit longer."

"I knew it! They think you murdered Dupree, don't they?"

"How did you know who—"

"Antoine said the police have arrested you!"

"*Non, chérie.* The police have not arrested me. *Est-ce que tu compris?* Antoine is an old gossip."

"You're not being held as a person of interest?"

"*Non. Pas du tout.* I am just helping them with their inquiries."

"But what do *you* know? How helpful can you be?"

"They need background on the monastery and the people who live there. That is all. I will tell you all about that when I see you, *chérie.*"

"When will that be? When are you coming home?"

"Not for a little bit but I need you to be strong and to behave yourself, *oui*? You are not to go investigating this on your own. Maggie? Promise me?"

Maggie wondered if he had somehow heard of her visit to *l'Abbaye de Sainte-Trinité* today.

"I mean it, *chérie.* No Nancy Drew this time, *oui?*"

"Yes, fine. I promise." But as she said the words she was aware of something in the back of her mind flitting about the edges of her thoughts. Something nagging and not at all comforting.

"As long as *you* promise to wrap up whatever you're doing with the police," she said. "And get back home as soon as possible."

"*Bien sur.* How are the children?"

"Jean-Luc spent the day with them. I had to go to Aix."

"Your father?"

Maggie sighed. "Actually more my mother this time. She couldn't work the stove and she didn't want to go shopping on her own."

"It is time for them to come to Domaine St-Buvard."

"I know. I know."

"I must go now, *chérie.* Stay home and wait for me, eh?"

"Yes, of course."

"Mind the little ones and give them a kiss from their papa," he said. She could tell he was in a rush now to get off the phone. "*Je t'aime, chérie.*"

"Me too you," she said as he disconnected.

She sat holding the phone wondering why she didn't feel comforted by having finally talked with Laurent when the front door opened and Jean-Luc stood there watching her questioningly.

She held up a finger to indicate she'd be inside in a minute and he nodded and went back in. She needed a second to collect her thoughts and to reconstruct the cheerful facade needed for the rest of the evening with Jem and Mila. She took in another long breath and just as she was about to leave the car, her phone rang again.

Thinking Laurent had forgotten to tell her something important, she snatched it up.

"Hello?"

"*Salut*, Maggie," Roger Bedard said. "Is this a good time?"

"You mean unlike all those *other* times throughout the day when I called and you never picked up?" Maggie said sourly. "What the hell, Roger?"

"I am sorry about that. Did you not think I would have answered the phone if I had anything at all positive to tell you?"

"Well, you could have just told me you had no news. That would've been better than being stonewalled! As it was, it made me go down a very dark road thinking maybe you thought Laurent was a suspect."

There was a pause on the line.

"Roger?" Maggie swallowed a sour taste in her mouth. "You... you don't think that, do you?"

"*Non*, Maggie. Of course not. *I* believe Laurent *absolument* when he says he had nothing to do with Dupree's death."

Oh God, Maggie thought. *No. No. No.* She felt as if the car was falling away beneath her, the trees outside swirling around her in a nauseating vortex of horror.

And still Roger's voice went on relentlessly.

"I am so sorry, Maggie. I wanted to call you with any other kind of information but this."

Maggie watched the light in the kitchen turn off as she stared at her home with her children waiting for her inside. Waiting for her and their father to come home.

"I hate to have to tell you that in spite of my best efforts and intentions today we arrested your husband as our prime suspect in the murder of Henri Dupree."

17

MONSTERS UNDER THE BED

The rain appeared to be finally stopping. Pierre peered out from the stable doors at the low overhang of fat grey clouds. There was a smell in the air of wet earth and stone that even seemed to overpower the fragrance wafting over from the stables.

Pierre stared at his hands, every finger bitten bloody. The police had been gone for hours and because of the bad weather Pierre had seen few people emerge from the refectory or their quarters in the upstairs dormitory. Even the monk had been invisible today—not like him at all.

The day had been an agony as Pierre had waited for the police to come and arrest him. If it hadn't been for his gut feeling —the one that never let him down—telling him to hold tight, that all was not lost—he would have lit out the minute he saw their cruisers drive up to the monastery.

But he'd held his hand. Just like *Oncle* Tito had taught him. He hadn't presumed and acted. Instead, he'd waited. He'd waited and swept the stable clean of every shred of hay or dung in the place. He'd waited and polished the pony harness—cracked and wet from years of ill use—until it molded in his hands like butter.

He'd waited and fed the pony and all the goats, re-supplied the kegs of grain and corn, and laid down new hay in all the stalls.

And when he saw the police leave and he realized that Noelle hadn't told on him after all—at least for now—he felt an overwhelming urge to slam his fist into the wooden slats that framed the door hinge and shout for pure joy.

And when the buzz of relief and pleasure wound down and left him exhausted and flushed, he sat on a bale of hay in the door of the stables and watched the night form into a spectacle of stars and moonlight and he realized...he still wasn't safe.

And I won't be as long as that girl lives.

He stood up and wiped his hands on his jeans leaving grease marks across his hips and knees.

He had two choices now.

He could run—which went against his every instinct at the moment. *Oncle* Tito had been right about that too, he thought grimly.

Run and the police are like a pack of dogs after a jack rabbit. Even if they weren't interested in you before, they'll chase you.

Running would signal the dogs to chase. It would mean Pierre would never again have a place to lay his head for longer than a night, he would never have a job he could count on, never emerge from the muck and mire of the underbelly of any city he ran to for fear of discovery.

A life on the run was no life at all.

His other option?

As he sat in the stable, miraculously he saw his other option take human animated form. Noelle appeared in the dusk, walking—alone—unmindful of the cold.

His only other option was to go to her and hear what she'd told the police. See if she could be trusted not to tell them the truth.

As Pierre watched her walk quickly around the corner of the refectory, he realized she was heading toward the monastery gardens, probably for a cigarette. He quickly slunk into the shadows of the stables and waited until she passed. He felt a spark of irritation that she hadn't even glanced in the direction of the stables. It seemed he wasn't on her mind right now.

Would he be tomorrow? After the pain of being newly bereaved had faded, would she remember him then? And pick up the phone to call the police?

He slipped out of the entrance and silently followed her, keeping to the shadows and the Mimosa shrubs that lined the high monastery walls.

Since he knew where she was going all he had to do was make sure she didn't see or hear him behind her.

Whatever happened when he reached the churchyard, *as long as it wasn't witnessed*, could not be connected to him. He shivered, sorry he hadn't taken the time to grab his jacket.

He heard a faint sob as Noelle's weeping was flung back at him on the wind. He felt a surge of elation.

She has no idea anyone is following her.

She pushed open the rusting iron gate in the front of the graveyard and walked to a stone bench among the headstones. It might have been a pretty churchyard once but now it was littered with Coke cans and cigarette stubs.

He waited at the lowest part of the stone wall that surrounded the graveyard until she bent her head to light her cigarette. Then he put his hands on the stone wall and vaulted over the top, landing softly on the damp dirt on the other side.

She never even looked up. The moonlight was enough to see by and the ember of her lit cigarette provided a target as vivid as a laser pointer's dot.

He launched himself at her, knocking her off the bench and onto the ground and pinned her beneath him.

She was so shocked she didn't fight him. Later Pierre would wonder if that was the reason that things happened next the way they did. He'd expected a quick, useless struggle. But instead she lay limply under him as if resigned to whatever he might do to her.

It was the only explanation that Pierre had for why he leaned over and instead of wrapping his fingers around her neck, he said in a low voice that didn't sound remotely like his, "Forgive me."

Just hearing his own voice say those words sent a shock wave through him. He was breathing heavily now in sharp labored pants, waiting for her response.

He saw her eyes dart about as if unsure of where she was or what was happening. She was so beautiful and so helpless.

"Noelle," Pierre said. "Do you understand? I'm sorry. I'm sorry about...what I did."

"You're sorry," she said, her words halting as if in disbelief.

He leaned close to her, his lips by her ear.

"Did you tell the police?" he whispered, his heart hammering in his chest as he waited for the answer he already knew.

If she'd told them, he'd be in jail right now.

"I...don't want to think about last night," she said and a tear escaped her eye and crawled down her chin.

Pierre shifted off her, suddenly aware that he wasn't sure what he was doing. He'd never felt this way before. And he hated the feeling.

"Noelle?" he said and he heard the pleading hitch in his voice.

"I forgive you," she murmured.

His head started spinning at the sound of her words and he felt a warmth radiate throughout his body. He pulled her to a sitting position.

"You forgive me?" he asked. "Really? And you won't tell?"

"I won't tell."

Pierre's relief coursed through him. "I love you, Noelle."

She looked at him, her face a mask of naked hunger and pain. "You do?"

Her hands clutched at his shirt and he pulled her to him,

pressing her tightly against his chest, his heart thudding loudly. An uncomfortable gurgling sensation spread through his gut.

"Yes," he said stiffly. "Of course I do."

Her shoulders began to shake and he realized she was crying. He held her and smoothed her beautiful hair down over her shoulders as she gave herself to her grief. His arms felt twitchy and prickling as if ants were crawling on them and he resisted the urge to jump up and rub them vigorously with his hands.

Instead he patted her on the back as she wept and clung to him.

What kind of woman could forgive such a thing? he thought as a wave of disgust slithered through his body.

18

A HARD RAIN'S A-COMING

Maggie wasn't sure how she got from the car into the house and then through the long evening of interacting with the children, making dinner and putting them to bed—all the while her mind in a constant turmoil of fear and dread.

Laurent is arrested.

Climbing into bed that night she felt the bare space next to her where Laurent should have been and her eye fell on the empty dog bed on the floor. Making sure the children were asleep first, she turned her face to her pillow and cried herself to sleep for the first time since she'd moved to France ten years earlier.

The next morning, she went through the motions of letting the dogs out, making breakfast and getting the children ready for church, amazing herself that she could go on autopilot so effectively without anyone noticing.

Later, as she was walking to the car after church in the little village church, she called Danielle to see if she and Jean-Luc were free to watch the children again today.

"I am at Grace's for the day," Danielle said. "The Americans have arrived and they are problematic, I'm afraid."

Maggie had forgotten about Grace's tour group.

"But I'm sure the children will be no problem if you want to drop them off here at *Dormir*," Danielle said.

"Is Jean-Luc there too?"

"Yes, he is working with Gabriel on a plumbing issue one of the Americans complained about."

"Are you sure they won't be in the way?" but Maggie was already pointing the car in the direction of Grace's *gite*.

Danielle's *mas* when she'd been married to Eduard Marceau was smaller than Maggie and Laurent's country house but it was imposing nonetheless. When Laurent bought the property from Danielle last summer after Eduard died he had the bathrooms renovated and put in an additional one and updated the kitchen. The rest he left to Grace when he rented her the property to to run as a bed and breakfast.

Maggie knew she could never have created the heart-stopping beauty of a place that Grace had done. She and Grace had spent many a Saturday morning last summer combing Provence and the Internet for just the right fabrics, pillow cushions, bed linens, artwork and *faience* in order to give any visitor the most iconic South of France experience possible.

A rental SUV was parked next to Danielle and Jean-Luc's older station wagon in the gravel drive.

As soon as Maggie parked her Renault next to Danielle's car, Jemmy and Mila scampered out and ran to the kitchen where Grace's twelve year old daughter Zouzou was sitting on a stool laboriously mixing a large bowl.

From the scent coming from the room, Zouzou was baking a cake of some kind and Maggie felt her stomach growl.

Grace stood in the living room, her hand on one hip, her hair tousled in waves of gold around her shoulders. Maggie had to admit that even as a harried inn keeper, Grace was beautiful.

Every hair in place, her makeup subdued but there, she wore what looked like a pair of Gucci pleated silk slacks with a jersey sweatshirt. Casual but perfection, like she just walked out of the pages of France Vogue. As usual.

Three heavyset women in tracksuits were talking earnestly to Grace who never stopped smiling as she listened to them. Danielle materialized from the far end of the kitchen, a wooden spoon in her hand. Maggie saw that she had been stirring some concoction on the stove, probably lunch. They greeted each other with a kiss.

"Things seem pretty tense here," Maggie said in French, assuming the Americans wouldn't understand her if they overheard.

"They are terrible people," Danielle said with a sigh. "I feel so bad for Grace. She is trying hard to do a good job."

"What's their problem?"

"There are many, I'm afraid and no time to describe them all."

"Was Jean-Luc able to fix the plumbing problem?"

Danielle nodded in the direction of the hallway off the living room beyond where Grace stood and Maggie turned to see Jean-Luc standing there now too, conferring with Grace.

Maggie hesitated. She didn't feel good about dropping the kids off when Grace had her hands full like this but Roger had agreed to meet her at Le Canard, the bar in St-Buvard, and she could not bring the kids with her when she met with him.

After much head nodding, Jean-Luc joined them in the kitchen and greeted Maggie with a kiss. Jemmy ran to him.

"I can help you, *Pépère*!" he said eagerly. "Papa lets me help all the time."

"Of course he does," Jean-Luc said to Jem. "And there is much for you to do here. Monsieur Gabriel will tell us, eh? Perhaps you could find him?"

Jemmy bolted out of the room nearly knocking over a small lamp in the process. Beyond him, Maggie saw that two more women had joined the first three in addressing Grace. One of them was raising her voice. Even from here, Maggie could see Grace's smile was wavering just a bit.

Maggie turned to Jean-Luc and Danielle and lowered her voice so that Zouzou and Mila couldn't hear.

"They've arrested Laurent for the murder of the guy found in our vineyard," Maggie said quickly.

Danielle gasped. "*Mais non!*"

Zouzou and Mila looked over but Jean-Luc just smiled and waved his hand to indicate it was nothing. They turned away again.

"I knew it," he said. "*Putains.* You cannot trust them."

"I assume you mean the police," Maggie said, "and in this case I'm afraid I have to agree. Laurent went willingly to give them whatever help they needed and they've grabbed for the first likely suspect."

"You must prove him innocent," Danielle said, her brows knit together in fierce determination.

"I'm meeting with the guy in charge at Le Canard," Maggie said. "He'll tell me what I can do."

Danielle looked toward the living room with dismay. "You were hoping Grace could help you, were you not?"

Maggie shrugged. "I guess. But she's got enough on her plate right now."

"But nothing as important as this, surely?" Jean-Luc said.

"No, Jean-Luc," Maggie said firmly. "I don't want to make Grace's life any harder than it is. If she knows I need her, she'll drop everything and she can't do that. She's supposed to be getting her life in order."

They all glanced at the living room. Now *two* women were raising their voices to Grace.

"If you can keep an eye on Jem and Mila until I return, Danielle, that would be all the help I need for now."

"You will keep us informed, *chérie*?" Danielle asked.

"Of course. You know I will."

Jean-Luc was chewing his mustache, his face flushed with concern.

Maggie paused just long enough to put a hand on his shoulder.

"Don't worry, Jean-Luc," she said. "It's all going to be fine."

The bar and restaurant Le Canard was the only place in the village of St-Buvard where one could get a drink let alone a sandwich. Over the years Maggie had spent many a happy hour after shopping with Grace or her mother sitting on the outdoor terrace that faced the main street that dissected the village.

The sky was still spitting rain when Maggie parked her car across from the café and hurried inside.

Roger was already seated with a cloudy glass of *pastis* in front of him. He'd ordered her a *kir*. As Maggie approached the table she didn't know if she was touched that he'd ordered her favorite drink or annoyed that he was showing off that he knew what it was.

She leaned over and they kissed on both cheeks, something it occurred to her that they did not normally do when Laurent was present and the realization unsettled her.

She sat down heavily.

"How did this happen, Roger?" she said tiredly. "Surely forensics has come back by now? Why are you still holding Laurent?"

Roger ran a hand across his face in frustration. It was probably too cold to be sitting on the terrace at this time of year but Maggie knew Roger had chosen it for the privacy it gave them. She was glad she'd worn her heavy pashmina over her jacket. She reached for her glass. Surely just a few sips wouldn't hurt the baby? She drank more than this at communion on Sundays. She sipped the *kir* and instantly felt some of the harsher edges on her nerves begin to soften.

"You know I answer to people higher up, right?" Roger said.

"I know that as far as this investigation goes the buck stops with *you*, Roger. So quit trying to dodge the responsibility. If Laurent is under arrest it's because *you* arrested him. So just tell me. What evidence do you have?"

"The knife lodged in the man's back," Roger said, his face pinched with tension. "It was Laurent's."

That fact startled Maggie. She took in a breath and tried to remember which of Laurent's knives she'd seen and what he used them for. He had many tools for cutting and trimming vine stocks but nothing specific came to mind.

How could Laurent's knife have been used to kill a man?

"You don't know for sure that the knife is Laurent's. And it's too early to get a DNA match."

"Laurent identified it as his."

Maggie's mouth dropped open. Why would Laurent admit that? Was he trying to show he had nothing to hide? Because even Maggie knew *that* wasn't wise.

"He said he lost it in the vineyard a few weeks back," Roger said.

Maggie swallowed down the rest of her *kir* but the alcohol didn't seem to be helping any more.

"Can you tell me how Monsieur Dupree died?" she asked.

"How did you know his name?"

There was no way Maggie was going to tell Roger that Frère Jean had called looking for Laurent to see if he knew where Dupree was because they'd had an altercation. She shrugged. "Everyone in St-Buvard knows," she said.

"And also you might have heard it when you visited *l'Abbaye de Sainte-Trinité*," Roger said, raising an eyebrow at her.

So he knew. Well, so what? It wasn't a crime and she'd been desperate for information.

She glared at him. "You were about to tell me how he was killed," she said.

"The autopsy isn't finished yet. But he'd been stabbed in the back. His hands were tied behind him and his forehead showed evidence of blunt force trauma."

Maggie frowned. "Was he killed in the vineyard?"

"Hard to say. There wasn't much blood from the back wound so there's a possibility that that wasn't even what killed him. We won't know until the lab results come back."

"So all you have against Laurent is that it was his knife?"

"That and the fact that he doesn't have an alibi."

"I was with him all night!"

"Really? Because he said he went out into the vineyard at eight o'clock and then again at midnight."

Maggie suddenly felt overly warm. She shook her head as if to clear it.

Why was Laurent telling Roger the truth? Especially when that truth looked so bad for him? She knew her husband. She knew he didn't believe in the justice of the process. He personally knew too many friends who were doing time because of circumstantial evidence for crimes they didn't commit. Being innocent meant nothing. *Appearing* to be innocent was always much more important.

Of course, they were the same friends who more often than not were guilty of other crimes that they hadn't gotten caught for, so Maggie thought it probably all balanced out. Perhaps that's the way Laurent looked at it too.

But if so it was very unlike him.

"Wow, he's really trusting you, isn't he?" she said.

A hurt expression formed on Roger's face. "Maggie, you know I'm going to do everything I can to make sure an innocent man doesn't pay for this crime. And I believe Laurent to be innocent."

Maggie nodded at his words but she took no comfort in them. After all, this was *Roger* talking.

Roger Bedard doing *everything he could* to make sure an innocent man didn't pay for the crime was practically as good as a guilty verdict for Laurent.

19

COLD, COLD HEART

The day after Henri Dupree's body was found, Guy sat alone in the refectory, a bowl of fish soup in front of him that he didn't have the heart to eat. He'd had several opportunities since yesterday to approach Noelle—to see how she was, to see if he could explain to her what she'd seen—but every time she spied him she ran away.

"This seat taken?"

Guy looked up to see the old widow Madame Montagne standing by his elbow, her lunch of bread and a banana in her hands.

"Help yourself," he said, nodding at the free chair. There were six empty chairs at his table.

"Did the police talk with you yesterday?" she asked, clearly ready to have a long detailed conversation about all the excitement at the monastery.

"Why would they?" he asked, wiping his suddenly damp hands on his jeans. "I have no idea how the old bastard got to the vineyard."

Madame Montage narrowed her eyes and Guy had the uncomfortable sensation that she could read his mind.

Hell, she could probably read his soul.

"They talked to lots of people yesterday," she said. "It is not a stupid question."

"No. They did not talk with me. Did they talk with you?"

"No."

"Well, there you are. Glad we got that cleared up." Just before Guy was about to jump to his feet and rid himself of the nosy old woman, it occurred to him that if he were to stop behaving so defensively he might actually be able to get some information from *her*.

If anybody knew anything about what was going on, Madame Montague would. But before he could put his thoughts together, she cackled loudly and pointed at the door forcing him to turn to look.

There, coming into the refectory was Noelle *holding hands with the gypsy bastard*.

Guy felt his muscles go numb as he stared, his mouth fell open in shock.

"Anybody besides me feel Henri turning in his grave?" Madame Montage said.

Guy lurched to his feet and cut the pair off as they made their way to the long table of bread and fruit at the side of the room.

"What do you think you're doing?" Guy said angrily as he shoved Pierre, separating his hand from Noelle.

A grimace of irritation flashed across Pierre's face before it was replaced by his signature smirk.

"Well, well, if it's not the ex-boyfriend," Pierre said. "Except Noelle said you weren't her boyfriend at all. It was all in your head. Pretty pathetic."

His face mottled with building rage, Guy clenched and unclenched his hands as he turned to Noelle. The look on her face stopped whatever he'd been thinking of saying. She wasn't looking at him, she was looking at her feet and her face was completely blank.

She looked drugged.

"Noelle," Guy said. "You don't have to be with him. You won't be alone."

"Are you a joke?" Pierre said derisively. "You think she's with me because she's afraid of being alone? Do you even have eyes?"

"Yes and I don't believe what I'm seeing," Guy snarled at him before turning back to Noelle.

"Noelle, please—"

"Don't talk to me!" Noelle shouted, looking him in the eye for the first time. "I'm with Pierre now. I was never with you. I was never going to be with you. Now leave us alone!"

Guy's stomach twisted at the look she gave him. It was worse than intolerance or even annoyance. The look she gave him was hatred.

Pierre laughed and draped his arm around Noelle's shoulders, reaching down to brush her breast with his fingers as if to rub into Guy's face his familiarity with her. Then, casually picking up a banana and a baguette Pierre pivoted Noelle back toward the front door.

As Guy watched them go, he desperately wanted to call out to Noelle to remind her that this *gitane* was not what her father wanted for her. It took every ounce of self-control he had not to scream out, *What would your father think?*

But he knew he didn't dare mention Henri's name. Not to Noelle. Not now. Not after what she saw him do that night.

20

BLOWING IN THE WIND

The next morning Maggie helped the kids dress for school and then drove them to Jean-Luc and Danielle's house. Before turning onto the drive Maggie saw the old sign, the faded letters *Domaine Alexandre* nearly obscured by time and the crowding olive trees. Typical of the old farmhouses in the area, their *mas* was built of rough fieldstone from the 1700s. It featured chipped blue shutters and terra cotta roofing and was set at the end of a long winding gravel drive.

Danielle was heading to *Dormir* this morning to pick up Zouzou and would drive all the children to school in Aix from there. They made arrangements for Maggie to collect them after school.

After Maggie kissed the children goodbye and helped load them up with their satchels and backpacks into Danielle's car, she waved them off and noticed that Jean-Luc was standing by the car, his hands on his hips.

"You are going to *l'Abbaye de Sainte-Trinité* today?" he asked.

Maggie was surprised. "How did you know?"

"It is where I would go to try to get answers on who killed the man."

"It's really all I have," Maggie said.

"That is not true," Jean-Luc said solemnly as he came around the car and slid in beside her. "You have me as well."

Maggie didn't know why she hadn't thought of it herself. Jean-Luc adored Laurent and was nearly as upset about what had happened as Maggie.

And just as driven to find information that would absolve Laurent.

As they drove to the monastery, she filled him in on what she knew about the murder so far.

"If the cops are still at the monastery, we probably won't get very far. But if they're not, I say we split up and talk to as many people as we can."

"*D'accord*," Jean-Luc said, his face set in a determined scowl.

The police were gone.

Maggie parked the car in the gravel parking lot in front of the monastery and she and Jean-Luc arranged to meet back at the car in an hour.

She debated whether to go inside the main hall of the monastery where most of the people seemed to congregate or back around the perimeter near the stables where she'd been before. In the end, she opted for the main hall. The sign next to the huge double doors bade all guests to please ring the bell but Maggie had always believed that giving anyone warning of her intentions was ill-advised. She grabbed the heavy wrought iron door handle and pushed open the smaller door.

The hall opened up into a main area featuring a high arched ceiling of rock over stone floors and walls with tall narrow windows. Metal and wooden tables had been set up in no particular order where at least two dozen people sat eating their midday meal.

Everyone stared as Maggie wove her way through the seated

throng. She did her best to smile at them—even though she'd been told over and over again by Laurent that the French don't smile at people for no reason unless they're doing it in a mental asylum. Smiling for no obvious reason was considered suspicious behavior.

But Maggie had been raised in the Deep South. She could no more have walked through a strange crowd and not smile than run naked through Lenox Square Mall.

The first person Maggie got eye contact with was an old woman sitting by herself. Maggie stopped in front of the woman. Reminding herself that if she was going to smile like a lunatic at least she could heed the other rules of French socializing and spend a few minutes chit-chatting with the woman before asking her where she might find Dupree's daughter or Frère Jean.

"*Bonjour*, Madame," Maggie said brightly. "It's a lovely day, isn't it?"

"It is pissing rain," the old woman said, but her eyes were amused.

"Well, no," Maggie said. "Actually it's cleared up. You might want to take a walk later."

She knew she wasn't very good at the whole small talk thing but she'd promised herself she'd at least try.

"Can I help you, Madame?" the woman said, her brows bunched together in a frown of curiosity.

"I'm hoping you can point out Henri Dupree's daughter to me," Maggie said.

"Do you know her?"

"I do not. That's why I need you to point her out to me."

The woman laughed, revealing a mouth of missing teeth. "Good point," she said. She twisted in her seat and glanced in the direction of the main dining table.

"See the girl in the blue tee-shirt?"

Maggie saw her. The girl was gorgeous. Even from this distance Maggie could see the shimmer in her jet black hair. Her skin was very lightly brown but whether from race or too much time in the sun, Maggie couldn't tell.

"She's beautiful," she said.

"Isn't she? And don't think the boys don't know it."

Maggie looked at the woman. "Does she have lots of boyfriends?"

"I don't know if I'd say *lots*. They flock. She runs."

"I see. What's her name?"

"Noelle."

"Pretty name." Maggie turned back to the woman. "Thank you so much, Madame..."

"Montagne."

"Thank you, Madame Montagne. Have you been at the monastery long?"

"I was the first person Frère Jean invited to stay." She waved her hand to indicate the rest of the people eating in the great hall. "And then *voila*."

"How does he feed everyone?" Maggie asked, her eyes on Noelle at her table of friends. She wasn't talking with the other girls but sat solemnly eating her lunch.

"The monastery is self-sustaining," Madame Montagne said. "The brothers grow all their own produce here. Even the grain that they feed the goats, the chickens and other livestock. They are truly inspirational."

"Very impressive," Maggie said, smiling apologetically before turning and hurrying toward Noelle.

She hadn't gotten ten feet before a shadow materialized in front of her. Maggie bumped into him and took a step back.

"Excuse me," she said and tried to go around him.

"What do you want with Noelle?" the young man said. When Maggie stepped back she could see he was a boy not yet in his twenties. He was handsome and blond, with piercing blue eyes and full lips. One of his lips was split. It looked like someone had punched him in the mouth.

"I'm sorry," Maggie said tamping down her annoyance. "Who are you?"

The young man hesitated and then puffed his chest out as if to compensate for being caught hesitating.

"I am Guy Dionne," he said loudly. "What is your business with Noelle?"

"I would say that it is none of yours," Maggie said politely, again attempting to step around him.

"If it has to do with Noelle, it is my business," he said. "She is upset over the loss of her father and is tired of answering questions."

"Maybe I'll ask *you* a question or two in that case. Like where were you the night her father was killed?"

She meant to unsettle him by the question but instead she saw fear and then fury flash in his eyes at her words. He licked his lips and took a menacing step toward her.

"You are not the police. I do not have to answer your questions." The young man leaned in close and it took all of Maggie's willpower not to step away from him.

"Leave Noelle alone," he growled, his breath pungent with garlic and onions. "I am warning you."

Before Maggie could respond, he twisted on his heel and stormed off and out the front door. Her heart was beating quickly as the sounds of his threat reverberated in her ears and she tried to calm herself. When she looked around her surroundings she saw that everyone nearby was staring at her.

But when she looked in the direction where Noelle had been, Maggie saw that she had disappeared.

21

INVITATION TO A HANGING

Directeur Général Albert Terrone was a large man with loose jowls that jiggled obscenely with every breath he took. His eyes were small and deep-set and lacked any discernible eyelashes. He sat at his desk and laced his fingers across his bulging belly as he observed Roger.

This was only the third time Roger had been in his superior's office over the last seven years. Except for performance evaluations that Roger felt Terrone was singularly unqualified to make about him, he had remarkably little connection with the man. Much of that was due to the fact that Roger worked Homicide and Terrone—as far as Roger could determine—worked on not being in the office as much as he could get away with.

Still, the man had been with the department for twenty years and was respected if not generally liked.

"We have a unique opportunity on our hands," Terrone intoned, deepening his voice and carefully enunciating each word as though Roger was hard of hearing.

"Yes sir?" Roger said. Ever since Terrone had asked to see him this morning Roger had tried to imagine for what possible reason. He had rarely commented on a single case Roger had worked and Roger wracked his brain to imagine why the Dupree murder would be any different.

"The man you have in custody for the Dupree case," Terrone said. "Dernier."

A needle of warning invaded Roger's gut at Terrone's words and he involuntarily tensed in his chair.

"I know him," Terrone said.

"Laurent Dernier is a well-known *vigneron* in this area," Roger said.

"Yes, well, I knew him before he was that," Terrone said, his lip curling over his small yellow teeth.

Roger knew for a fact that Laurent had no official criminal record. He also knew that years ago he had made his living as a con man on the Riviera. The people he consorted with—many of whom *did* end up in prison—and the victims he'd robbed were well-known to most law personnel on the Cote d'Azur.

"Dernier has no record," Roger said.

"I am aware of that," Terrone countered, leaning forward in his chair and pushing the heavy metal desk forward a few inches in the process. "Are you not familiar with the Henderson case? In the late nineties? Or the Diaz case? One million euros worth of South African diamonds never recovered. I worked both those cases back in the day. Did you know that?"

"How are those thefts connected to my murder case, sir?"

Terrone curled his lip and looked at Roger in a cold, flat gaze.

"They are *connected*, Bedard because we finally have the bastard who pulled them off."

Roger suddenly had difficulty breathing.

"I'm not understanding you, sir," he said. "Dernier is a person of interest in my case because he—"

"I know that!" Terrone bellowed, rattling the window behind him. "I'm talking about two con men working the Cote d'Azur in 1998 who stole a million euros worth of diamonds. Are you listening? Two con men. An Alsatian and an Englishman who teamed up to pull off a series of swindles that summer who were never apprehended. Can I tell you how humiliating that was for me and my department, *Inspecteur* Bedard? It was international news!"

"I can imagine, sir," Roger said, his mind racing to get ahead of wherever it was that Terrone was going. Surely the man didn't think he could charge Laurent with a twenty-year old cold crime? With no new evidence?

"We know Dernier's accomplice Roger Bentley died two years ago in London," Terrone said. "But now we have Dernier."

Roger was sweating. He knew Terrone couldn't help but notice.

"Dernier isn't Alsatian," Roger said.

"Don't be an idiot," Terrone said with disgust. "Dernier has been alternately Morrocan, Belgium, Swiss and at one point Austrian. He was whatever was necessary for the particular job. The point is, he's finally made a fatal mistake and now I have him."

"I should tell you, sir," Roger said, licking his lips in growing nervousness, "that the evidence against Dernier for Dupree's murder is weak. So far the forensic indications are only circumstantial. And once the complete pathology report comes in—"

"It is enough for what we need," Terrone said.

"I don't understand," Roger said, feeling a chill slice through him in spite of his perspiring. "Are you suggesting we charge Dernier with one of these cold cases? Has new evidence come in?"

"Don't be stupid," Terrone said. "If anything, the trail is so cold that I could have an eyewitness to both crimes and we still couldn't arrest him for the thefts."

"Then I don't understand why—"

"All you need to know, Bedard, is that as far as you're concerned the Dupree case is closed. You are not to go looking for any other perpetrator."

"But the real killer—" Roger said blinking rapidly and licking his dry and cracking lips.

"Screw the real killer! Are you not listening? *Dernier* is on the hook for this! You have the murder weapon! You have the DNA! You have motive, means and opportunity! Tighten the noose! Do I need to have Detective Inspector Girard present Dernier with his options? Because if I do I'll need to question what *else* you are unable to do in your present position as *Police Commandant*."

"What...what is it you're asking me to do?" Roger said helplessly.

"Get a confession on the diamond heist. Present Dernier with the facts. He can go down for Murder One and spend the rest of his life in prison or confess to the Cannes thefts and get out of prison in time to walk his daughter down the aisle. His choice."

Roger got up out of his chair, his thoughts flying about the room like panicked birds.

"Oh, and Bedard?" Terrone called after him.

Roger paused, his back still to his supervisor.

"Come back to me with anything else than Dernier's confession and I'll have to seriously reconsider your career trajectory."

22

BOTH SIDES NOW

By the time Maggie and Jean-Luc headed back to Domaine St-Buvard the rain had eased. While Maggie had not found either Noelle or Frère Jean—or even a glimpse of the sly gypsy boy she'd seen before—during her hour at the monastery, Jean-Luc had met several people whom all confirmed Guy Dionne's assessment of the murder victim: he was a bad-tempered man who they all tried to stay clear of.

"Always nice to know when the murdered guy is hated," Maggie said as she pulled into the gravel drive at Domaine St-Buvard. "That way everybody including the pious monks have a motive for killing him."

"It does make things more difficult," Jean-Luc agreed. He squinted into the sky and Maggie wondered if his hip hurt him. Recently he'd been using a cane but she noticed he didn't bring it today. He probably didn't want to remind her of his weaknesses—not when she needed a strong partner to help her free Laurent.

As Maggie parked the car, she turned to face Jean-Luc. There had been something on edge about him ever since he'd gotten in the car from the monastery. She was pretty sure the news that Dupree had been an unpleasant man wasn't the reason for it.

"You know, Jean-Luc," she said. "If we're going to be partners, it's important you don't try to protect me from stuff you learn."

He regarded her with widening eyes. "How did you know?"

"I'm getting better at reading people. So what aren't you telling me?"

He sighed heavily. "It is true what the people said about Dupree. But that's not *all* they told me."

"I'm listening."

"I talked to three people who witnessed an unfortunate altercation between Dupree and Laurent the day Dupree died."

Maggie sucked in a quick intake of breath. "What kind of altercation?"

But Maggie knew before Jean-Luc even said the words.

"It was physical. Apparently there was a problem in the fields and Laurent..." Jean-Luc shrugged.

"Laurent what?" Maggie pressed, feeling her heart drop into her stomach.

"He threw Dupree against a tree."

"Oh well if that's all—"

"And I think punched him in the nose."

"You *think*?" Maggie watched Jean-Luc's face for a moment and then turned to stare at the house. "Not good," she said with a sigh.

"There were several witnesses."

"I'm sure Laurent had his reasons."

"They said Dupree was mistreating a small boy. I would have done the same." There was a pause. "Even so."

"Agreed. Bad timing."

They sat quietly for a moment, until Maggie shook off the disquiet the information fostered in her gut. She couldn't change the past. The only thing that would help Laurent now was for her to go forward and find the facts that would lead them to the true killer.

"So," she said, turning to Jean-Luc. "Are you up for a walk in the vineyard?" As soon as the words were out of her mouth she nearly bit her tongue for the look on Jean-Luc's face.

"*Mais bien sûr!*" he said, swinging agilely out of the car.

Maggie didn't miss the wince on his face as he steadied himself and turned toward the path that wound around the *mas* toward the vineyard. She ran into the house to let the two dogs out of their crates and then hurried through the back terrace to catch up with Jean-Luc.

The recent rains would mean that the dogs would come back muddy and since Maggie didn't have the energy or time to give the two rambunctious animals baths, she made a mental note to at least try to towel them off and put them away dirty. She could always brush the dirt off them when it dried.

Izzy and Buddy—named by the children—sprinted ahead of Maggie. It occurred to her as she watched them surge past Jean-Luc who was definitely beginning to limp now—that she had no idea of how she was going to get the dogs back inside.

She pushed the thought from her mind. Jean-Luc would help her corral the dogs and right now she had bigger *poisson* to fry.

The vineyard that surrounded their *mas* was forty hectares of neatly groomed rows of vines. It was cut into fourths by an ancient tractor road and a one-lane country road that led to the village. At this point in the year with the harvest behind them and the hard work of pruning and tidying up dead stalks still months away, there was little reason for anyone to be here.

Maggie watched Jean-Luc's straight back as he worked not to limp or look weak before her. He called to the two half-grown poodles and Maggie's mouth fell open to see the dogs reverse course and run to him.

Jean-Luc always had a way with animals. Laurent had mentioned on more than one occasion that he was surprised

Jean-Luc hadn't replaced his beloved hunting dog Marie when she died of old age last year.

Jean-Luc walked to the southeast quadrant—the one closest to the village road—and turned to wait for Maggie to join him.

Although the police had finished processing the scene the day before, there was still bits and pieces of crime scene tape fluttering from the branches of the vinestocks.

"Is this the area?" Jean-Luc asked.

Maggie looked around. "I think so."

They both stood and looked around where the end of the rows met a narrow, muddy footpath.

It had rained the night of the murder—and the two nights since—so there were no visible tracks except for the ones she, Jean-Luc and the dogs were currently making.

"Can you see anything?" she asked. Like so many men in the area, Jean-Luc used to hunt. Maggie hoped he might be able to make out something the police had missed.

"The rain has destroyed anything there was to see," Jean-Luc confirmed.

"I was afraid of that."

He walked down one of the rows to the end, the dogs loping beside him. Maggie rubbed the chill from her arms through her jacket and pushed her collar up for all the good it did. She felt a heaviness in her body with every step she took.

She'd done everything she could not to think too much of what Roger had said last night. But she keenly felt his betrayal —*he was supposed to be a friend!* The police had their suspect and they would go forward now to do everything they could to cement their case against Laurent.

As usual in these things, they wouldn't be looking outside their own jailhouse at this point.

That would be Maggie's job.

Mine and Jean-Luc's, she reminded herself with a flicker of comfort.

"Maggie?" Jean-Luc called.

Feeling a pulse of excitement, Maggie turned to Jean-Luc at the row nearest the village road.

Had he found something? Something the cops had missed?

"What is it?" she asked breathlessly as she hurried over to him.

He was squatting and looking at something on the ground that looked remarkably like a huge muddled cow patty.

"This shouldn't be here," he said, pointing at the pile.

Maggie frowned. This didn't look like much of a clue to her. She felt the disappointment settle onto her shoulders.

"What is it?" she asked, more to be polite than from any real interest. Jean-Luc seemed to think the pile of crap was somehow important. Had she been wrong to think he would be a help?

"It is from a horse," he said. "Not a very big one, either."

"Okay," she said tiredly. "Is that important, I guess?'

He looked at her, his blue eyes glittering with intelligence and amusement.

"What is a horse doing in your vineyard?" he asked.

Slowly, Maggie began to see what Jean-Luc was getting at. She felt a quickening of interest.

"Are you sure it's horse poop?" she said, squinting at it and wondering if possibly someone's goat had wandered into their field.

"I rode a horse every day of my life until I was sixteen. I think I know it when I see it."

Maggie looked at the nearby village road. While the rain would have destroyed any evidence of horse tracks from the road to the vineyard, the droppings made it clear that one had indeed been inside the vineyard at some point. And while a goat might get loose and wander about the countryside for a day or so, there was no way a horse would go missing for that long without its owner out looking for it.

"You think the murdered guy rode here on a horse?" she

asked, glancing down the row of vines to where the body was found.

"I think it is more likely that whoever killed him was riding the horse," Jean-Luc said.

"Right," Maggie said, her pulse quickening. "Because that way he would have ridden off on the horse. Otherwise the horse would be wandering around loose."

"*Exactement.*"

"So it's possible our killer was on horseback," she said, her brain trying to fit that in with the whole scenario. "It's just that it's a hard picture to imagine, you know? Dupree wandering around our vineyard at night and he comes upon some guy on horseback who kills him?"

Jean-Luc straightened up and called for the dogs who had found the village road.

"I think," he said, "it makes more sense to imagine that Dupree and his killer came together."

"Riding double you mean?"

Jean-Luc shrugged. "We don't know that the horse was saddled. It could have been a wagon. Because as you say it makes no sense that Dupree would be here alone in the night."

"You're suggesting Dupree was killed elsewhere and *brought* here by a wagon?" Maggie's excitement intensified.

"It would certainly fit," Jean-Luc said ominously as the two dogs began jumping excitedly around him.

23

TOO FAR GONE

Roger spent the better part of the rest of his day locked in his office. He sat and he paced. He stared out the window and he watched his cellphone light up with call after call from Maggie—none of which he took. He looked at the photograph on his desk of his daughter, Chloe, eleven years old and the light of his life. Since her mother died a decade earlier, he had done everything he could to be both mother and father to the child.

If he were to fail to do what *Directeur Général* Albert Terrone ordered him to do—get a confession from a suspect—he would without doubt fail his daughter and break every promise he'd made to her dying mother.

His career would be over in the department, perhaps anywhere else in France. What Terrone was doing was illegal of course but it was unthinkable to go to Internal Affairs with this. They were even more hated than the pimps and drug dealers Roger's group hauled in off the streets. Going to IA would simply mean his career was over in a different way.

He dragged a hand over his face and felt his muscles stiffening into tense contractions.

With one last look at the photograph of his smiling angel, Roger checked his watch and then got up and left his office.

The holding cells were located in the bottom two floors in the subterranean cavity of the police department building. Roger jabbed the elevator button, oblivious to the noise and clamor that surrounded him of people walking the halls, laughing or talking. Behind him, facing the bank of elevators, was a large waiting room. As he stepped into the elevator and faced the waiting room he noticed a man in monk's clothing seated there, his head bowed in prayer.

Was he from l'Abbaye de Saint-Trinitie? Was he here because of the Dupree case? He would ask Girard for a full report later that day. Meanwhile as he rode down the elevator Roger cursed the fact that he had handed this particular investigation off to Girard. Roger should've handled this himself.

For all the good that would have done.

Roger walked to the security outpost, showed his badge and signed in. The young policeman walked him to the interview room. A small window was set high up the wall and allowed in a glimmer of sidewalk level activity outside and daylight.

Laurent stood with his back to the door, looking up at the window. He turned when Roger walked in. They shook hands but didn't speak. Roger turned to the guard.

"Turn off all recording devices for this room," he said.

"I will need to make a record of the request," the guard said. "And you'll need to sign off on it."

"Fine. Just do it." Roger turned and gestured for Laurent to sit at the lone table in the room.

Laurent watched him but in no other way did he betray that he was anxious or curious about what was happening. Roger could imagine he had been a very good con man in his day. Even now, he gave nothing away.

"We have a problem," Roger said.

"Let's hear it," Laurent said, his face impassive, his gaze unreadable.

"My boss, Albert Terrone, does not care about the murder of some refugee."

"And yet I am still here," Laurent said and a faint sad smile tugged at his lips as if he'd already jumped ahead to the end and knew exactly what Roger had come to say.

"He wants you for the ninety-eight Cannes theft," Roger said.

"Is there new evidence?"

"No."

Laurent nodded. "I see." There was a pause. "Is there an offer on the table?"

"None that is not reprehensible and disgraceful," Roger said bitterly.

"I'd still like to hear it."

Roger took in a breath. "Confess to the twenty year old heist or go down for Murder One."

Laurent nodded again. "How is the evidence against me for the murder? Or does that matter?"

Roger had difficulty swallowing and felt the nagging pain again in the back of his throat.

"There's enough to go to trial," he said. "Or there will be."

"And you are no longer searching for the real killer?"

"It wouldn't matter, Laurent. Even if Dupree's killer waltzed in here and confessed, he'd be sent away. Terrone has the power to suppress or even destroy any evidence that might cloud the certainty of your guilt." Roger hesitated. "I have nothing concrete to base that on but because he doesn't trust me, I probably wouldn't be in the loop anyway."

"This puts you in a bad spot, doesn't it?" Laurent said.

"Forget about me. What will you do?"

Laurent looked back toward the high window in the interview room. There was no way Roger could discern what the man was thinking.

"I'm sorry, Laurent. It's a hell of a thing," Roger said.

Maggie will hate me until the day I die.

"It is what it is," Laurent said.

"Can I do anything for you? I know the names of several good defense lawyers."

Laurent continued to stare toward the small patch of daylight from the window. He turned and smiled sadly at Roger.

"Never mind," Laurent said, his face giving away nothing. "If what you say is true, all the defense lawyers in France won't help."

24

TIGHTROPE

Back at the house, Jean-Luc took a hose and washed off both dogs while Maggie made coffee. Her mind was swirling with the possibilities of what they'd discovered in the vineyard.

It wasn't so farfetched. There was no other explanation for why a horse would be wandering around the vineyard at night. The droppings—although deteriorated from the rain—could easily be seen as fresh enough to have been recently deposited.

Jean-Luc's theory about a wagon made so much sense. But Maggie knew she didn't have any evidence to put before Roger. Finding horse poop when there shouldn't have been any wouldn't be enough for him. But it buoyed her anyway. It gave her and Jean-Luc another avenue to go down.

Now they just needed to find someone with access to a horse and wagon or pony cart. Once they added some kind of motive to the mix, they were half way there. When Maggie had asked Jean-Luc if there was any hope of finding pony cart tracks in the vineyard, he only shook his head. The recent rains had destroyed any hope of that.

Maggie tried calling Roger but her call went to voicemail. Fighting her annoyance, she quickly texted him: <There is reason to believe the monastery stables are involved in the murder. Did you check them out?>

She finished making the coffee and as she was pulling out a tray of goat cheese and *tapenade paniers* from the oven where she'd warmed them up, Jean-Luc came in after putting both dogs back in their crates.

"That smells nice," he said. "Danielle just called. She's in Aix shopping and is happy to pick up the children from school."

"Oh, my gosh," Maggie said, her mouth falling open. "I totally forgot about them!"

"*Pas de problème*," Jean-Luc said seating himself at the kitchen counter as Maggie poured his coffee.

"I'm a terrible mother," Maggie said picking up the plate of *paniers*. "Let's go in the living room where it's warm."

"You are a wonderful mother," Jean-Luc said as he took his coffee mug and followed her.

When they settled down in the living room, Maggie felt a pulse of anguish. Always before Petit-Four would be here too, especially if there was food on the coffee table. She pushed the sad thought away.

"I saw a stable at the monastery," Jean-Luc said as he reached for a *panier*.

"I was thinking that too," Maggie said. "Is there a way to check the poop from the vineyard with one of the horses there, do you think?"

Jean-Luc laughed. "I don't know anyone who could do that for us."

"We need a police lab and we're fresh out. I went ahead and asked Bedard anyway but I don't think what we found today is enough to get him to act."

They sat in silence for a moment.

"How did Laurent sound when you talked with him?" Jean-Luc asked.

"He flat out lied to me is how he sounded," Maggie said. "He said he was *not* being held as a person of interest and he'd be home for dinner."

"*Vraiment?*"

"Well, he didn't say dinner but he did make it sound like it was no big deal."

"He is concerned then."

Maggie realized suddenly that Jean-Luc was right. Laurent was trying to convince her not to worry, *because he was worried.*

"You know him so well," Maggie said. She knew Jean-Luc would take that as high praise. Laurent was the most enigmatic person on the planet.

Jean-Luc sipped his coffee and looked very serious. Maggie wondered if he was remembering how he first met Laurent. How he had come to Laurent as a friend in order to hide the fact that he was doing Eduard Marceau's dirty work. It had taken a very long time for Laurent to trust him again.

As if reading her mind, Jean Luc cleared his throat.

"Having Laurent Dernier's trust and regard is the highest achievement of my life. Even more than my relationship with my brother, Patrick."

That surprised Maggie but only a little. Jean-Luc's brother Patrick had been a decorated Resistance hero and the pride of Jean-Luc's family until he was arrested and indicted for a triple murder and ended up committing suicide in prison.

Fifty years later, Maggie had uncovered evidence that proved Patrick's innocence. And forever endeared her to Jean-Luc.

"I wish I could have met your brother," Maggie said.

"I will never forget what you did for me and my family," Jean-Luc said, his voice gravelly with emotion. "Or how I rewarded that kindness with treachery." He stared into his coffee mug.

"That's all water under the bridge now, Jean-Luc. You are

Pépère to my kids and Laurent loves you like a father. It goes without saying that I love you, too."

His eyes watered. "I was a lonely old man until you and Laurent came to St-Buvard and today I have a wife, grandchildren, and a happiness I thought had passed me by."

Maggie leaned over and squeezed his hand.

"We'll get him back, Jean-Luc," she said. "Do not doubt that."

Jean-Luc smiled and patted her hand. "I don't," he said softly. "*Pas du tout.*"

An hour later, after rehashing their vineyard discover every way imaginable and outlining the various farms and houses nearby they could check out—in addition to the monastery stables—Maggie sent Roger two more texts urging him to examine the monastery stables before Danielle arrived with the children. As Jemmy and Mila ran into the house to free Izzy and Buddy from their crates, Maggie walked Jean-Luc out to where Danielle waited in the car.

"Is everything all right?" Danielle asked as Jean-Luc got in the car.

"Good as gold," Maggie said. "But can I have Jean-Luc again tomorrow? We found a clue that means we need to go back to the monastery in the morning."

"That is fine," Danielle said, smiling fondly at her husband. "But I have promised Grace I will be at *Dormir* with her tomorrow afternoon."

"No worries," Maggie said. "If you can take the kids again in the morning, I promise I'll remember to pick them up. And thank you so much, Danielle." She caught Jean-Luc's eye and he gave her a slow wink.

She felt a surge of confidence just knowing they were doing this together.

Together, how could they fail?

. . .

That night after feeding the kids and supervising their homework, Mila sat on Maggie's bed in her pajamas, her hair damp from her bath as Maggie combed it. Jemmy stood next to Maggie's bed. He was holding Petit-Four's bed.

Sighing, Maggie pulled both Mila and Jemmy into her arms.

"She's dead, isn't she?" Jemmy said solemnly. Maggie saw he was trying to be brave.

"I'm afraid so," Maggie said gently to the children. "I didn't realize it at the time but Petit-Four was very sick."

"It wasn't because she was old?" Mila said, her voice trembling.

"Yes, well it was that too," Maggie said. "She was old *and* sick."

"Where is she now?" Jemmy asked quietly. "What happened to her?"

"*Pépère* and I wrapped her up in her favorite blanket..." Maggie's voice broke.

"My baby blanket," Mila said, a tear rolling down her cheek.

"Yes, sweetheart. The one she loved so much. And when Papa comes home from...his business trip...we'll bury her in the garden."

"I miss her," Jemmy said, sniffing.

"I know, darling," Maggie said, kissing his hair and holding them both close. "I miss her too."

That night after the children were asleep, Maggie reviewed her day and tried to feel the optimism she'd felt earlier when Jean-Luc left. But she was tired and her emotions were raw from telling the children about Petit-Four and she only felt the failures and dead-ends of the day.

She glanced at her phone wishing Laurent would call, wondering what he was doing when suddenly her phone lit up.

She saw the photo of her mother show up on the screen. Her stomach clenched.

Oh, no, she thought. *Please no.*

"Mom?" she said hesitantly, picking up.

"Oh, darling," her mother said. "I just wanted to call to say everything is fine here on this end and your father had a good day today."

Finally some good news.

"I'm so glad, Mom. That's great."

"Isn't it? I just wanted to let you know that I think perhaps your father is settling in and that both of us shouldn't worry so much."

After they'd spoken a moment more and Maggie disconnected, she couldn't help but think: *that's what they always say just before the sky falls.*

Before she put her phone down on the bedside table, she impulsively typed in Grace's number and Grace picked up immediately.

"Darling, is everything all right?" Grace asked breathlessly.

"Yes," Maggie said. "How about on your end? Things looked tense last time I saw you."

"Oh, I got it sorted. But I'm so glad you called. I feel terrible about being such an absentee friend during this of all times."

Grace sounded like she was about to burst into tears. Maggie shifted her phone to her other shoulder.

"Please don't feel bad about it," Maggie said. "You have your hands full right now and you know Laurent would want you to do your best at the *gite,* Besides he's already forbidden me to work this case in any way."

"Like *that* ever did any good."

Maggie laughed.

"I can't believe Bedard isn't more help than he is," Grace said. "What's the point of having a friend in the police if he can't pull strings?"

"Well, you know Roger," Maggie said. "I'm sure he thinks he's doing all he can."

"Please try not to worry, Maggie," Grace said. "It sounds like the police have only very weak evidence against Laurent. He didn't do it so they can hardly find proof that he did. They'll have to let him go eventually."

"You're right. Of course, you're right." Maggie began to feel a swell of comfort in Grace's words. And it was true. Unless the cops tried to *frame* Laurent, there was no way the knife or the proximity of the body were enough to convict him.

"How are your American guests?" Maggie asked.

"Ugh. Don't ask. I hate them all."

Maggie laughed and then saw she was getting another call. It was Roger.

"Hey, Grace. I need to take this call. I'll ring you tomorrow."

Maggie switched to the incoming call.

"Hey," she said. "Did you get my texts? After you check out the stables at the monastery I bet you'll be able to wrap this up. Want to know why?"

There was a pause on the line.

"Roger?"

"Maggie," Roger said, swearing under his breath. "*Merde.*"

Maggie caught her breath and a tremor of anxiety rippled through her. "What? What's happened?"

"Something...I don't know how to tell you."

She felt her legs go weak and the room seemed to darken and grow smaller.

"Just spit it out, Roger," she said, her jaw clenched. "I can't bear this."

"I was hoping to ask the judge to allow Laurent to be released today on his own recognizance but now that's not possible."

"Why not? Because of a knife he lost weeks ago? Are you kidding? A dead guy he barely knows was found in our field? You have *nothing* on him!"

"As of this afternoon, I'm afraid we do," Roger said tiredly.

"What? What could you possibly have?" Maggie heard her voice rising in agitation. "Just tell me one thing!"

"A confession," Roger said. "I'm sorry, Maggie. We have a signed confession."

25

GOING NOWHERE FAST

The refectory hall opened up into the main dining area which was dappled with the light from dozens of tapers and votives placed on the scarred wooden dining tables.

The monks wove among the diners like silent waiters, their heads bowed, their hands tucked in the long flowing sleeves of their dark robes.

Guy watched Noelle walk through the refectory and get in the food line. Two girlfriends joined her. Guy could swear there was a purple bruise forming on Noelle's cheekbone.

His nostrils flaring, he felt the blood pounding in his ears as he worked to control himself. He sat gripping the baguette in front of him until he'd torn in half without realizing what he was doing.

Except for that one time Pierre didn't walk with Noelle or eat with her or do any of the normal things a man in love did. On the one hand, that was a relief to Guy not to have to see her with that bastard.

On the other hand, it meant Pierre was only using her.

And now obviously abusing her.

"Guy, stop that!" old Monsieur Bledot said from across the table. "You are ruining my digestion with your gnashing of teeth."

"Sorry," Guy murmured.

The old man turned to his wife. "Some people don't know what's best for them even when it's staring them right in the face."

The elderly woman looked at Guy and snorted but Guy didn't care. He barely registered their derision.

Some people don't know what's best for them when it's staring them in the face!

Of course! Noelle needs my help.

She can't do this on her own. She needs me to step in and save her.

Guy felt a wave of elation as he wondered why it had taken him so long to see it.

26

EVIL IN THE AIR

Maggie got very little sleep that night. After hanging up with Bedard she finally gave up on trying to sleep and spent the next two hours scrubbing the kitchen floor which didn't need it and cleaning out the fireplace. After a second shower, she went to her office—the one that Laurent had created for her that overlooked the back garden—and wrote out everything she knew about the case against her husband.

The facts didn't fill a whole paragraph.

She fell asleep with her head on her desk, waking the next morning to the sounds of the two dogs whining to be let out.

Fueled by her determination to get back to the monastery to get some answers from Frère Jean, Maggie raced the children through breakfast and drove them to Danielle and Jean-Luc's house. Jean-Luc was waiting for her in the driveway when she drove up. Jemmy and Mila jumped out of the car and ran skipping into Danielle's house.

"What has happened?" Jean-Luc asked as he got in the car.

"You are not going to believe it," Maggie said, making a sharp turn in the drive to head back to the main road. "Bedard called me last night to tell me that Laurent confessed to the murder."

Jean-Luc sucked in a sharp intake of breath.

"*Incroyable!*"

"Yeah, that's what I said—or words to that effect with a few more cuss words thrown in. It turns out that the head monk of the monastery was in the Aix police station yesterday answering questions and when he was done one of the other detectives—or maybe it was Frère Jean —I don't remember the details—anyway one of them asked if he wanted to visit Laurent—which by the way, how come he gets to see Laurent when I can't?"

"They're probably not worried he will be slipping Laurent a nail file in a cake."

"Anyway, supposedly, while the monk was there, I guess giving comfort to Laurent, Frère Jean says Laurent *confessed* to him that he killed Dupree!"

Jean-Luc frowned. "It's not believable. Never would Laurent confess to such a thing. Even if he did it."

"Exactly! There is no way and besides, monks don't do confessions! Honestly, Roger is an idiot."

"We will get to the bottom of it."

"Damn straight we will."

By the time they arrived back at the monastery, thick bands of rain clouds threw the ancient stone building into deep shadow creating an ominous affect. Maggie and Jean-Luc divided up again. She would track down the elusive Frère Jean to get some answers—if not to wring his neck—and Jean-Luc would snoop around and talk to anyone who was willing to talk.

"Walk the entire perimeter," Maggie said, pointing at the edge of the main building the furthest point from the stable. "Start there looking for anything that's odd or different and finish up at the stable. I'll meet you there in an hour."

Maggie hurried to the main building. This time when she tugged on the iron handle, it didn't budge. Frustrated, she looked around for anyone who might be able to let her in. There was nobody in front of the monastery so she hurried to the side where the rectory stood. There on his knees in the flower bed in front of the building was a man in monk's robes.

She hurried over to him.

"Excuse me," she called. "*Mon Frère?*"

The monk turned, startled, and looked up from the small patch of turned earth he was patting down with a trowel.

Maggie had never met Frère Jean before but she had a tingling sensation across her scalp that this was the guy. He had the look of a guy who was in charge.

"*Oui?*" he asked, frowning at her. "May I help you, Madame?'

"Are you Frère Jean?" Maggie asked.

The man had a cap of white hair and a sparse beard, although he probably wasn't out of his forties as far as Maggie could guess. He stood up with the guilt-ridden manner of someone who had been caught doing something he shouldn't.

He licked his lips and seemed to openly assess Maggie. She was wearing jeans and sneakers with a pullover sweater under her rain jacket.

"And *you* are?" he said, his eyes darting behind her as if looking for a way out.

"I am Maggie Dernier," Maggie said, feeling her face flush with anger. "I'm Laurent's wife."

"I cannot talk with you, Madame," Frère Jean said turning to grab the handle of the door behind him to the rectory.

"You went to the police last night and swore a false statement, *Mon Frère*," Maggie said tightly. "You could get in a lot of trouble for that."

"I only told the truth," he said over his shoulder as he hesitated on the doorstep.

"The police have recording devices activated at all times. If

Laurent really confessed like you say he did where's the recording of it?"

"The confessional is sacrosanct. The police respected that when I asked them to turn the devices off."

"That is BS! Monks don't take confessions! You had them turn it off so you could lie and get away with it."

"I understand you are upset, Madame," Frère Jean said. "I am sorry for your troubles."

"And after everything Laurent has done for you and the people here. You should be ashamed of yourself."

The monk had the door open now but Maggie saw him falter at her words.

"I...I am sorry, Madame," he choked out before lurching into the rectory and slamming the door behind him.

Maggie stood there staring at the closed door in her face. She couldn't help but think if she had to put a name to the expression on the monk's face when he'd made that less-than-sincere apology to her, the word she would have used was *guilty*.

27

MAN IN THE MIRROR

"What part of *getting the confession* are you having trouble with?" Terrone said, his voice tight with control, as he stood in front of his office window, his spittle flying against the glass. "We now have a deposition from a credible source saying Dernier committed the murder but *you* can't turn that into a confession for a lesser crime?"

Roger flinched at the sight of the man reddening in the face, his flabby chins quivering in fury.

"I'm sorry, sir," he said.

"*Screw* sorry!" Terrone bellowed. "Get me that confession or you'll be directing traffic in Nimes by the weekend!"

"Yes sir," Roger said, taking the man's threat as his dismissal. He left the office, his heart pounding. He walked down the hall toward his office, grateful that only Terrone's secretary could have heard the screaming.

Did that even matter? At this point Roger was headed either for career obscurity and disgrace or an outright ejection from the *Police Nationale*.

His breath was coming in short, labored pants by the time he reached his office and closed the door. He'd seen Girard loitering in the hall—clearly hoping to witness the bloodletting from Roger's meeting with Terrone—and been assailed by a smirk and a knowing look.

It took all the strength Roger had not to bury his fist in the man's face.

But since Yves Girard was also Terrone's nephew on his mother's side, that would pretty much finish off any hope Roger had of continuing in the police service anywhere in France.

He fell into his seat in exhaustion, his eyes falling on the photo of Chloe on his desk. In the picture she was dressed as a belly dancer for the performance at the *Théâtre du Jeu de Paume* in Aix last year. Her dream was to be a dancer when she grew up. To that end Roger had enrolled her in the summer dance program she'd begged him for. The one that cost two thousand euros, not counting board.

He looked at her beaming little face and imagined telling her that she could not go to the summer program after all. Or continue with her dance lessons with Madame Picot. Or even stay in Aix where all her friends were since they would be moving away, perhaps somewhere up north.

He raked both hands through his hair in frustration.

And for what?

To save Laurent from paying for a crime that everyone knows he committed? That Laurent *himself* would readily admit he committed? At least off the record.

Roger's anger and resentment threatened to boil over.

My daughter should pay with tears and heartbreak because I don't want Laurent to face the music?

There was no question that Laurent did the heist twenty years ago. After his first talk with Terrone, Roger had gone back and read the files on the theft in depth. Every detail of the con had Laurent's signature all over it.

Why wasn't Laurent admitting to the cold case? Roger

wondered in agitation. Why wasn't he offering up a confession to the theft? What was he waiting for? A miracle?

Was Roger supposed to sacrifice his own daughter's happiness so that Laurent could play whatever long con he had in mind to avoid prison and go home to his children unscathed?

To his children, Roger thought bitterly.

And to Maggie.

28

ONCE MORE WITH FEELING

That afternoon after picking up Jemmy and Mila from Danielle's and dropping off Jean-Luc, Maggie once more went through the motions of a typical school night at home. She reheated a *coq au vin* Laurent had made a few days earlier, helped Jemmy with his homework only to discover that at seven years of age his French was already more fluent than hers, orchestrated baths for the children and somehow managed to let the dogs out without losing them.

At the monastery that afternoon Jean-Luc had never made it as far as the stables. He'd been promptly confronted by a pair of stone faced monks who had strict orders to keep all non-residents off the premises. He was escorted back to where Maggie had parked the car where he waited for her in ill humor until she finished her conversation with Frère Jean.

As for that, all Maggie could really take away from her interview with the monk was (a) he wasn't telling her the truth and (b) he looked guilty as hell.

Neither observation was much to go on and both she and Jean-Luc had finished the day depressed and disconsolate.

By the time she fell into bed hours later, exhausted and

discouraged at another day passing without hearing from Laurent or uncovering any information that might help free him, Maggie was too tired to let her thoughts and worries keep her up another night. She slept the whole night through.

The next morning, she drove the kids to school in Aix and rang Grace to let her know she'd be happy to pick up Zouzou after school.

"Funny you should call," Grace said. "I'm just dropping her off at school right now."

"You're in Aix?" Maggie said as she maneuvered her car into a parking spot not far from her parents' apartment building. "I imagined you'd be knee-deep in catering to demanding Americans by now."

"Yes, well, they're gone," Grace said tensely. "Got time for a coffee? I'll tell you all about it."

After making plans to meet at Nico's, one of Maggie's favorite cafés on the Cours Mirabeau, Maggie hurried to the eighteenth century apartment building off of rue des Marseillais to check on her parents.

When she used her key to enter the apartment she was surprised to see her father standing in the kitchen waiting for the kettle to boil.

"Dad?" she said, coming in and dropping her purse on a chair. She looked around the apartment. The door to the bedroom was closed.

"Hello, sweetheart," he said, turning and smiling. "This is a nice surprise."

So is this, Maggie couldn't help think as she went to him and kissed him. He did this from time to time. Less and less but it was always a gift when it happened. It was like the brain cells had all regenerated, sloughing off the clouds of his disease for a brief period of time—and gave her father back to her again.

"Where's Mom?"

"She's lying down." Her father took the kettle off the cooker and poured the boiling water into a large teapot on the kitchen table. "I thought a cup of tea might make her feel better."

Tears sprang to Maggie's eyes as she watched her father being the caretaker for once. She couldn't help the panoply of images flashing through her mind of her father through the years. Strong, good-humored, sage and balanced. She reached out to touch his arm.

He glanced at her with bemusement as he replaced the teapot lid.

"Everything okay, darling?" he asked, his brows knit together in concern. "Laurent fine? The children?"

Her father mentioning Laurent hit Maggie solidly in the solarplexus. It took everything Maggie had not to collapse into his arms in tears. How she would love to lean on him, to get his advice, to hear his words of comfort and support. But she didn't dare.

"Yes, all good," Maggie said hoarsely. "But a cup of tea sounds perfect."

She watched her father's face clear as he turned to pull a mug from the open shelving in the small kitchen.

"Nothing a cup of tea won't cure," he said affably. "Haven't I always told you that?"

"You have, Dad," Maggie said as she sat down and watched him pour the amber fluid into her mug. "And you were always right."

An hour later, Maggie left her parents to their English newspapers and radio and their tea, promising to bring them back a couple of *chocolatines* when she returned from her visit with Grace. As she closed the door behind her and hurried down the stairs—too impatient to wait for the ancient lift—she knew there was every possibility that the man she'd just left in the apartment would be gone when she returned, receded into the fog of his disease, where no stretch of love or good intentions could reach him.

She walked briskly down the cobblestone alleys to the main thoroughfare, coming out between the side entrance of MonoPrix and a series of tiny boutiques that faced it. Nico's was directly across from Bechard's on the Cours.

As Maggie hurried down the famous avenue, she saw Grace sitting at an outdoor table nearest the promenade.

Most Aixoise didn't let a little cold keep them from enjoying their cafés or apéros on a pretty day on the terrace so while the diners were all bundled up against the chill, nearly every table was filled.

She and Grace kissed as the French do and Maggie took a seat at the table. Grace had already ordered her a coffee and a croissant.

"Oh, yummy," Maggie said, cupping the steaming cup in her hands. "Thank you."

"Parents okay?"

Maggie took a long sip and then nodded. "I'm not sure it's not worse when he's lucid, though, you know? It just reminds me of what we're missing all the other times."

"Oh, darling," Grace said. She wore a bright floral Valentino cotton shirtdress and the sunlight that strove to break through the grey bank of clouds picked out glints of gold in her hair.

"Enough of that," Maggie said, shaking herself out of her melancholy mood. "What happened to the Americans?"

Now it was Grace's turn to pause before speaking—almost as if she were trying to compose herself. Which was so unlike Grace who was *born* composed.

"Grace?"

"I threw them out!" Grace said.

"What?"

"I did. I'm sorry. I couldn't help it. I didn't mean to. I mean it didn't start out like that."

"What happened?"

"Oh, Maggie, they were vile. All of them and I was falling over myself to accommodate them and be... *gentil*, you know?"

"I know. I saw them yesterday when I was there," Maggie said. "They did look difficult."

"They were *horrid*. To everyone. They made Zouzou cry."

"No!"

"Yes, they said her biscuits were inedible. Can you imagine? Zouzou's biscuits are to die for. They didn't act at all like they were in someone's home. They treated us like servants."

"I'm so sorry, Grace. But how is it you ended up throwing them out?"

Grace took in a long breath.

"I went to bed two nights ago berating myself for being such a wimp. I thought, *you can still be a good hostess without being a doormat!* So the next morning when one of them—the leader, she was the worst—told me she didn't intend to pay full price when she had to wait ten minutes for the shower water to get hot, well, I....I....told her to deal with it or get out."

"You didn't!" But Maggie was smiling. She needed this. She needed to hear Grace's stories, bask in the near sunshine on the Cours and feel the rest of the world—and her troubles—float away for just a few minutes.

"I did. And well, in the movies when the heroine stands up to the bully, the bully apologizes and the whole storyline takes a rousing victorious upswing for the heroine."

"Uh-oh. I take it that's not what happened."

"No. She started ranting at me and getting the rest of her crew up and packing and she said she intended to flood TripAdvisor with the worst imaginable reviews for *Dormir!*"

"Oh, well, Grace, she might have said that..."

"No, Maggie, she's done it!" Grace pulled out her cellphone and began scrolling to a website. "*Disaster in Provence* is the headline," Grace said, her face stitched with misery. "She writes,

Dormir might mean sleep in French but it really translates to uninhabitable dump in English."

"Grace, that's terrible! Can she do that?"

"She's done it," Grace said, dropping her phone on the table. "And she goes on and on. She must have gotten her whole crew to do it too because I woke up this morning to six new reviews—all one stars."

"Maybe they'll get buried in all the other reviews?"

"There are no other reviews!" Grace said fretfully. "And now nobody will book at *Dormir*. I'm ruined."

"You're overreacting," Maggie said. "It's not wonderful but this is early days for the *gîte*. You're still getting your legs. These first terrible reviews will be buried by glowing ones before next summer. You'll see."

"Laurent will be so disappointed in me," Grace said sadly. "He was counting on me not screwing this up."

"Laurent will understand," Maggie said firmly. A flinch of pain flitted across her brow at the thought of him. She'd gone a full fifteen minutes without thinking of where he was right now.

"Speaking of which, any more news on his situation?" Grace asked, putting her phone away as if realizing that in the scheme of things, her troubles were trivial.

"Well, none of it good," Maggie said. "It turns out that one of the monks at *l'Abbaye de Sainte-Trinité* was allowed to visit Laurent yesterday and claimed that Laurent confessed that he murdered Henri Dupree."

"That's absurd."

"Yes, well, the police are treating it as the real deal."

"Isn't Roger helping you?"

"He says he's doing what he can. But the murder weapon belonged to Laurent and since I fell asleep during the approximate time of the murder, I can't serve as an alibi for Laurent."

"You're scaring me, Maggie. Is there any good news?"

"Jean-Luc found horse poop in our vineyard near where the body was found."

Grace frowned. "How does that help?"

"It helps because it could explain how the body got there and *that* helps because it means Dupree might not have been killed in our vineyard."

"But surely modern forensics can tell the police that?"

"You'd think. I'm trying to get Roger to get his forensic guys over to the monastery. They have a horse stable and if there's any connection, it'll take Laurent out of the frame."

"Will he do it? Roger?"

"He says he'll do whatever he can to help but honestly so far it's been only words."

"He's still in love with you, you know."

"Which is not as much help as you'd think," Maggie said wryly.

"So what are you going to do?"

Maggie broke her croissant apart and licked the buttery flakes her fingers.

"Until I can get Roger to move, I intend to go looking for clues at the monastery stable myself. I can't tell you how much help Jean-Luc has been. I think he was really looking for something to do. You know how much he loves Laurent."

"We all do. And now I've got time to help too," Grace said.

"If you want to help, I'd appreciate you giving the kids a lift to school for the next few days. Mornings are the best time for me and Jean-Luc to ask questions at the monastery. If I could drop the kids off with you in the morning, I'll pick all of them up in the afternoon in Aix."

"Are you sure, darling? That doesn't seem like much help."

"It's immense. Really. But now I need to get back to my folks."

"Of course. Give my love to your parents."

They hugged and kissed again but Maggie hesitated before leaving.

"There'll be other guests, Grace. Trust me. This is just a hiccup."

"I'm sure you're right. And don't worry about Laurent. He's innocent. That's what you need to hang onto. The cops can't just lock up an innocent man."

29

BURNING BRIDGES

Guy waited until he was sure Pierre was in the stables. It had taken him all night after his initial brainstorm about Noelle to devise a plan. All night when he finally realized she didn't know what she was doing and needed him to step in before she ruined her life.

It made so much sense. Without a father to guide her, Noelle needed Guy to show her the mistake she was making.

He walked to the large holly bush opposite the stables and pulled out the lantern he'd hidden there earlier in the day. He had no doubt his confrontation with the gypsy would get physical and he didn't want to be thrown out of the monastery afterward for fighting.

Fighting of course was prohibited in the monastery. Guy hated lying to the Brothers but if Pierre went to them to say Guy had attacked him, Guy would need to be able to convince them that was not true.

He could tell by the way Frère Jean looked at the gypsy that he didn't like him.

It shouldn't be too difficult to convince him of Guy's version of the truth.

With a lantern Guy could shut the barn doors behind him to block the view from the outside while still being able to see what he needed to do.

His mouth was dry and he felt a sharp and insistent breathlessness as he ran over his plan in his mind.

Guy had never fought anyone in his entire life. His older brothers had been in fights but because he was the youngest it had never been necessary.

They never tell you how amazing it feels to fight for someone you love, he thought as the adrenaline surged through him.

He entered the stable and immediately saw Pierre, his back to him, at the rear of the building. He was sitting on a hay bale, smoking.

Smoking! With hay and livestock!

Fury wove its way into Guy's gut as he set the lantern down and turned to close the doors behind him.

"Hey! What are you doing?" Pierre yelled, jumping to his feet.

Pierre was tall but Guy figured he outweighed him by twenty pounds. In Guy's view beating the crap out of Pierre would accomplish two things. It would scare him away from Noelle—and perhaps the monastery as a whole—and it would make Guy feel a lot better.

"Time for you to go, gypsy scum," Guy snarled, slamming his fist in his hand to make his point unmistakable. "Go now and I won't beat the hell out of you."

Pierre sauntered down the aisle, his cigarette hanging out of his mouth, his eyes flashing with amusement.

"Have you ever even slapped another human being?" Pierre said, laughing. "Or are threats your limit?"

"I guess we'll see, won't we?" Guy said, a thin sheen of perspiration beginning to form on his top lip. He formed his hands into fists.

The soft glow from the lantern distorted both their shadows into elongated forms against the walls of the stable.

"You look ridiculous," Pierre said, his weight on one hip in a relaxed stance.

"I'm warning you," Guy said. "Leave Noelle alone or you'll be sorry."

"I'm not afraid of you, Guy," Pierre said. "You're pathetic."

Guy felt his vision dim as his fury pushed up his throat and into his brain. Adrenaline felt like it was shooting out from his extremities.

Why was he laughing at me? Why was he not afraid?

"Perhaps you will not be laughing when I tell the police I overheard you threaten to kill Henri Dupree," Guy said.

Pierre stopped smiling. Guy felt a surge of elation.

That did the trick! He's afraid I'll tell.

"Go ahead," Pierre said. "Tell them. And then Noelle will tell them you raped her."

Guy staggered backward a step, his skin tingling and stinging like razor blades were scraping against it.

"She would never do such a thing," he sputtered.

"She would if I told her to."

Propelled by pure fury, Guy charged Pierre. He registered the gypsy's startled look as he hit him and brought him down hard onto the hay-strewn ground. The pony in the back stall whinnied loudly but all Guy was aware of was the feel of his tormentor—Noelle's tormentor—on the ground beneath him.

He straddled Pierre and pulled his arm back to slam his fist into the gypsy's face but before he could he felt the red hot cramp of a knife slicing into his side. Screaming, Guy fell off Pierre, grabbing for his hip. He touched the still lighted cigarette that Pierre had jabbed through his shirt.

Before he could brush the burning cigarette off him, he felt pain reverberate up his spine as Pierre slammed his head against the wall of the nearby stall.

Pierre leapt up, his wiry body uncoiled and grabbed Guy by the throat, pinching off his airway, his face a visage of demonic intention. Guy began to panic as he struggled to breath, his hands beating uselessly against Pierre's hands where they gripped him. In desperation, Guy brought up a knee hard into Pierre's crotch and felt the gypsy let go.

Guy scrambled away, fighting for breath. Pierre was bent over, cursing. Guy kicked out viciously, aiming for his ribs. He connected with Pierre's knee hard enough to knock the gypsy over but the wild fury on Pierre's face told Guy he'd done no real damage.

Bringing his fists up to his face again Guy tried to guess what Pierre would do next.

"Had enough?" he said, his voice scratchy and damaged from the punishing pressure on his windpipe.

Without warning, Pierre swiveled on one leg and slammed his fist into Guy's stomach. Guy's breath rocketed out of him, his fists dropping to his sides. He felt Pierre grab him by the hair and agony shot through his scalp as Pierre jerked him around and drove his fist into his face. Guy felt one tooth go and his mouth filled with blood.

He dropped to his knees, blood dripping off his chin. Somewhere in the back of his head he could hear the labored panting of Pierre's breathing. Or was it his own?

Suddenly he heard the stable doors creak open and a blast of cool air rushed in, making Guy want to fall face first into it.

"You idiots!" a man shouted. His voice sounded far away as if in a dream. "Get out of here before you kill yourselves!"

Guy turned to blink at the man and realized it was one of the monks. His dark robes flapping around his legs, the Brother rushed into the stall and grabbed Guy by the arm. He pulled him to his feet and shoved him out the door. Guy staggered outside and fell to his knees again. The agony in his face, his skull and his stomach all rivaled each other. His ears rang and his vision was wobbly.

A crowd had gathered outside the stable and someone

pushed him out of the way just as one of the monks came out of the barn leading the pony.

Guy watched in numb shock and finally saw what he'd been too focused on killing Pierre to see before.

Flames were shooting out from the slats in the stable doors, voraciously eating the ancient rafters overhead. Black ash swirled around the next figure—Guy realized in horror that it was Pierre—who ran from the barn herding three terrified goats in front of him.

Guy watched Pierre direct the panicked animals down the path toward the monastery garden. As he watched in dull horror, he felt the heat of the stable fire against his face, felt it burning the very breath in his lungs.

Oh, God. What have I done?

30

MARKING TIME

After saying goodbye to Grace, Maggie went to Bechards and loaded up with *chocolatines* for her parents before visiting the fishmongers shop that faced *place de Richelme*. The market had been dismantled hours earlier—the crushed ice long hosed from the slate pavers of the square and replaced with outdoor tables—but the shop was still open.

Maggie decided she had just enough time to make the fish and put together a little gratin of eggplant and sliced tomatoes for her parents' supper. Her mother had emerged from the bedroom looking frail but in good spirits. By the time Maggie returned with the fish, her father had started to stare at her like he couldn't place her.

Swallowing her disappointment, Maggie quickly cleaned and prepped the fish before slicing a lemon and mixing up a vinaigrette and then setting the fillets in a hot pan coated with olive oil.

Her mother sat at the kitchen table and stared out the window at the rooftops of Aix. An *International Tribune* sat on the table in front of her unopened and unread. Maggie's father was lying down in the bedroom. Maggie kept her eye on the fish while she assembled a casserole dish with the eggplant and tomatoes. Gratin was one of the dishes Laurent made that Maggie adored because it was good on just about everything—from fish to pasta to omelets. It was easy to make and would last her parents the week.

She added crushed garlic and lots of grated Parmesan cheese on top, sprinkled it liberally with olive oil and popped it in a slow oven.

She set the timer for three hours. She would be long gone by the time it was ready but all her mother had to do was take it out and turn off the oven.

"Your phone, Maggie," her mother murmured.

Maggie ran to her purse where she could hear her phone vibrating from deep within. She prayed it was Laurent.

Roger Bedard's photo was on the screen.

Tucking it between her chin and her shoulder, she moved back to the stove to make sure the fish didn't scorch.

"Hey, Roger," she said. "Do you have news?"

"Are you in Aix?"

Maggie moved the phone to her hand. "I am. What's up? Did you find something? Did you go to the monastery and check out the stables like I asked?"

"Maggie, no. In fact, there was a fire at the monastery today that destroyed the stables but we believe it is unrelated to the case."

Maggie sat down hard on a kitchen chair beside her mother, the oil in the pan with the fish popping loudly.

"How can you say that?" she blurted. "It's not at all unrelated! Now you can't run your forensic tests in the stables!"

"What do the stables have to do with anything?"

"I told you! I found horse manure at the crime scene yesterday."

Maggie glanced at her mother and wasn't surprised to see she wasn't even listening to what normally must have sounded like a very bizarre phone conversation.

"So?" Roger said impatiently.

"So that is *not* a usual thing to find in a vineyard! I was hoping you could check out the monastery stables so—"

"Maggie, please do not go snooping around the monastery! If the Benedictines complain about you it will look very bad for me and I will not be able to help you as much."

Maggie was dumbfounded for a moment before she felt the rage build up inside her.

"Excuse *me* if how you look isn't my main concern at the moment, Roger," she said bitingly.

"Maggie, the fish," Elspeth said tiredly.

Maggie turned to the stove and turned the heat down under the pan.

"Look, Maggie, the main reason I'm calling is to tell you I've arranged for you to see Laurent today."

Maggie stood up. "When?"

"Right now if you're able."

Maggie glanced at her watch. It was only a little after one. She didn't need to be at the school to pick up the kids for another three hours.

"Right now works," she said, pulling off her apron and then eyeing her mother. "Hold on a second, Roger." She turned to her mother. "Mom, can you watch the fish? It's almost done but I have to leave early today."

"Leave?"

Maggie felt a flare of impatience invade her gut. This was the woman who organized a cotillion for two hundred people only five years ago! When had she crawled into this shell of a woman expecting everyone else to handle her life for her?

"Mom!" Maggie barked, trying to snap her out of her fog. "I need you to finish the fish. Can you do that?"

When Elspeth turned to look at her, a slightly panicked look in her eye, Maggie cursed and spoke into the phone.

"I'll be at your office in twenty minutes," she said before disconnecting. She turned off the stove and the oven and went to the cupboard where she found a box of Kix cereal. She turned to her mother.

"There's fresh milk in the fridge. I'm sorry, Mom. I have to go." She kissed her mother and grabbing up her coat and purse, ran out the door.

31

DROWNING

Frère Jean leaned against his desk, using the firmness of it to hide the trembling in his hands. The two young men stood before him, waiting patiently.

They probably think my making them wait is by design, he thought. *When it's only because I am so upset I have no idea of what to say to them.*

He looked at their faces. They couldn't be more different from each other.

Guy—as handsome and unselfconscious of the fact as a Greek god—standing respectfully and contrite, his shoulders straight, his eyes cast downward.

And then the other one.

Frère Jean fought his natural inclination against Pierre. He had to believe it wasn't racism. It was just that the boy was so inherently difficult. His curly hair was plaited and twisted into a thick ponytail that ended at his neck and his olive complexion was spotty and slick with grease.

Unlike Guy's respectful stance, Pierre stood with his weight on one hip, casual and indifferent, the perpetual sneer on his lip.

"I've met with the other brothers," Frère Jean said. "They

opted for leniency in this case but I'm inclined to ask you both to leave *l'Abbaye de Sainte-Trinité*."

"*Mon Frère, non,*" Guy said, his voice suddenly wheedling.

Frère Jean hardened his heart to the sound. He knew the boy was in love with Noelle—and that she was now with the gypsy boy. What a mess. Even if he didn't throw them both out he would need to throw *one* of them out to eliminate any future problems. But if he threw Pierre out—his preference—would Noelle feel as if she should go with him?

Frère Jean ran a hand across his face.

"What caused the fire?" he said suddenly.

"It way my fault, *Mon Frère,*" Guy said forlornly. "I brought a lantern into the barn."

It infuriated Frère Jean that Pierre refused to take his share of the responsibility. After the fire, one of the brothers had found several cigarette butts in the debris. As far as Frère Jean knew, Guy didn't smoke.

"I meant, *why* were you fighting?"

"He cannot accept that I am screwing his girl," Pierre said. "Except she was never his. Not like she is mine. Every night she is mine."

"Shut up, Pierre," Frère Jean said, hating the fact that he'd been baited into losing his temper with the boy. He could see Guy stiffening in rage at Pierre's words and that in itself infuriated Frère Jean although he could not say exactly why.

"If you are in fact engaging in sexual congress with Noelle," Frère Jean said between clenched teeth to Pierre, "then both of you will go. You and Noelle."

"No!" Guy said. "That's not fair!"

Frère Jean laid his most disgusted gaze on Guy and the boy had the good sense to drop his eyes in shame for his outburst.

"If there had been any loss of livestock," Frère Jean said, "I would have had you both arrested on top of thrown out. As it is, the two of you will work together to create a shelter for them before winter."

Both young men paused to glance at each other. Frère Jean didn't have much hope that they would be able to work together but it sounded like the sort of thing a normal, balanced and loving father might suggest as punishment.

Instead of the very un-Christian thoughts that Frère Jean had in mind that involved a good deal of blood-letting and public humiliation.

"That is all," he said, turning his back on them. "One more fight and you're both gone. Now, go."

Frère Jean waited until he heard the outside door close behind them before his shoulders sagged with dejection and he sat down heavily in his desk chair. He held his hands out in front of him and watched the trembling as if they were an interesting specimen and he merely an objective scientist.

And then, as he'd done every day since Henri's murder and his own subsequent escape from any punishment, he pulled open the bottom drawer of his desk and carefully pulled out a stiff dark towel. He spread it gingerly on his lap and smoothed out the creases in it as the dried blood cracked and crumbled into flakes onto the floor and the folds of his robe.

He took in a deep breath and made his hands into tight fists to prevent them from shaking.

This wasn't just the towel that had covered Henri's dead ody on that fateful pony cart ride.

It was his own very real cross to bear.

32

JUDAS

The Commissariat d'Aix-en-Provence was housed in a modern building of steel and glass on Avenue de l'Europe across the street from a McDonald's restaurant. Maggie parked on a side avenue off Avenue de l'Europe, pausing only long enough to pinch some color back into her cheeks and add a quick swipe of tinted gloss to her lips.

As she assessed her appearance in the car's rearview mirror she knew she looked like she hadn't slept in a couple of nights but it couldn't be helped. The thought of seeing Laurent again filled her with a sad longing.

The office of the Commandant de Police was at the end of a long hallway. After having her bag searched and a scanning wand waved over her body, Maggie was given a visitor's badge and told to wait in one of the metal chairs that lined the hallway. She sat and quickly texted Roger. <*Je suis ici*>

He appeared almost immediately in the hallway and motioned for her to follow him to his office.

The last time Maggie had been in Roger's office had been right around when he'd first moved into it nearly seven years ago. At the time she and Laurent had come here to argue with him for arresting Jean-Luc for a charge that they felt sure would prove to be false—as it was—and would only end up making Roger look bad. As it had.

Why do I get the feeling I've done this before? Maggie thought, her stomach twisting as she sat in one of the cushioned chairs facing the wide metal desk where Roger had retreated.

Oddly, the office looked exactly as it had the last time Maggie had been here. There were no new photographs or artwork, no trophies or memorabilia—nothing to show that Roger had been doing this job for longer than a week. When she tore her eyes from the furnishings to settle on Roger, she was shocked.

He looked as if he'd just pulled an all-nighter.

With a gin bottle.

His hair was unwashed, his eyes were bleary and deeply sunken. Even his lips which he continually licked were cracked and peeling.

As eager as she was to get to the point where he was walking her to wherever Laurent was in this building, Maggie couldn't help but feel a tremor of guilt. She hadn't been in touch with Roger in months—nearly a year in fact. Not since he'd grabbed Laurent to go racing to Grenoble in order to be a part of the search and rescue effort after the avalanche.

Maggie wracked her brain to try to remember if she'd ever even thanked him for the work he'd done to help locate her. She had no idea what was going on in his life these days. Was Chloe okay? Roger rarely talked of her but Maggie had to admit that was probably because when she saw Roger it was never a social circumstance. Was he dating someone?

Something was going on with him.

"You look terrible," Maggie said, putting on her most appropriately concerned look while fighting the urge to ask him to move things along to the point where they were walking to wherever Laurent was.

"Thanks," he said. He shuffled a few pages on his desk and then picked one up and placed it in front of her.

Maggie saw the heading said *Laboratoire de Lyons Police*.

"Is this the forensics report?" she asked, picking it up. Most of the numbers and percentages didn't make sense to her. "Can you translate it?" She looked up at him.

"It basically says there was straw found embedded in the crepe soles of the victim and it definitively ties the knife to Laurent," he said wearily, his face bleached of color. He picked up another piece of paper on his desk and waved it at her.

"This is the preliminary pathology report. Turns out Dupree wasn't killed in the vineyard and the knife wasn't the murder weapon."

Maggie's eyes widened. "Well, that's good news!"

"Is it? Because my colleagues don't think it changes anything and I'm afraid I have to agree."

"The knife you have tied to Laurent is not the murder weapon," Maggie said with deliberate frustration. "How is that not good news for us?"

"It doesn't prove anything one way or the other," Roger said.

Maggie pushed the lab results sheet back across the table to Roger.

"So if he wasn't stabbed how was he killed?" she asked.

"He was hit on the head with a blunt object." Roger pointed to his right temple.

"Like with a bat or something?"

"We don't know."

"Is that an odd place to hit someone? The forehead?"

"It reveals that the assailant was right handed and suggests he was very tall."

"Are you saying the wound placement on the vic's head indicates *Laurent* fits the bill for hitting him?"

"Look, Maggie, I know this isn't what you want to hear. I'm

just trying to keep you in the loop and frankly it would probably be worth my job if anyone knew I was telling you this much."

"Really? Because it doesn't feel like proprietary information to me. It feels like the kind of thing I could read in the newspaper."

"Well, what you won't read is that we feel we have a motive now."

"We?"

"*Merde*, Maggie! I'm on your side but I'm also trying to do my job! Would you have me withhold evidence? Or pretend to not see something I can't help but see?"

"What kind of motive?"

"The fact that it appears Laurent attacked Dupree the day of the murder."

"So you're saying Laurent's *motive* was that he wasn't finished beating up Dupree? That's lame, Roger. Even for you," Maggie said with disgust.

A pulse of silence stretched between them that Roger broke by jerking open his desk drawer and rummaging in it for a moment before bringing out another sheet of paper. He hesitated a moment before tossing it in Maggie's direction.

Maggie picked it up with slow movements. But she knew what it was. She knew even before she read the header, *Deposition de Police Nationale de Aix-en-Provence*.

It was the confession that Laurent supposedly gave to Frère Jean. Maggie scanned it and then folded it and tucked it into her purse.

"That's only a copy," Roger said.

"Then you won't mind if I take it. Who else have you spoken to at the monastery beside this monk? There are three others there, I believe?"

"The other three were at a retreat of some kind in Dijon," Roger said. "It's well-documented."

"So no point in talking to them, I guess."

"Look, Maggie, I am sorry. I don't know what else to say,"

Roger said. He looked as if the air had deflated out of him and he had barely enough energy to shake his head in sadness across the desk from Maggie.

"Don't worry about it," she said formally. "You did your best. Thank you for keeping me informed. May I see my husband now?"

"Maggie, please," Roger said, his face creased with despondency. "If you only knew how my boss is screaming at me for a fast conviction on this one. I'll be honest with you. The fact is I haven't done an amazing job in this position since I came here."

Maggie couldn't help but soften toward him at this. For Roger to admit what she'd long suspected was very much out of character for him.

"This is my chance to put it all back together," Roger said. "Can you understand?"

Maggie didn't trust herself to speak. She didn't want to be glib and she didn't want to let him off the hook either. This was too important.

"I want you to do well in your career, of course, Roger," she said, keeping her voice even. "Just as long as Laurent being convicted of a crime he didn't commit isn't part of the price for that."

"I'm actually glad to hear you put it that way," Roger said softly.

"What way?"

"Never mind." He stood up and Maggie noted that it looked as if he'd slept in his clothes last night. His shirt was stained and rumpled and he was missing his belt. "Come," he said. "He's waiting for you."

33

A REASON TO BELIEVE

The room Roger led her to was bare except for a small metal table and two chairs facing it. A window was set high up, preventing anyone from seeing out but allowing a trickle of pale light into the room.

When the uniformed policeman who stood at the door opened it for them, Roger muttered an excuse and turned and walked back down the hall.

That was fine with Maggie. She strode to the table and dumped her purse onto it and turned to face the entrance, her heart beating in double-time as she waited for Laurent to walk through the door.

She didn't have to wait long.

Although the door had been closed behind her, she was able to hear what sounded like friendly voices outside. When the door opened, she took one look at Laurent and burst into tears.

He was inside the room in two strides and took her into his arms. Somewhere in the distance she heard the heavy door clang shut behind him.

"I'm sorry," she wept. "I didn't want to..."

He kissed her face, her eyelids, her hair, murmuring gently to her.

"*Non, non, chérie.* I am here."

For one moment, Maggie flashed back to the first time she'd heard those words from him—over a decade ago in her mother's Buckhead garden when Maggie had never expected to see Laurent again.

One minute she was cutting roses for her mother's dinner table and the next, this handsome six-foot five Frenchman was standing before her.

I am here, chérie. Laurent is here.

Maggie cried harder.

Laurent pulled one of the chairs out and sat down, taking her onto his lap. He rubbed her back and spoke softly to her until she was able to wipe away her tears and take a long breath.

"It will be all right, *chérie*," Laurent said.

"Will it?" Maggie shook her head. "Do you really think so?"

"*Bien sûr.* Of course. You are not to worry."

Maggie turned to face him. "That's what you said yesterday just minutes before Roger told me you were their prime suspect."

Laurent made a sound of disgust. "The man's an idiot."

"Yes. Yes, he is," Maggie said. "And he holds the power of life and death over you."

"You are being overly dramatic."

"Am I?" Maggie jumped up and waved to the room they were in. "Tell me which part of *this* is hyperbole, Laurent, because I'd really like to buy into that."

Laurent sighed. "Bedard has no control over anything," he said. "I think, for us, that is the problem."

"What do you mean? He insists he's helping us."

"Except he cannot. His hands are tied."

"You mean because he wants to look good for his boss? So I guess an easy conviction is what would do that?"

Laurent hesitated for a moment. It was a hesitation that Maggie would come back to reflect on days later.

"*Oui*," he said. "That is what I mean." He stood up and took Maggie into his arms again and she lay her cheek against his chest.

"I want you to come home," she said softly, her chest aching with the effort not to cry.

Laurent took in a breath as if to answer but only let it out again.

Maggie looked up at him. He did not look as if he'd just spent five days and nights in a prison. While it was true she had no idea as to the comfort level of the accommodations, they must be at least decent for Laurent to look so unruffled. But then again, nothing ruffled Laurent.

Laurent looked as if he'd been out shopping for asparagus in the Richélme *marché*.

Bedard on the other hand looked like he'd just come off the Bataan Death March and *he* was in charge of the investigation.

"Do you have any idea how your knife wound up lodged in Henri Dupree's back?" she asked.

"Maggie, *non*," Laurent said firmly, narrowing his eyes at her. "You are to leave this case alone. Do you hear me?"

"Do you really trust Bedard's minions to do their best for us?" Maggie said incredulously. "Are you that comfortable with *the idiot* as you called him making sure you don't go to prison for this?"

"I need you to promise me you will not involve yourself with this."

"Sorry, no," Maggie said, shaking her head. "Not going to happen."

Laurent dropped his hands from her waist and took a step back, his eyes snapping with mounting ire.

"I insist," he said, his voice cold and unfamiliar to Maggie.

"Why did Frère Jean come to visit you yesterday?" she asked, doing her best to ignore his tone.

For a moment he looked as if he would not allow himself to be distracted but clearly he'd been giving that some thought himself.

"It was a deliberate act so that he could fabricate my confession," Laurent said.

"Any idea why?"

"To protect someone he cares about, I assume."

"The killer, you mean."

"Maggie..." Laurent said in a warning tone.

"I have to tell you that Roger is *not* doing all I think he should be in order to help us. Jean-Luc and I found horse droppings in the vineyard close to where the body was found and Roger has yet to send his crime tech people to either our vineyard to examine it or to the monastery which has a stable. Or at least had one."

Laurent rubbed a heavy hand across his face wearily.

"Jean-Luc?" he said.

"He's helping me," Maggie said. "Since Roger seems happy with the evidence he has so far, someone needs to be out there—"

"*Non!* Maggie, if ever I have asked something of you, now is when I need you to listen to me. *Attends!*"

"Laurent, I—"

"*Non!* You will *not* investigate this case. You will trust Commandant Bedard to do his job. Do you understand me?"

Maggie faced him, her mouth a firm line. "I understand you. But I don't understand why."

Laurent drew her back into his arms. "It could be dangerous," he said softly.

"Talking to a bunch of monks?" Maggie said incredulously. "Poking around an old monastery?"

"Someone was murdered," Laurent reminded her. "The murderer is still out there. I don't want you any where near him."

Maggie felt a flush of frustration. She could see Laurent's point of course. He was inside and feeling helpless and couldn't bear the thought of Maggie walking into a murderer's lair.

"I wish you'd trust me," Maggie said. "Jean-Luc and I are close to getting some answers. I really feel we are."

"It doesn't matter, *chérie*," Laurent said.

Maggie pulled away. "How can you say that? *Evidence* matters! Just today Roger gave me a copy of Frère Jean's deposition."

"He should not have done that." But he softened his words by kissing her. "Enough of this," he said. "Tell me of the children. What is happening at Domaine St-Buvard?"

Instantly Maggie's eyes filled with tears.

"Oh, Laurent," she said, but before she could form the words to tell him, his eyes softened and she knew he'd guessed.

"Little Petit," he said sadly. "I am so sorry, *chérie*. She was a good pet to our family."

Maggie cried. "She really was. I can't bear how much I miss her."

"*Courage, chérie*," Laurent whispered into her ear. "This too will pass. There will be another Petit-Four someday,"

"Never," Maggie said, blinking back her tears.

She closed her eyes and felt the relief and sanctuary of his strong arms around her. He didn't argue with her. He didn't tell her better days were coming.

In fact, Laurent didn't give her the confident, encouraging words she'd always counted on him for when times were hard.

For once he looked as if he didn't have any answers at all.

34

TUMBLING DOWN

The drive back to Domaine St-Buvard that afternoon was a somber one. Zouzou, who'd gone through a bad stage the year before, was now almost always in a good mood—matching Mila for all the giggles and shrieks that came from the back seat.

Jemmy sat next to Maggie in the front seat, studying a game he was playing on his iPad.

Maggie didn't see the streets that led from their school to the A7 exit. She didn't see the traffic on the ramp to the exit or the mile after mile as they flew by as she drove due west toward home.

All she could see was Laurent's face and his insistence that she stop investigating his case—as well as the utter and complete discouragement that came from every pore in his body.

This was a Laurent she didn't know. He'd given up. Worse, he'd accepted someone else's interpretation of his future and was doggedly resisting any attempts to change that interpretation.

It just didn't make sense!

But one thing she knew for sure, the feeling of hopelessness was contagious.

From the minute she'd been forced to let go of him and walk out of that police station, it no longer mattered what she knew, what help Roger did or didn't give her, what new clue Jean-Luc might discover, or what Frère Jean's deposition revealed.

It was over. Their future was decided.

And their future wasn't good.

How had Laurent lost hope so quickly? Was there something they knew that Maggie couldn't see?

On the face of it anyway, his case wasn't hopeless! Barring the confession which surely wouldn't hold up to scrutiny, the evidence was strictly circumstantial. The forensics could tell any of a couple of different stories just as factually depending on the point of view.

Did Laurent know something that Maggie didn't?

Did *Roger*?

Is that why they both acted so fatalistic?

Could there be evidence that they knew pointed more damningly to Laurent? If so, why hadn't she been told about it?

But she knew why. Laurent would be trying to protect her.

She worked to tamp down her feelings of mounting stress when the phone rang. She saw it was Jean-Luc.

"*Allo*, Jean-Luc," she said. "I saw Laurent today."

"That is wonderful! How does he look?"

"So-so. I'll fill you in later. Do you have news for me?"

"Not really. *Tant pis*. I drove to two surrounding farms that have stables for the tourists but they insist none of their horses have been out and certainly they wouldn't ride them through a vineyard."

Maggie sighed with frustration although she hadn't expected anything different.

"I have one more to visit," he said. "But it is the one at the monastery that really matters."

"Well, you can forget that. It burned to the ground this morning."

"*Vraiment?*" Jean-Luc said in astonishment. "Isn't that suspicious?"

"Hell yes it is. We need to find out who was responsible."

It wasn't until the words were out of her mouth that Maggie realized she intended to defy Laurent. She quickly reran the visit in her mind to see if she'd specifically told Laurent that she *wouldn't* investigate the case but she knew in the end it didn't matter.

He'd asked her not to. If she did, it was a betrayal. Pure and simple. Maybe not technically in a court of law.

But definitely in the court of Laurent.

"*Bien sûr,*" Jean-Luc said. "There are still more clues to be found."

"Where are you now?"

"Meeting a friend for a drink in Velaux. Did you need me?"

Maggie glanced at her purse where Frère Jean's deposition was.

"No. Enjoy yourself. We'll meet up tomorrow."

As soon as she hung up, Maggie dug out the deposition from her purse and unfolded it, trying to keep one eye on the road.

"*Maman*, can we stop for *la glace?*" Mila asked. "Please?"

Even Jemmy looked up from his electronic game to see Maggie's response.

"Not today, sweetie," Maggie said, flapping out the sheet of paper and squinting at the small type. "It'll spoil your supper."

"Papa says not to call it *supper,*" Jemmy said refocusing on his game.

"Yes, well, whatever it's called," Maggie said, trying to read the deposition. She made out the line, *Dernier said Monsieur Dupree would need to pay for his crimes and he didn't trust the police to do the job properly.*

"*Maman,* look out!" Mila squealed.

Maggie felt the car edge off the highway at the same time

Mila screamed. She quickly corrected the move and dropped the deposition.

"Okay, guys," Maggie said, turning on her turn signal. "Ice cream after all."

Cheers erupted in the car as Maggie took the next exit. She wasn't exactly sure where she was since she'd never had reason to exit this far away from Aix or St-Buvard before but she drove until she found a *tabac* with a sign out front with a big pink flamenco on it that also announced *la glace*.

She parked and turned around to face the two girls in the back seat.

"Zouzou?" Maggie said. "Can you do this on your own or do you need me to come in?"

"*Non, Tante* Maggie," Zouzou said eagerly. "I can do it."

"Hey, I'm the man," Jemmy said. "It should be me."

"Yes, but Zouzou is the eldest," Maggie said, giving her firstborn a quick kiss on his head. She handed a ten-euro note to Zouzou and watched the children scramble out of the car and run into the *tabac*.

Quickly, she picked up the deposition and read it. It was only half a page long but even after ten years in France Maggie was surprised to find a phrase or two that she didn't know. In the end it didn't matter, she was able to translate enough of it to get the picture.

And a black, damning picture it was.

She took in a long breath to steady herself. If she had Frère Jean in front of her right now she wasn't sure she wasn't capable of burying a knife in his back herself.

She re-read the deposition a third time and tried to see what she was missing. She now knew what the monk had said and while she and Laurent had made a pretty good guess about *why* he'd said it, she still needed to know for sure.

Knowing *why* would lead them directly to the murderer. On that Maggie had absolutely no doubt.

She picked up her phone and called Grace.

"Hey," Grace answered. "Is everything okay?"

It was amazing that *that* was the first thing any parent said when they got an unexpected call from someone who was supposed to be in charge of their children.

"Everything's fine," Maggie said. "I've effectively ruined Zouzou's appetite for dinner tonight with ice cream so there's that."

Grace laughed. "No worries. She monitors herself so well these days I'd be surprised if she eats more than a few bites of the ice cream. What's up?"

"Is there any way you can come collect the kids?" Maggie asked. "I hate to ask especially after we made our deal today but—"

"Not a problem. I'm literally doing nothing but watching the grass refuse to grow. Where are you?'

"That's just it. It might be a little tricky to find me. If Google Maps is to be believed I'm at a point that will take me directly to the monastery if I stay on this road."

"So you'd like to stay there and let me come to you? No problem. Can you give me an idea of where you are?"

Maggie squinted at the map on her phone and tried to figure out where *Dormir* was in relation to her position.

"I think if you take the St-Buvard village road due north for a few miles it eventually connects with D10. You know, the one with the even bigger aqueducts?"

"Don't you just love that we get to use thousand year old Roman aqueducts as direction reference points?"

"And then take that road about, I don't know, maybe another ten miles over country roads, you should come to Le Pechou and hang a left there. Or I guess I mean go south. Not sure how far from there we are. Maybe five miles. But you can't miss us. We're on the side of the road with a big pink flamenco advertising a traditional French *tabac*."

"Of course it is," Grace said with a laugh. "Be right there."

The kids came out of the *tabac* and Maggie was surprised to see that, sure enough, Zouzou had only taken a few bites from her ice cream before tossing it in the trash.

We should all have such willpower, Maggie thought.

The three children sat at an old wooden picnic table out in front of the *tabac*. Mila was growing so fast. Her legs were long and shapely even at five and for the first time ever, Maggie was stunned to realize that Mila looked like Maggie's sister Elise. Something unpleasant and sad churned in her stomach as she realized that.

But when Maggie's eyes moved to Jemmy—the spitting image of what his father must have looked like at that age—all Maggie could do was gaze at him through tear-filled eyes and pray.

Please give him the chance to grow up knowing the amazing man his father is.

35

FOUNTAIN OF SORROW

Serving the evening meal in the refectory was generally something Guy preferred to do because it was so social. But the Brothers were very strict about making sure that everyone took a turn so nobody got stuck with a bad job for longer than a cycle.

Guy knew the older residents disliked the work because it meant a solid hour on their feet. And the chronically shy also usually balked at it. It occurred to him that Pierre had yet to work the food line and Guy wondered if that was because the monks didn't trust him not to spit in the food or otherwise disrupt what was supposed to be a quiet, monastic part of the day.

In any case, Guy's work ladling soup and handing out baguettes was accompanied by a good deal of explanation on how the stable could have burned down and how he got the cut over his eye and who started the fight. After the fifteenth person asked him if he ran into a door he began to wonder if Frère Jean hadn't moved him up in the roster to soup duty deliberately knowing how the constant barrage of questions would be a fitting consequence of his actions.

But Guy didn't mind. The people here were curious and for

the most part they liked him. He knew that being a part of a big family often included teasing in equal measures with expressions of concern.

He saw Noelle the moment she entered the refectory and his heart began to beat in double time. She was alone.

She stopped at a table full of her friends while Guy waited for her to get in line. There was only one line tonight. Everyone came to Guy for their soup and then moved down a long table where they picked up bread and then on to where Madame Dumas poured them either coffee or handed them a water bottle. Carafes of wine sat on each table with thick-rimmed glasses that would later be Guy's job to wash when he cleaned up after mealtime.

He spilled soup twice in his rush to hurry the people through the line so he could be face to face with Noelle. She waited, her eyes downcast, while he meticulously ladled up the thick creamy celery and white fish soup into a ceramic bowl for her.

As he handed it to her she looked up to take it and said quietly—still not looking at him—"I will never forgive you for fighting with Pierre."

Guy did not release the bowl but stared at her in surprise.

"What?" he said.

"You got Pierre in trouble," she hissed, her hands gripping the bowl along with Guy's. "And now *Mon Frère* says there's no stable so there's no job for him!"

Pierre was leaving? Guy's spurt of joy was quickly tamped down by the sudden thought that Noelle might leave too.

He had heard that Noelle had given up her place in the little house on the fringe of the vineyard and moved back to the monastery dormitory. He had also heard that Pierre was secretly spending nights with her there, just down the hall from where her father had been killed.

Guy flinched at the sound of those words in his head. He'd done everything he could to blot out the memory of that night.

He released the soup bowl. As Noelle turned to shove two

demi-batons in her shoulder bag, Guy tried to think of something that might help him understand *why* she'd turned to Pierre—a filthy, scheming, lying gypsy—instead of...but of course he knew why she didn't turn to *him*. He accepted now that that could never be.

But Pierre?

"I'll never believe you love him," he said to her now.

"That is not something that matters to me," she said.

"What, *love?*" he said in astonishment.

"No. What you believe." Her eyes found his now but they were cold and unforgiving.

"Just tell me why," he said helplessly, unmindful of the woman waiting patiently for her soup. "If Pierre really makes you happy..." He couldn't finish the thought.

How could that be?

"Pierre and I have a special bond," Noelle said archly. "I can't explain it and you wouldn't understand. I hold his life in my hands."

He watched her walk away. But his heart was heavier than before he'd seen her.

Because one thing Guy knew better than anyone—holding someone's life in your hands could end very badly indeed.

In fact it usually did.

36

THE LAST NAIL

Laurent guessed the cement blocks measured eighteen inches by six inches each. They were stacked in a bricking pattern up to the ceiling on three of the four walls, the exception being the wall that held the door to the hall. *And freedom.*

Laurent rested his hands against the blocks and did a series of pushups against the wall, banishing those two words as quickly as they'd formed in his head.

This wasn't the first time he'd been in custody of course. He and Bentley had shared a cell in St-Tropez for a few days one summer before a compatriot bailed them out before their false passports could be double-checked.

The nineties, he thought. The police were just beginning to discover DNA. Even Interpol's criminal computer database was in its infancy.

Could he even have worked the Cote d'Azur if he were still in the business today?

It was an idiotic question. Which was testimony to how the long hours in solitary confinement were getting to him.

It had never been a matter of having the right identification papers. It was always a matter of people and what they would believe. What they wanted to believe. What they could be made to believe.

He pushed off from the wall. *Enough,* he chided himself.

Yesterday is a long time ago.

He sat on the cement bench built into the wall on the wall opposite the door. His meal sat on a tray by the slot under the door waiting to be picked up. Something congealed on top of a brown sort of meat. The heel of the baguette actually broke into three crumbling pieces when it fell from his plate. He hated not eating. He didn't want to weaken and he didn't want his jailers to think any of this affected him. But even being incarcerated for a murder he did not commit in order to be charged for a crime he most certainly did, he could not eat bad food.

An image of Maggie's face came to him. She'd looked so beautiful today. She always did when her expression held that singular combination of vulnerability and intensity she got when she had a problem she could not let go of.

What was it Jean-Luc would say? *Like a terrier with a bone.*

He smiled in spite of his surroundings. He refused to think of Jemmy or Mila. Thinking of them could only weaken him. But imagining his wife's face—even if it didn't solve anything—at least it gave him comfort.

For now.

Until he found himself wondering when he would hold her again. And if the next time there would be iron bars separating them.

He stood and walked to the door and then back again. With his long legs, he could easily do it in two steps—one if he tried. Pushing the image of Maggie back to the corner of his mind he thought instead of the question Roger had asked him.

"What are you going to do now?"

Pushing aside the fact that Laurent was not at all convinced *le flic* would honor any deal he made with them, he would be a fool not to confess to the lesser charge.

Just the thought of that gave him a visceral reaction that twisted in his gut.

Confessing to anything at all went against everything he knew. As long as he didn't formally put his name to a confession there was always a chance that something might come up, some miracle might present itself.

Perhaps *Directeur Général* Terrone would have a heart attack after a particularly large and satisfying meal of *steak au poivre* with a rich helping of *pommes anna* which would make the whole matter fade away.

Should he instead count on the murder charge not holding up in court? There was no real evidence against him. A moron of a defense attorney should be able to plead the case successfully.

Unless.

Unless Terrone had something more persuasive up his sleeve.

As of course he would.

You didn't need to be a criminal mastermind to figure out that a man's wife and children were his weakest link. Before Laurent married there existed no leverage under the sun to force him to do what he didn't want to do.

Not so now.

Now there were any number of things Terrone might threaten Laurent with that would make life miserable for Maggie and *les enfants*. He could even outright harm them. With Laurent in jail, they would be defenseless.

It was too much to hope that Terrone wasn't base enough to use his family against him.

Laurent heard the sound of the bar releasing from the door and he stepped back to the cement bench to face whatever was coming.

The little *singe* Girard had been in to wheedle a confession out of him twice already in two days and twice Laurent had refused to give a definite answer.

It was time for them to raise the stakes.

The door swung open and Detective Inspector Girard stood there grinning before taking a step into the room and putting a foot in Laurent's uneaten dinner tray.

The man slipped and put his hand against the wall to steady himself. He swore and barked out for the guard to come and remove the tray.

Laurent watched Girard's eyes. He was a petty man and he was now feeling foolish. Laurent knew that could only feed the man's spite.

"Enjoyed your meal, I see?" Girard said as he stepped into the room. He left the door open behind him. A guard stood outside.

He's afraid I might attack him.

Laurent's stomach tightened at what it was that Girard had come to tell him today that might make him want to do that.

"I think, Monsieur," Girard said, smirking, "that we have finally found something that will make our offer irresistible to you."

37

HIGH HOPES

In the end Grace had gotten lost twice on the way to the *tabac* and by the time she finally drove up in her classic Citroen 2CV, Maggie was about to jump out of her skin with impatience. She estimated that she could probably have driven the kids to *Dormir* and stopped for a coffee in half the time it had taken Grace to find them.

As a result she arrived at *l'Abbaye de Sainte-Trinité* in the late afternoon. She parked in front of the rectory and sat for a moment trying to get her thoughts straight about the questions she had for Frère Jean. A light glimmered from one of the windows in the rectory and as Maggie watched the door opened and three men dressed in monks' robes filed out, their hands pressed together in prayer. Once outside they walked toward the gardens in the direction of where the stables used to be. It was impossible to tell if one of them was Frère Jean.

As Maggie was trying to decide whether to follow them or knock on the rectory door to see if Frère Jean might be inside, a woman came out of the main building. The giant double doors—easily sixty feet high—had embedded in them a smaller wooden door through which the woman emerged.

Maggie recognized Madame Montagne immediately. The old woman stopped outside the huge double doors in her rain jacket and lit a cigarette. Maggie immediately left the car and hurried over to her.

Madame Montagne watched her approach through hooded eyes.

"*Bonjour*, Madame Montagne," Maggie said cheerfully. "Enjoying the afternoon air?"

"You are very *droll*, Madame," the woman said, puffing on her cigarette, but her lips twitched in the direction of a smile. "I see you cannot keep away."

"I was wondering if I could ask you a few more questions."

"What will you give me to do this?"

"How about the satisfaction of knowing you helped free a man unfairly held for a murder he didn't commit?"

The woman made a face.

"Ten euros?" Maggie said.

"What do you want to know?"

"Is it true everyone hated Henri Dupree?"

"He was a despicable human being."

"So why was he allowed to stay?"

Madame Montagne took in a long drag on her cigarette. "His daughter, Noelle for one. Why should she be punished because her father is a *putain*? And people felt sorry for him."

"Why is that?"

Madame Montagne tossed her cigarette on the gravel and ground it out with the toe of her espadrille. It was much too cold to be wearing open-toed shoes and Maggie wondered if they were all the woman owned.

"Because of what happened the year before."

"Okay, Madame Montagne," Maggie said in impatience. "Can we speed things along here? I need to talk with Frère Jean today too and get home to my children before they graduate from college."

Madame Montagne scowled at her. "Why do you want to talk to *Mon Frère*?"

Maggie debated lying to her but the old woman was sharp and could probably see through it.

"Frère Jean claims my husband killed Henri Dupree," Maggie said. "I want to know why."

Madame Montagne shrugged. "Perhaps because it is the truth?"

"It *isn't* the truth so I want to know why Frère Jean would say it is."

"There is not a person here who does not love and respect Frère Jean," Madame Montagne said, her eyes snapping.

Maggie quickly began to rue her honesty with the woman.

"Frère Jean is a saint," Madame Montagne continued, fully angry now. "There is no job too difficult or disgusting for him to do if it benefits his flock. He would sacrifice himself for any of one of us."

"Okay, that's great," Maggie said. "No disrespect intended. You mentioned that people felt sorry for Dupree for something that happened the year before. What was it?"

Madame Montagne glared at Maggie as if not ready to forgive her for maligning the monk. Maggie dug out the ten euros from her billfold.

The old woman hesitated only a moment before snatching the bill from Maggie's hands.

"Henri and Noelle came to the monastery after a fire killed his wife."

"That's terrible."

"And twin sons."

Maggie felt her stomach clench and she involuntarily put her hand on her abdomen.

"So if he wanted to be a bastard from time to time or drink too much," Madame Montagne said, "there were few who could fault him."

"I thought you told me he didn't drink."

Madame Montagne shrugged. "He said he was an alcoholic and had given up drinking. But there are some who said he was drinking again. Can you blame him?"

As Madame Montagne turned away, Maggie reached out to touch her sleeve.

"Madame? One more question?"

The woman sighed but paused.

"Any idea of how the stables burned down?" Maggie said, speaking quickly. "Or who was responsible?"

At first Maggie didn't think the woman would answer but she shoved the money in the pocket of her old worn coat and looked over her shoulder at Maggie.

"Two boys fighting over Noelle," she said. "Pierre and Guy."

Maggie remembered Guy introducing himself to her two days earlier.

"Which one is Pierre?" she asked hurriedly as Madame Montagne opened the door.

"The *gitane*," the woman spat before disappearing inside. *The gypsy.*

Maggie stood with her hand on the doorknob.

So the two men in love with Henri Dupree's daughter had *jointly* burned the stables down? Was that significant?

Her fingers went cold and she felt the familiar feeling of dread welling up in her chest.

There are no coincidences. Of course it's significant.

Roger sat alone in the back of the bar, his cognac on the scarred wooden table in front of him. He knew he probably should eat something to mitigate the effects of the four shots drunk on an empty stomach. But he didn't have the energy or inclination to order food.

Chloe had been so excited this morning as she got ready for school. Her dance instructor had said she was to be the lead dancer at the recital next spring. Chloe had also related how all her friends were so envious of her going to the summer dance camp in Nice.

"It made me feel so special, Papa!" she'd said with delight as she pirouetted and skipped around the room, every word out of her mouth sinking Roger lower and lower into the depths of despair.

And now? Was he really going to destroy all that for her? Was he really going to take her away from her friends, the school she loved, her dance teacher who cherished her as if she were her own daughter?

Roger drank the dregs of his brandy and lifted his glass to the waiter to indicate he wanted another.

The words reverberated in his brain ...*as if she were her own daughter*...and he got an image of Choltilde that brought tears to his eyes. He quickly wiped away evidence of the emotion as the waiter brought him his drink and also a small bowl of nuts.

Was this what he'd promised Choltilde as she lay dying from cancer ten years ago? That he would break their daughter's heart and crush her spirit? Was Choltilde looking down at him even now with disgust and revulsion at his betrayal of all his promises to her?

No, he said firmly as he drained his glass. *No, I will not do that to my only child.*

You are asking too much of me, Maggie, he thought. *As usual. Too much.*

As he got up to leave, unsteady on his feet, he felt the whiskey like a sour taste in his mouth and before he could stop himself, the thought came to him...

This must be what betrayal tastes like.

38

FADING AWAY

Maggie turned and wandered to the side of the building where the stables used to be.

The walls still stood but little else. The roof must have been the first thing to go, she thought as she stepped into the thick ash of what had once been the interior of the stable.

In some spots the area was even still smoking. But the rectory and the main monastery building containing the refectory—the two closest buildings—were made of stone and brick. There was no worry that they might be affected by a still smoldering fire.

The first and last time Maggie had seen the gypsy boy Pierre was here. If cleaning the stables had been the work he did at the monastery, he was now likely out of a job. She walked through the ash, amazed that Roger didn't think this was worthy of another look.

What is with him? He says he wants to help but he isn't at all.

"Madame? You should not be here!"

Maggie turned to see Frère Jean himself marching toward her. The second he recognized her, his face changed from irritation to shock and then to what looked to Maggie like fear.

"Frère Jean," Maggie said. "Just the man I want to talk to."

He put his hands up, palms out as if to shield himself from her. "I have nothing to say to you."

"Really?" Maggie called loudly. "Even if I tell you the cops know you lied?"

Another monk appeared from around the corner on the path that led from the monastery gardens. Behind him, Maggie could see a few stalks of corn although even she knew it was too late in the season for them. The monk glanced at Maggie and Frère Jean.

Frère Jean spoke quickly to him.

"It is nothing, Frère Ambrose. A woman has gotten lost and I am giving her directions back to the village."

The other monk nodded and continued down the path until he disappeared around the corner of the main building. By then, Maggie was standing directly in front of Frère Jean.

"The cops know you lied," she said. "Your so-called confession that you claim Laurent made to you is riddled with factual errors."

The monk blinked rapidly and looked around as if afraid someone else might overhear them.

"I don't know what you're talking about," he said, licking his lips nervously.

"The statement you made to the police said Laurent killed Henri Dupree by stabbing him in the back," Maggie said, "but Dupree was killed by being bashed on the head with a bat."

"Is that true?" Frère Jean had been in the process of turning away from Maggie but her words stopped him.

"Plus your statement said that Laurent killed Dupree in our vineyard and the cops know now that he was killed elsewhere and brought there."

"How do you know what is in my statement?"

But Maggie was ready for him. "You mean the official police statement that will be read at your obstruction-of-justice trial just before they defrock you and put you in GenPop? *That* one? I read it online."

He gasped. "No! Is that true?"

It shouldn't have surprised Maggie that the monk was not technologically savvy. There was a hope that that might work in her favor.

"Oh, yeah. It's public record now, baby. It's all over the Internet. And the cops are scratching their heads because *your* version of the facts—the version you say you got from Laurent—bears no resemblance to the forensic evidence of the actual murder. How about that? So any minute now the cops are going to start wondering why you lied. *I'm* wondering why you lied."

Frère Jean grabbed his head as if it would explode, his eyes darting maniacally.

"You are trying to confuse me!" he shrieked suddenly. "I am a Benedictine monk! They came to *me*! Besides who would people believe? A man of God or a criminal who made his living lying and stealing?"

He turned and ran down the pathway leading to the garden.

Maggie walked to the wall of the nearby building and put a hand on its stone wall to steady herself, Frère Jean's verbal assault ringing in her ears.

She felt an insistent hollowness in her chest and she breathed slowly in and out several times.

What had she expected? That Frère Jean would break down and apologize for trying to implicate Laurent in the murder? The man was lying for a reason. Obviously a very powerful reason.

She turned back toward her car. In the distance a dog began to bark and Maggie thought of her own two dogs at home. It was growing dark. She still needed to collect Jemmy and Mila from Grace's place.

Her limbs felt heavy as she got into the car. She couldn't remember the last time she'd eaten. The ancient soot-stained brick buildings of the monastery seemed to loom over her, blocking out what was left of the late afternoon light. She struggled to fight off the wave of hopelessness descending over her.

By the time she turned the car around to head away from the monastery and was driving back through Pont l'Abbe the rain had started back up again in a slow steady drizzle that dripped off the rooftops of the village houses and filled the stone gutters in the middle of the cobblestoned road.

She flipped on her headlights and felt like crying.

Frère Jean was right about one thing. Everyone would believe him over Laurent. He was a *monk*. He did good works. He was beloved in his community.

She felt a throb of discouragement.

Why was he lying? Who was he trying to protect?

Something else Frère Jean said bothered her and Maggie reran the conversation in her mind trying to remember what it was but she was too tired and it was too deeply buried in a lot of emotional conversation.

But something wasn't right and it hovered just outside the fringes of her thoughts—pulling at her.

She reached for her phone to tell Grace she was on her way when she saw the screen light up, revealing her mother's number. Without thinking and for the first time in her life, Maggie pushed *Decline*.

Immediately she pulled off on the side of the road. She wiped a thin veneer of perspiration from her top lip, took in a long breath and called her mother back.

"Maggie, thank God you're there," her mother said in nearly hysterical tones. "It's your father. He's fallen off the toilet and I can't get him up."

Maggie felt twin waves of relief and fear collide as one.

"Is he on the floor right now?" Maggie asked.

"Yes! Yes, he can't seem to find his legs. He's just sitting on the floor!"

"Get him a blanket and make him comfortable and I'll be there as soon as I can," Maggie said.

"Maggie! I need you here now!" her mother wailed.

"I know, Mom. I'm on my way." Maggie disconnected the phone and pulled the car back onto the road. She called Grace to ask her to keep the kids tonight. She spoke briefly to Mila about something that happened at school today and then focused on the road and the long drive back to Aix.

As she drove she called Jean-Luc to see if he could run by the house to feed the dogs when he got back from his drink with his friend.

"I didn't go," Jean-Luc said. "I got this idea so instead I went back to Domaine St-Buvard. I have already let the dogs out. I will feed them too."

God bless this man, Maggie thought as tears sprang to her eyes. *Is there anyone else on the planet who is actually making my life better these days?*

"Thank you, Jean-Luc," she said. "I don't know what I'd do without you."

"Did you have any joy at the monastery?"

"No. Frère Jean is definitely hiding something but he's not at the point of breaking down and recanting his testimony. Why did you cancel out on drinks with your friend?"

"Because I got an idea and I knew if it rained one more night I would not be able to do it," Jean-Luc said.

Maggie squinted through the windshield and the downpour as she climbed onto the A7 and saw the highway sign, *Aix 28 kilometers.*

"You are being very mysterious," she said. "What was the idea?"

"I went back to the vineyard where the *merde* was," Jean-Luc said, "and collected a large sample of it. You are not going to believe what I found embedded in it. Corn kernels."

Maggie wasn't sure what she'd been expecting to hear but it hadn't been that.

"Is that significant?" she asked wearily.

"Most of the farms around here buy their feed supplemented with other agents for their animals," Jean-Luc said. "This corn wasn't processed."

"You mean it might have come from the monastery's cornfield?"

Maggie remembered what Madame Montagne had said. The monastery made its own livestock feed.

This was proof that the horse in the vineyard had come from the monastery!

"Only a lab test will tell us for sure," Jean-Luc said. "But we don't need the stable intact for this. I put the sample in your refrigerator. Make sure the kids don't think it's *paté*."

"Jean-Luc you're an angel."

"Not at all," he said, but she could tell he was pleased at her praise.

"How was your visit with Laurent?" he asked.

"He's discouraged," she said. "It's so unlike him."

"Ah, well. You have told him that you and I are on the case together, yes?"

Maggie smiled. She could already see the lights of Aix on the horizon. Laurent was there in that glow and that thought cheered her some.

"I did," she said. "And you're right, Jean-Luc. I think that must have made him feel a lot better."

She knew it certainly made her feel better.

"All we have to do now is get your friend in the police to run the tests on the *merde*," Jean-Luc said. "Once the sample is confirmed and can be matched against..." He paused.

"Jean-Luc?"

"Did all the animals get out alive from the monastery fire?"

"They did, yes. Six goats and one horse."

"*Bon*," he said happily. "So as soon as we prove it was the monastery horse that was in the vineyard that night, we are half way home. And then so is Laurent."

At his words Maggie felt a surge of happiness welling up beneath the crust of the day's disappointments.

Yes, she thought, her heart lighter than it had been since hearing that Laurent was arrested.

We are halfway home.

39

HELL IN A HAND BASKET

That night, helping her mother get her father off the floor of the bathroom took Maggie almost thirty minutes and cemented in her mind the conviction that the present situation wasn't working. When it was all over her mother had been so glad to have the night's crisis resolved, that she immediately shepherded Maggie's father into their bedroom and Maggie didn't hear any more from either of them for the rest of the night.

Normally, seeing her parents so helpless would have been cause for another sleepless night for Maggie. But her day had been so intense—and the resulting emotions so draining—that she fell asleep as soon as her head hit the pillow and she slept soundly until eight the next morning.

When she awoke, she quickly showered and dressed. Even then her parents were not yet up, so she hurried downstairs and across the bustling *marche de* Richelme where she bought a bag of apricots, a large wedge of Sainte-Nectaire cheese and a baguette still warm from the oven.

Once back upstairs, she boiled water for the French press and ground the beans. By the time she was pouring the coffee, her parents were both up.

"Good morning," Maggie said as she set plates out on the small bistro table in the kitchen. "Did you sleep okay?"

"Well, enough," John Newberry said as he took his coffee. Maggie glanced hopefully at him. *Was he having a good day?*

"But Ben will be late for school if he doesn't shake a leg," John said.

Maggie didn't look at her mother. The disappointment was too sharp and it didn't help to see it reflected in Elspeth's face too.

"Do you have to leave right away?" her mother asked as she picked up the baguette and then put it back down.

"No. I'll stay for the day. Grace brought Jemmy and Mila to school so I'll collect them and Zouzou this afternoon."

"Oh, that's nice," Elspeth said.

"Do you think you'd like to check out the market?" Maggie said. "You do know it's two steps from your doorstep."

"Maybe another time," Elspeth said.

"What market?" John asked.

"The produce market, Dad," Maggie said. "There's also cheese and lavender and fresh fish and they have a wheel of nougat that's as big as a Volkswagon."

"I like nougat," he said after some hesitation.

"Then it's settled," Maggie said. "Mom? You can come too or if you'd rather have an hour to yourself…"

"What would I do with an hour to myself?" Elspeth said bitterly and looked away as if embarrassed at her outburst.

Maggie glanced at her phone. She'd already put two calls in to Roger and several long texts. None of which were returned.

"Right then," she said brightly to her father. "I guess we're going shopping."

. . .

The rest of the morning spun away in a blur of walking around the famed Aix food market. Maggie's father ambled slowly but seemed to enjoy the sights and sounds of the market. Elspeth had her arm looped firmly through his allowing Maggie to shop without having to keep a constant eye on them.

It seemed the rain was done for now. Although there were still puddles in the irregular surfaces of the cobblestone streets, the sun had made a weak but definite appearance, brightening the moods and spirits of everyone tired of the week's grey weather.

Her father seemed mesmerized by a huge bundle of beets, most of them still encrusted with the dirt they were grown in. At lunch time, Maggie stationed her parents at a nearby café and ordered them coffees while she finished shopping. She bought several ounces of the Bleu d'Auvergne cheese that she knew her father liked and a quart of citrus-spiced Niçoise olives.

Whenever Maggie came to the Aix markets she imagined the pleasure of living right down the street from all this bounty and selection. Although she was grateful that St-Buvard now had its own *boulangerie*, it boggled her mind to imagine how lovely life would be with so many cafés and shops—not to mention the convenience of Mila and Jem's school—so close to where they lived.

Her last stop was a small bakery where she bought four *jambon* sandwiches. Although she could easily make them herself with the ingredients she'd bought today, she decided she would wrap and freeze these for her parents to enjoy days from now.

As she shopped, she continued to check her phone but there was no reply from Roger. As she stood before a booth with bucket after bucket of several dozen different kinds of olives, she rang him again. Her call went to voicemail.

Forcing down her annoyance at not being to touch base with Roger, she put a call into Jean-Luc to see if he could meet her at Domaine St-Buvard later that afternoon to put their heads together over what their recent discoveries might mean. He didn't answer his phone either so she left a message and went to find her parents.

Her father was in a much better mood after their outing and if possible, perhaps even a little clearer headed. But the morning had also tired him and he went immediately to his room to nap while Maggie put away her purchases. Her mother watched as Maggie cleaned and trimmed the vegetables and fruits.

The gratin she'd made yesterday had ended up in the garbage bin uneaten when Maggie had had to leave quickly. She'd bought another glossy eggplant and more tomatoes this morning to make another one.

Her mother watched silently as Maggie pared and sweated the eggplant slices, then grated a fresh block of Parmesan cheese and began to pit some of the olives.

"Something on your mind, Mom?" Maggie said as she began to fry the eggplant slices in small batches in a large skillet on the apartment's small cooker.

"Ben called yesterday," Elspeth said.

Ahh. That explains why Dad flashbacked to Ben as a boy.

"Everything okay with him?" Maggie asked as she preheated the oven. She knew that—barring a miracle—everything was *not* okay with Ben. He was recently divorced, unemployed, on the edge of being disbarred, unemployed and clinically depressed. And he was still calling to complain to his parents—who had much bigger emotional fish to fry—that life had treated him unfairly.

"He doesn't really understand why your father and I are here," Elspeth said. "I wasn't sure what to tell him."

Maggie felt a flash of anger that she swallowed down.

"Well, I hope you told him you're here because you wanted to be near me and your grandchildren."

"Well, really it's because you refused to come back home to Atlanta," Elspeth said.

Maggie picked up a chef's knife and thinly sliced four large tomatoes before arranging them in a large casserole dish with the fried eggplant slices. She forced herself not to respond.

"He thinks we should come home," Elspeth said.

"What do *you* think? Because you should definitely do what you think is best for you and not what Ben thinks you should do."

"Why are you angry at your brother?"

"I'm not at all," Maggie said, as she began to coarsely peel and chop six large garlic cloves.

"Well, you sound like you are."

"I don't mean to," Maggie said blithely, forcing herself not to look at her watch. She had to be out in front of the school by four o'clock. She was hoping to have a little bit of time to herself before then. She mixed the grated cheese with the chopped garlic and sprinkled it over the eggplant and tomatoes.

"I told Ben we might be coming home. I think that's what he was suggesting we do."

Is this what love is? Maggie thought as she chopped a handful of the pitted olives and scattered them on top of the dish before covering it with foil. *Is love trying not to rock the boat and upset your loved ones? Or is it pressing your agenda when you believe you're right and they're wrong?*

"Maggie?"

Maggie glanced at her mother.

"Would you be okay with us going back to Atlanta?"

"Does it matter what I think?"

"Don't be like that."

"Like what? Like someone who sees you about to make a mistake but doesn't want to upset you so she keeps her mouth shut? You mean like that?"

"I just don't understand you."

"I know." Maggie wrapped two of the four *jambon* sandwiches and popped them in the freezer. Then she slid the gratin inside the oven and set the alarm. "This will be ready in time for dinner.

When Dad wakes up he can have one of the sandwiches. I've left two on the table. I also got some fresh pasta. It boils up in seconds. Just spoon the gratin over the top, okay?"

"I think I know how to make pasta," Elspeth said peevishly, turning away to look out the window.

"That is a relief to me," Maggie said cheerfully, trying to lighten things up with a little good-natured teasing. "I need to pick up the kids from school."

Elspeth frowned and looked at her watch. "This early?"

"I have a few errands to run first."

"Of course you do," Elspeth sniffed.

"Is there something else you need me to do, Mom?" Maggie asked.

"No. We've inconvenienced you quite enough as it is."

"It's never an inconvenience, Mom," Maggie said, reaching for her purse. "I hope in your heart you know that."

Elspeth didn't answer so Maggie leaned over and kissed her on the cheek.

"I'll call you later," she said and hurried out the door.

40

TIME TO GO

Maggie felt as if she were escaping and she hated feeling that way. She ran down the stairs of her parents' building until she stepped outside and took in a breath of fresh air.

The morning market had already been disassembled. The pavers had been hosed down, the corns husks, flower stems and fish heads gone, the wet cobblestones gleaming. In place of the produce and cheese vendors' booths the square was now covered in outdoor tables, many with umbrellas in case of the unlikely return of the Provençal sun.

Already waiters scurried around tables taking late lunch orders or early *apéro* drink requests. Maggie wove between the tables to make her way across Place Richelme toward the street where she'd parked her car the night before.

It hurt to think that this amazing panorama of activity and magical color was now lost on her parents. If they'd come even a year ago, Maggie knew they would have loved wandering through Aix and claiming it as their own.

But they were a year too late to enjoy the enchantment of this amazing town.

Maggie hurried down rue Laurent Fauchier, passing art galleries and clothing boutiques along the way. There were dozens of children's clothing shops in Aix—and she'd shopped them all. Laurent liked to tease her that their children were the best dressed people under ten years of age in all of Provence.

Her heart flinched at the memory of Laurent teasing her in happier times.

No! She told herself. *I will not be pessimistic. Our life together is not over. I'm going to make sure it isn't.*

She glanced for the hundredth time at her phone but there was still no reply from Roger.

He can't pretend to be helping us now, she thought angrily. *He can't expect I'll believe his easy words and promises any longer.*

She slowed her steps. But if she didn't believe Roger could help her, where did that leave her? Wasn't there at least some hope that the police could be reasoned with to take another look at this crime with Laurent out of the frame?

Without Roger what hope did she have?

She came to a stop in front of a bakery she wasn't familiar with. The glossy braids of *fougasse* studded with cherry tomatoes and olives in the display window glistened. When she glanced in the front door she could see a woman in a white apron beyond the cash register was pulling a tray of croissants out of the oven. It was unusually late in the day for fresh baked goods and the aroma of the pastries drifted out to the street and pulled Maggie inside.

There were two tiny bistro tables inside the bakery. Maggie glanced again at her watch and then walked to the counter.

Ten minutes later, she had a steaming cup of hot chocolate—because why not?—in front of her and a still-warm-from-the-oven *chocolatine* on a dish. She propped her phone on the windowsill so she would be sure not to miss any calls—and to remind her of the time so she wouldn't be late picking up the kids—and pulled out a small notebook from her purse.

Nobody else came into the little bakery and Maggie was glad for that but sorry too. With the magnificent Bechard's just across town, this bakery like all the others probably struggled to find regular patrons. Yet the pastries were exquisite, probably every bit as good as the ones at Bechard. Or at least as far as Maggie's palate could tell.

She took a bite of the croissant. The flakes of sugar shattered in her mouth and she closed her eyes to fully enjoy every moment of the bite. Her eyes opened at the thought that she had no idea what Laurent had had for breakfast—or lunch—today. She swallowed the bite and washed it down with the hot chocolate, burning her tongue in the process.

She looked down at her notebook and wrote down the name *Henri Dupree*. Under his name she wrote: *the victim—maybe a drinker maybe not—found face down in our vineyard—his hands tied behind his back and Laurent's utility knife in his back.*

She thought for a moment and then wrote:

He'd suffered blunt trauma to his head which the police believe is what killed him and that the knife was just for show.

She looked out the window.

But show for who?

She thought back to the lab report that Roger had let her see.

She wrote down:

There was straw on the victim's shoes. And a horse had been in the vineyard at some point. All other tracks had been destroyed by the rain that night.

Next she wrote down Laurent's name and under that she drew a frownie face.

Laurent was seen assaulting the guy by at least five witnesses —*really, he needs to work on his temper.*

She wrote:

Laurent got physical with Dupree the day of the murder.

She tapped her pen against her lip and then wrote next to the name *Henri Dupree—a man nobody liked.*

Then under Laurent's name she wrote:
Frère Jean—a very credible source swears Laurent confessed to killing Dupree.

Just writing it down made Maggie mad all over again. She circled the line. Was this the key? The fact that this monk lied to the police? He had to know the truth, right? Or else why would he make up this fiction?

She revisited in her mind the hysterical outburst that Frère Jean had blasted her with yesterday evening. Suddenly she remembered more precisely his words when he made it clear that he knew all about Laurent's criminal past.

"Who are they going to believe? A Benedictine monk or a man with a criminal history?"

Maggie thought back to those first few months with Laurent. It was true he'd kept his past from her right up to the point where she'd discovered on her own how he made his living with Roger Bentley as a high stakes Riviera con man. Even now it was easy to see that tendency to dissemble still in him. Laurent was naturally mysterious, prone to fixing a problem with a lie before the truth, and endlessly enigmatic.

But how had Frère Jean known about Laurent's past? She was positive Laurent wouldn't have told him and the monastery was too far from St-Buvard for him to have believably heard it through idle village gossip.

Someone had told him.

Was that someone connected to the murder? Perhaps even the killer himself?

The foot traffic outside the bakery window had picked up and a woman came in with a toddler. Maggie glanced at her phone. It was time to go.

As she was gathering her things from the little bistro table her eye fell on where she'd written Laurent's name on her notepad. Quickly, she wrote, *No alibi.*

And of course that was because of *her.*

As she slipped out the door of the bakery, she felt a creeping annoyance that, like Roger, Jean-Luc hadn't gotten back with her either.

She called Roger one more time as she hurried toward her parked car.

"Hi, Roger. Me again," she said to the voicemail that she was not at all surprised had picked up. "That poo sample I was telling you about? Please make arrangements for it to be tested. I know it won't prove anything one way or the other but it'll at least tell us if the horse in the vineyard belonged to the monastery. Okay? Thanks. Call me."

She tossed her phone into her purse. Somewhere during the long day it had occurred to her that she needed Roger and being derisive to him was not the best way to get him to help her. She would stop short of apologizing for being snippy to him earlier but she knew she couldn't afford to light any matches to that bridge.

At least not until Laurent was a free man again.

The bedlam in front of the International Bilingual School of Provence which Jemmy, Mila and Zouzou all attended was only slightly less organized than Maggie imagined any normal American carpool might be. While the French didn't typically believe in queues, there was a kind of order to how they let the kids out.

A favorite for ex-pats in Provence, the school was unique in that they had a section for what Americans called *grade-school level* as well as middle school. As a result Zouzou—who would have been in the fourth grade back in the States—was able to go to the same school as Jemmy and Mila.

Jemmy was very smart and the school administrators had immediately suggested he skip first grade in favor of more challenging curriculum. Because of that, he was in the third grade—

just a grade behind Zouzou—although he was only seven years old. Mila was in first grade and happy there.

As Maggie waited in her car and watched as many of the French mothers marched up to the front door to retrieve their children, she thought of how balanced and orderly her life was.

Or at least had been.

Jemmy and Zouzou appeared in the doorway and Maggie watched her son as he scouted the street until he spotted her car. He was already at the point where he didn't want to be retrieved by her but would cross the street on his own—holding little Mila's hand—like the very big boy he considered himself to be.

The street in front of the school was blocked at both ends during drop off and pick up times so Maggie didn't worry about traffic which was why she felt comfortable answering her phone when it rang without her usual dread.

Because she'd enjoyed at least five minutes of thinking how lovely her life normally was, for once the ringing phone didn't immediately remind her that Roger hadn't called. Or that her mother might call with yet another crisis to be dealt with.

With relief, she saw that the call wasn't her mother at all but Grace.

I've been so unreliable lately, Maggie thought with a twinge, *she's probably checking to make sure I'm picking up the kids.*

"Hey," Maggie said into the phone. "Never fear. I've got them."

She saw the children poised on the opposite curb—Jem, Mila and Zouzou, all holding hands, waiting for the crossing guard to give them the okay.

"Are you alone?" Grace said, her voice tight.

The tone of her voice alerted Maggie immediately. She sat up straight, her stomach suddenly churning. "What's happened?" she said.

Her mind raced. It couldn't be the kids, she was looking at them. It couldn't be Maggie's parents. They wouldn't call Grace.

"It's Jean-Luc," Grace said, beginning to cry. "Sweetie, I'm so sorry. It's Jean-Luc."

41

PORTRAIT IN BLUE

The drive to Danielle's house that afternoon was a blur for Maggie.

She took her time pulling herself together before breaking the news to the children as gently as she could while her heart pounded in her chest in denial.

While Mila cried and the other two sat in mute shock, Maggie called Danielle as she maneuvered the car out of the city and pointed it toward home.

"Danielle," Maggie said, her eyes filling with tears. "I am so sorry. So desperately sorry. Are you alone? What can I do?"

"I am not alone, *chérie*," Danielle said softly, her voice trembling. "Grace is here and also Madame Dulcie."

"Can I bring the children there?"

"Of course, *chérie*. I would like that. I must go now."

Maggie could hear voices in the background.

"We'll be there soon," Maggie said. As soon as she disconnected, she took in another long breath. She couldn't go to pieces. The kids needed to know she was in control.

"It's going to be okay," she said to them and then cursed her words.

Was Jean-Luc going to be alive again? Of course it wasn't going to be okay.

Thankfully, none of the children really heard her. She put the radio on and let them have their separate thoughts—their separate memories—and drove over the speed limit to reach Danielle and Jean-Luc's house in half the usual time.

Once there, Maggie was surprised to see all the cars. When Danielle had been married to Eduard, she'd socialized very little and had almost no friends in the village. Since marrying Jean-Luc—a confirmed bachelor—her society hadn't changed that much. It had always just been her and Jean-Luc.

But this was St-Buvard—a village in rural France. You didn't need to be the head of the village guild for them to gather around when you needed them.

Everybody was there. The postmistress, the butcher, the new baker Antoine and his wife. They filled every square foot of the house and even spilled out onto the front drive, standing, talking, drinking.

"*Tante* Maggie?" Zouzou asked as Maggie parked in the circular drive out front of the house.

Maggie turned to her. While all the children loved Jean-Luc, Zouzou's special relationship was with Danielle, the woman who had coached her and taught her to bake. As much as it hurt Zouzou to lose Jean-Luc, whom she loved like a grandfather, it was breaking her heart to imagine her beloved Mémère in such pain.

"Yes, sweetie?" Maggie said as she gathered up her purse and got ready to leave the car.

"Can I bake for Mémère?" Zouzou said, her eyes full of unshed tears.

Maggie rubbed the girl's arm.

"I think she would like that very much," Maggie said.

. . .

Inside the house Maggie found most of the village women had taken a page from Zouzou's book and were making coffee and warming up whatever casseroles or baked goods they had brought.

Most of the men were in the salon—a cold and barren affair that was a throw-back to how Jean-Luc had lived before Danielle. The men were drinking and looking at old pictures on the walls —mostly scenes from the village during the second world war. Maggie heard mention of Jean-Luc's brother Patrick and she realized that even though most of these men had not been alive during the war they all knew the stories.

It killed her that Laurent wasn't here with them.

How was Laurent going to process this all by himself in jail? Maggie thought and then shook the thought away and hurried into the annex room off the kitchen where Grace sat with Danielle. Maggie went to Danielle and knelt by her, taking her hands.

"Danielle," Maggie said, and then bowed her head and wept.

No foul play.

Just a heart attack. Just the one that snuck up when he wasn't looking and led Jean-Luc away from the people who loved him.

He had left home early this morning to let Maggie's dogs out and he didn't return.

Hours later, tired of not being able to reach him on his phone, Danielle went to Domaine St-Buvard and found him face down in the vineyard.

"Doing a favor for me," Maggie said sadly.

"*Non, chérie,*" Danielle said with a smile. "Doing what he loved. Helping his family. I cannot imagine a better way for Jean-Luc to leave us."

Maggie nodded. She felt a heaviness in her arms and legs.

Hours later Grace encouraged Maggie to take the children

home and stick to her routine as much as possible. She and Zouzou would stay with Danielle. They had no guests at the moment at *Dormir*.

"We'll take care of her," Grace said. "You go on."

"I can't believe this has happened," Maggie said. "I can't believe he's gone."

"I know. Have you called Laurent yet?"

A wave of hopeless pain rifled through Maggie's chest.

"I put in a request to have him call me," she said. "I said it was urgent. He'll probably think it's my dad."

"Would calling Roger help speed things up?"

Maggie snorted. "Roger's no help at all. No. All I can do is follow the rules. They'll let Laurent call me when they do. If they do."

"What an awful time for this to happen," Grace said. "Laurent will be crushed."

"I know."

Suddenly Maggie's phone rang and she saw the words *Unknown Caller* appear on the screen. The numerical prefix was the same as the Aix police station.

"This might be him," Maggie said.

"Go on, sweetie," Grace said gently. "I'll keep the kids distracted until you've told him."

Maggie took the phone outside welcoming the hard bite of cold against her neck and bare arms.

"Laurent?" she said into the phone.

"*Oui, c'est moi*," he said hurriedly. "What is it? Is it John?"

"No, it's not my dad," Maggie said, feeling a lump form in her throat. "Laurent, I am so sorry to tell you this but it…it's Jean-Luc."

Silence met her statement.

"Laurent? Did you hear me?"

"*Oui*," he said softly. "How?"

"A heart attack," Maggie said, feeling the tears streaming down her face again. "It was quick."

"Where?"

Dear God, why would he ask that?

"In our vineyard," she said and held her breath.

A silence curled around them before he spoke again. "Then that is good. He loved the vineyard."

"He did," Maggie said, gulping back her sobs. "He was so happy there."

"How is Danielle?"

"She's fine. We're all here. The whole village is here. I wish so much that you were here."

"*Moi aussi*," he said. "When is the funeral?"

"Sunday. Will you be able to come?"

"I will be there, *chérie*. Can you hand the phone to Danielle? I would speak to her."

"Of course," Maggie said, wiping her face as she hurried back inside.

Danielle was standing in the kitchen in front of the window over the sink where Maggie realized she must have been watching her.

"It is Laurent?" Danielle asked.

Maggie nodded and Danielle smiled sorrowfully and held out her hand for the phone.

42

FUNERAL FOR A FRIEND

The next two days passed in a haze for Maggie.

She drove the children to school both days and then over to Danielle's for the evening meal. Like the rest of the women in the village, Maggie made casseroles to stack in Danielle's freezer. There was easily enough food stored to last Danielle for the rest of the month.

Every time Maggie came in through the door with the children Zouzou instantly went to the kitchen and tied on an apron. The child had learned quickly—whether through Laurent or Danielle herself—the power of food to sooth and comfort.

Danielle, ever gracious, usually sat in the annex room by the Franklin stove with a cup of coffee on the table beside her. Sometimes Maggie heard her on the phone talking with the priest or the undertaker. Except for dropping off more food than anyone could eat in a lifetime, the village women no longer came to stay for long visits. Maggie wasn't sure that Danielle herself hadn't told them enough was enough. Danielle had always been very private. Jean-Luc had been the outgoing one of the two.

. . .

On the day of Jean-Luc's funeral, Maggie got up early and made a full breakfast for Jemmy and Mila. Like most children, they'd bounced back somewhat from their initial heartbreak at the loss of their beloved *Pépère*.

That's as it should be, Maggie thought sadly. They loved him. They respected him. They'd never forget him. And today they would say goodbye to him. But before that they had to do one more very sad thing.

Jemmy was the first one down. He wore jeans and a long sleeve t-shirt and took his seat at the kitchen counter where Maggie placed a plate of scrambled eggs, toast and cheese grits.

"Is Mila awake?" she asked as she poured his orange juice.

"Yeah," he said, picking up his fork.

"Say a blessing, please," Maggie reminded him absently. He paused, closed his eyes for a moment and then dug into his breakfast.

Minutes later Mila came skipping down the long timeworn steps—always making Maggie's heart falter for how dangerous the slick stairs could become with one wrong step. As both Maggie and her brother Ben had heart-breaking reason to know.

Mila wore a navy blue cashmere cardigan with a pleated wool skirt. It was cold so she still wore thick stockings under her skirt but Maggie couldn't help but smile at her daughter's fashion sense. She was more like her grandmother in that way than either Maggie or Elise whom she favored physically more and more every day.

Elspeth loved clothes and the more expensive the better. Maggie hoped that Grace's influence would temper any inclination Mila had in that direction. Grace was the most stylish person Maggie knew—and she was definitely a clotheshorse—but she didn't choose her clothes based on how much they cost.

As Maggie placed Mila's plate in front of her she felt a twinge of foreboding at the thought that this might be how things were for the three of them from now on.

Maman making the meals and all of them wondering when they would see Papa again.

"Mom?" Jemmy asked. He'd begun calling her that more and more lately. Maggie assumed it was Zouzou's influence who had been in the States just long enough to stop calling her own mother *Maman*. Maggie missed the French version and hoped Mila wouldn't pick up the American alternative from him any time soon.

"Yes, sweetie?" Maggie leaned a hip against the massive Cornue stove—Laurent's pride and sipped from her coffee mug.

Jemmy looked around the kitchen and then over his shoulder. "So, where is she?" he asked.

Maggie sighed. "Finish your breakfast, Jemmy," she said. "Plenty of time for that."

She appreciated that he didn't seem to be looking at the upcoming task with horror or loathing. If anything, the thought of burying little Petit-Four seemed to generate the same amount of curiosity as he might have about a stunned bird on the back terrace. And that was probably good.

After both children had eaten, Maggie made them put on their jackets while she went to the basement. Her heart sank with every step that took her to the bottom where her eyes landed on the small bundle that Jean-Luc had placed on the wooden bench by the tower of stacked crates of empty wine bottles.

With trembling fingers, Maggie picked up the bundle and held it to her chest as she climbed back up to the kitchen.

Knowing she couldn't add a single iota more of sorrow to Laurent's load or wait any longer, Maggie led the way to the back garden. Jemmy carried a long-handled spade and Mila clutched the paper cone of flowers Maggie had bought yesterday in Aix for the occasion.

"I think right there," Maggie said, pointing beside the tool shed where the back garden ended and the vineyard began.

"*Non, Maman,*" Jemmy said. "She liked to chase the voles here. Remember?"

Jemmy pointed to the stonewall that divided the garden from the vineyard.

Maggie's heart caught as she brought to mind an image of Petit-Four dashing through the undergrowth in search of mice and voles. She'd had a happy life, Maggie reminded herself, with a loving family and a giant vineyard to scamper about.

"You're right," Maggie said. "It's perfect."

Maggie and Mila waited silently while Jemmy dug a small hole. At one point, Mila reached up to gently pat the little bundle in Maggie's arms and Maggie took in a long breath to steady herself.

This dog had been her friend and her comfort when she first moved to France and couldn't speak the language and was so homesick for home and everyone she knew there. Petit-Four always spoke Maggie's language. And she had done so from the very beginning.

After Maggie laid the dog in the hole still wrapped in Mila's blanket, she found herself wishing she'd let Jean-Luc do this when he'd asked. He loved all dogs so much and he was especially fond of little Petit-Four since his own niece had given her to Maggie.

"Rather than say a prayer or something," Maggie said as Jemmy covered the hole back in with dirt, "why don't we each remember something about Petit-Four that we really loved?"

"I loved how she always came into my bed with me when she knew I wasn't feeling good," Mila said as she watched Jemmy work.

"I loved how she made the doves scatter when she pounced on them in the garden," Jemmy said.

He patted down the mound with his spade and Mila carefully laid the flowers on top. Maggie couldn't help but think how proud Laurent would be of Jemmy right now.

"What about you, *Maman*?" Mila asked as they began to turn back to the house to get ready to go to the village church.

Maggie took Mila's hand and reached out for Jemmy's. "I loved how she taught me to be a mother," Maggie said, "before the real thing came along." She wiped the tears from her eyes, but she smiled as she spoke.

After they'd bathed and dressed for church, Maggie drove the half mile to the small village Catholic church that she and the children attended every Sunday and where Jean-Luc would be laid to rest. On the way she called Grace to confirm that she and Zouzou would drive Danielle to the church.

The early afternoon clouds were heavy and gray and there was a distinct bite to the air that smelled of snow to Maggie. But it was only the second week of November and snow was unlikely.

Just thinking of Thanksgiving made her want to collapse on a chair and cover her face with both hands.

Surely Laurent would be home for Thanksgiving? Or definitely Christmas? Just the thought that he might not be home for Christmas added a weight of heartbreak to Maggie's shoulders.

Tucked on the perimeter of St-Buvard, the village church was half hidden in a copse of trees near the side of the road. Its gray stone work blended into the dingy blue-gray of the landscape making it nearly invisible if you didn't know it was there. The steeple presided over a small graveyard enclosed by a frail wrought-iron fence.

Most of the village was in attendance of course. Around two dozen cars were parked in the dirt and gravel lot by the church. There were also bicycles leaning against the crumbling stonewall that Laurent had told her had been there since the time of Philip II in the early twelfth century.

Maggie hadn't told the children Laurent would be at the church just in case he couldn't make it after all. She was so excited about seeing him again—to touch him and feel his arms around her—that the disappointment of *not* seeing him would be almost too much to bear. She couldn't allow Jem and Mila to feel anything like that.

Both children darted out of the car looking for Zouzou. The wind was brisk and cold but Maggie had dressed for it. She tightened the belt on her leather jacket and quickly searched the group of people milling around outside the church.

The first thing she saw was a shiny new Audi Q5 and her heart caught. Unless Jean-Luc had uptown friends, it could only be Roger Bedard's car. Maggie's heart began to pound as she walked quickly toward the car.

"Papa! Papa!" Jemmy's voice was shrill and excited and Maggie felt her insides collapse in relief and joy.

As she came around a heavy rose bush, its thorny stems still climbing the doorway of the church, she saw him.

Laurent stood, taller than anyone else in the crowd, with Mila already in his arms—her little arms tightly around his neck and covering his face with kisses—and Jemmy beside him, looking up, Laurent's big hand on his shoulder, his face animated with love and, for a moment, happiness.

When Laurent looked around scanning the crowd, she knew he was looking for her. In spite of the sad occasion, she couldn't help smile when his eyes met hers. Nearly stumbling over the broken pavers in the church walkway, she hurried over to him. He immediately wrapped an arm around her waist and pulled her close.

"Thank God," she breathed, closing her eyes for a moment to revel in the simple nearness of him.

He gave her a firm squeeze before releasing her and setting Mila down. Maggie turned to see Danielle walking toward them. Laurent went to her and embraced her. He murmured in her ear in low, thick French and Danielle nodded, the tears finally spilling out over her lashes and down her cheeks.

Maggie reached for both children's hands and saw Grace standing nearby, the saddest smile on her face.

Laurent was here and now that they were finally all together they would say goodbye to their beloved friend.

43

TEARS ARE FALLING

Later that day at Danielle's house, Maggie finally saw Roger. She knew he'd been at the church but in all the excitement, she'd not had a chance to look for him.

Most of the village had come back to Danielle and Jean-Luc's house after the service and filled the large living room. Maggie and Grace were in the kitchen laying out massive quantities of *tagines, cassoulets* and other savory casseroles as well as pastries and bread while Danielle spoke to everyone and thanked them for coming. Maggie knew this was hell for Danielle on so many different levels. A shy person—who'd just lost her best friend in the world—she was probably longing for the day to be behind her.

Laurent stood in the doorway of the kitchen and raised his eyebrow at Maggie. She couldn't help but grin because she knew he was asking her if she needed help in the kitchen.

"We're good," Maggie said. "Does everyone have something to drink?"

"Darling, go be with your husband," Grace said from behind Maggie. "Today of all days, if you've got one, enjoy him."

"Are you sure?" Maggie said, glancing around the kitchen. Zouzou was washing dishes and things did seem to be in order.

"I'm positive," Grace said firmly. "Go."

Maggie snatched off her apron, and hurried after Laurent who had gone back into the living room. Roger was standing by the hearth jabbing at a nest of blazing kindling.

She caught Laurent's sleeve and he turned and slipped his arm around her, drawing her near.

"You look tired," he murmured into her ear. "You need to stay off your feet."

"I'm fine," she said, her eyes going to Roger who was studiously working not to look at them. "How did you manage to be let out?"

Laurent shrugged. "I am working with them," he said. "They were happy to accommodate me."

Maggie pulled back, mindful of the two villagers in the room close enough to hear everything she said and no doubt keen to hear what they could.

"That's bull," she said, her hands planting themselves on her hips as she faced him. "You just spent seven days in jail and expect me to believe that?"

"Maggie..." Laurent said warningly, his eyes going to the villagers in the room behind her.

"No! I want *answers*, Laurent," she said, dropping her voice and glancing at Roger.

This time, Roger looked up. He tossed the stick into the fire and stepped over to them.

"I'm sorry for your loss," Roger said. "Laurent, we should be going."

Maggie shot a hand out and poked Roger on the chest. "No!" she said. "You're not going anywhere until I find out what is happening. Why are you still keeping him? Why haven't you called me back?"

Laurent pulled Maggie away from Roger and swung her to face him.

"*Chérie, non*," he said sternly. "We talked about this..."

"No. We *have not*," Maggie said between gritted teeth. She hated that she was ruining the one moment with Laurent where they weren't separated by steel bars. Any second now he was going to go back to Aix and this might be the last moment they had together for God knew how long. But she couldn't help herself.

"I want to know why you've given up and why our so-called friend here is being absolutely no help at all! Did he tell you that Jean-Luc found horse manure in the vineyard and that we have a sample in our fridge for the police to test but they won't even—?"

"Maggie, stop this *immediatement*," Laurent growled, his eyes glinting with intent. "You will not discuss it. Do you understand me? Not here. *Not today*."

Maggie's cheeks burned and she glanced around the room to see that three more villagers had joined the others and were unabashedly listening to their conversation. Laurent was right. This day wasn't about anything except Jean-Luc. She would have been horrified if Danielle had overheard her.

"I'm sorry," Maggie said, ashamed. She looked at Laurent and saw his anger soften and then dissipate. He drew her close again and that in itself told her how worried he must be. Laurent never kissed her or held her in public. *Ever*. For him to do it now with an audience of nearly half a dozen villagers—not to mention Roger—struck fear into her heart.

"You will be there for Danielle, *chérie*," Laurent whispered to her.

"Of course," she said hoarsely. "You know I will be."

"*Bon*. Take care of her. And *les enfants*." He nodded at her abdomen. "*All* of them, *oui*?"

Before Maggie could react Jemmy and Mila ran in from

outside. Instantly Laurent scooped up his daughter and again rested his hand on Jemmy's shoulder.

"Are you leaving again, Papa?" Jemmy asked. "Did Maman tell you how I was the one who buried Petit-Four?"

Laurent glanced at Maggie and she read the anguish in his eyes.

"She did, *mon vieux*," Laurent said to his son. "It made me very proud. That was a hard thing to do."

Jemmy grinned, basking in his father's praise. "Not too hard for me though."

"I miss you, Papa," Mila said softly. "Are you coming home soon?"

Laurent kissed her. "You are your Papa's special angel, *oui*, Mila?" he said. "My own treasure."

"Laurent..." Roger said, looking down at his shoes. "We need to get back."

Without answering him, and still holding Mila Laurent knelt by Jemmy until they were eye level.

"Take care of your *maman, mon fils*," Laurent said, cupping Jemmy's head with his hand.

"I will, Papa," Jemmy said seriously. "And Mila, too."

Laurent kissed Mila and set her down. "Yes, and Mila too." He looked up at Maggie and it took everything she had to smile bravely at him when he was so clearly saying goodbye to his children for a very, very long time.

44

SHINE ON

Maggie waited while Laurent said goodbye to Danielle and then to Grace. He kissed the children one more time and she walked with him to where Roger was waiting by the car.

Laurent turned to her and ran his hands up and down her arms. She'd left her coat inside.

"Go inside, *chérie*," he said, kissing her. "It's cold."

"Please do a better job of staying in touch with me," she said, hating the plaintive tenor to her voice.

"I will, *chérie*." He kissed her slowly and put his hand to her cheek. "Stay out of this, Maggie. I am serious."

"I hear you," Maggie said past the lump in her throat.

"*Bon.* I will call you later. *Je promets.*" He kissed her once more and then opened the car door. "Go inside, *chérie*."

She took a step back toward the door to allow Roger to pass her as he reached for the handle on the driver's side of the car.

"You're pregnant?" he blurted out, not looking at her.

"Is that a problem?"

"No. Of course not. Congratulations." Roger glanced into the car where Laurent sat, his gaze directed away, his thoughts already far away. "Look, Maggie, I'm doing everything I can to help get this sorted out."

"That would be a nice change of pace," Maggie said and immediately cursed her lack of self-control. "I'm sorry," she said quickly. "Thank you, Roger."

"I really am sorry about Jean-Luc. He was a great guy."

Maggie rubbed the chill from her arms. "He was."

Roger got in the car and drove down the drive. Laurent glanced back long enough to note that she was still there and even from this distance she thought she could see his eyes narrow in annoyance that she hadn't gone inside as he'd told her to.

But that wasn't what kept Maggie standing outside in the cold long after the car had disappeared from view. It was the air of—not just pessimism but downright obstruction—from Laurent that made her stand there shivering, her mind in a confusing whirl.

It's almost like he doesn't want me to find the real killer.

Back inside the house most of the villagers had already gone home. Grace and Danielle sat in the annex with a platter of pound cake and berries and a scattering of tea cups in front of them. Zouzou and Mila were wiping up spills from tabletops in the kitchen as well as the living room while Jemmy sat on the sofa next to Danielle and played a muted video game on his iPad.

Maggie came into the room and sat down next to Danielle, leaning over and kissing her first.

"How are you doing, Danielle?" she asked.

"It has been a long day," Danielle answered.

Maggie caught Grace's eye. Danielle never complained and she certainly never complained about being tired. As brave and strong as she was, it appeared she had met her match on the day she buried her husband and best friend. Maggie's heart ached for her.

"We're happy to stay the night," Maggie said.

"Zouzou and I will stay, too," Grace said. "Is everything all right with Laurent?"

"Not really," Maggie said and then bit her tongue. The last thing she wanted to do was give Danielle something else to worry about. "But he'll sort it out," she added hastily.

Danielle smiled sadly at Maggie.

"You gave Jean-Luc some of the happiest moments of his life this last week. Did you know that?"

Maggie took Danielle's hand. "I'm glad."

Danielle looked apologetically at Grace. "I am going to bed now."

It wasn't yet five o'clock but the light had already faded from the sky.

"Can I get you anything?" Grace asked her. "A cup of tea? A brandy?"

"No, *chérie*," Danielle said. "Just sleep. That is all I want."

Deliverance, Maggie thought. *She needs a respite from the conscious state of knowing that Jean-Luc is gone forever.* Maggie's heart felt like it was breaking.

She and Grace watched Danielle make her way slowly back to her bedroom—the one she would never share again with another living soul.

"I need a drink," Grace said.

"I need to go," Maggie said.

Grace looked at her in surprise.

"I hate to ask," Maggie said, "but can I leave the kids with you for a few hours?"

"Of course. But where in the world are you going?"

"Back to the monastery," Maggie said setting her jaw.

It had been rattling around in her brain for the last several hours—maybe ever since she'd heard that Jean-Luc had died.

She knew the answer to this whole mess was at the monastery and after today she knew she was the only one who was in a position to find it.

Jean-Luc had discovered the one big clue that pointed them in the right direction—the horse manure. He'd also realized even before Maggie that connecting that manure with its source would put them on the path to finding out who it was who was in the vineyard the night Henri Dupree was murdered.

Jean-Luc had found that out and by God Maggie was not going to make his discovery meaningless today of all days. She was not going to ignore the hard work he'd done just because he wasn't here to help her process it.

In a way, going to the monastery on the day of Jean-Luc's funeral felt to Maggie—even more than the flowers and the kind words and the mass itself—the best way she could think of to honor him.

"At this hour?" Grace asked in surprise.

"I think the later hour will actually work in my favor," Maggie said, picking up her purse. "I need to talk to Dupree's daughter. I need to talk to both the two young men who were in love with her—the ones who apparently burned down the stable—and I need to find out if there's a connection to that stable and the horse in our vineyard the night Dupree was killed."

"I wish I could come with you," Grace said with a frown.

"You're a bigger help to me here minding the kids. And being here for Danielle."

"Promise me you're not going to do anything dangerous," Grace said. "Right? Maggie?"

"Don't be silly," Maggie said as she gave Jemmy a kiss. He never looked up from his game. "I'm going to a *monastery* for heaven's sakes."

45

BREAKAWAY

Thirty minutes after leaving Danielle's house, Maggie pulled into the monastery parking lot. For the whole drive over all she could think of—like a mantra—was *if the horse came from the monastery it meant the killer did too.*

Regardless of what Laurent was keeping from her—and she was more and more convinced he was definitely keeping something from her—she knew that the answer to *who* killed Henri Dupree was at the monastery. Now that Jean-Luc was gone, Maggie was literally the only person on earth who knew that.

Or cared.

As she got out of the car she reminded herself that one thing she knew for sure was that there was no point in speaking with Frère Jean. As agitated as he was the last time she saw him, it was probably best to avoid him altogether.

She left her purse in the car, taking only her phone, car keys and the flashlight she kept in the glove box, then walked silently in the dark across the grass and gravel parking lot to the front door of the monastery.

The ancient doors were easily six inches thick. There was no way she could hear anything from inside. She decided it was just as well since going inside would only call attention to herself. While it was likely that Noelle and the two men she wanted to talk to, Pierre and Guy, were somewhere inside—either at dinner or in their lodgings—Maggie wanted to have a quick look around the outside surroundings first.

On the drive over she'd thought a lot about Laurent—how he'd looked and his general affect. While she knew he was happy to see her and the children today, he'd behaved with such emotional restraint it was as if he were holding himself back.

Like the way you do when you don't want to get hurt later so you try and keep your feelings in control.

That was Laurent in a nutshell. He was all about control. But this time he was struggling. Even she could see it. He knew something he didn't want her to know—probably because he thought he was protecting her—but whatever it was, it was killing him.

When Maggie reached the corner of the main monastery building and the rectory, she saw the shades weren't pulled in the windows allowing the lights inside to illuminate the dark pavement below.

That either meant Frère Jean was home or the other monks were.

She hurried down the path that had led her that first day to where the stables had once stood. The remnants of the stables loomed like a ghostly fortress. The loan remaining beam that had supported the south wall—the one closest to the rectory—and the only one still in upright position gave an eerie minaret effect.

Looking over her shoulder to make sure she was alone, she turned on her flashlight and stepped into what had been the interior of the burned stable. In the distance she heard a horse whinny and she felt a twinge of relief that the animals had been rescued in time.

Everywhere she shone her light she saw nothing but rubble and ash. The lovely scent of horses and leather and feed and even manure that she had experienced before had been replaced by the overpowering stench of smoke. On the blackened beam that was still standing—and Maggie was careful not to touch it in case it crumbled beneath her touch—she could see rusting hooks where the last time she'd been here she'd seen bridles and leather cinches hanging.

She moved further to the area she guessed the tack room would have been. She stepped over the pitchfork she'd last seen clutched in the hands of the angry gypsy boy Pierre, its handle mostly gone but still attached to the black tines.

The wood of the tack room's many barrels of grain had completely burnt away leaving only piles of the metal bands that had held the barrels together. Maggie went to the bottom of the first barrel and knelt, unmindful of the fact that the scorched ground was ruining the knees of her jeans.

She wondered if people in France bought their feed in plastic or paper bags. Either of course would have been destroyed in the fire. In any case she found nothing in the way of commercial feed bags. She reminded herself that it didn't mean anything that she couldn't find them. If she really did succeed in getting Roger on board with her view of the investigation all he'd have to do would be to interview the people at the monastery to determine if their animals were fed with store-bought grain or home-grown feed.

Something caught her eye and she reached down and found a charred stub of corncob with several uncharred kernels still attached. She held the corncob in her hand and felt her excitement grow. She hadn't examined the sample that Jean-Luc had put in her fridge yet—but corn was corn.

And this in her hand was as unprocessed as it came.

Maggie tucked the corncob in her jacket pocket and walked out of the stable. She looked up at the side of the building facing her and could see six windows. Lights were on in two of them. The others were dark.

She glanced at her watch. Roger had left Danielle's house two hours ago. That meant he was surely back in Aix by now.

Let's see if he means what he says.

She walked to the building and stood with her back against it and texted him.

<which room at the monastery belonged to the vic?>

She directed her flashlight on the ground where she saw a scattering of hay stems. The pathology report said there was hay stuck in Dupree's shoes. She played her light beam along the ground and down the path leading toward the garden. That might not mean much since there seemed to be a lot of hay everywhere but particularly around the stable. Still it at least meant that Dupree was near the stables that fateful night.

Just then a group of four men and women walked up from the direction of the garden. The men were smoking and they nodded a greeting to Maggie.

"*Bonsoir,*" Maggie said as they passed. She listened until she heard—with the sudden influx of noise and laughter—the moment the small inset door opened at the entrance as the couples entered the refectory.

Her phone chimed and she looked down to see a text from Roger.

<No! I forbid it! I'm warning you!>

Maggie read the text and nearly laughed outloud.

Interesting how he ignores me when I want a favor but responds straightaway when it looks like I'm about to do something he doesn't want me to.

Annoyed but encouraged at having discovered a way of getting Roger to at least respond to her, she texted him back.

<Tell me which room is his and I promise I won't go in.>

She put a hand on the smooth bark of the giant plane tree so close to the building that it nearly leaned against it. It must have been no more than a seed dropped by a passing bird when the monastery was built. She glanced up at the upper windows of the building wondering if they were bedrooms. She noticed that the trunk of the tree stood close enough that it formed a natural ladder down from one of the windows.

She quickly sent Roger another text.

< *if you don't tell me I'll knock on every door in the place until I find it myself*>

Her phone rang immediately.

"Maggie, I need you to stay away from the monastery," Roger said breathlessly.

"And I need you to do your job so I don't have to," Maggie said.

"You're already there, aren't you?"

"I told you why, Roger," she said biting off every word but lowering her voice in case she was overheard. "I found a physical link to this place that's connected to the murder. So are you going to help me or not?"

"Look," he said after a brief pause, "if I tell you which room was Dupree's, you must solemnly swear to me—on the heads of your children—alive and unborn—that you will not go there. Do you swear?"

"Yes, of course, Roger. I swear. Now which one is it?" She craned her neck to scan the length of the building. One of the upstairs lights blinked on as she watched.

Silence.

"Roger?"

"It is in the dormitory on the second floor of the main building. On the south side."

"Is that the side facing the stables?"

She heard pages rustling.

"I don't have that information."

"Wait," Maggie said, her voice rising. "You mean you haven't been out here?"

"I have people I trust who do my legwork for me," Roger said, his voice trailing away.

"So you've never been to the monastery?"

"I think we've established that. As far as I know *l'Abbaye de Sainte-Trinité* is not a crime scene."

"Then why do you care if I'm here snooping around?"

"Because it is an invasion of privacy for the Brothers. Surely you can understand that?"

"I do understand that, Roger. Just like I understand Laurent being held in a jail cell when he should be home is an invasion of privacy."

"It is not the same thing. Those monks did nothing to have the serenity of their daily round disrupted."

"And Laurent did? Is that what you're saying?" But Maggie could have bitten her tongue. She reminded herself that she needed Roger on her side.

"You know I don't believe that, Maggie," Roger said with exasperation. "But there are...other things in play here that you... aren't aware of."

"Do I need to be? Are they germane to what I'm doing?"

"No," Roger said quickly but even to Maggie he didn't sound convincing.

"Thank you, Roger," she said as she walked to the side of the building that faced the stables. Once there she saw that there was no door leading in or out on this side of the building.

"Remember, Maggie," Roger said, still on the line. "You promised."

"I remember, Roger. And thank you again."

Maggie disconnected and slipped the phone into her jeans pocket as she ran around the side of the building to the front door. This time when she pulled on the door's ornate handle, the door tugged open and she was able to step into the cavernous room filled with the sounds of people eating and talking.

Quickly getting her bearings, she saw a set of flag-stone steps that led to the upper floors. Forcing herself not to look around first—always the glaring hallmark of suspicious behavior—she darted up the steps to find a corridor lined with half a dozen doors. One of these rooms was Dupree's room, she thought as she walked down the hall.

Unless I'm on the wrong side of the building.

She put her ear to the first door she came to but heard nothing inside. Was this one of the windows she'd seen from outside that had been dark? She looked down the long hallway of doors.

Was she really doing to have to try every single door?

"What are you doing up here?" a strident voice demanded imperiously.

46

TROUBLE KNOCKS ONCE

Maggie whirled around to see Madame Montagne standing on the top step of the stairs watching her.
"Oh, it's you," Maggie said.
"What are you doing up here?" Madame Montagne repeated as she approached.
Maggie turned to the old woman, her eyes flashing.
"Okay, here's the deal," Maggie said. "I'm fresh out of euros so you'll just have to trust that I have reason to be here."
"Before I go and inform the Brothers that we have an intruder," Madame Montagne said, "perhaps you could tell me what that reason is."
"I'm here to find evidence that my husband is innocent."
"By laying the blame at someone else's feet?" Madame Montagne gaze went to the hall lined with doors.
"What? No! Well, laying it at the feet of the real murderer, yes. Do you have a problem with that?"
The old woman cackled and reached out to take Maggie's arm and shook it.
"I knew I liked you once I learned who you were married to. You know all the women here are in love with your husband?"

"Tell me something I don't know. Does this mean you'll help me without my having to cash in my kids' college fund?"

"That depends. What do you want to know?"

Maggie turned in frustration at the long line of rooms. "Which one of these rooms was Monsieur Dupree's?"

The woman didn't hesitate. She walked past Maggie to the third door. "*Et voila*," she said, and pushed the door open.

Maggie hurried to stand beside her and stared inside, her heart beating in double time. She glanced around the room. A half coil of greasy rope lay next to a pile of old boots, a crumpled weatherproof jacket and a broken kerosene lantern.

The space was sparsely furnished with nothing on the walls and no curtains on the narrow window that indeed looked out over the stables but the view outside was blocked by the large plane tree Maggie had leaned against a few minutes earlier.

Maggie went to the lone cot in the room. She had absolutely no qualms about breaking her word to Roger. First she didn't imagine he'd ever find out about it but also because she didn't feel like she owed him honesty when he was doing so little to help Laurent.

"Are all the rooms like this one?" Maggie asked as she stepped over a potted plant that was on its side, its dirt spilled out across the wooden slats of the floor.

"Pretty much. Henri was an unhappy man. I am not surprised to see he lived like a *cochon*."

"Noelle didn't share a room with him?"

"She has a room on the other side of the building."

"What about Pierre and Guy? Where do they live?"

"Guy lives in a room on the first floor of this building. I have no idea where Pierre sleeps at night. Perhaps the pig sty."

Maggie stepped over a chair that was on its side. A stack of books were scattered on the floor.

"Do you know what the fight was about that Monsieur Dupree had with Laurent?" Maggie asked.

"I heard it was because Henri was hurting a boy," Madame Montagne said with a shrug.

Yep. That would do it, Maggie thought.

Maggie saw a small wooden table that the books might logically have been sitting on. Someone had knocked them over or deliberately pushed them onto the floor.

"Didn't you tell me Monsieur Dupree lost his own two boys last year?" Maggie asked. "How old were they?"

"Twins. Eight years old. As I said before, Henri had much to be unhappy about. Nobody denies that. But he still had Noelle."

Maggie turned to look at her. "I thought you said Noelle was beating the local boys off with a stick."

Madame laughed, showing missing teeth in the process. "It's true. It wouldn't be long before she left with one of them."

Maggie went to the window and looked out.

"How well do you know Guy Dionne?" Maggie said.

Madame Montagne shrugged again. "I know everyone here."

"Even Pierre?"

This time Madame made a face. "Gypsies," she said with disdain.

Maggie drew closer to the window to peer out. It was definitely the same tree she'd leaned on from the ground directly across from the stables. The tree was close to the window but upon closer examination, she didn't think it would have been possible to climb into it from the window. The nearest branch was several feet below the window.

Maggie turned to look at Madame Montagne. "Aside from being a gypsy, is there anything else wrong with him?"

"Only everything. The way he looks at the girls. Like he is going to salt and pepper them and eat them for dinner."

"So not just Noelle?"

"All of them. Myself included. I saw him watch me."

Maggie turned her head so the old woman wouldn't see her hide a smile. As she turned back to the window with the tree outside she saw something she'd missed before. Maggie threw back the sash and leaned out the window.

"Be careful, Madame!" Madame Montagne said from behind her.

But Maggie was too excited. She rested her hip on the window ledge and grabbed the window frame to lean out as far as she could. Whipping out her flashlight, she directed the beam at the speckled bark of the tree trunk.

There, on the side of the tree was a dark stain that she first thought must be resin.

But, the closer she looked, she could see it could only be one thing.

Blood.

47

LADY BE GONE

Maggie teetered on the edge of the window and nearly dropped her flashlight.

Blood! On the tree. Twenty feet above the ground.

Maggie's mind began to whirl as she tried to imagine how it could have gotten there. She got a sickening image of someone throwing a man out the window, bashing his head against the tree or on the heavy branch jutting out just below the window.

That would work.

She pulled herself back into the room.

"Madame?" Madame Montagne said from the hallway where she had retreated.

Maggie glanced around the room. All of a sudden it didn't look like a messy, disorganized room that might belong to a bachelor.

All of a sudden—the chair overturned, the books on the floor, the potted plant on its side—*it looked like a room where a struggle had taken place.*

How many people had been in this room since the murder? she wondered. How badly compromised was the crime scene?

Because there was no doubt in her mind that that was what she was looking at—a crime scene.

She took a few careful steps away from the window and then turned and looked at it with an eye for murder.

The limb below was the exact right place to be struck by a body thrown out the window.

"What is the meaning of this?"

Frère Jean pushed past Madame Montagne who quickly disappeared down the hall. He stood gaping at Maggie from the doorway, the veins in his neck straining under the skin.

"Get out!" he shouted, dramatically pointing his finger toward the hallway at the same time he reached in his cassock and pulled out a cellphone. "This time I will see you in jail for this trespass! Get out! *Allo?*" he said into the phone. "Yes, get me the police. There is a crime in process at *l'Abbaye de Sainte-Trinité* monastery. I need police! Hurry!"

"Oh, come on," Maggie said, brushing off paint flakes from the windowsill from her jeans. "You know very well I'm not stealing anything."

"I know you will be taken away in handcuffs," the monk hissed. "*Oui?*" he said into the phone. "Yes, it is outside the village of Pont l'Abbe. How soon can you get here? Please hurry. The perpetuator is Madame Dernier and she is still on the premises."

Maggie turned to look at the tree again and then at the monk. When Frère Jean put his phone away, she saw him glance out the window too.

Did he know about the blood?

Did he help put it there?

"You know what happened in this room, don't you, *Mon Frère?*" Maggie asked before pointing to the tree outside. "Kind of sloppy not cleaning that up," she said. "Or did you expect the rain to do it?"

"The police will be here in only moments now."

"Awesome. Do *you* want to show them the big-ass blood

smear on the tree outside Dupree's room or is that going to be my honor?"

There was no doubt about it this time. The man was sweating. His eyes flicked again to the tree outside. He actually pulled at the cowl of his habit as if he was hot, yet with the open window it was actually chilly in the room.

"I will ask you to leave this room at once," he said stiffly, scraping a hand through his hair in agitation.

"Probably a good idea," Maggie said as she moved out into the hall. "While the scene has already been contaminated I imagine that unless it rains in the next thirty minutes—or someone takes a hose to it—that tree out there is all the evidence the cops will need to reroute their investigation."

"Now the only question," she said looking him in the eye as she passed him in the doorway, "is did *you* do it or are you just protecting the one who did?"

48

BONES IN THE SKY

Pierre watched in growing panic as the American woman leaned out from the window ledge and then withdrew. Up until that moment he thought there just might be a chance for him to finish this chapter without any more bloodshed.

Right up to the moment that that nosy bitch Madame Montagne told him at lunch how the American woman was determined to talk with Noelle about her father's death.

Pierre felt a wave of nausea. It had been all he could do to convince Noelle not to tell but he knew how women were. As soon as the American sat Noelle down for a nice little chat, the stupid bitch would spill everything she knew about that night. That damnable, cursed night! If only Pierre could go back and relive it. Would he have done anything different?

He snorted. What difference did that make?

The problem right now was that the American was determined to talk to Noelle and when she did she'd find out the truth and then Pierre would be running again.

Unless.

He felt a satisfaction and a peace come over him when he

realized he was going to have to do something that most people would be too uncomfortable to do.

Something terrible.

Something final.

And he would have to do it soon.

While Frère Jean didn't appear to Maggie to look any more confident in how things were going than before he'd ordered her downstairs, he at least had the presence of mind to close the door to Dupree's room and stand guard to make sure no further damage could be done.

That was fine with Maggie. The fact that the room showed signs of a struggle was helpful but probably didn't definitively add up to anything—at least not a full week after the murder. But there was nothing the monk could do about the evidence on the tree.

Frère Jean knew about the blood on the tree. He knew Dupree was killed here. And how would he know that unless he was the one who did it?

Now Maggie had a very good idea why Frère Jean had lied.

It's because he killed Henri Dupree.

That was certainly motive enough for why he tried to set Laurent up for it.

As she hurried downstairs she found herself asking *why* the monk would kill Dupree but she quickly shook off the question.

Motive would be revealed later. Now that she had found enough reason to get Roger to put the wily monk in handcuffs he could take over and *do his job* to sweat out the reason why Frère Jean did it.

She felt a flush of excitement. As soon as the police tech team tested the blood to confirm that it was Dupree's—and Maggie had no doubt they would—that would take Laurent off the hot seat and move the blame to where it had always belonged—at the monastery.

As Maggie reached the bottom of the stairs and the opening to the dining room she glanced over at all the tables full of people talking and eating. She scanned the group looking for Noelle or the two young men and instead caught sight of Madame Montagne waving for her to join her at her table.

Madame Montagne was sitting with two other older women. Maggie walked over and sat down.

"This is Madame Cuillerier," Madame Montagne said, nodding at a thin rail of a woman who looked to be well into her eighties. "And Madame Nouveau." A much plumper woman with a permanent scowl raised an eyebrow at Maggie.

"I did not call for reinforcements," Madame Montagne said. "I want you to know that. Frère Jean just happened to come up the stairs."

"It doesn't matter. I was finished anyway."

"What was it you found?" Madame Montagne asked as she pushed her soup bowl away.

"Just the murder scene," Maggie said. She knew she probably shouldn't have revealed that. Not until the cops had a chance to cordon it off anyway.

"How can that be?" Madame Cuillerier said, her eyes lively and inquisitive. "We were told Henri was killed in a vineyard,"

"That's what the killer wanted everyone to think," Maggie said.

"This is Laurent's wife," Madame Montagne said to her friends. "It was *her* vineyard."

"Ahhh!" The other two women nodded and seemed to be more interested in Maggie after that.

"Can I ask you a few questions?" Maggie asked the women.

"Didn't I tell you?" Madame Montagne chuckled as she addressed her friends. "She is like Inspector Poirot, this one."

"I'm told Monsieur Dupree didn't get along with very many

people," Maggie said, hoping one of the women would pick up the ball and run with it.

"That is true," Madame Nouveau said, tearing her baguette and dropping the pieces into her soup. "He was depressed about his tragedy. You know of this?"

"I told her," Madame Montagne said.

"But also because he'd started drinking again," Madame Cuillerier said, nodding her head knowingly.

"Really?" Madame Nouveau said. "I never saw him take a drink."

"He did it in private," Madame Cuillerier said. "So you wouldn't."

"Well, who could blame him, eh?" Madame Montagne said.

Maggie filed away the fact that Dupree could possibly have been intoxicated the night he died. Odd that Roger hadn't mentioned it. She hadn't seen it on the toxicology screen he'd showed her either.

"How did Monsieur Dupree get along with Frère Jean?" Maggie asked. "Did you ever hear them fight?"

"Henri fought with everyone," Madame Nouveau said. "But no, I don't remember a time when he and Frère Jean fought."

Maggie gnawed her thumbnail and tried to think of another question that might implicate Frère Jean.

"Frère Jean would not fight with anyone," Madame Cuillerier said. "He is above such things."

"The man's a saint," Madame Nouveau said. "He goes above and beyond always. If it weren't for him, my husband and I would be starving on the streets of Lyons."

"Same here," Madame Montagne said. "There's not a job too disgusting or onerous for him. He wouldn't ask you to do it if he wasn't willing to do it himself."

The other two women nodded in agreement. Maggie was about to leave the Frère Jean Fan Club since it was pretty clear that even if they'd known something damning about the man, they wouldn't share it with her.

"That is absolutely true," Madame Cuillerier said earnestly. "Did I tell you I saw him making a delivery last week *at night* in the pouring rain?"

"I am not at all surprised," Madame Nouveau said. "The man is a saint," she repeated.

"What kind of delivery?" Maggie asked, breathlessly. "When? What night?"

Madame Cuillerier looked around the room as if suddenly bored with the conversation. "A week ago, I think."

A week ago would be around the time of the murder.

"Do you know what the delivery was?" Maggie asked trying not to show her excitement.

Madame Montagne patted Madame Cuillerier's hand and gestured to Maggie.

"I should have told you she gets like this," Madame Montagne said. "If you can't remember, Michelle, there's no shame in that. She will pay you if that will help your memory."

"I can remember," Madame Cuillerier said indignantly but she frowned as she looked at Maggie as if struggling to put the pieces together.

"I don't know *what* he was delivering," she said finally, "but I'm assuming it was probably perishable and he was in a hurry since he was driving the pony cart."

49

NEVER ENDING

The minute the words were out of the woman's mouth, Maggie felt a tingle of triumph.
Frère Jean is the murderer! This proves it!
"You're sure about that?" Maggie's pulse was racing. "You saw Frère Jean driving the pony cart *at night* last week?"
"Yes, of course, I'm sure," Madame Cuillerier said, sniffing. "I don't have dementia."
"Not yet," Madame Montagne pointed out to her friend.
Maggie sat back in her chair and dug out her cellphone. This couldn't wait. This was the nail in the proverbial coffin for old Friar Jean. If Roger didn't respond to *this* information then he truly was working for the enemy.
She quickly punched in his number and stood up to give herself privacy from the women's table.
As soon as the phone started ringing, she heard another phone—inside the dining room—also ringing.
Confused, she turned and saw the very moment when Roger who was striding toward the table stopped to look at his ringing phone.

Behind him, Maggie saw Frère Jean, a look of determination mixed with malice on his face.

"Roger!" she called. "I'm so glad it's you!" She hurried over to him as he jabbed his phone back in its holster and reached out to grab her roughly by the arm.

"All right," he barked. "Let's go. Enough of disturbing these good people."

Before Maggie could close her mouth that had fallen open in shock, Roger had twisted her around to face the door and was driving her forward past Frère Jean.

"I'll cuff you when we get to the car," he said loudly, "and read you your rights." He nodded gruffly at the monk and pushed Maggie out the door and down the gravel path to where both their cars were parked.

"Why must you always do this to me?" he muttered to her, his hand still tightly on her arm.

"I was about to say the same thing to you," Maggie said coolly, telling herself to give him the benefit of the doubt before she launched holy hell on his arrogant French ass.

As soon as they reached the cars, Roger glanced over his shoulder behind him.

"Are they watching?" she asked.

"No, but I probably should give you a good wallop just in case they are." He turned her to face him and finally released her. "You promised you would not use the information I gave you!"

"And *you* promised you'd help prove Laurent's innocence," she retorted. "What did you *think* I was going to do with the information? Write a blog about it? Of *course* I was going inside and you knew very well I was!"

"It's a miracle that I heard the call come in," Roger said. "Anybody else and you'd be in the cell next to Laurent's right now. Even so there'll be a record of it and I'll have to explain why I didn't bring you in."

"Gosh Roger, it never occurred to me to consider the incredible stress you must be under," Maggie said, her voice laced with sarcasm.

"They're going to expect me to put you in my car," he said, glancing again back at the monastery.

Maggie frowned. For the first time she was sensing that there was something more than just Roger's natural hesitancies happening here.

"What will happen if you aren't seen to follow protocol?"

He glanced at her to see if she was being snide and when it appeared she really wanted to know, he just shook his head as if he'd already said too much.

"Tell me what you found," he said.

Maggie watched the breeze whip a handful of dead leaves in the gravel parking lot into a vortex of dust. She shivered in the cold.

"I think I have evidence that proves that Frère Jean killed Dupree," she said.

He glanced again back at the monastery. In Maggie's mind, he should have been way more excited about what she'd just said.

"What evidence is that?" he asked.

"Before I tell you, did your crime team examine the vic's room in the monastery?"

"Of course."

"Really? Because it seriously looked like it hadn't been touched. In fact it looked like somebody had a knock-down drag-out brawl in there."

Roger rubbed a hand over his face as if trying to blot out Maggie's words.

"And directly outside the window," Maggie said, "there's a huge smear of blood on the tree limb right below the window."

"Tree limb?" Roger said frowning.

"Yes, Roger. As if someone had, oh I don't know, thrown a

man out the window and he hit his head on the tree? Did the autopsy say anything about any bones being broken? Because that would have been a long way to fall without breaking something."

Roger nodded but his eyes seemed unfocused, staring off into the horizon.

"His left arm and his left leg," he said.

"Damn it, Roger! And you didn't think that was worth passing on to me? The guy was stabbed, had his brains bashed in *and* he had broken limbs?"

Although as Maggie thought back she realized she had looked at the pathology report so quickly she could easily have missed it.

"No, Maggie. I didn't think to pass it on to you," Roger said heatedly. "I have competent, capable men working this case."

"I beg to differ. You've got a prime suspect and no reason to look any further. I'm ashamed of you, Roger." Maggie held her chin up high and glared at him. "And you call yourself a friend?"

Roger's face hardened and he looked back at Maggie.

"Is that it? Blood on a tree and some fantasy about a monk—who's been written up in all the local papers for doing good works by the way—being a cold-blooded killer?"

"No. I have a witness," Maggie said. "Someone *saw* Frère Jean leaving the monastery with the pony cart the night of the murder! The pony cart was loaded down with a dead body—"

"Wait. Your witnesses saw a body?" he asked incredulously.

"Well, no, but you can connect the dots, can't you? It all makes sense! Dupree was pushed out of his own bedroom window! He was then taken to *my* vineyard to implicate Laurent!"

"Why would anyone want to do that and what does a pony cart have to do with anything?"

"Do you not even read the texts I send you? I *told* you. Horse droppings were found in the vineyard near where the body was."

"So?"

"So, we don't own a horse!"

"There are riding stables in the area are there not? Perhaps someone was riding a horse."

"Through our vineyard? Who would do that? *At night*? And besides Jean-Luc checked the other stables in the area. There are two that cater to tourists. And he confirmed that they hadn't lost any horses in the middle of the night at any point last week. No, the only logical place where a horse might have come from was the monastery stables—the one that very conveniently burned down two days after the murder."

Roger shook his head but Maggie thought a part of him was starting to see the pattern, too.

"I'm telling you, Roger, Frère Jean is *lying*. You need to hold his feet to the fire and get the truth out of him."

"I can't bring a Benedictine monk in to the police station and work him over! France is a civilized country! My people have taken his statement—"

"A statement that you and I both know is a lie!" Suddenly before she knew she was going to, Maggie burst into tears.

Without hesitation, Roger pulled her into his arms. He held her for a moment as she fought to pull herself together. And she let him. God help her, she needed someone to lean on today if just for a few seconds.

"Sorry," she said, wiping her wet cheeks with the back of her hand.

"This is a lot for you to deal with," he said softly. "You've got so much going on right now."

"You have no idea."

Maggie looked up and saw Roger's eyes—tortured, pained and yes, full of love. She knew then he really did want to help her.

But wanting to wasn't going be enough.

She took in a long breath. "You have to help me, Roger. I can hire an independent laboratory to check out the sample but it'll have more weight in court if the police are the ones who run the test."

"Maggie..." Roger looked down at the ground between them. "The sample is in my refrigerator. Follow me back there tonight and I'll—"

"It's contaminated."

"The *weather* contaminated it! *I* preserved it!"

"It still won't be admissible."

"Fine. How about this? You see that horse over there?" She pointed to the far pasture where a lone horse stood with his head hanging over the black fence slats watching them. "Turns out that is the only horse the monastery has. Talk about making your job easier, Roger. And you don't have to worry about *it* being contaminated because it comes to you in the original package."

"What are you—?"

"Get one of your men to test the dung from that horse with what I have in my refrigerator. If it isn't a match, no harm done. But if it's the same then you're at least on the right path. And isn't that what we all want?"

Roger sighed heavily and watched the horse in the pasture.

"Please, Roger," Maggie said. "I'm begging you. Please test the horse. Please test the blood on the tree. For the love of God. Please."

"All right," Roger said quietly. "I will." He lifted his hand to touch Maggie's cheek and his eye dropped to her abdomen in case she thought for a moment he'd forgotten she was pregnant.

"Get in your car," he said. "I'll follow you to Domaine St-Buvard."

Maggie felt a sudden rush of relief collide with a grinding exhaustion to have finally worn him down and won. It wasn't the key to Laurent's jail cell but it was a start.

She opened her car door and her phone rang. When she

pulled it out she saw her mother's picture materialize on the screen. Her stomach knotted immediately.

"Hold on a second, Roger," she said and answered the phone.

"Mom? Is everything okay?"

"No, everything is not okay!" her mother screeched. "Your father is not in his room and I can't find him anywhere!"

50

A TIME TO ACT

Frère Jean watched from the front window of the rectory as the detective and Madame Dernier talked in the parking lot. He could see even from here that there was going to be no chance that the detective would put her in his car and drive away with her.

There was something about the way they stood together—too closely if you asked him—that told him they were *conferring*. She wasn't defending herself. He wasn't admonishing her.

Did it matter?

The American was leaving and she knew now that Frère Jean would call the police if he caught her at *l'Abbaye de Sainte-Trinité* again. And the police had demonstrated to him that they would respond when he called.

And respond quickly.

He could feel safe now.

He should feel safe now.

As he watched Madame Dernier get into her car and the detective in his, he felt a spasm of annoyance. Clearly she had used her feminine wiles to get him to let her go.

Not that Frère Jean wanted to see her in jail. It was bad

enough that her husband was there and he knew she had children.

But he wanted her to stay away.

Would this be enough? Was this the extent of the police's intimidation? Frère Jean seriously feared it might be.

He watched as the two sets of taillights glowed brightly and then disappeared into the darkness.

Would he be strong enough to do what was necessary to stop her if the police weren't able to?

He would simply have to and beg God's forgiveness for it later.

There was too much at stake to stop now.

51

DANCE AWAY

Roger felt better than he had in weeks. Maybe it was seeing Maggie and being on the receiving end of her gratitude. Maybe it was the burgeoning belief that maybe—just maybe—there was a way to pull this off without sacrificing his career *and* his daughter's happiness. If he was careful, if he talked to the right people, he could get the information he needed—the information Maggie had been haranguing him for. And if he was able to lay it out in a coherent order, maybe he could trump Terrone's plotting.

Of course! Why had he just assumed he was helpless? Terrone had enemies. Terrone wasn't Teflon. If Roger was able to solve this murder and prove that Laurent wasn't involved—and do it before Laurent signed a damn confession—what other leverage would Terrone have?

Even if he tries to demote me, Roger thought with growing determination, *I can fight it. I can bring it to IA and to hell with what the world thinks. Do I always have to cave? Just once can't I fight for the right reasons and win?*

Feeling a surge of optimism and rising confidence, he put in the call to the tech lab and gave the order for a crew to get to the monastery of *l'Abbaye de Sainte-Trinité* first thing in the morning to take a DNA sample of the horse they found there and the blood on the tree.

He even joked with the tech who took the order who had a good laugh at the order but promised to have a crew out first thing in the morning.

I suppose it does sound ridiculous, Roger thought. *As ridiculous as me deciding to give up without even a fight on helping Maggie when she needs me.*

He put another call into his daughter's phone. He knew she was still rehearsing for the coming weekend's dance recital and when she didn't answer, he texted her that he would be out front to pick her up promptly at seven.

He frowned remembering how worried Maggie had looked when she got the call about her father. Perhaps after he picked Chloe up he would swing by to see if everyone was okay. After all, Laurent would appreciate Roger looking in on his in-laws.

The drive back to Aix was relaxing and as he accelerated down the highway Roger put music on to match his improving mood.

When had he gotten in the habit of thinking of himself as a coward? Or unimaginative? When had he gotten into the habit of just giving up when he hit a brick wall? He flushed uncomfortably thinking of how he'd been drinking himself sick the last few days.

That's how I handle a problem? he thought with disgust before reminding himself that that was the old Roger.

The new Roger had found a way to save Laurent, protect his own career, and find the real killer of Henri Dupree.

He felt a warmth radiate through his body in waves.

And earn Maggie Newberry's undying respect and affection in the process.

His cellphone vibrated loudly where he'd dropped it in the console and Roger picked it up and saw it was Terrone's number.

He hesitated for a moment and then took in a long breath, reminding himself that he could handle this.

"Bedard here," he said.

"Tell me you're on the way back to the station with Dernier's wife in handcuffs in the back of your car," Terrone said.

A flicker of anger pierced Roger. He wondered how Terrone knew about the monk's call into the station.

"No crime was committed," Roger said flatly. "I issued a warning and released her."

"I'll just bet you did," Terrone said tightly. "May I inquire why *you* responded to the call instead of sending a police car?"

"I was in the area," Roger lied, feeling a thin line of sweat dribble from his neck down the back of his shirt.

"I see. And do you have an answer for the phone call I just received notifying me of an order to send a team of crime techs to the monastery tomorrow?"

Roger felt the chill finger of panic tighten around his throat.

"I have reason to believe—"

"I don't care what you have reason to believe," Terrone interrupted. "I told you to back off that case. We have our suspect."

"And if he agrees to confess to the lesser charge?" Roger blurted. "Then who do we have for Dupree's murder?"

"This...that is not your concern!" Terrone sputtered.

A sudden terrible thought slid into Roger's brain like a water moccasin seeking water.

Is it possible Terrone will take Laurent's confession for the Cannes theft and still hold him for the Dupree murder?

"And you took Dernier out of lockup today?" Terrone continued, his voice becoming shrill. "Are you out of your mind? He could have run!"

"And left his family?" Roger said, his mind spinning with desperation. "It was a *funeral*, sir. I know the man. He wouldn't have run."

"That's the problem, Bedard. You know the man. Too well, I

think. You are to report to me immediately first thing in the morning."

"Yes sir," Roger said, and then as he saw his one grand gesture to Maggie disappearing in a puff of smoke and because he had to know, he said: "Did you cancel the crime techs?"

"Of course I cancelled it, you idiot. You're lucky I don't write this up. The DNA of a *horse*? You've lost your mind."

Roger bit his lip. Arguing wouldn't help or change anything. If he called the tech team back they'd only report it again to Terrone. He felt a sour taste in his mouth as a lump formed in the back of his throat. His mind was an eddy of images and thoughts, none of them good. As he focused back on the phone conversation, he realized Terrone had been talking for the last several seconds.

"Excuse me?" Roger said. "Could you repeat that?"

"I said I've decided not to wait for tomorrow to tell you in person. You are officially off the Dupree case, Bedard. I've reassigned it to Detective Inspector Girard. You'll hand over all files tomorrow morning. Any more involvement in this case—and that means any contact with Dernier or his wife—and I'll see you're struck off the force."

Terrone disconnected.

Roger drove another five miles before he realized he was still holding the phone in his hand.

52

A DAY LATE

Maggie took two steps into her parents' apartment building and the first person she saw sitting in the building lobby flipping through an old *International Tribune* was her father. He looked up at her in surprise.

"Hello, darling," he said. "Home from work already?"

Maggie felt her whole body relax and tears welled up in her eyes.

The long drive to Aix from the monastery had been a blistering maelstrom of panic and fear and guilt for her. She knew that if anything happened to her father, the blame for it must lie solely at her feet.

She gave her father a quick hug.

"What are you doing down here, Dad? Thinking about taking a little walk?"

"I used to love my daily afternoon ambulations," he said wistfully.

"As long as it involved a golf cart."

He laughed and the sound of it—reminding Maggie of so many happy times in her childhood—made her want to cry. She escorted him up the elevator and into the apartment where her mother sat at the kitchen table drinking down a bottle of wine that Maggie knew had been in the kitchen for at least three months.

Not for the first time, Maggie wondered if the real problem with her parents wasn't more her mother than her father.

Without a word Elspeth met them at the door and took Maggie's father's arm to lead him back to the bedroom. Maggie realized with a shock that her mother had stopped coloring or styling her hair. It hung around her shoulders in long gray waves, framing a face more and more haggard and lined than the day before.

It was close to nine o'clock by the time Maggie and her mother got her father sorted out and in bed. She called Grace to tell her she'd be back late to Danielle's tonight but that she was definitely coming back.

Maggie went to the kitchen to see that the casserole she'd made the day before was still in the oven, baked but untouched. She sighed, grateful her mother had at least turned the oven off. She scraped the casserole into the garbage, then wiped down the counters, poured the rest of the wine down the sink drain and turned to face her mother, her back against the kitchen sink.

"You are moving to Domaine St-Buvard with me," Maggie said. "I'll help you pack this weekend."

Her mother shook her head.

"We've been all over that," Elspeth said. "Your father and I need to be near the doctors and a hospital."

"I can get you to a hospital when you need it. What I can't do is continue to drive back and forth to Aix every day."

"I am sorry if we are such a burden to you, Maggie," Elspeth sniffed. "I wish your brother were here. He never had any problems taking your father to his medical appointments or calming him down."

"Tell me *one* time Ben took Dad to anything but a golf match and that was five years ago! You can wish for Ben all you want but you're stuck with me."

"I wish we'd never come to France! Everything is harder here! Everything!"

"I know, Mom, and I'm sorry." Maggie took in a long breath. "This isn't the way I wanted to tell you this but Laurent is in trouble and there's another baby on the way. I can't be racing back and forth to Aix on an hourly basis. I'm sorry. You and Dad are moving to Domaine St-Buvard. And that's all there is to it."

An hour later, Maggie was back on the road, her back aching from all the driving and her head thick with fatigue and the drama of the two screaming arguments she'd had tonight.

At least the one with Roger had resulted in him taking her house key and promising to retrieve the horse poop sample to run a test on it. It didn't seem like much on the face of it but on this day—the day when they'd buried their dearest Jean-Luc—it felt like a giant step forward.

Jean-Luc would have been relieved to know the sample he was smart enough to recognize needed to be examined was being tested. And because of that, very possibly because of that, Laurent would soon be free.

As Maggie approached the exit off the A7 she put in another call to Grace to tell her she was almost there.

"Darling," Grace said. "You sound exhausted. Please don't drive into a ditch in the process of doing everything you can to make everyone happy."

"I won't. I guess the kids are asleep?"

"I put them to bed hours ago. Just come on and we can share a glass of wine and you can bunk down here tonight."

"I can't," Maggie said with a groan. "I have to go back to Domaine St-Buvard and let the damn dogs out."

"Well, at least you should get a good night's rest," Grace said.

"I'll bring the kiddies to school tomorrow. I can pick them up too if you..."

"No, you've done enough, Grace. I'll collect them tomorrow and thank you."

"You are very near your limit, Maggie," Grace said. "I'm officially worried about you."

"I know. I'm a little worried about me too. But I've sorted out my folks tonight at any rate."

"How?"

"I laid down the law. They either come to Domaine St-Buvard or they go home. At this point I'm not sure I care which."

"How did they take it?"

"Ask me in two weeks when I'm not fighting to save my husband from prison. I'm sure I'll have the emotional energy to care about their problems by then. But today, no."

"I'm worried about you," Grace repeated.

Maggie pulled into the driveway of Domaine St-Buvard and saw that the place was totally dark. Normally Laurent left the lights on over the front steps or at least the landscape lighting by the hollyhocks and the stonewall. But Maggie hadn't thought to do it and now she was welcomed back to a darkened house.

She was already depressed and exhausted as she stopped the car. She could hear the dogs barking as soon as she opened the front door. They'd probably heard her car in the front drive. It was, after all, why Laurent got them, so they could alert the household to strangers.

Maggie dropped her purse and coat on the antique bench in the front foyer.

If they weren't just such puppies, she thought wearily as she hurried to the room off the living room where their crates were. She heard the frenetic scratching as the noise of their nails joined their howls of delight as she came into the room and undid the latches on the crates.

Unlike the welcome-home greeting of little Petit-Four, these two were already big enough and untrained enough to nearly knock her down in their exuberance.

"Stop it!" Maggie said, pushing their paws away from her face. "Down!"

She went to the French doors, the dogs leaping at her feet, and flung the doors open. They bounded out into the night.

Maggie watched them disappear into the vineyard wondering if she'd seen the last of them and deciding she was probably too tired to care. She came back inside and went to the kitchen where she mixed up their dinners and set them on the tile floor outside their crates.

She opened the back door again and looked out but still couldn't hear or see them. She came back into the house where today's mail had been shoved in the slot by the front door. She picked up the letters, mostly bills and put them on the table in the foyer. When she had a moment she'd move them to her desk.

Glancing in the direction of her office she felt a tremor of guilt at how long it had been since she'd written on the newsletter. She was supposed to release a new one every month—chocked full of tips and sales, special offers and proprietary tips for shopping the area. It was supposed to go out in five days and she hadn't even started it.

Turning the light out in her office, she went to the kitchen and took a bottle of Perrier out of the fridge and used it to chase down the two ibuprofen she hoped would take care of the relentless ache creeping up her spine from the hours in the car.

Where were those stupid dogs?

She went to the French doors again and tried to hear them but there was only silence.

"Izzy! Buddy!" she called. A splinter of annoyance was swamped by another feeling. A burgeoning trepidation. She waited to see if they would respond to being called and then she went inside and checked to make sure the front door was locked. She passed the antique Saint Remy cherub clock on her way back to the kitchen. It was just shy of midnight.

She went to the first kitchen drawer and pulled out a flashlight.

Damn dogs.

She hesitated at the French doors before stepping out onto the terrace. Normally the lights in the garden were motion-activated. She'd gone several steps away from the house before she realized the lights hadn't come on. Were they battery-operated instead? She wasn't even sure. But whatever they were, they weren't working.

She hurried to the end of the terrace feeling the cold wind bite into her thin cashmere cardigan.

"Izzy!" she called. "Buddy! Dinner time!"

This is when you're glad you don't have neighbors close by, she thought. *When you're out bellowing your dogs' names at midnight.*

Except she couldn't help the creeping sensation on her scalp that seemed to make her wish—just for tonight—that she had a close neighbor or two.

Suddenly she heard a dog yelp. One dog. In the vineyard.

"Buddy?" she called as she flashed her light in the direction of the sound. There was nothing but a pool of darkness around her. It suddenly occurred to her that she hadn't locked the door behind her.

Someone could slip into the house while she was out here.

She turned to flash her light at the doors leading into the house just as a shadow leaped out at her, slamming her to the ground.

And snuffed all the light out of her world.

53

TOUCH AND GO

It was the warm and wet sensation on her face that made her realize how cold she was.

Maggie groaned and heard a whimper in her ear, close and hot.

Another tongue raked across her face and she lifted a hand to push the dog away. Her hand grabbed its collar and she held on.

Maggie opened her eyes. It was dark and so cold.

She pulled herself to her knees. The movement sent stars shooting off inside her skull. She leaned over and threw up on the pavers, then waited for the nausea and the trembling to stop.

Neither would.

Suddenly she remembered the form that had slammed into her.

She'd been attacked in her garden.

She lifted her head and scanned the terrace, her heart pounding in her chest. Her fingers trembling and still clutching one of the dogs, Maggie staggered to her feet. She saw her flashlight lying on the terrace, its beam directed into the pomegranate bushes next to the back terrace steps. She made no move to retrieve it.

Moving slowly and with dread, she stumbled toward the house. The other dog was there pawing at the door to be let in. She opened the door and both dogs shot inside going straight to their food bowls.

Maggie shut the door behind her and locked it.

She still couldn't get her heart to stop racing as she ran to her purse in the foyer and her phone.

∼

A few hours later Maggie came downstairs lured by the beckoning fragrance of coffee being made. For one sickening, gut-wrenching moment she thought that Laurent was back.

When she reached the bottom tread of the marble staircase, she saw Roger Bedard in the kitchen using the French press coffee maker. A large potted lavender plant sat on the breakfast counter. He looked up and watched her as she approached.

"You were pretty confident your attacker wasn't in the house with you," he said as he handed her a mug of coffee. "After you called me you went upstairs and just went to bed?"

"I don't remember doing that," Maggie said, taking the coffee and closing her eyes to enjoy the fragrance of it before taking her first sip. "Did you leave Chloe home by herself?"

"She's on a sleepover. You didn't tell me he struck you," Roger said, his lips pressed together in a white line of determined self-control.

"He didn't," Maggie said, gently touching the lump on her temple. "I think that's where I hit the terrazzo."

"You have a black eye too."

"I don't know then, Roger. One minute I was calling for the dogs and the next minute he was between me and the house."

"He?"

"I'm sure it was a man. That's all I'm sure of."

"Do you have any idea who might want to hurt you?"

Maggie shook her head and was instantly sorry she had. She moaned and Roger shook out three ibuprofen into his hand.

"Here, take these." He slid a bottle of water toward her.

She swallowed the pills and drank all the water. "Don't you dare tell Laurent about this," she said.

"Why? Because then he'll know you deliberately disobeyed him?"

She winced and sat down on the kitchen stool, cupping her hands around the coffee mug.

"Our marriage doesn't work like that. I just don't want him to worry."

"Well, he's married to you so I'm pretty sure he's in a constant state of worry."

"I know you're mad, Roger. I get it. And I also know that you think I brought this on myself somehow with all the questions I've been asking. But I'm doing what I have to because *you* won't actively help me,"

"I *am* actively helping! I handed over an official police deposition to you! Which by the way Frère Jean is convinced you published on the Internet. I let you see a copy of the lab forensics—"

"That is not good enough!" Maggie said, feeling her head vibrating with the pounding pain. "My husband is being railroaded by circumstantial evidence! And you're just letting it happen because you don't want to upset your next promotion!"

"That is a monstrous thing to say."

"Well if the shoe fits, why don't you kick yourself with it?"

"If that is an American idiom, it is terrible."

After a beat, both of them burst out laughing.

"It's a modified American idiom," Maggie admitted.

"Remind me not to learn it."

"Your English is still very good."

"And your French is so good that now I never get to practice my English."

"I'm sorry for being so hateful to you, Roger."

He turned to pull a bag of frozen peas out of the freezer and handed it to her. "I deserved it. I know you don't think I'm very good at my job."

Maggie pressed the frozen bag to her temple and felt some of the throbbing in her head begin to ease.

"If it's any consolation, I always thought you were way more caring than most cops."

"Caring." He nodded. "I cannot say I ever saw that on my job application when I joined the service."

"Doesn't mean it's not important."

"Sometimes I think there is a piece missing in me for being able to do this job."

"God, Roger, even Laurent couldn't do your job."

Roger laughed. "You don't really believe that."

Maggie grinned. "You're right. Because Laurent does everything well. But maybe being a detective isn't your thing. There's no shame in that."

"Unless a man's life is hanging in the balance."

"You're just not going to let me say something nice, are you?" She smiled sadly at him. She knew he was struggling with something and she still didn't know what.

"You always at least try to do what's right," she said. "And not every cop does. And unless I'm way off track here, it feels to me like you're at war with yourself right now because you know you can't be a good friend to me and do your job too."

"I'm ashamed for even having the war. It should be *évident*."

"Yeah, but life isn't like that. It doesn't matter. It only matters that you're on the same page with me now."

"Yes, of course," Roger said, not looking at her.

He seemed to be suddenly very focused on winding his watch and turning to check the time on the kitchen clock. Maggie knew he had a smart phone and thought his preoccupation with his watch was a little strange.

A tremor of doubt rippled through her. What was she missing about what he was *not* telling her? What was she not seeing?

Because whatever it was, it was definitely something.

54

WHAT THE HEART KNOWS

Maggie watched the morning clouds hanging low and gray over the vineyard. There was a bite to the air that promised more rain later. She let the dogs out and stood with Roger on the back terrace and watched them run into the vineyard.

"It'll be hell trying to round them up again," she murmured.

"I'll catch them."

Maggie looked at him. He still looked like hell. Like he hadn't slept in days—or showered. His eyes were bloodshot so he was probably drinking too much on top of it all.

"Chloe okay?" she asked.

He looked at her in surprise. "Of course. She's got a small recital next weekend."

"Mila would love to come."

He smiled but didn't take his eyes off the vineyard and the horizon. "I think I can manage to get tickets."

"And everything else is all right?" she pressed.

"Yes, of course."

Of course, Maggie thought, because he *always* looks like he just dragged out of bed with a hangover and no hope for the future.

What is going on with him?

"It occurred to me that the guy who attacked me last night might be the murderer," she said.

He glanced at her. "I thought you said the monk was the murderer."

"He's on my short list," she said.

"But you don't think the monk was the one who attacked you?"

"No. Frère Jean is older and not tall. This guy was bigger. I got the brief impression he was young."

"But basically it could have been anyone," Roger said, glancing around the terrace. There were no obvious signs of the attack. "I think for your own safety, you need to stop doing whatever it is you're doing, *chérie*."

"Don't call me that, Roger."

"How am I going to tell your husband?" Roger said, pinching his lips together. "What am I going to tell him if something happens to you?"

"Well, for starters you're going to keep your mouth shut and *not* tell him anything. I thought we discussed this."

"If something happens to you I will never forgive myself and Laurent will murder *me*."

"Well, not if he's in jail so let's start by changing that situation, shall we?"

"This man who attacked you may well do it again. Don't you see? You are putting yourself in danger."

"Don't *you* see? If that's true then it means I'm getting close. That alone should tell you that you have the wrong guy."

"Maggie, I *know* we have the wrong guy," Roger said in frustration. "You don't have to convince me. But even if the lab results come back saying the blood on the tree is Dupree's and the room shows signs of a struggle and the horse was in the vineyard, it is still not good news for Laurent. Don't you see that?"

Maggie turned to face him, her stomach roiling at his words

"The prosecutor will just argue that Laurent went to the monastery, found his way to Dupree's room, argued with Dupree and then tossed him out the window," Roger said. "How does the fact that Dupree died at the monastery and not your vineyard prove Laurent's innocence? *Pas du tout*. It doesn't."

Maggie's mouth went dry and she held her shoulders tightly as if to protect herself from his words. His relentless words.

"But if Laurent killed Dupree," she said, "why the hell would he take the body to his own vineyard? That's crazy!"

"Agreed," Roger said with resignation as he turned his attention back to the vineyard.

Maggie could see the dogs loping back toward the house.

"Maybe Dupree killed himself?" Maggie said. "People said he was depressed."

"With his hands tied behind his back?"

Maggie felt a wave of discouragement. "I forgot about that."

"Look, Maggie, let the police do their work, eh? The forensics team will process Dupree's room and the stables and the tree. We'll talk to all the same people again but ask different questions this time, yes? I will personally talk with Frère Jean and ask him if he took the cart out that night."

"I can't tell you what a relief it is that you're finally with me on this," Maggie said. She thought she could literally feel the burden on her shoulders begin to lift.

As the dogs joined them on the terrace, Roger turned back to Maggie and cupped her cheek with his hand. He took a step toward her, closing the distance between them.

"As wonderful as it is to hear you say that," he said, his voice hoarse and low, his eyes on her lips, "I will not ruin your trust by taking advantage of it."

Maggie snorted and pulled her head away from him.

"Well, that's a relief since ending this Hallmark moment by me clocking you would be a serious disappointment. Really Roger? *That's* what you took away from all this? You're a hero because you *won't* make a pass at me while my husband is in jail? —a place where *you* put him?"

Roger winced and turned to herd the dogs inside the house.

"It sounds bad when you put it like that," he said over his shoulder. "But I am French. It is not in my makeup to give up on *amour.*"

Maggie followed him inside and he turned to her with a charming shrug and a grin.

"Even if nothing ever comes of it," he said, "At least I know there is something between us and you know it too."

"What I know is that you're being an ass, Roger. Please knock it off."

Maggie led the dogs to their crates and locked them in. She turned and stood facing Roger, her hands on her hips.

"When do you think the forensics team will have results on the blood?" she asked.

"It takes awhile."

"At least we're moving forward. And I thank you for that, Roger. I'm not going to kiss you or anything but I'm grateful."

"*De rien.* I'm just doing my job."

"Now if I can just get you to reconsider Frère Jean as the killer. Will you talk with him today?"

"I will." Roger didn't look at her.

If she had to put a name to it she'd say he was evading direct eye contact with her and somehow she didn't think it was because she'd rebuffed him on the attempted kiss.

"If you will stay here," he said, "and stay out of trouble, I will make some calls and determine where he was during the time of the murder."

"Thank you," Maggie said, picking up the bag of frozen peas

and holding it to her temple. She winced at the sting of coldness. She'd skinned her cheek too when she fell.

"Are you sure you don't want me to make a formal complaint about the attack last night?" he said.

"Very sure. I don't want a single jot of police effort directed away from the task of finding Dupree's real killer. I'm sure whoever hit me was either just a prowler or...well, probably just a prowler."

"If you're sure then I'll go now. Meanwhile, promise me you'll stay here and wait for my call?"

"Yes, Roger. I promise. I'll be here."

After a quick call to Danielle's to talk to both Jemmy and Mila and then Grace—while being careful not to mention last night's attack—Maggie took the dogs out on long leashes for a walk around the nearest border of the vineyard.

There was no evidence of her attack last night except for the flashlight whose battery had since gone dead. She picked it up and slipped it into her jacket pocket.

Was the attacker just some random prowler? Didn't it make more sense that he was someone from the monastery? Regardless of his possible *other* murderous tendencies, Frère Jean just didn't strike her as the jump-out-of-the-bushes type of attacker.

Guy or Pierre on the other hand...

After bringing the dogs in, Maggie barricaded them in the living room with assorted dog toys and went upstairs to shower and dress.

She debated calling her mother but after yesterday's showdown she thought they both could use some emotional distance. Maggie had already made it clear that her mother and father were to start packing up and she'd help them move in by the weekend.

Back downstairs Maggie checked her phone but there was nothing from either her mother or Roger. She knew these things took time and she resolved to distract herself for the morning until it was time to collect the children from Aix.

Going into her office gave her a lurch of sadness thinking how Laurent had created this room for her as a surprise. It backed up to the terrace and featured tall floor-to-ceiling windows that — except for the upstairs bedrooms—afforded the best view of the vineyard. He'd had a local craftsman forge rustic wrought iron *fleur de lis* brackets on the hand-carved barn door that led into the cozy bookcase lined den. A thick Moroccan rug that she'd found in a Paris flea market lay on top of the blue patterned Italian tile floor.

She went to her computer and booted up. She had a list of artisans expecting to be showcased in November's newsletter and a file full of jpegs that she'd collected featuring their various products and art pieces. Pushing thoughts of Laurent and her parents away, Maggie focused on putting together the newsletter, writing airy commentary to aid all American and British Francophiles to imagine a charmed life in Provence.

By the time the dogs began to whine to be let out again, two hours had passed without her realizing it. Ready for a break, Maggie took the dogs into the garden on leashes and walked out into the vineyard where the body had been found.

There was nothing left to indicate that anything terrible had happened there. Even the spot where Jean-Luc had found the manure now looked no different from any place else. The recent rains had erased every trace.

A nagging thought in the back of her mind made her cut the walk short in order to hurry back to the house. Letting the dogs have the run of the place at least momentarily, she went to the kitchen and pulled open the fridge.

She found what she was looking for in seconds. A small

plastic container sat on the top shelf with a note on top that said *ne mange pas.*

Don't eat.

Maggie stared at the sample, imagining Jean-Luc putting it there. She closed the fridge and stared at the door covered with snapshots of Jem, Laurent and Mila and several of Nicole too. There was a spelling test from Jemmy with *bon travail!* scrawled across the top in red, and a note in Laurent's handwriting that looked like the start of a grocery list.

But all Maggie really saw as she stared at the closed refrigerator door was the fact that the sample was still there.

Which meant Roger hadn't taken it.

Which meant he wasn't running any tests.

Later Maggie made herself an omelet with left over asparagus spears and forced herself to eat even though she wasn't hungry in order that she could take more ibuprofen for her headache. Her eye was puffing up nicely now and turning a dark blue and the abrasion on her forehead was already scabbing and looking much worse as a result.

Too antsy to go back to her office, she pulled a disk of *pâte brisée* from the fridge and began to roll it out to fit her pie pan. Her hands were coated in flour when her phone rang but she didn't bother wiping off the excess before she snatched up her phone.

"Hey," Grace said. "I'm going into Aix this afternoon so I'll pick the kids up. Everything okay on your end?"

Maggie's shoulders slumped in disappointment.

"Yeah, that'd be great," she said. "How's Danielle?"

"She's coming with me. We thought a couple hours shopping might be a nice afternoon."

"Good idea. Give her my love. Want to come here for dinner tonight?"

"We were thinking of doing something at Danielle's. You've got enough to worry about. I'll bring the kids straight here. Just come over when you're ready."

"Thanks, Grace."

The screen on Maggie's phone began to morph into another image—this one of Roger.

"Grace, I've got another call," Maggie said hurriedly. "I'll see you tonight." She disconnected and breathlessly answered the phone.

"What did you find out?" she asked.

"The tests will take time. I don't have a report on them."

Maggie couldn't help but glance in the direction of the refrigerator where the horse sample still was. But she'd vowed to herself that she wouldn't call Roger on it. She needed his help and couldn't afford to risk him turning away. Besides he might be talking about testing the tree trunk blood or the monastery pony.

"I did have a conversation with Frère Jean," he said.

"And?"

"Maggie, it's not him."

"How can you say that?" she said in agitation. "Of course he'll deny it! Did you ask him what he was doing driving the pony cart at eleven o'clock at night?"

"He admitted that was him but said it was hours earlier. Your witnesses must have gotten their times confused."

"You can't believe him just because he's a monk! Wake *up*, Roger!" Maggie said in frustration.

"Maggie, he has an ironclad alibi," Roger said firmly. "Are you listening to me? He was celebrating *mass* during the time of the murder."

"Says *him*!"

"Yes, says him," Roger said tiredly. "Says him and thirty other people in the congregation including one of my own men."

55

POISONING THE WELL

Roger hung up the phone and for a moment it was all he could do to stare at it in his hand as he replayed in his head the sound of Maggie's disappointment. He'd have given anything—in what was turning out to be his last official duty in his current position—if he could have given her news that would actually cheer her.

He'd gone out on a limb to talk to people he knew would end up reporting back to Terrone in order to get the information that the monk's alibi put him out of the frame for the murder. And for what? So Maggie could thank him with that voice full of sighs and dejection when in her heart she and he both knew he'd failed her?

His vision was clouded with fury as he turned back to his computer and opened up his emails. He'd made two phone calls both of which would absolutely cement his ruin within the department and he didn't even get the benefit of being a hero to Maggie for an hour.

He ground his teeth in repressed frustration as he scanned the list of emails. None were specifically addressed to him. He'd been only copied on all of them. But he didn't need to look at his interoffice communications to know that things had already changed. Word had gotten out.

Roger Bedard, Commandant de Police, was everything but finished in the Aix-en-Provence Police *Nationale*.

The detectives he'd worked beside for the last seven years were suddenly too engrossed in their work to look up from their desks to greet him when he came through the office.

He'd torpedoed his career.

And for what?

Laurent will still go to prison. The Dupree murder case will still go unsolved. And he and Chloe will still have to move.

And Maggie will always remember me as the man who couldn't help her in the one thing she needed me to do more than anything else.

He swallowed hard and his eye fell on the stack of case files for the Dupree murder at the edge of his desk. Girard still hadn't come by to pick them up.

And why should he? Even though his name was officially on the case as lead investigator, Girard had no more interest in solving that murder than he had in meeting His Holiness the Pope for lunch.

Not now that he had Laurent exactly where he wanted him.

Maggie hung up the phone and sat in her kitchen, tapping her fingers against the granite counter top.

She tried to imagine a single scenario by which Frère Jean could have possibly killed Dupree, disposed of the body and still gotten to the mass on time.

The autopsy said Dupree had been killed between eight and ten o'clock. The mass had been held at eight and fellowship afterward had gone on until eleven. Frère Jean was completely accounted for. And while technically it was possible that the monk could have killed Dupree minutes before he celebrated mass, even Maggie couldn't believe that.

But if it wasn't Frère Jean, then who? And why was the monk acting so suspiciously?

She moved listlessly to the living room and sat on the couch. Her head had stopped hurting but she knew she looked like she'd gone two rounds with Mike Tyson. The only benefit to Laurent being in jail, she thought sadly, was that he wouldn't see her like this.

She picked up her phone again and put a call through to the only number she had for Laurent at the jail. She'd thought about asking Roger to patch her through earlier but had forgotten when she had him on the line. When she reached the jail switchboard, she asked to speak to Laurent Dernier and was put on hold for several minutes until she was finally disconnected. Sighing, she sent a quick text to Roger to see what he could do.

She knew that both Roger and Laurent were holding something back from her but it wasn't until this moment that it occurred to her that it could very well be the same thing. A tremor of dread rippled across her shoulders.

They're protecting me from something. But what?

What could be worse than going to prison for murder?

She glanced at her watch. Grace and Danielle would be picking the kids up about now. That meant Maggie had plenty of time to clean the kitchen floor, scrub all three bathrooms and finish baking the quiche Lorraine to bring to Danielle's tonight—as if Danielle needed more food.

Just as Maggie was trying to decide if she should call her mother after all, the doorbell rang.

Wondering when was the last time she'd heard the doorbell ring, Maggie picked up her phone, dialed nine-nine-nine and poised her finger over the SEND button as she opened the front door.

Guy Dionne stood on her threshold, his motorcycle propped up behind him against the stonewall that bordered the driveway.

"May we talk?" he said briskly, slapping his leather driving gloves together nervously.

Knowing he expected her to invite him in, Maggie stepped outside and pulled the door closed behind her. She held her phone ready to dial for help if necessary.

"Happy to," she said. "Was that you who paid me a visit last night?"

He frowned and tucked his chin into his chest in confusion. "Last night?" he said.

"Never mind. What did you want to talk about?"

Guy rubbed his hands against his jeans. It was cold out but Guy wore an expensive leather jacket. The thought occurred to Maggie that the jacket was awfully nice for a homeless guy living at a monastery.

"I heard someone told you that Frère Jean was seen driving the pony cart the night of the murder," Guy said, not looking directly at her. "I'm here to tell you they were mistaken."

"How do you know what they did or didn't see?"

He glanced at her and his eyes flashed angrily and it occurred to Maggie that the shadow who attacked her last night could have been wearing all black—like Guy was now. It could easily have been him

"My source seemed pretty sure they recognized Frère Jean driving the cart that night," she said.

"If you ask them again you will find they didn't see his face. All they saw was a man wearing a monk's robe driving the pony cart in the rain at night."

"Are you saying it was one of the other monks? Because I heard they were all away from the monastery that night."

Guy shook his head. "Anyone can dress in monk's robes." He shrugged. "It's a monastery."

"So you're saying it was someone dressed as a monk? What for? To put suspicion on Frère Jean?"

"I don't know. But I do know *who* was driving the horse in the right that night because unlike Madame Cuillerier, I saw his face."

"I'm listening," Maggie said.

"It was Pierre Guillaume."

"The gypsy boy? Are you sure?"

Guy crossed his arms over his chest and fixed her with a deliberate stare.

"I saw his *face*," he said peevishly. "I couldn't see what was in the back of the cart but I recognized him and I wondered what he was up to. I thought it was very suspicious him taking the cart out at that time of night in the pouring rain."

"Where's the cart now?"

"Destroyed in the fire."

Naturally.

Maggie frowned as she tried to digest what Guy was telling her. Had the police talked to Pierre? Did he have an alibi? *Did Guy?*

"I just thought you should know," Guy said earnestly. "It was Pierre. Not Frère Jean."

Boy, everybody sure loves Frère Jean.

"Did you tell this to the police?" she asked.

"No. But if it looks like they are going to arrest Frère Jean, I will."

"Well, you don't need to worry about that," Maggie said. "It seems Frère Jean has an airtight alibi."

"*Bon*," Guy said, turning away. "That is all I came to say."

There was something about the young man that made Maggie feel unafraid of him. She knew not to always trust her instincts about people—especially when she first met them—but she couldn't shake her impression that this young man was more gruff bluff than threat.

"Wait," Maggie said, taking two paces off the front steps to follow him. "You haven't told me *why* Pierre would want to kill Dupree."

"Why?" Guy looked at her as if the answer was the most obvious in the world. "Because he was in love with Dupree's daughter."

"Why does that matter?"

Guy was fidgeting now, rubbing his hands against his jeans, clearly ready to leave.

"The very day Monsieur Dupree was killed he told Pierre— loud enough for everyone in the monastery dining hall to hear— that he would rather die than have a filthy *gitane* be with his daughter."

"That doesn't mean any—"

"I personally heard Pierre say under his breath that perhaps that could be arranged."

Guy turned and jumped on his motorcycle and revved the engine before roaring out of the driveway, spraying an arc of gravel behind him.

Well, Maggie thought as she watched him disappear down the village road.

That would certainly qualify as a motive.

56

DREAM ON

Maggie spent the rest of the afternoon cleaning house and trying to process what Guy had told her. If it was true that Frère Jean really was off the hook as Roger insisted then why was the monk trying to implicate Laurent? She and Laurent had both guessed that Frère Jean might be trying to protect someone. Could that someone be Pierre?

She knew she'd been asking the wrong questions up to now. Asking Frère Jean to unstick from his deposition was always going to be a brick wall. But backing him up against it with the truth—that he'd been caught trying to protect Pierre—the true killer—at the expense of an innocent man? Well, that might just get the dam breaking.

Feeling a little better since Roger's disappointing phone call, Maggie hurriedly let the dogs out one more time and then filled their dinner bowls.

She didn't for a minute let Guy off the hook in all this. Not only was he the right size for whoever attacked her last night, but according to Madame Montagne he was a romantic rival of Pierre's. That might not make him a suspect for the murder, but it would definitely discredit his testimony if he were trying to hang it on Pierre.

She locked the dogs back in their crates and pulled on her coat and collected the quiche. She felt a lightness in her chest. Guy's visit had given her a new direction in the middle of a dead end. She would need to go back to the monastery first thing tomorrow and track down Pierre. At the very least he had motive —and one that most Frenchmen regarded as ultimately credible —*la belle femme*.

As she placed the pie on the floorboard of her car, she thought about calling Roger to tell him what she'd learned but ultimately decided against it.

Roger talked a good game and she was sure he'd love to be a hero in her eyes but in the end he wasn't really interested in finding the killer. If he were, he wouldn't stop with the dead end of Frère Jean and his alibi. He'd keep digging until he found another thread he could follow. And if that fizzled out, he'd go looking for another.

She hated to admit it but it was true: she really was all alone in this.

Jean-Luc and Danielle's country *mas* was an easy walk by way of the vineyard but it was two miles from Domaine St-Buvard by car. Maggie had thought about bringing the dogs with her but the kids had spent the last two nights away from home. Tonight they would sleep in their own beds with their own mother making their breakfast in the morning.

When she arrived Jemmy was outside tossing a ball in the air. Maggie was surprised but pleased to see it. He normally spent too much time in front of the TV or with his iPad. She didn't know who had chased him outside—Grace or Danielle, although her money was on Danielle—but she was glad of it.

"*Maman!*" he said, running to give her a hug. "I missed you."

"I missed you too, sausage," Maggie said, kissing the top of his head and juggling the quiche and her purse as she hugged him. "Everything okay at school today?"

"I got an award in science class," he said with a shrug.

"Jemmy, that's great!" Maggie said.

"It's inside. I kept it to show Papa."

Maggie felt her heart sink. "He'll love that."

They walked inside the house and Maggie saw that Zouzou and Mila were in the kitchen—the fragrance of a cake baking filled the cheery little room.

Grace and Danielle were sitting in the annex room in front of the fire. Both were holding coffees.

"Darling, you're here!" Grace sang out. "There's fresh coffee. Come and join us."

Maggie slid the quiche onto the kitchen counter and poured herself a cup of coffee.

"Hey, you two," she said to Mila and Zouzou, "that smells amazing!"

"We are cooking cake, *Maman!*" Mila said happily.

"I can tell."

"What happened to your face?" Mila said, her eyes suddenly troubled.

Oh, crap. Maggie had intended to camouflage it with makeup before she came over but Guy's visit had distracted her.

"One of the puppies banged into me," she said.

"It's a shiner!" Jemmy crowed, laughing.

Maggie left the laughing children and entered the annex where she went immediately to Danielle and gave her a kiss.

"Hey, Danielle," she said. "How are you today?"

"*Chérie*, what happened to you?" Danielle said in surprise.

"Maggie, your eye..." Grace said, covering her mouth with a hand, her eyes wide.

Maggie touched it and grinned sheepishly. "Yeah," she said. "Unexpected run-in with a dog's head."

"Come sit down," Danielle said, gesturing to the place beside her on the couch. "Tell us about these bad dogs."

"Oh, they're not bad," Maggie said, sitting down and reaching for a macaron on the dish on the coffee table. "They're just young and untrained."

"Jean-Luc said they came from a good breeder," Danielle said, frowning.

"They're good dogs," Maggie insisted. "I just wasn't paying attention."

She caught Grace's eye and realized she wasn't believing a word of it. Before Maggie could decide whether to lay it on a little thicker or switch the subject, her phone rang. She pulled it out and saw the words UNKNOWN CALLER on the screen.

"*Allo?*" she said, answering it and standing up in case she needed to take it somewhere private.

"*Chérie?*"

She turned to Grace and Danielle. "It's Laurent," she said, her heart beating quickly, her eyes overly bright. "I'm going to take it outside, okay?" Without waiting for an answer, she hurried toward the front door.

"How are you?" she asked breathlessly. "Any news on your front?"

"*Non, chérie,*" he said softly. "I am only calling to hear your voice."

The inflection in his voice made Maggie falter as she pushed the front door open and stepped outside into the cool of the late afternoon.

His voice sounded tired and drawn. If Maggie had to come up with one word to describe how he sounded, she would pick...discouraged.

"Laurent, Roger has a whole bunch of new information on the case that—"

"Maggie, *no*," Laurent said, a veneer of anger creeping into his voice. "I told you—"

"Yes, I know," Maggie said hurriedly. "But that was before I—"

"I do not want you doing this!"

Maggie tried to remember the last time Laurent had raised his voice to her. She couldn't remember a time.

She knew how helpless and frustrated he must feel in that jail cell. He was asking her to do one simple thing—and he was powerless to make her do it.

She sat on the stone bench in Danielle's front garden facing the driveway and shivered in her thin sweater. She'd forgotten to grab her coat.

"I want to make sure you know certain things in case communication going forward becomes difficult," he said.

Maggie felt a sliver of ice insert into her spine.

"Why would communication become difficult?" she asked softly, her eyes going to the tops of the cypress trees that squatted at the end of Danielle and Jean-Luc's drive. She could see birds in the trees. *They must be cold* she thought dully.

Ignoring her question, Laurent's voice returned to a businesslike tone.

"The life insurance policy is in my desk drawer," he said, his words stabbing her in the heart.

Why is he doing this?

"I know where it is," she said.

"*Bon.* There are a few things that have come up here." He paused and Maggie found herself holding her breath. "A few more charges."

Maggie's stomach plunged as she bit back a gasp.

"Charges? What kind of charges?" she stuttered.

"Right now that doesn't matter," Laurent said. "What does matter is you promising me that you will allow the *avocat commission d'office* to handle my case. Do you understand?"

Maggie's mind whirled. The *avocat commission d'office* was the French equivalent to a public defender in the States. She and Laurent were borderline wealthy ever since his Aunt Delphine made him the sole heir to her considerable fortune three years ago.

"No, I don't," she said. "If you're in trouble, we need to hire a good lawyer."

"*No.* That is exactly what I do not want," he said firmly.

"That doesn't make sense!" she said, standing and throwing up a hand in frustration. "We have the money!"

"I will not have Jemmy and Mila's inheritance—the money *you* need to live on—squandered on my defense fund."

"Squandered?" Maggie said, almost speechless. "Are you serious? Do you think any of us care about a stupid inheritance? Jemmy and Mila want their father back!"

"*I* care about the inheritance," Laurent said firmly. "I very much care and I forbid you to spend any of it for a defense that does not exist."

"What do you mean *does not exist*? Why are you acting like the case against you is over? *What are you not telling me?*"

"You know what you need to know, *chérie*," he said wearily. "I must hang up now."

Oh hell no.

"You said *a few other charges*," Maggie said hurriedly. "What charges?"

"I have to go, *chérie*. Promise me. For just this once I need you to do as I say. *Promise me.*"

"No."

"Maggie..."

"*No.* You must have had a stroke since the last time I saw you if you think I won't spend every dime we have to get you released. I don't know what they're feeding you in there but just *no*. No effing way. Nope."

"Maggie," he said angrily. "I insist you do as I say!"

"Laurent, if you won't tell me what's going on, my only recourse is to spend everything we have for your defense. Even if it means the kids and I have to move into a garage apartment in the back yard of my folks' house back in Atlanta."

She could hear him sputtering in furious frustration on the end of the line and then without another word from him the connection broke.

57

RUNNING ON EMPTY

Maggie sat holding the phone and tried to control her emotions. She wanted to believe that the reason their connection was cut off was because Laurent's time was up and they were automatically disconnected rather than think he was so upset with her that he hung up on her.

She sat down heavily on the stone bench and felt the tremors start in her stomach and work their way up to her shoulders. She'd goaded him by painting a horrific picture of her and the kids impoverished. Why had she done that? She knew he was worried about exactly that. And she'd landed a bulls-eye. Right in his weak spot.

Tears gathered in her eyes and she blinked them away.

He'd been so unhappy with her. So terribly, very unhappy.

"Maggie?"

Maggie looked up to see Grace standing in the doorway watching her questioningly. Maggie tried to smile but only ended up putting her hands to cover her face to stop further tears. She felt Grace drape a heavy coat over her shoulders and settle down next to her.

"What happened?" Grace said softly, putting an arm around

Maggie and squeezing her gently. "Whatever it is we'll fix it, darling."

Maggie wiped her eyes and shook her head. It was all so hopeless.

"Oh, Grace," she said. "He said they have even more charges against him now."

"On top of the murder charge?"

Maggie nodded miserably. "And he won't tell me what they are and he doesn't want me to get him a decent lawyer either."

"Well, that's just crazy."

"He sounded so...flat. Like he'd given up. I just...I just..."

Grace squeezed her arm and Maggie lay her head against Grace's shoulder.

"Can't you ask Roger what's going on?" Grace asked.

Maggie shook her head. "Roger's useless," she said. "Totally useless."

They sat quietly in the cold. The drive to Jean-Luc and Danielle's house was framed on both sides by a small forest and a low knee wall of fieldstone draped in verdant cascades of ivy.

Finally Maggie took in a long breath. She had never openly defied Laurent's wishes before as she had just now on the phone. She'd fought with him plenty of times but never flat out refused to negotiate or compromise. Her stomach roiled at how much she knew she had upset him today.

"One of the guys at the monastery said he saw the gypsy Pierre driving the pony cart the night of the murder," Maggie said, sniffing and wiping the last of her tears away.

"Is that significant?"

"Remember I mentioned that Jean-Luc and I had a theory that Dupree's body was placed in our vineyard by way of a horse and cart?"

"I do."

Maggie felt a little better as she talked. She turned to face Grace, her energy and hopefulness returning.

"Well, before this afternoon I thought it was the monk who killed Dupree since someone at the monastery told me she'd seen him driving the cart in the rain the night of the murder."

"The monk? You mean Frère Jean?"

"Yes, but Roger called a few hours ago to tell me Frère Jean was at mass during the murder window. And that's confirmed. Whatever else the guy's done, he couldn't have been driving that cart."

"Is the cart so important? If you give up your theory, maybe it will put Frère Jean back in the frame."

"I can't give it up. It's all I have. If I give it up I'm literally at a dead end," Maggie said dejectedly.

"You said somebody told you it was the gypsy boy driving the cart?"

"Yeah, this afternoon this guy from the monastery came to Domaine St-Buvard and told me he saw the gypsy—whose name is Pierre—driving the cart that night. But he and Pierre are rivals for the dead man's daughter, Noelle."

"So perhaps he was lying."

"It's possible. I spoke to Pierre once and it wasn't pleasant, but now I'm pretty sure I need to go talk to him again."

"Was he interviewed by the police?"

"I doubt it," Maggie said.

"Are you going to tell me how this happened?" Grace said gesturing to Maggie's black eye.

Maggie sighed. "Somebody was skulking around the garden of Domaine St-Buvard last night. When I let the dogs out I ran into him. Literally."

"Did you recognize who it was?"

Maggie shook her head and glanced again at the sky. "No. It was too dark. Grace, I need to go."

"Are you really going to the monastery? *Tonight?* Darling, I don't like this." Grace bit her lip, her gaze moving to Maggie's black eye.

"I'll be fine. Watch the kids for me? I don't know how long I'll be."

"Darling, I really don't like this," Grace said again. "Shouldn't you tell Roger about this gypsy boy?"

"I don't think it would help," Maggie said dispiritedly. "I don't know what's going on with Roger but I'm not sure he can help *himself* at the moment, let alone me."

A few minutes later as Maggie drove the darkening roads to the monastery her stomach was tied in knots. Never before had she deliberately done something she knew would upset Laurent like she was doing right now.

He'd asked her—well, *demanded* actually for all the good that would do—that she not involve herself in this case. If he knew she'd been attacked at home last night and was now going to confront the person most likely to have done that...well, Maggie knew her husband well enough—and his temper well enough—to know how unhappy that would make him.

No, she thought as she maneuvered through Pont l'Abbe on the north side of the monastery. *This is not what Laurent wants or Roger. Or Grace.*

And nobody needed to tell her it was dangerous. Especially after the assault on her back terrace, she *knew* it was dangerous.

She felt a surge of resolve as she parked the car and touched her tummy without thinking.

She didn't know if what she was doing was good or bad, right or wrong.

All she knew for sure was that she had to do it.

58

LOOSE ENDS

Roger sat in front of his computer and scrolled through the long list of names. He'd spent four hours in the middle of the day drinking his lunch and while nobody would care if he hadn't returned, he had nowhere else to go except to another bar.

As he watched the litany of names in the national crime database roll by monotonously, he could only think of how many people had done terrible things in this world. And for all the people that they had a record of, like in this database, there were so many more who, like Laurent, had never even been put in the system. Until now.

Laurent's confession to the nineties crime would change all that. And not just for the reasons that Terrone had given. Surely Laurent must know that Terrone wouldn't stop with Cannes. He would dig up every unsolved con or swindle on the Cote d'Azur in the ten years before Laurent became a *vigneron* and lay them at Laurent's door.

"Did I say you'd get out in time to escort your daughter down the aisle? How about your granddaughter? Sign this new confession or I'll make sure you never get out."

Once Laurent signed that first confession to the Cannes theft, the dominoes would start to fall. And they would never stop falling until Laurent died an old man in prison.

And until she drew her last breath Maggie would spend her life hating me.

"Well, it is official!"

Roger looked up to see Yves Girard leaning against the doorjamb of his office. Roger's stomach convulsed and for a moment, he thought he might throw up on his keyboard just at the sight of the man.

"What is official?" Roger said, careful not to slur his words.

"Dernier," Girard said, stepping into the office and wrinkling his nose as if he'd encountered a bad smell.

"What about him?" Roger said with mounting trepidation.

"He's agreed to make a full confession on the Cannes theft and also one in St-Tropez that we added yesterday, including information that only the thief could know."

Roger felt a slight flutter in his stomach.

"But he hasn't signed anything?" Roger said.

"Oh, he will," Girard said. "Let's just say I was able to encourage him to see the wisdom in signing."

"What do you mean?"

"I told him that an old property lien was found on Domaine St-Buvard calling into question his uncle's ownership of the property and therefore Dernier's ownership through inheritance. I told him there might be a need for his family to move from the property immediately."

Roger wondered if he'd ever hated anyone as much as he hated this man.

"But there is no lien, is there?" Roger said.

"What a suspicious mind you have, Bedard!" Girard said with a mocking laugh. "Does it matter?" He turned on his heel and walked away, leaving Roger's door open to the sounds of the bullpen outside.

Roger watched the man walk away. He watched him until Girard disappeared into the bullpen no doubt to brag about his accomplishment of having secured the confession of one of the Cote d'Azur's most infamous con men.

Roger looked back at his computer screen. What was he even doing here? Pretending to be a detective? Hadn't he always done exactly that? Faked it and somehow that had been good enough? And in the end, failed at even being a friend.

I'm not a hero. I'm not a brave man. I'm just a father who wants to give a good life to my child.

Could he even call himself a policeman? Most of his solved cases—*all* of his solved cases—were solved by Maggie Newberry, a woman he loved but could never have.

And in the end had ended up betraying.

It didn't matter that Laurent had in fact committed the crimes he'd go to jail for. As much as Roger might tell himself it did. He knew in his heart that wasn't the issue. Not even close.

This was a matter of honor.

And it was Roger's biggest failure yet.

Suddenly, his eye caught a name in the line of rolling database names he recognized. He grabbed his mouse and scrolled back up.

Pierre Guillaume. Why did that name ring a bell? Turning to a file on his computer desktop he clicked the basic information from the Dupree case and went to the list of refugees living at the monastery. He found the name on the list. *Pierre Guillaume.*

He frowned and tried to assimilate what this might mean. Many of these people were refugees and all were homeless. Likely half of them had criminal records. It didn't mean anything.

Plus Roger was off the case.

He clicked on Guillaume's name in the database which immediately sent him to a somewhat lengthy juvenile rap sheet. Theft, battery, cruelty to animals. And an active warrant in Nice which was why his name had popped up.

For sexual assault.

The moment Roger saw those two words next to Pierre Guillaume's name he got a sensation he'd never felt before in his fifteen years of detective work. It was a weird tingling sensation in his brain—something Maggie called a "spidey sense." She once told him that it was something every great detective gets—an indefinable trigger that tells him something was important.

Without thinking or knowing even what he was going to say, he picked up his cellphone and called Maggie. He let it ring until the call was about to go to voicemail and then he disconnected.

But he continued to stare at the name on the computer screen.

What did it mean? How did it fit? Was he trying to connect an open rape charge against a seventeen year old with a murder that had no other evidence pointing to the boy?

But there was that tingly sensation. Did that mean anything? Should he pay attention to it?

He'd been told to stay away from all the players in the Dupree case while Girard was wrapping it up.

And besides, a gypsy with a sexual assault complaint was like a bird with feathers. It meant nothing. It certainly wouldn't move Terrone off his determination to nail Laurent for the Cannes job.

Roger's shoulders sagged in defeat.

So basically it was a blind. Something that looked important but was a sham.

Like everything about Roger's life up to now.

Even the spidey sense was a sham. It made him feel for a moment like a real detective. And in the end it was as artificial as everything else in his life.

He shut down his computer, and watched the gypsy's name disappear. Even if Guillaume was the murderer, it wouldn't matter. Roger was out of the game. The sooner he accepted that the sooner he could move on to something else and put all this behind him.

He picked up the phone and called his mother who answered on the first ring.

"*Allo, chéri*," she said happily. "Are we seeing you and Chloe for lunch this weekend?"

"Yes," he said tiredly. "Can you pick her up at dance class tonight? I have to work late."

"Of course. It is not a problem. But I worry you work too much, *chéri*. You look like you have lost weight."

"Thank you, Mother. I will see you this weekend."

Roger hung up and grabbed his jacket, feeling a little woozy and steadied himself on the desk before he put his jacket on.

He'd lately been getting strange looks at his neighborhood bar.

Tonight he would need to find some place new to drink.

59

THE DEVIL YOU KNOW

The monastery walls looked ominous in the dark. The two cylindrical turret towers in front loomed over her, reminding Maggie of past sieges of desperate, beleaguered people. She wondered how many over the centuries had died violently behind these stone walls. She shivered and turned off her car. She'd parked further away than usual, very nearly on the perimeter of the village.

On the drive over she rehearsed her strategy for finding Pierre. Short of barging into the dining hall—probably not a good idea if she didn't want Frère Jean to call the cops again—she would need to surreptitiously explore the perimeter of the complex first. She'd brought a headscarf just in case she needed it to enter the dining hall and walk through it head down.

But that would be a last ditch effort.

It was important that Frère Jean didn't see her. She'd been lucky that Roger had caught the call that had come into the police station from Frère Jean. She couldn't expect her luck to hold a second time.

Grateful for the fact that her coat was a dark navy and would help her blend into the night she held the collar close to her throat.

She skirted the parking lot—absent of vehicles at this time of day—and congratulated herself for not parking there where her car would be immediately recognized. She hurried to the side of the main monastery building.

She stayed in the shadows—or near enough to be able to jump into them in case the small inset wooden front door swung open.

In the week she'd been visiting the monastery she'd gone around the main building to the south stable side and seen the entrance to the monastery garden. She thought she remembered Jean-Luc had explored the north side but she didn't remember what he'd found there.

Edging around the side of the monastery, Maggie saw a partial stonewall that glistened in the dark as if it were sweating. It jutted out from the side of the main building and disappeared into the night.

Maggie followed the wall until she was sure she'd found what had once served as the community churchyard. The wall surrounding the yard stood chest high in some spots and no more than knee high in others where the stones had crumbled or broken away. She placed her hands on the wall and it them—icy and ungiving—beneath her fingers.

She passed the eerie remains of what appeared to have been a massive medieval fireplace. A broken section of spiral stone stairs leading to empty sky hinted at the likelihood that this area had once been indoors and part of the main monastery.

She entered the churchyard and walked amongst the lichen-covered headstones and tombs and immediately saw a girl sitting on a stone bench.

Noelle Dupree was smoking a cigarette and staring up at the sky, her thoughts far away, oblivious to Maggie's presence.

Maggie moved as quietly as she could, painfully aware of

every rustle of the dry weeds and broken stones beneath her shoes.

When she was about twenty feet away, Noelle jerked her attention to where Maggie stood. She threw down her cigarette and stood up.

"I'm sorry," Maggie said quickly. "I didn't mean to disturb you."

Noelle was truly beautiful—the kind of beauty movie directors and photographers discover and make famous. Her clear, perfect skin was offset by thick dark lashes and full lips.

If her eyes hadn't held so much stark terror in them, Maggie would have said Noelle was the most beautiful woman she'd ever seen.

"I'm Maggie Dernier," Maggie said, moving a step closer to the girl.

"I know who you are. Everyone knows who you are."

Maggie wasn't sure if that was good or not.

"So then you know my husband is being held for the murder of your father," Maggie said, knowing that making such a blunt statement could go one of two ways: either it would disarm Noelle or it would make her run.

Maggie could see the battle between exactly those two options race across Noelle's face and Maggie forced herself not to interrupt while the girl decided.

Finally Noelle sat back down heavily in resignation. She dug out another cigarette without looking at Maggie

"Do you smoke?" Noelle asked listlessly.

"Yes, of course," Maggie lied, deciding she'd mainline heroin if it meant keeping the girl talking to her.

Noelle lit a cigarette and handed it to Maggie. Maggie took it gratefully and sat down next to her. She'd been saved the embarrassment of trying to light it herself and demonstrate without a doubt that she'd never done it before.

Now she just needed to smoke it without coughing up a lung.

"I'm sorry about your husband," Noelle said. "I liked him. He was kind."

He still is, Maggie wanted to say, but didn't.

"I have reason to believe your father was killed in his room at the monastery," Maggie said gently. "And that his body was taken to my vineyard."

"You're wrong!" Noelle said sharply. "It's not true!" Noelle's voice edged up into shrillness. Maggie felt a budding revelation as she watched the girl.

She knows her father was killed here. What else does she know?

"Guy Dionne came to my house today," Maggie said putting the cigarette to her lips, sucking in and quickly blowing the smoke back out into the night air.

Noelle's eyes darted around the cemetery. She looked like she was trying to get control of herself after her outburst but she still puffed anxiously on her cigarette.

"He thinks that Pierre killed your father because he wouldn't give his blessing to you dating a gypsy."

Noelle turned to look at Maggie in amazement. "*Guy* told you that?"

"Is it not true?"

Noelle shook her head but not in denial. Even with a cigarette in one hand, she put the other to her mouth to gnaw on her nails. Maggie noticed the nails on both Noelle's hands were chewed to the quick.

"I hate men," Noelle said bitterly. "I hate them all to death."

Maggie wasn't sure how to respond to that or why her comment about Guy might have triggered it so she kept her mouth shut and tried to look sympathetic. She put the cigarette to her mouth again and blew, making the ember glow in much the same way as if she'd taken a real drag.

Finally, no longer able to stand the silence, Maggie said, "Men can certainly be a trial."

Even to her own ears it sounded lame but she needed Noelle to start talking again. As if on cue, Noelle turned to Maggie.

"He raped me," she said, her eyes angry and glistening with tears. "I still can't believe it."

Maggie was stunned. *Who? Guy?*

Noelle twisted the scarf around her neck and shifted in her seat as if she couldn't get comfortable. Her foot swung constantly in agitation.

"Oh, he says he loves me. *Now*," Noelle said bitterly. "And he was very sorry about it *later*." She took another drag off her cigarette and flicked it against the headstones. Maggie immediately threw hers away too.

"That's terrible," Maggie said wondering if the assault was somehow connected to the murder. If Guy raped Noelle, maybe Henri Dupree intervened and was killed in the scuffle?

"Did you tell the police?" Maggie asked.

Noelle's face reddened. "Why in the world would I? I told you. He said he was sorry."

Oh well then, Maggie thought, and she felt her anger beginning to build. *If he said he was sorry...*

Noelle stood up in agitation and rubbed her arms through her jacket.

"*Mon Frère* said we're supposed to forgive," she said, raising her voice, her eyes on the cemetery gate. "And he said he was sorry."

"*Who* was sorry, Noelle? Who are you supposed to forgive? And for what?"

"I forgave him for what he did," Noelle said bitterly, not hearing Maggie now. She looked down at her hands in the picture of dejection. "He asked me to marry him."

Maggie felt a sick cramp in the pit of her stomach.

"Tell me you're not thinking about marrying the guy who sexually assaulted you," Maggie blurted out before she could stop herself.

"I told you! Pierre said he was sorry about that!" Noelle shrieked, her eyes wild and glassy.

So it was Pierre. Not Guy.

"What happened?" Maggie asked gently. "Was Pierre sorry because he attacked you? How about your father? Was Pierre sorry about hurting him, too?"

"Don't talk about it!" Noelle said and put her hands over her ears. "He said he was sorry!"

Fighting her frustration, Maggie tried again. "The night your father died—" she began.

"I don't want to think of that night! I don't want to remember it! He told me it would be better if I forgot what I saw! Leave me alone! Leave both of us alone! He didn't mean to do it! He's sorry for what he did! He told me so!"

"Noelle, wait," Maggie said as the girl lurched to her feet.

But Noelle was done. Pushing Maggie away as she ran to the entrance of the graveyard, the girl ran sobbing into the night.

60

READY OR NOT

As Maggie watched Noelle disappear through the churchyard gate she saw a picture coming together of the young gypsy Pierre beyond Madame Montague's racist epithets. The fact was, regardless of the unfortunate circumstances of his birth or race and the unfair way that the world perceived that, it was beginning to look like Pierre was *not* a good guy.

He raped Noelle.

But did he kill Henri Dupree?

Maggie felt a shiver of anger as she got up to walk back to the monastery. She was sure Pierre hadn't been interviewed by the police. They had their prime suspect safely locked up and felt no need to look at anyone else.

If what Noelle told her was true, then Maggie knew that Pierre had done something terrible the night Dupree was killed. And if the idiot girl was shrugging off sexual assault as a misdemeanor that could be covered by an apology, what else might she excuse?

Murder?

Maggie felt a ripple of excitement. Pierre had motive and

means for killing Henri Dupree—especially if Guy Dionne was telling the truth about Pierre driving the pony cart that night. All that remained now was pinpointing an opportunity for him.

Noelle seemed certainly stupid enough to give her rapist an alibi. Maggie could well imagine it: *"Pierre couldn't possibly have killed my father that night! He was too busy attacking me!"*

Maggie shook her head in disgust. Was Noelle's life so twisted up that she couldn't see she had value? In her mind, what had been done to her—a sexual attack—might warrant an apology but not much more? What had happened to Noelle growing up that could have created such a mindset?

The wind was blowing in sharp angry gusts as Maggie made her way out of the graveyard and around to the front of the refectory. There she saw a small group of men smoking in the front of the main monastery building. She quickly joined them, wishing she had a pack of cigarettes to offer as entrance fee. She needn't have worried. Two of the five men were clearly drunk and all of them were only too happy to have Maggie join them.

In her experience living in France this sort of easy social inclusion was highly unusual—unless of course the French person you were attempting to engage with was seriously hammered.

"*Bonsoir*," Maggie said. "It's cold tonight, isn't it?"

One of the men—easily in his fifties, clean-shaven with bright blue eyes—slipped an arm around Maggie's waist and drew her close to him to the general merriment of his friends. Maggie grinned but felt her shoulders tense. If she had to, she was inches away from kneeing this guy in the family jewels.

Fortunately, his intentions seemed focused more on drunken camaraderie than sex.

"I'm looking for Pierre Guillaume," Maggie said, trying to gauge how her question would be received. If these men leaned toward Madame Montague's point of view, she'd need to amend her approach accordingly.

One of the men spat on the ground. "*Putain*," he said, his eyes looking at Maggie with new and unfriendly interest.

"Because I think he stole my wallet," Maggie said hurriedly.

Instantly the tension in the group dissipated and the men indulged in a few moments of loud racist invective.

Poor Pierre, Maggie couldn't help but think. He probably never had a chance here. On the other hand, he didn't do himself any favors, she remembered. He'd been aggressive to *her*, threatening her with pitchfork, and between what Noelle and Madame Montagne said, possibly even a rapist.

Still. It's always nicer to be judged on your actions, not your race.

"He left," the man with his arm around her said. He released her when he decided he needed two hands to light another cigarette.

"Left for where?" Maggie asked.

"Who knows? Who cares?" another man said. He pulled out a flask from his coat and offered it to Maggie who knew enough about asking questions to readily accept it and pretend to drink.

"*Merci*," she said. "Are you sure? Because I don't want to go to the police about this."

They all laughed. "Good luck with that!" they chortled.

"I thought I heard that the police were here today?" she asked innocently.

They all shook their heads and confirmed to Maggie that if the police had been at the monastery today they would know.

"*Tant pis*, Madame," the one who'd held her said. "Because if the filthy *putain* were still here we would happily kick the shit out of him for you, eh?"

All the other men raucously agreed and Maggie thanked them profusely for their threats of retribution on her behalf before turning and walking toward the other end of the monastery building in the direction of the stables.

She was pretty sure she knew what she was going to see before she got there.

Standing beside the building, she could see not a flutter of crime scene tape or a dropped ball point pen to indicate that the police had been there at all today.

Strike Three, Roger, Maggie thought bitterly.

What good would it do for her to tell him that she had someone—*two* someones—who could give evidence against Pierre for the murder? It seemed Roger was determined to hold on to Laurent regardless of the facts.

The sound of a window opening overhead made Maggie take several steps away from the side of the building. In her experience it wouldn't have been totally improbable to have a jug of dirty water—or worse—dumped on her head.

"*Bonsoir*, Madame Denier!" a woman's voice called out. "Is that you?"

Maggie squinted up at the window and then went to pull out her phone to use the flashlight function before realizing she must have left it in the car.

"Madame Montagne?" Maggie called out.

"You will have to decide if you are going to move in here with us at the monastery or not!" the woman cackled.

"I think Frère Jean will probably block my application," Maggie called up to her to a chortle of laughter. "I was hoping to find Pierre. Is he still here, do you know?"

"No, thank God," Madame Montagne said. "I saw him leave with his rucksack on his shoulder. Gone for good, I'm told."

"When did he leave?"

"First thing this morning," the old woman said. "I was surprised to see him up that early."

First thing this morning would fit if he was the one who attacked me last night.

In any case, in Maggie's mind Pierre running away was a definite admission of guilt.

But there was no way Roger was going to see a gypsy picking up and leaving in the early hours of the morning as significant.

After all, isn't that what gypsies do?

"*Bonne nuit*, Madame Montagne," Maggie said.

"*Bonne nuit*, Madame Dernier. I hope you get your husband back."

Maggie turned back toward her car, her shoulders sagging with discouragement. As far as she was concerned, Pierre leaving was an obvious admission of guilt—at least to something. Maybe he was afraid Noelle would press charges after all?

Relieved that she hadn't bumped into Frère Jean but not sure what her night of questioning had really revealed, Maggie hurried the last few steps to her car, sorry now that she'd parked so far away.

She surprised herself when she reached the car and slipped inside with a feeling of relief. Her heart was pounding as if she'd been followed.

Was she being followed? Did some part of her unconscious brain pick up footsteps behind her? She took in a long breath to steady herself and quickly turned on the ignition.

The car wouldn't start.

A creeping dread began to climb up her arms. She looked at the dashboard but could see nothing that would indicate there was any trouble with the car. She made sure the car was in neutral, she checked that the headlights hadn't been left on—although surely she would have noticed that—and she picked up her phone to shine a light on the darkened dashboard.

Her phone was off.

A needle of fear pierced her as she stared at the phone. She never turned her phone off. Could it have just died? She turned it back on and while she waited for it to boot up she tried the car's ignition again. It still didn't start.

Trying to push down the building panic that was inching up her throat, Maggie debated whether to call Grace or a tow truck.

But when she went to select Grace's phone number in her list of contacts, it wasn't there.

Wiping a sheen off perspiration off her lip, she flipped frantically through her list of contacts and saw in mounting disbelief that they were all gone.

How can that be? How can all my contacts be gone? she thought in growing panic.

Should she call nine-nine-nine? Would that even work? If she called the cops would they arrest her for trespassing?

She heard a sound outside the car, like the crunching of gravel underfoot. She jerked her head around to see but it was too dark. Only the vague gloomy outline of the monastery with its turrets jabbing into the night sky was at all visible.

Maggie swallowed hard and looked back at her phone. Her fingers were now trembling as she started to punch in the emergency number.

At the same time her driver side door wrenched open.

Harsh hands grabbed her by the shoulders and jerked her out of the car.

61

BY THE SKIN OF YOUR TEETH

Maggie's breath left her body in an agonizing explosion as she hit the ground, gravel slamming into her face. She flailed out her arms out to push him away, but her attacker sat on her and wrenched her arms behind her back.

She needed to scream but her breath came in jagged, hysterical puffs, the air knocked out of her. Her heart pounded in her chest like a trapped bird's. Her mind raced and a thought came to her, not fully formed as she registered the realization—hovering on the edges of her consciousness—but in her terror and panic what it meant was just out of grasp.

Her attacker grunted and swore as he secured her hands tightly before pulling her over on her back and stuffing a rag in her mouth. Maggie closed her eyes involuntarily, sure that he would strike her.

She tasted the rag and felt the duct tape secure it, taping over hanks of hair too. She struggled to breathe through her nose, blinking back tears. Her eyes still closed, she felt a burlap sack go over her head and the glimmer of moonlight was blotted out.

Gasping at the sudden darkness Maggie felt her attacker grab her by her jacket and jerk her upright before slinging her over his shoulder.

For one terrible moment she thought she would vomit behind her gag. She clenched her eyes shut to fight the maelstrom in her head of the jostling movement as he walked.

The second she heard the car trunk open, her mind cleared.

And she began to fight.

She couldn't let this happen. She struggled, her movements sluggish and impotent. She felt herself fall as he twisted around abruptly and let her slide off his back into the trunk.

Seconds after he dropped her into the trunk, she heard the lid slam shut. Her body vibrated in the sudden stillness and abrupt lack of physical contact.

She sucked in a long breath, her lungs desperate for air and smelled the stink of damp mildew and petrol. Her ears rang in the silence.

What would he do when the car wouldn't start? He could hardly kidnap her without a car!

Could he?

A splinter of hope pierced her. If he left her here, the car would be discovered by morning.

But why had he taken her at all if he intended to just leave her?

Maggie felt the nausea of her fear and panic threaten to overwhelm her.

He wouldn't leave her. When he couldn't get the car started, he would take her somewhere else.

He would kill her here if he couldn't kill her there.

She had landed on her back with her arms and hands pinned under her weight and she twisted to relieve the pressure from them. She tried to think what she could do when he discovered the car wouldn't start.

She needed to be ready for that. She needed to be poised for when he opened the trunk—to hit him in the face with both feet.

She squirmed around to position herself so she could kick out when the time came and then took a moment to try to calm her ragged, desperate breathing. She didn't seem to be able to take in a big enough breath to satisfy her straining lungs. It felt like she was asphyxiating. She closed her eyes and told herself to *get ready.*

She would have one chance when he opened the trunk once he realized the car wouldn't start. She needed to be ready for him.

The next sensation she felt was a vibrating movement as the car slowly backed out of the parking lot.

He'd gotten the car started.

62

WHAT HAPPENS NOW

Maggie lay in the trunk, her stomach lurching with every turn the car made. Her astonishment that the vehicle was working was quickly swamped by the realization that her attacker must have somehow temporarily disabled it.

So he was waiting for me to return to the car.

She breathed in shallow pants as she tried to calm herself. All she knew about her attacker was that he was male and she was sure he wasn't Frère Jean. Her attacker was muscular and young. She shuffled through the faces of the other monks living at the monastery—none of whom had ever even glanced at her. They were all quite stout.

Her attacker was slim.

She had failed to prevent him from getting her into the car. She needed to make sure that wherever he was taking her—likely some place remote and uninhabited—she was ready for the next opportunity for escape.

Her stomach gurgled and she forced her thoughts away from the baby she carried. She needed to be strong. She couldn't fall apart or give up. She didn't have that luxury.

Suddenly she heard the ring tone that she'd assigned to her phone for Grace. The sound was muffled but definitely coming from the front seat where she'd dropped her phone. Maggie felt a surge of hope that was quickly dashed when the musical chime was abruptly cut off.

He must have declined the call, she thought, her heart sinking at the thought of Grace back at Danielle's house trying to reach her.

The airless atmosphere of the trunk prompted another wave of nausea as the driver took yet another sharp turn. Maggie felt every bump on the ill-kept village roads. Her hands groped behind her for whatever was in the trunk when she suddenly remembered the tire iron Laurent had tossed in the trunk some time last week.

Laurent was very tidy and never more so than when it came to his tools. But as Maggie remembered, something had been going on that day that might have prevented him from putting the tire iron away.

Her heart pounded in her throat as she fumbled desperately with her fingers, a prayer on her lips.

Within seconds her fingers curled around the tool.

She felt a flush of gratitude. Just holding it made her feel better. She tried to imagine how she would use it with her hands tied behind her back. She tried to envision a scenario in which her holding a tire iron with both hands tied behind her back was going to work in her favor.

Pushing the pessimistic thought from her mind, she gripped the tire iron tighter.

It was at least something and even though she had no idea how it might help her in the end...

...she hung on to it for all it was worth.

She felt the car slowing down and after taking a last turn, it stopped. Maggie's muscles tensed and she felt her fingers vibrating as they gripped the iron. She heard the emergency brake being set and the driver's side door open and shut. She felt the car raise a little when her attacker got out of the car.

Her brain humming with fear and desperation, she squirmed around, praying she was facing the right way, and drew her legs up to her chest, ready and poised for when he opened the trunk lid.

63

THE BITE IS ALWAYS WORSE

The trunk lid creaked open. Maggie tried to determine which direction the sound came from but in the end she knew it was irrelevant. If she was facing the wrong way, nothing would matter.

She kicked out violently with both legs and made solid contact against his chest.

She heard him curse. Before she could sit up, he grabbed her foot and yanked her hard, slamming her into the side of the trunk.

"Stop it right now!" he snarled. "You can do nothing about this!"

Underscoring his words, he took her by the shoulders and pulled her roughly out of the trunk. As soon as Maggie felt the ground beneath her feet, she lashed out with a foot but he grabbed her from behind and pulled the tire iron from her hands. He lifted her off the ground.

"Stop it!" he shouted into her ear as he carried her.

Instead, Maggie kicked out with her legs and fought for all she was worth, kicking and flinging her head back into his face. She hit him solidly with her head and he yelled in pain and let go for one brief second. Just as she found her balance, he grabbed her again and threw her over his shoulder still cursing.

"You broke my nose!" he said angrily as he walked.

As she hung on his shoulder Maggie felt her terror ratchet up higher. She kicked again with all her strength. He pivoted sharply and Maggie's stomach lurched. She felt the bile coming up her throat and pressing against the gag in her mouth. She made a choking sound and darkness began to spin around her.

Seconds later she felt an ocean spray on her face. Her head throbbed but she could breathe again. Her eyes fluttered open and she licked her lips. The gag was gone. The sack was off. Her face was wet.

"Drink this," he said. "If you throw it at me I'll tie you up again."

Her eyes fought to adjust to the light, when she realized her hands were unbound. She squinted at her surroundings. She lay on a hard tile floor, her attacker looming over her, holding out a plastic bottle of water.

She blinked, trying to bring her surroundings into focus. Her arms continued to vibrate in a steady aching agony from being twisted under her in the trunk.

Maggie looked from the water bottle to his face.

It was Guy.

"If you don't want it, fine," he said.

She reached for the water bottle, the effort making the muscles in her shoulders scream. She let out a small whimper of pain but brought the bottle to her lips and drank thirstily.

She looked around and realized she was inside one of Laurent's small houses that he'd built for the vineyard workers. This one didn't look finished yet.

"Why have you done this?" she croaked.

Guy stood facing her, his face unreadable. "Why couldn't you have just stayed away?" he muttered. "How is any of this my fault?"

Maggie shifted slowly to a sitting position, her head pounding. She put her hand to her head. Her skull was reverberating with pain and she wondered if she'd hit her head when he'd deposited her on the floor.

"Don't try anything," he said. "I'm warning you." He watched her and cracked his knuckles nervously.

He doesn't know what he's doing, Maggie thought, a small desperate hope beginning to bloom inside her.

"If you let me go," she said, "there's no harm done yet."

"Are you kidding? I kidnapped you! Do you think I'm stupid?"

He ran a hand across his face and turned from her, standing at the small window that looked out over the Domaine St-Buvard vineyards.

He doesn't know what to do with me.

"Was that you last night in my garden?" she asked.

He whirled around. "I already told you, no. Pierre was bragging how he was going to take care of you. So it was probably him."

"Wasn't Pierre worried you might tell the cops what he did?"

"Why the hell would I?"

Maggie tilted her head to look at him. She thought Guy hated Pierre.

Didn't he try to convince me that Pierre was the killer? Why wouldn't he go to the cops if he heard Pierre threatening to harm me?

Unless Guy had a worse secret he needed to hide.

Guy rubbed the back of his neck and refused to look her in the eye.

"Look," he said, "just tell me what Noelle said to you tonight. She told you it was me, didn't she? She told you I killed her father?"

Maggie's eyes widened in astonishment.

Guy killed Dupree? And Noelle knew all along?

"I saw you talking to her!" Guy shouted. "I saw her run off. I am not going to prison for this. Do you hear me?"

"Noelle didn't tell me it was you," Maggie said. "If anything, it sounded like she was saying Pierre killed her father."

"*Pierre?*" Guy's eyes widened in surprise. "She said *Pierre* killed Henri?" He shook his head in bewilderment. "Why would she say that?"

"Maybe she was confused. I know I am. Why are you so shocked that the killer might be Pierre? Isn't that exactly what you told me this afternoon? You told me he was driving the wagon with the body in it."

Guy turned away in disgust. "Whatever."

What was going on? So Guy *didn't* think Pierre killed Dupree?

Afraid he was shutting down, Maggie searched for a way to get him talking again. And then it occurred to her.

"All Noelle told me," she said innocently, "was that Pierre raped her the night of the murder so she—"

"What? What is this you're saying? He raped her?" Guy's face was mottled with outrage and shock. He took two steps toward the door and then stopped.

"If you're thinking of wringing his neck, you can forget it. He's run off."

Maggie pulled herself up to sit on a wooden chair near her. It was cold in the room and her body temperature had dropped. She tried to calm the shaking in her limbs that suddenly seemed to have magnified.

"So are you saying that when you saw me and Noelle talking in the churchyard," Maggie said, "you thought Noelle was telling me it was *you* who killed her father? Is that what Noelle thinks? Why would she think that?"

The fight seemed to have gone out of Guy as the news of Noelle's rape sank in. He shook his head, his shoulders hunched in despair.

"Because it is the truth," he said, his voice thickening.

"You killed Henri Dupree?" Maggie asked breathlessly.

Guy's shoulders slumped as if he'd given up. "I was with him that night," he said. "She came in on us in his room."

An image of the destroyed room came rushing back to Maggie.

"Did she see you fight with him? Is that what happened?"

He nodded miserably.

"What were you fighting about?"

"It doesn't matter."

Maggie wasn't entirely sure how she was going to get Guy to confess to the murder without him then feeling the need to kill *her* to keep it secret.

"The knife in Dupree's chest," she said. "That's not what killed him."

"It was in his back," he said, narrowing his eyes at her. "Was that a trick? You still don't believe I was the one who stabbed him?"

"Okay, fine. But like I said, that's not what killed him. So if you did stab him—and that's all you did—you didn't kill him." She paused a beat. "Why did you stab him?"

"I did it to make it look like...look like..."

"Like he'd been stabbed?"

"Don't mock me," he said fiercely. "I killed him by throwing him out his bedroom window and then took his body to your vineyard in the pony cart."

Whoa. That's pretty much how Jean-Luc had it figured, Maggie thought in a mixture of excitement and dread. But there went any chance of Guy pleading to accidental manslaughter.

Pretty hard to accidentally fling someone out a window

"Why did you take the body to the vineyard?" she asked.

"So people wouldn't suspect it was me, of course."

"Were you wearing gloves? Because your prints will be on the knife handle."

He snorted. "I am not a criminal, Madame. You will not find my prints in any criminal database. And the police have not asked to *take* anyone's prints at the monastery. They have the one they want in custody."

It was something about the way he said that last line—a sentiment that of course Maggie had believed all along—that had a strange ring to it. When Guy said the words *They have the one they want in custody* Maggie's mind suddenly ricocheted back to her first conversation she'd had with Frère Jean.

She felt her pulse speed up as she realized what it was she hadn't been seeing.

Until now.

She'd gotten so distracted by the fact that Frère Jean knew about Laurent's criminal past she had completely skipped over the part where he said *the cops had come to him.*

The revelation stunned her. If she had remembered the comment at all she'd probably just assumed Frère Jean was referring to when the police had come out after the murder to take everyone's statement.

But what if that wasn't what he meant?

"Do you know anything about the statement that Frère Jean gave to the police?" she asked. "The one where he claimed Laurent confessed to him? Do you know if the police asked him to do that?"

"I don't know what you're talking about." He began to pace restlessly and rub his hand over his head and down his arms.

It was possible Guy didn't know. But that didn't matter. Because Frère Jean knew. In a sudden sickening moment of awareness, the unwanted, inescapable thought came to her—

Which means Roger knows.

It would explain so much. Laurent's discouragement, Roger's torment and lack of help, the fact that the police weren't looking anywhere else for a suspect.

Could they really all be dirty?

"You said you didn't plan this," Maggie said. "But you had a gag handy and a bag to put over my head. Not to mention the zip ties."

"I carry the ties with me because of my job at the monastery garden. I use them to stake the corn stalks. The bag I use for collecting rain in the garden. The gag was my own handkerchief."

"Okay, well, now what?" she said quietly. "If you don't let me go, what's next?"

He licked his lips as if he truly hadn't thought that far ahead.

"I'm sorry we don't have a handy window to fling me out of."

It wasn't that she didn't think Guy was dangerous. He was foolish and emotional and obviously had poor judgment. But he was also undecided and confused.

From what little she'd seen, she didn't think he was a cold-blooded killer. What had happened with Dupree must have been a crime of passion. Guy seemed contrite and tortured.

Not the mindset of most murderers.

"I could strangle you," he said, still rubbing his hands on his arms as if to wipe the tension from them.

"I think you'll find it's not as easy as they make it look on TV."

A sheen of sweat coated his cheeks and forehead as he continued to rub the back of his neck in agitation.

"Why couldn't you just let it alone?" he asked plaintively.

"Because my husband is being held for the murder."

He looked around for the sack that had been over her head and found it on the floor. He picked it up and stared at it as if trying to figure out how to use it.

Maggie felt a flinch of fear. Had she misjudged him? She hadn't thought him capable of callous, cold-blooded murder. But when pushed to the limit, one thing she'd learned long ago was that most people are.

"Just let me go," she said.

"I can't."

"Sure you can."

"You will go to the police."

"As soon as they start processing the scene at the monastery they're going to know it was you anyway."

But that was a lie. The police weren't going to process anything now that they had Laurent.

Did Guy know that?

"Listen to me, Guy," Maggie said, her panic beginning to build in her as she saw him stare at the bag, "Maybe Dupree's death was as an accident. But if you kill *me*, there's no question at all. And because I'm an American citizen, you'll be extradited to my home state of Georgia and given a one way trip to Old Sparky."

"Old...?"

"The electric chair. You do know we still have capital punishment, right?"

Guy looked started. "Can...can they do that?"

"Oh, yeah. You kill me and the French government will hand you right over for immediate execution. Are you even a French citizen? You look Greek or Spanish to me."

"I, well, uh," he said nervously.

"Never mind. It doesn't matter. Accidentally killing Dupree is one thing, but killing an American citizen on purpose? You'll be toast. *Literally.*"

"Dupree's death was no accident," Guy said.

Maggie was surprised. And now suddenly worried. If Guy really did kill Dupree on purpose...if she really was that wrong about him and what he was capable of...well, it didn't bode well for *her.*

Maggie had given Guy every opportunity to say Dupree's death was an accident and that kidnapping her had been an unplanned and now regretted impulse. Guy didn't seem interested in grabbing for either way out.

"I don't want to hurt you, Madame, but what choice do I have?"

"You have every choice!" Maggie said stridently as Guy

dropped the bag and pulled out a length of short rope from his pocket. He stared at it for a moment, emitting a guttural sound that resembled an animal whimper.

Holding it in both hands, he took a step toward Maggie. She watched him come in frozen shock.

"I am sorry, Madame," he said. "May God forgive me."

64

RIVER DEEP, MOUNTAIN HIGH

"Stop it this instant!" Maggie said, her voice firm as she fought to hide her tremors as he stood over her, the section of rope in his hands. "Why would you untie me or give me water if you were going to kill me? You're *not* a murderer."

"I *am* too!" Guy moaned, curling his arms over his head in a protective gesture.

"I don't believe it," Maggie said. "I don't know what happened with Henri Dupree but you're not a killer."

She saw his arms drop to his sides as his shoulders began to heave with the sobs that wracked his diaphragm.

Just then a deep voice from outside boomed out.

"Open up! This is the police!"

Guy reacted quicker than Maggie, turning and wrenching open the back window. He crawled through seconds before the front door exploded into splinters of board and plaster as Roger Bedard burst into the room followed by Grace's handyman Gabriel.

"Maggie, are you okay?" Roger said, running to her.

"Yes! Hurry! He went out the back window! It's Guy Dionne!"

"Take her back to Madame Van Sant's!" Roger shouted to Gabriel as he ran to the back window and hoisted himself out.

Maggie turned to Gabriel. "Don't just stand there! Go help him!" she shouted.

As young as Guy was, his head start clearly hadn't been enough. Maggie ran to the back window in time to see Roger tackle the young man to the ground. She nearly cheered out loud.

Within moments Roger came back through the front door, dragging Guy between him and Gabriel, the young man's hands handcuffed behind his back.

"I thought I told you to go to Grace's," Roger said to Maggie, but she could tell by the flush of excitement on his face that he wasn't really angry with her.

"He killed Dupree," Maggie said. "He confessed to me." She knew her word wouldn't be enough. Who would believe the wife of the prime suspect?

"I know," Roger said. "He confessed to me too."

"He did?" Maggie narrowed her eyes at Guy who was staring at the floor, chewing his lip and looking the picture of mulish resistance. "Oh. Well, that makes things convenient."

"I've called for back up," Roger said as he slammed Guy into the chair that Maggie had been sitting in. He gestured to Gabriel. "Watch him." Then he motioned for Maggie to follow him outside.

"I can't believe he confessed to you," she said. "And Gabriel heard it too?"

Roger nodded. "There seems little doubt he will recant. He was eager to tell me the truth. Maggie, you are hurt."

Maggie stared down at the rip in the knee of her jeans where she'd hit the gravel parking lot when Guy pulled her out of the car. She gingerly touched her cheek too but the abrasion had stopped bleeding.

"I'm fine," she said. "How did you know how to find me?"

"First tell me what happened," Roger said firmly. He was still eyeing her as if checking for injuries. But there was a lively sparkle in his eye that Maggie had not seen in a very long time.

"I went to the monastery to talk to Pierre Guillaume," she said.

"Dear God, why?" He wiped his face with a hand and then stood facing her with both hands on his hips.

"Well, because Guy told me he saw Pierre driving the pony cart with Dupree's body in it."

Roger frowned. "When did he tell you that?"

"This afternoon. He came to Domaine St-Buvard."

He sighed and shook his head. "Go on."

"So I came to the monastery to find Pierre and I ran into Noelle who seemed to confirm that Pierre had in fact killed her father. So I went looking for him but it turns out he's run off."

"Thank goodness you went looking for a suspected murderer on your own," Roger said. "That was quick thinking."

"Are you being sarcastic?" Maggie said, frowning.

"What an idiotic thing to do!" Roger made an effort to control his temper. "I put a country-wide alert out on Guillaume this afternoon."

"Really? So you suspected him too? When? Why?"

Roger waved away her questions. "What happened after you talked to Noelle?"

"Well, since Pierre had made a run for it I figured that was an admission of guilt so then I went to leave but my car wouldn't start."

Roger glanced at Maggie's car now parked in front of the cabin.

"Guy must have disabled it so he could grab me," Maggie said. "He put me in the trunk and drove me here where he confessed to killing Dupree. He thought Noelle had already told me."

"So Noelle Dupree knew? Did Dionne tell you *why* he killed Dupree?"

"He said he went to Dupree's room to complain about his behavior with Noelle and they fought."

"*D'accord.* I need you to leave now, Maggie," Roger said tensely. "Gabriel will drive you back to Madame Alexandre's."

"Why can't I stay? I can give my statement to the detectives when they arrive."

Maggie could hear a police siren in the distance growing closer.

"I have just taken your statement, *chérie*," Roger said. "While in the end I will not be able to keep you completely out of it, it would be best if you were not here right now."

As Roger turned to go back into the cottage, Maggie said, "So how did you know I was here?"

He laughed, again, mirthlessly. "It was the tracking app you put on Grace's phone a few days ago."

Maggie's eyes widened. After Grace had gotten hopelessly lost trying to meet Maggie on the road, Maggie had downloaded the app to her phone.

"When I came looking for you tonight and couldn't reach you," Roger said, "I called Grace and drove to her when she said she could track your location with the app you downloaded for her. She mentioned Laurent has one on his phone too?"

"For all the good it does him in the kitchen drawer. He never uses it."

"He might after tonight."

By the time Gabriel and Maggie arrived at Danielle's house it was past midnight. Maggie had called Grace to tell her she was coming and Grace had run to Domaine St-Buvard to pick up the two dogs and bring them to Danielle's.

When Maggie got out of the car in Danielle and Jean-Luc's

driveway, she felt every inch of having been thrown to the ground, stuffed in a trunk, and manhandled. She ached all over and walked slowly to the front door where both Danielle and Grace awaited her.

Wordlessly the two women opened their arms and drew her in where they held her for long moments before the two big dogs began jumping around them forcing them to move into the house. A fire was in the hearth in the annex room and Maggie saw evidence of knitting and embroidery. Pretty clearly as soon as Roger had shown up hours earlier, Grace and Danielle had begun their vigil.

It's even harder on the ones waiting at home, Maggie knew.

Grace settled Maggie onto the couch with an afghan across her knees while Danielle made her a stout cup of tea.

"Tell us everything," Grace said. "We've been worried to death."

Buddy jumped up on the couch next to Maggie and snuggled against her hip. Because he was a standard poodle he had the same curly hair as Petit-Four.

"Guy Dionne forced me into my car and took me to one of Laurent's unfinished houses," Maggie said.

"Whatever for?" Danielle said as she set the tray of hot drinks down.

"He thought that Noelle—the victim's daughter—had told me that she saw him kill her father."

"*Mon Dieu!*" Danielle said. "*C'est terrible!*"

"Yeah, so he was very upset. Danielle, do you have any ibuprofen?"

"*Oui, chérie.* He hurt you?"

"No, just grabbed me and pushed me around a bunch. I'm going to be a mess of bruises tomorrow. Thank God Roger was able to use the tracking device on your phone, Grace."

"Well, thank goodness you put it on there. Remind me to put one on Zouzou's phone when she's a little older."

Danielle came back with a glass of water and handed Maggie the pills.

"So Guy killed Henri Dupree?" Grace asked.

"He confessed it all to me," Maggie said. "And also to Roger."

"Does that mean Laurent will be released soon?"

Maggie shrugged helplessly. "Honestly, something's going on with Laurent that I don't think is even connected to the murder."

"What did Roger say?"

"Not much," Maggie said. "He wanted me gone before his men got there. I thought that was weird too, you know?" She sipped her tea. "Oh, Danielle, this is perfect. Thank you."

"We were so worried, *chérie*," Danielle said and she reached over and took Maggie's hand.

"I know and I'm sorry," Maggie said. "I just wish Jean-Luc could have seen the end and how it all turned out."

"Are you hungry?" Danielle asked, brushing away her tears and smiling. "I have a very good *coq au vin* that only needs to be reheated. In fact I have three gallons of *cassoulet*."

All three women laughed and Maggie said, "That sounds wonderful. Need help?"

"*Non.* You have done quite enough for tonight," Danielle said.

Once Danielle left, Maggie turned to Grace. "Tell me the kids weren't too badly freaked out?"

Grace hesitated. "They know something's going on but they're okay."

There was a knock at the door and Maggie felt a stab of fear.

"Who would be visiting at this time of night?" Maggie said with consternation as both dogs bolted, barking for the door.

Possibly Roger? Did the police want to take her statement after all?

Grace hurried to the door but Maggie's exhaustion and apprehension kept her rooted to the couch.

Whatever it was, Grace would deal with it.

Maggie heard his voice in the hallway like out of a dream and before she even recognized it for sure, her body reacted to it. She was off the couch and running.

He filled the foyer, his hair windswept and wild about his shoulders, his eyes darting from Grace over her shoulder to the one he sought.

"Laurent!" Maggie cried.

In two strides, he reached her and swept her up into his arms.

65

EDGE OF GLORY

Later Maggie would remember the details of seeing Laurent again—the joy of watching his eyes crinkle when he smiled, of feeling his arms around her, holding her close. But when the moment actually happened, she only felt and saw the fact that he was finally with her again.

After greeting both Grace and Danielle Laurent stood in the kitchen and told them how it was he came to be released. He made garlic toast to go with *foie gras* and onion and pear chutney to go with the *coq au vin*, while Buddy and Izzy jumped and paced around him. It was nearly two in the morning.

At one point after Danielle had persuaded Maggie and Laurent to stay the night so that the children didn't have to be awakened, she and Grace went to make the guest room ready. Laurent went to where Maggie stood by the fire in the annex room.

She expected him to kiss her or take her into his arms but instead he cupped her face with one large hand, his eyes worried and serious.

The black eye must look even worse today, Maggie couldn't help but think. Not to mention the gravel that had gotten scraped into her chin when Guy jerked her out of the car.

"It's nothing, Laurent. I'm fine."

"I know," he said, but his eyes were clearly registering something else. Was he remembering how she refused to do what he'd asked when he was powerless? How she'd endangered not only herself but their unborn child? Was he remembering how when the chips were down, he couldn't count on her to help him not worry about her and the children?

She swallowed and put her hand on his.

"I love you, Laurent," she said, her eyes filling with tears. "I couldn't just let them take you."

"*Je sais,*" he said. *I know.*

"Forgive me," she said, because she knew right or wrong, it had to be said.

He leaned over and kissed her. "There is nothing to forgive."

Later that night in Danielle's guest room, with the two dogs overfed and finally settled down on a rug on the floor in their room, and after a long hot shower, Maggie snuggled up against Laurent in bed.

It was almost impossible to believe that a few hours earlier she'd been riding in a car trunk—her own car trunk—anticipating a fight for her life. She wasn't sure how much Roger had told Laurent—or even if the two had spoken tonight—but she hoped very much that the details of her night wouldn't need to be revealed completely to her husband.

He's been through enough.

"How is it they were able to release you in the middle of the night?" she asked with a yawn as Laurent turned off the bedside light.

"I think Bedard was pushing all the buttons by then," Laurent said. "He was like a man possessed. When he gave orders for my release it was to be done immediately and without question."

"Took him long enough."

Laurent turned to face Maggie as they lay in bed.

"*Chérie*, you know Roger was under considerable pressure. I never expected him to do what he did."

"What do you mean? I practically laid out the evidence for him."

"The evidence was not the problem."

"Why are you being so mysterious? What *else* was the problem?"

Laurent leaned over and kissed her and Maggie got the idea it was to soften the blow of whatever he intended to say next.

"He'd been taken off the case, *chérie*," he said. "What he did tonight will finish him in Aix as *Commandant de Police*."

Maggie sat up in bed. "What? What do you mean? Why was he taken off the case?"

"Lie back down, *chérie*," Laurent said, patting the bed. "Morning will be here soon. We both need sleep."

"*Why* would releasing you result in a demotion for him?" Maggie pressed. "I don't understand. He's a hero."

"*Non, chérie*," Laurent said tiredly. "He used the rank of his command to have me released and to find you and the real murderer tonight but he disobeyed a direct order from a superior officer to do it."

"Well, in the scheme of things that doesn't seem like a very terrible—"

"And he made a formal charge of corruption against his immediate superior."

"I knew it!" Maggie said excitedly. "I *knew* there was something rotten going on! And you did too, didn't you? But you wouldn't tell me."

"There was nothing anyone could do, Maggie. All your sleuthing and questioning...even uncovering the real killer...none of it was going to fix this. Only Roger could do that. And he needed to destroy his career to do it."

"But...but Roger made the arrest! He found the real killer," Maggie said.

"Yes, *chérie*, but he betrayed his division to do it. There's no one there who will trust him again."

"That makes no sense."

"It does if your job is to work as a team," Laurent said.

"His team was rotten!"

Maggie remembered how haggard and ill Roger had looked this past week. How distracted and tortured. He'd been wrestling with the dilemma of needing to do the right thing—at the cost of his career and livelihood.

"It's not fair," she said softly, lying down again next to Laurent.

A moment passed and Maggie turned and felt Laurent pull her to him, his arms wrapping around her. The bliss of having him beside her was so intense, she felt tears gathering in her eyes.

It was over. It was all over.

Almost.

"There are still a few things left to sort out," she said. "Like *why* did Frère Jean lie? I think I already figured out that the cops probably approached him with the idea."

Laurent murmured. "My understanding is that he did it to protect the killer. The real question is why did Frère Jean suspect Guy in the first place?"

"That's easy. He probably saw Guy leave that night in the pony cart wearing monk's robes. And then when Guy came back, Frère Jean likely found evidence in the cart, like bloody clothing, that he couldn't understand. Then the next morning when he found out Dupree was missing, he assumed the worst about Guy."

"Frère Jean's life will be ruined now," Laurent said darkly. "A human rights hero or not, he could go to jail." He shook his head. "Why would he risk everything?"

"My guess? He felt protective toward Guy in a way that isn't condoned by the Catholic Church."

"Ahh."

Maggie turned around in Laurent's arms to face him.

"Just like I think Guy confessed to killing Dupree to protect someone else," she said.

Laurent looked at her in astonishment. "You don't think Guy killed Dupree?"

"I know for a fact he didn't."

66
AIN'T NOTHING LIKE THE REAL THING

The next morning began with pancakes *á la* Laurent, the fragrance of which brought squeals of delight from all three children as they ran downstairs to join the two puppies jumping around Laurent's knees.

Danielle, Grace and Maggie watched the activity from the annex where they sat with their morning coffees.

"I can't believe he's back," Grace said, smiling over her coffee mug. "Watching him in there like the French Pied Piper, it's like he never left."

"I know," Maggie said.

"So tell us again," Grace said. "Roger's department is corrupt? And they were holding Laurent on the barest shreds of circumstantial evidence so they could get him on other charges?"

"I don't know the details," Maggie said. "And I probably never will. You know Laurent. But that's roughly the size of it."

"And Inspector Bedard sacrificed his career to right this wrong?" Danielle asked.

"In a nutshell," Maggie said and when Danielle frowned at the American idiom, she said. "*Exactement.*"

"Poor Roger," Grace said. "Do you think this will mean he has to move from Provence? I know his little girl takes dance lessons in Aix, doesn't she?"

Maggie had forgotten about that. What Roger had done had caused celebration and thanksgiving in this household but it was likely a very different story in Roger's home.

One of the dogs ran into the annex looking around frantically as if for a treat or one of her toys and then bounded back to the kitchen where the children had now settled down at the kitchen island while Laurent plated up stacks of his famous crepes.

"It is so quiet when you are not here," Danielle said softly.

Both Grace and Maggie reached over and took her hand. Maggie knew that in the few days since Jean-Luc died Danielle had yet to be alone. Her house was always filled with the sounds of children, animals and well-meaning neighbors. But of course Danielle knew that could not last.

"I was thinking maybe," Grace said carefully, "that you might want to come to *Dormir* to live with me and Zouzou. I'm not trying to get live-in domestic help," she said hurriedly. "But it's a big place. I mean, you should know. It used to be your house."

Tears filled Danielle's eyes and she looked gratefully at Grace.

"Oh, *chérie*, are you sure?" she said.

Grace laughed and threw her arms around Danielle. "Am I sure?" she laughed, choking back her own tears. "Gosh, yes, Danielle. I would love it."

Maggie basked in the love and camaraderie of her two dearest friends and relished the sounds of laughter from the kitchen along with Laurent's voice in his low timber underpinning the chatter and the noise.

And she couldn't help but think how much Jean-Luc would have loved to have seen this morning.

∽

That afternoon after a quick visit to check on her parents, Maggie and Laurent sat in the waiting room of the Aix Police Station. At first she'd suggested that Laurent not come with her. After all, she could only imagine having to return to this place after only a single night away from it.

But Laurent wouldn't hear of it.

Even though Maggie had spackled heavy makeup over the slowly yellowing bruises of her run-in with Pierre Guillaume three days earlier, the signs of the encounter were there to see.

And Laurent had very good vision.

Maggie had tried several times to reach Roger on his phone but while the texts she sent came back as *Delivered*, no answers followed. Laurent encouraged her not to take it personally. Roger had a lot on his plate these days and none of it good.

A phone call from Laurent, however, had obviously connected because Roger had been able to set up this meeting today with the team who'd taken over the Dupree homicide case. While no longer in charge, or even an Inspector any more, Roger still had enough clout to insist Maggie be allowed to visit Guy Dionne in custody.

The detective who ushered them into the interview room was grim-faced and intractable. He was young and Maggie didn't remember seeing him around the station. It seemed likely that he had been brought in from outside the district.

And was none too happy about it.

The detective who'd come to get them from the waiting room now paused at the door to the interview room before opening it and leading Maggie and Laurent inside. There, two other detectives sat staring sullenly at them.

Guy Dionne sat at a metal table in the center of the room. His hands were cuffed to a steel loop on the table, his head was in his hands. He looked up when they entered, his freshly broken nose had not been set since Maggie saw him last. Guy looked first at her and then, whitening, at Laurent.

He's probably glad he's in a police station about now, Maggie thought. She felt Laurent stiffen with fury beside her.

The two detectives didn't bother introducing themselves but one of them stood up, vacating the chair opposite Guy. The other detective stood and the two leaned against the wall, both of their arms crossed on their chests.

Maggie didn't see any sense in prolonging anyone's misery. She strode to the chair and sat. Laurent took up his position beside her, glaring at the two detectives as if they were personally responsible for his recent eight-day incarceration.

"Good afternoon, Guy," Maggie said tartly. "I'm going to begin by saying I haven't brought a charge of attempted murder against you since I'm going to assume you wouldn't have been able to go through with strangling me."

"I swear I could not have done it!" Guy said, addressing Laurent, not Maggie.

"Yes, well, I'm going to give you the benefit of the doubt on that," Maggie said primly.

"I've only come here to see if there's any way I can talk you out of throwing your life away for nothing."

Guy's glance flickered to the detectives.

"Please look at me, Guy," Maggie said.

When he did, she leaned across the table toward him.

"I know you didn't kill Henri Dupree," she said.

He swallowed and Maggie heard one of the detectives snigger.

"You know what else I know?" she said quietly. "I know that Noelle is a very confused girl and right now she thinks you killed her father."

"I did kill him," Guy muttered, looking down at his handcuffed hands.

"And I know," Maggie continued, "that if you go to prison for this...if you let her believe you killed her father, she'll have been betrayed by everyone she ever trusted." Maggie let the silence fill the room before speaking again.

"She's strong enough to hear the truth, Guy."

"She will blame herself," he said softly.

"Maybe at first," Maggie said. "But she'll come to grips with it, I promise. You need to tell the police how Henri Dupree really died."

At first she wasn't sure Guy would talk and so she waited. The detectives, clearly used to waiting for a suspect to eventually break down and speak, were silent and unshifting in their stances.

Finally, Guy sighed and tears gathered in his eyes.

"He treated her like a dog," he said in a low voice. "Especially that day."

"Speak up, please," one of the detectives said. "The mike can't pick up your voice when you mumble."

Maggie forced herself not to glare at the detective. *It was almost like he doesn't want to hear the truth.*

Guy cleared his throat.

"I went to Monsieur Dupree's room to talk to him about Noelle. About why he was being such a *putain*. I knocked on the door but there was no answer. I knew he was there so I just went in and when I did..." He held out his hands as if not sure how to describe what he saw.

"He was standing on the chair, wasn't he?" Maggie said. "In the process of hanging himself."

Guy nodded.

"He had a rope around his neck," Guy said. "I ran to him and said *what are you doing you crazy bastard*? I ran to him and dragged him off the chair. He fought me. He wanted to be allowed to die."

"That's how you got your split lip, isn't it?"

But Guy didn't hear her. He was remembering that night.

"He didn't want to live with the pain any more," he said

morosely. "He'd been drinking and he hated himself for that too. He'd had a fight with Noelle at dinner and she said she hated him." He looked up at Maggie in appeal. "You see how I couldn't let her know what he intended to do? Noelle is very religious. It would have killed her."

"She came in and saw you fighting with her father, didn't she?" Maggie asked gently.

Guy nodded. "I'd had a bunch of zip ties in my pocket from working in the garden securing the corn stalks to stakes. I figured if I tied his hands I could talk with him without him doing something crazy...but when Noelle came in, I was distracted for just a moment..."

He shook his head and the tears rolled down his cheek.

"He ran for the window and jumped," he said.

The silence in the room was oppressive. Maggie looked up to see that the two detectives were looking at each other.

Maggie knew she was doing the best she could for Guy—allowing the truth to give him some chance at a life. Whether the cops believed him or whether Guy's defense attorney could convince a judge or jury—that was out of her hands.

"Noelle ran away before her father jumped," he said. "So she didn't see him do it. When I looked out the window I saw him all crumpled underneath the tree." He covered his face with his hands. "I ran outside but it was dinnertime so nobody had seen or heard. I knew I had to get rid of the body. If I'd just left him there everyone would know it was a suicide."

"So you took the pony cart and took him to my vineyard?" Laurent said.

Guy looked at him, his face stricken with guilt.

"I wasn't trying to frame you for it," he said. "I was trying to get the body away from the monastery. I've seen enough American television to know the police would process the scene and eventually discover the truth."

"And the knife?" one of the detectives asked.

Maggie thought the detective asking questions was a good sign.

"I saw it glinting in the moonlight between the rows in the vineyard like a gift from God," Guy said. "I was trying to make it look like it wasn't suicide."

"Weren't you afraid Noelle would tell what she'd seen?" Maggie asked.

"I was at first. But then I thought her thinking I killed her father was at least a little better than the truth. I can't let her know *she* was the reason her father died. Because if she only hadn't distracted me..."

"Guy, no. Noelle isn't the reason her father died," Maggie said as she stood up from the desk. "*Her father* is the reason."

"But if she hadn't come in right then," he said disconsolately, "I would've stopped him."

"And he'd just have done it another time," Maggie said sadly.

67

TWO WEEKS LATER

Maggie ran over the grocery list to make sure she didn't need to go to the *boulangerie* in St-Buvard that afternoon when she was in the village. Laurent had already taken her parents and the kids there once today and they had all the *ficelles, brioche* and *pain de campagne* that any family would need for at least twenty-four hours.

After a rough few days her parents had settled into life at Domaine St-Buvard and Maggie could already see evidence of her mother's improved spirits after two short weeks.

Elspeth was more relaxed and had taken an interest in the back garden. Maggie began to see glimpses of the mother she'd known all her life, the one who was interested in learning new things and wasn't afraid to walk alone in the village.

As for her father, Laurent took long walks with him and Jemmy and Mila both gave him and Elspeth as much attention as any family had for beloved grandparents. It wasn't always smooth but they shared the burden now and it felt right. Maggie's brother Ben was planning on bringing Nicole—who had spent the fall living with friends in Atlanta—over for the Christmas holidays and both her parents were excited about that.

It was a cold afternoon—the week before Thanksgiving—but even now Maggie could spot her mother in the garden getting some sun on her face and relaxing as she had gotten into the habit of doing every afternoon when Maggie's father went down for his afternoon nap.

Jemmy and Mila were both at *Dormir* this afternoon helping Zouzou bake cupcakes in advance of the holidays. Danielle had officially moved to *Dormir* and she and Grace had made their partnership legally binding. Every time Maggie saw either of them it was very clearly a very good fit for both of them.

Maggie glanced at her watch and realized she was running late. She still needed to drop by the post office and the *charcuterie* before meeting Laurent and Roger at Le Canard although she was fairly confident the two men would find something to talk about before she got there.

Laurent leaned back in the chair of Le Canard, a *pastis* in front of him. It was too cold to be sitting outside so he and Roger had the outdoor terrace to themselves. Roger faced him across the table with a glass of beer by his hand.

He looked better, Laurent thought as he regarded Roger. His hair was longer and he wore a shaggy pullover under a wool pea coat—much less tidy than his usual attire. But all told, he looked rested and at peace.

"I don't want to tell you before Maggie gets here," Roger said, "and end up repeating myself."

Laurent lifted a finger to Gaspard Theroux Le Canard's proprietor to indicate another round.

"I'll fill her in later," Laurent said. "Let's hear it."

He didn't mean to sound abrupt. He was aware of what it had cost Roger to finally do the right thing. There were people in the world—mostly women—and certainly his own wife—who would lavish endless praise on Bedard for doing what he should have done initially. Bedard wouldn't expect it of Laurent.

After all, Bedard was very familiar with the inhospitable accommodations at Clairvaux Prison in northern France. He knew exactly what Laurent had been facing.

And it had still taken him a full eight days to put the brakes on the out of control train rushing down the track.

Laurent didn't spend much time wondering what he would have done if Roger hadn't come through. Terrone was good at what he did and his last play had been flawless. When Laurent had been threatened with the loss of Domaine St-Buvard and their family home he'd had no other recourse but to capitulate.

Well, there had been one other recourse.

Even now he wasn't sure he would have done it. And since in the end he hadn't needed to there was no point in dwelling on it.

But if he'd had to do it, he knew it would have altered his life going forward forever. And not in a good way.

Doing it would have fundamentally changed him such that he would have no longer been the man that Maggie married. Nor possibly would she have wanted to continue to be married to him. But losing her, although worse than a lifetime in prison, even that was not as bad as his children losing their family home.

In the end, he hadn't had to do the unthinkable.

Not this time anyway.

"Why did Frère Jean falsify the confession?" Laurent asked.

"To protect Guy Dionne who I take it the monk was in love with or something."

"Why did he believe Guy had killed Dupree?"

"He saw Dionne leave the monastery in the horse wagon and later when he returned Frère Jean went to talk to him and failing to find him, looked inside the wagon." Roger grinned wryly. "I think the good monk was afraid that Guy had taken the wagon out for a rendezvous with a lover—and instead he found bloody towels. Not knowing what to make of them, Frère Jean instinctively took the wrappings to his room intending to ask Guy about them later."

"Anyway," Roger continued, "the next morning when Noelle came to him asking if he'd seen her father, Frère Jean didn't connect Dupree's disappearance or the bloody towels with Guy. That's when he called Maggie hoping to get a hold of you to see if you'd seen him. When the police showed up to say Dupree had been found murdered in your vineyard, Frère Jean put the pony cart and the bloody towels together and came up with the young man he was besotted with as a killer."

"Did he ever confront Dionne?"

"No. I guess after the initial horror of it all he became solely focused on protecting Guy to make sure the boy didn't ruin his life over what he'd done."

"Over committing murder."

"I'd say it's safe to say the good brother was not thinking clearly."

"And the false testimony?" Laurent asked as Theroux dropped off two more drinks and quickly left the chilly terrace.

Roger ground his teeth and his face hardened.

"Yves Girard had a private conversation with Frère Jean that very first day," he said, "and picked up that the monk was trying to protect someone. Girard told Frère Jean he needed to create a false deposition to keep the real killer safe from prosecution and he told him exactly how to do that."

Roger pulled out an envelope and pushed it across the table to Laurent.

Laurent saw his name scrawled on the outside.

"It's from Frère Jean," Roger said. "He asked me to see that you got it. I'm pretty sure it's a heart-felt apology for trying to make it look like you were the killer."

Laurent picked it up and slid it in his jacket pocket.

"Is there any *evidence* of this private conversation with Girard?"

"Not any that would end up in an indictment against him or Terrone. They covered their tracks fairly well."

"And they're still in the force."

"They were transferred to Normandy."

"It's nice up there."

"It's not the south of France," Roger said.

Laurent shrugged. "What is next for Frère Jean?"

"He'll be indicted for giving false testimony, defrocked and likely forced to serve some kind of probationary period," Roger said.

Laurent nodded. Even before he read the monk's letter, he knew he'd be asking Frère Jean to continue his work at *l'Abbaye de Sainte-Trinité*. Frère Jean had made a mistake because he was human. But he would do just as good work for the community as a defrocked monk as he had before. And Laurent was pretty sure it wouldn't alter the man's relationship much with the Almighty.

Laurent saw Maggie's car pull into a parking spot in front of the *charcuterie* and a smile played on his lips. He loved watching her when she didn't know it. She was studiously unselfconscious as she moved—graceful yet deliberate. Like most American women, her strides were purposeful and determined.

"One last question," Laurent said, "before we are joined by *ma femme*."

Roger turned to see where Laurent was looking and Laurent noticed he sat up straighter when he saw Maggie.

"Yes?" Roger said.

"How did you know to go looking for Maggie the day she was attacked by Dionne?"

"Surely Maggie already told you?"

"The important parts. You will tell me the rest. How did you know?"

Roger grinned. "It was really the damnest thing. I was in my car driving to Eguilles to this bar I know, intending to get drunk minutes before I pulled off the road and made a course correction."

Laurent lifted his eyebrows in query.

"Maggie told me once years ago about something she called a spidey-sense," Roger said. "I had never heard of it before but as I understand it, it means that undefinable sensation one gets when, even in the absence of recognizable facts, you just *know* something. Or if you don't know it, you at least start to wonder about it. I'd never felt that until that afternoon. Scrolling through a national crime database on an unrelated case I came across a name that I recognized as one of the refugees at the monastery. Pierre Guillaume. Seemed he was wanted in Nice for sexual assault."

"What did that mean to you?"

"In itself nothing," Roger said with a shrug. "See? It didn't mean anything on its own but I got that tingling feeling in the base of my skull that said it was something."

"But Guillaume was not the murderer."

"No, but he was a key piece of the puzzle. He was also the thing that was luring Maggie that night, drawing her to the monastery, although I didn't know it at the time."

"And so you stopped your car and decided to go to the monastery?"

"Better than that," Roger said proudly. "I decided to be a policeman for a change. I called an APB on the kid with the last known address as *l'Abbaye de Sainte-Trinité*. And then I began to drive to the monastery to make the arrest while trying to get a hold of Maggie. You won't be surprised to know Laurent that your wife called or texted me an average of a dozen times a day while you were incarcerated. And now she was unreachable?"

"Was that so hard to believe?"

"For a mother with children? Maggie would never leave the house with her phone not fully charged nor would she go anywhere without it inches from her fingertips. When I couldn't reach her, my new-found spidey-sense went crazy. I called Madame Alexandre who handed me off to Grace Van Sant who was there at the time. When I spoke to Grace, she told me where Maggie had gone and she also told me that she wasn't able to reach her either. She said it didn't make sense because when she tracked Maggie's phone—"

"She was able to track Maggie?" Laurent said in surprise.

"I'm surprised Maggie didn't tell you this," Roger said. "Yes. The device pinpointed her whereabouts exactly. I drove to Grace's, picked up her phone with the tracking device, recruited her handyman, Gabriel Près, and we went charging out with regimental flags flying to the little pulsating dot on the phone screen." Roger grinned in spite of himself.

"Just in the nick of time," Laurent said dryly. No he hadn't heard the details of that night, just seen the evidence of Maggie's bruises and her evasive answers. If Roger hadn't had a change of heart accompanied by his ridiculous spidey sense, God only knows what would have happened to her that night.

Roger looked at his drink and then finished it in one swallow.

"Maggie told me once that I was no good at my job," Roger said. "I never knew how right she was until this last week."

Laurent signaled for the waiter again.

"I think," Laurent said with a smile, "she was never more wrong about anything in her life." He stood up to embrace his wife who was hurrying across the terrace to join them.

After Maggie had a lovely coffee festooned with a dollop of pure whipped cream, she could feel the pleasure of the hot drink warm her up from the inside. Madame Dulcie had cut a lovely leg of lamb for tomorrow's roast and Maggie knew that Laurent—who normally bought his meat in Aix—would be pleased with her purchase.

"All right," she said, looking from one man to the other. "Tell me what I missed."

"Roger was just filling me in on a few details you failed to mention to me," Laurent said.

Maggie turned to look at Roger but she could see that both of them were laughing.

"Very funny. Okay, Roger, start with Guy. What's happening to him?"

"You know I'm not in the loop with all that any more," Roger said.

"I know you know more than we do," Maggie said. She was glad to see Roger relaxing. His face looked fuller as if he'd been eating better lately too.

"Okay, let's see," Roger said. "He was charged with moving a dead body, and obstructing justice. Since you didn't feel the need to press charges on him kidnapping you, I didn't mention that whole resisting arrest incident either. I don't think he'll do any time or if he does not much. Thirty days maybe."

Maggie couldn't help but think wryly that the French law enforcement definitely had Guy Dionne's prints in their database *now*.

"Do you know what he'll do when he gets out?" she asked.

"I heard he's planning to return to the monastery," Roger said. "He talked with some of the Brothers about working to rebuild the stable."

"That's a nice fit," Maggie said, looking over at Laurent, who merely shrugged.

"As for Pierre Guillaume, you heard he was picked up the same night he ran off and is back in Nice, right?" Roger said.

"I did."

"Noelle Dupree refused to press charges against him but he has quite a bit else going on to keep him locked up for a good while."

Maggie had also heard that Noelle had left the monastery to live with a relative on her mother's side in Dijon.

"I guess that about wraps it," she said. "What about you, Roger? What will you do now?"

"Turns out I'm going to be able to stay in the south after all. There's a job for me in Nice. Still a detective. Working in the Department of Motor Vehicles. Did you know the rate of motor vehicle theft in France is two hundred and sixty two cases per one hundred thousand population?"

"I did not," Laurent said.

"The money's not as good and Chloe and I will still have to move, which she is not happy about but it could be worse."

Maggie winced. Even she knew that chasing stolen cars was a big career drop from being the head honcho in charge of homicides.

"Will the new job be compromised because of what happened here?" Maggie asked.

"I'll come to Nice with the stink of having refused a direct order from a superior officer—never a good recommendation for a new job."

"I am sorry, Roger."

He waved away her apology. "It was past time to go. I just couldn't see it."

Laurent stood up and put his hand on Maggie's shoulder.

"*Chérie*, I see Bernard Medoc inside Le Canard. I would have a word with him. Roger?" He and Roger shook hands. "Thank you for your help, *mon vieux*. I hope we will see you and Chloe before you leave."

"I'd like that, Laurent," Roger said.

As Laurent moved inside the bar, Maggie turned to Roger.

"I was right, wasn't I?" she said. "About the part you do best? You came through like I knew you would."

"You mean the detective with a heart of gold?" Roger laughed.

"For all the good it'll do me in the Department of Motor Vehicles."

"There are different ways of going forward."

"My friend the philosopher," he teased. "Perhaps you should put that in your blog? I think Americans especially would eat it up."

"Is Chloe broken-hearted about leaving Aix?" Maggie asked, ignoring his good-natured ribbing.

"She's not thrilled but honestly not as upset as I'd feared. My mother is more distraught than my daughter."

"I'm so sorry it all shook out like this," Maggie said.

"I'm not," he said with a smile finishing off his drink. "Even with my career in tatters, my daughter not speaking to me, and Aix in my rear view mirror, I'm not at all sorry. In fact, if you want to know, Maggie," he said with a grin, "all things considered, I feel pretty damn good about myself at the moment."

68

ALL THE COLORS OF THE SUN

That evening, Laurent made his special *bouillabaisse*. Elspeth and John sat in the living room afterwards with Danielle planning the details of Thanksgiving dinner at Domaine St-Buvard. Their voices rose and fell, interspersed with occasional laughter. Maggie missed having Grace and Zouzou and now it looked like they wouldn't be at Domaine St-Buvard for the holiday. Business had finally picked up at Dormir and Grace was expecting a full house for Thanksgiving week.

"You don't feel thrown out of your own kitchen, do you?" Maggie asked as she and Laurent stepped outside onto the back terrace with the two dogs for their evening walk through the vineyard.

"It is only one day," he said. "And in the end, I will likely end up cooking most of it."

"Except for the cranberries," Maggie said teasingly.

He made a face. "Never the cranberries."

He put his arm around Maggie and they walked through the back terrace to the edge of the vineyard. Behind them, Maggie could see both children's bedroom lights still on.

Before Laurent could say anything, she said, "It is the weekend."

He frowned but didn't argue.

Maggie had been wondering if Laurent was in any way different after his eight days in the Aix Police jail, and she could confidently say there was nothing that she could detect. Given what she knew about Laurent, that was probably compatible with titanic shifts having happened inside him. But she would never be able to pick up on them.

Even so, after several long conversations, Maggie was confident he'd told her the truth about what had happened—all about the deal that Roger's superior had attempted to push through. And while Laurent said it had never been close, the fact was Maggie would never really know.

They walked to the shed and gazed out over the vineyard for a moment.

"I know you miss him," Maggie said putting her hand in Laurent's pocket where she found his hand.

Laurent made a noise in his throat—a Laurent noise that could mean anything but in this case Maggie knew meant he was agreeing with her.

Even though they'd both seen how Jean-Luc had slowed down in the last year, the end had still come so suddenly and the shock continued to reverberate in everything they saw in the vineyard. It was so hard to believe that Jean-Luc wasn't just over the next rise, ready to come and talk endlessly with Laurent about the vines, or throw a ball with Jemmy.

Laurent called to the dogs and they appeared from deep within the vineyard and ran past them to wait by the French doors at the back of the house.

"Danielle said Jean-Luc died the way he would've wanted to," Maggie said. "In the vineyard doing something to help the people he loved."

Laurent grunted and again said nothing. But Maggie felt his

sorrow and his love for his friend as he stood in the vineyard the two had shared and loved.

"Where did you bury Petit-Four?" Laurent asked.

"Over by the stonewall where you grow the oregano."

"Ahhh, very good," he said. "She loved to chase voles there."

"That's just what Jemmy said."

They turned to walk back to the house, the upstairs bedrooms' lights out now but the glow in the living room bright through the French doors.

Maggie had a moment of memory of when Pierre had come to her house to scare her. It seemed he had panicked when he saw the dogs and accidentally knocked her down in his hurry to flee.

She still hadn't mentioned that to Laurent. And didn't see any reason to now.

"You know," she said lightly, "if you hadn't punched Henri Dupree in the nose that day, the cops would have had one less thing to lay at your feet. Something to think about."

He raised an eyebrow at her and she thought she saw a corner of his lips twitch in a near-smile.

"*Peut-être*," he said.

"Maybe you should take some anger management training or something."

"You are very amusing tonight, *chérie*."

"I kind of am, aren't I?" she said seconds before Laurent grabbed her up in his arms and swung her off her feet.

"Perhaps I should start working on my impulses right now, eh?" he said kissing her neck.

Maggie squealed and threw back her head.

He put her gently back on her feet but before he let her go, he held her chin with his fingers and gazed into her eyes.

"*Le bébé*?" he said questioning.

Maggie shook her head. "It just...disappeared. I wasn't that far along and the doctor said it happens sometimes. I was going to tell you tonight. Are you disappointed?"

He kissed her on the mouth and cupped her cheek as he gazed into her eyes.

"Yes. Of course. But that doesn't mean we should have another. For me, ten more would not be too many but also the two I have are enough."

"Sounds like classic French thinking to me," Maggie said, leaning into him as they turned to walk to the house. With every step she felt his strength and his warmth transfer to her in a steady infusion of love and deep connection.

And on this starry brisk night so close to Thanksgiving—and on all the nights that stretched out ahead of them in her little corner of France—Maggie couldn't help but feel that the future and everything it held for them was going to be just fine.

To see what happens next, order *Murder in Arles, Book 13 of the Maggie Newberry Mysteries!*

DANIELLE'S VINTNER GRAPE CAKE

You'll need:
- 2 large eggs
- 2/3 cup sugar
- 4 tablespoons melted butter
- 1/4 cup cooking oil
- 1/2 cup whole milk
- 1 teaspoon pure vanilla extract
- 1-1/2 cups unbleached all-purpose flour
- 3/4 teaspoon baking powder
- A pinch of salt
- Grated zest of 1 lemon
- 10 ounces seedless grapes
- Confectioners' sugar, for garnish

Preheat oven to 350 degrees F. Generously butter and flour a 9-inch spring form pan, tapping out any excess flour. Set aside.

Beat eggs and sugar until thick. Add butter, oil, milk, and vanilla extract, and mix until blended.

Sift flour, baking powder, and salt into a large bowl. Add lemon zest, and toss to coat with flour. Spoon mixture into batter and stir until blended. Scrape down sides. Set aside for 10 minutes to allow flour to absorb liquids.

Stir 3/4 of the grapes into batter. Spoon batter into prepared cake pan.

Bake for 15 minutes, then sprinkle top of cake with remaining grapes. Bake more until top is a golden brown and cake feels firm, about 40 minutes, for a total baking time of 55 minutes. Cool.

After 10 minutes, run a knife along sides of pan, release and remove sides of spring form pan. Sprinkle with confectioners' sugar and serve at room temperature.

WHAT'S NEXT

Interested in seeing what happens next to Maggie and Laurent? Check out *Murder in Arles, Book 13 of the Maggie Newberry Mysteries!*

Here are the first several chapters of *Murder in Arles*.

I

Maggie surveyed the crimson and bright yellow leaves scattered across the terra cotta pavers of the back terrace of Domaine St-Buvard.

She knew if she opened the French doors that separated her from the terrace and garden she would smell wood smoke and with it the promise of the coming coziness of winter. As long as she had been living at Domaine St-Buvard, winter was always defined by long hours curled up in front of the fire, cashmere throws across her knees, a good book, and a steaming cup of tea at hand.

Even with two children, a thriving Internet business, and an active social schedule, winter always tended to be a time to rest, rebuild, and rejuvenate.

Even Maggie's best friend Grace, who ran a bed and breakfast a few miles away, didn't expect any more bookings for the next five months. Maggie knew Grace would use the time to ramp up renovations on her property. But even for Grace—and Danielle too who Grace now ran the *gîte* with—winter was a time to push the pause button and rest.

Maggie stepped outside, her arms laden with the place settings for tonight's dinner which they'd eat on the stone table that faced the vineyards. She was sure it would be one of the last meals they'd be able to eat outdoors this year.

A few more leaves scuttled across the tiles of the terrace which was bordered on one side by a walled garden and on the other by their vineyard. The house that Maggie's husband Laurent had inherited ten years earlier, known in the nearby village as Domaine St-Buvard, was a very old stone *mas* situated deep in the heart of Provence.

Originally connected to a small but prime vineyard that Laurent had cultivated for the *vin de pays* he produced, now his land had grown to nearly three hundred hectares.

"You should have Mila do this."

Maggie turned to see her husband standing in the doorway of their *mas*. He was frowning, a wooden spoon held loosely in one hand.

Laurent was six foot five—unusual for a Frenchman—and he used his height alternatingly with moderation and to his advantage.

"I enjoy doing it," Maggie said, feeling a lightness in her limbs as she regarded him. It always surprised her, his effect on her.

In spite of the ten years—and two children—behind them, Laurent could still set her pulse racing with just a glance. What surprised her even more was when she reminded herself that she'd met this mysterious, sexy man when she'd come to France to find the truth about her missing sister while he was in the middle of pulling a con.

On her family.

What Maggie had discovered on that fateful trip eleven years ago was a man who resonated with her on nearly every level and who offered her a life more exciting than she could ever have imagined in her wildest dreams.

"*Chérie?*" Laurent said, a wry smile tugging at his full lips. His hair was brown, thick and he wore it nearly to his shoulders. He was broad shouldered, yet he moved with the grace of a cat.

"I was just thinking," Maggie said, blushing.

He knew his effect on her and she knew enough to know how rare what they had together was.

Not that it had always been easy.

"I sent Mila and Jemmy off to find whatever flowers might be left in the lower garden for the centerpiece," she said.

"Did you remind Mila to feed the goat?"

Two months ago their eight-year old daughter had begged them for the little goat and in a moment of weakness they'd relented on the condition that she take care of it.

Meanwhile Maggie was becoming proficient in feeding and tending to an energetic and very naughty twenty-two-pound goat.

"You are too indulgent with them," Laurent said, joining her on the terrace.

Maggie knew Laurent's own childhood had not been a pleasant one, although in many respects it had been privileged. He'd lost his parents early and had been raised by a wealthy elderly grandmother who had too many ghosts to chase to give much thought to Laurent and his younger brother Gerard.

In Gerard's case, the old woman's ambivalence had triggered the beginning of the end.

"You're only a child once," Maggie said. She wasn't the disciplinarian in the family. That would be Laurent. The kids knew it too. They moved easily around Maggie, manipulating her at will. But they were sweet children, compliant and unspoiled—largely thanks to Laurent.

Laurent slipped an arm around Maggie's waist and drew her to him. She turned on tiptoe to kiss him. He smelled like lemons and rosemary. A tinge of smoke clung to his hair and his lips were cool.

"Will you set the braziers up?" Maggie said. "It's getting colder."

Their dinner guest tonight was Danielle Alexandre, their neighbor and the widow of their beloved Jean-Luc who'd passed away the summer before.

Laurent turned to regard the table as if seeing it for the first time.

Maggie suddenly knew it was already too cold to be eating outdoors.

"Should we move things inside?" she asked.

"*Non*," he said, running a hand down her back and then stepping over to where the braziers sat by the side of the house. "Danielle will prefer to eat on the terrace."

The sounds of childish laughter tumbled down the garden path and Maggie turned toward the vineyard. The light was just fading to a soft dark blue. She saw the dogs first, bounding up the pathway toward the house.

"Mila?" Maggie called.

Both children appeared from the bottom of the garden. Ten year old Jemmy was the eldest. He arrived with his face flushed, his eyes glittering with merriment in the aftermath of their footrace. Clutched in his fist were several stems of bedraggled zinnias. Mila hurried behind him. With her blonde hair, she looked like she was glowing in the dusk.

Mila ran immediately to Laurent and although she was too old for it, he scooped her up and held her in one arm.

Now who's indulgent? Maggie thought with a smile.

But the rules didn't often apply to Mila. At least not where Laurent was concerned. He was much harder on Jemmy but there was little that Maggie could do about that. Laurent was chauvinistic and his expectations for his first-born son were different than for his princess. The fact that Mila was feminine as well as beautiful only underscored her irrefutable role to her father.

"Jemmy," Laurent said, kissing Mila and setting her down. "Position the braziers near the table."

Mila came to Maggie to show her the flowers she held—none of which had an intact stem to support it in a vase. Maggie took them from her and put a hand on her hair.

"Go wash your hands, sweetie," Maggie said before turning to Jemmy who was attempting to position one of the bulky braziers.

"Laurent, he's too small to do that," she said.

"No, I'm not!" Jemmy said hotly and tugged harder on the brazier. Laurent shot a hand out to keep the tall heater from crashing to the stone pavers of the terrace.

That was my fault, Maggie thought as she bit her lip. *I should have just let him get on with it especially since Laurent was clearly watching out for him.*

"Perhaps your mother is right," Laurent said. "Go to the kitchen and start chopping the garlic."

Jemmy flushed angrily and turned to leave. Laurent's hand came down firmly on his son's shoulder and Jemmy froze. After the briefest of moments, Jemmy nodded.

Laurent released him and watched him go inside.

"Why didn't you give him a second chance with the braziers?" Maggie asked.

"Because this way he'll remember what happened when he let his temper get the better of him."

"I don't want him hiding his emotions, Laurent."

Laurent moved the two braziers into place and said nothing.

"Laurent?"

"I heard you, *chérie*. Don't you think you should dress? Danielle will be here any minute."

Maggie knew Laurent was not going to discuss with her how to handle Jemmy. She'd learned that from long experience.

And as for teaching the boy to hide his emotions, well, she also knew that that was something that Laurent frankly saw great merit in.

2

Dinner was *coq au vin* with individual artichoke soufflés. The meal was mostly quiet amidst the evening sounds of the vineyard and the garden—the far off barking of the neighbors' dogs and the rush of the wind among the trees.

Once the last course was served and eaten the children were excused to clear the table and go do their homework.

Maggie couldn't help but wonder if on her own she would have insisted on such perfect table manners. But for a traditional Frenchman—which in so many ways Laurent was— there was no other way. His children would be obedient, silent and well-behaved especially at the dining table.

"Mila and Jemmy are perfection as usual," Danielle said fondly as she watched the two children scamper into the house. "They will give you great comfort when you are my age."

A spasm of pain throbbed in Maggie's heart. She'd always felt sorry for the fact that Danielle and her first husband Eduard had not had children. By the time Danielle had married Jean-Luc it was too late.

Maggie leaned across the table and touched Danielle's hand. The older woman looked tired tonight, Maggie realized. It had been a hard year for Danielle—not the least of which was trying to learn to live without Jean-Luc.

While Danielle now kept busy working with Grace at *Dormir*, Grace's *gîte*, she obviously had many a lonely night to remember and miss her soulmate.

A chill breeze came down through the dogwoods that bordered the terrace, rattling the branches, the leaves long since gone, and flapped the cotton tablecloth. Maggie shivered as an image of the *mistral* darting through Provence formed in her head.

Laurent had gone to oversee the children's chores and activities and came back now with a tray holding three heavy cut crystal glasses and a decanter of Calvados.

"You will stay the night, Danielle?" he said.

Even though it was phrased as a question, Laurent didn't look at Danielle for her answer. Maggie knew he would insist she stay.

Maggie always marveled at how expertly Laurent was able to size up any given situation. It was probably what had made him such a good con artist, she thought wryly. He would know, of course, that—with the constant hum of children in the background—Danielle would naturally prefer to stay the night at Domaine St-Buvard than go back to her quiet room at Grace's.

"*Oui, Laurent. Merci,*" Danielle said.

Maggie leaned back in her chair and surveyed the table—a pleasant *tableau* of glasses showing varying depths of wine or water, and flickering candles. She glanced at Laurent at the end of the table as he poured the drinks. He looked relaxed although Maggie, of all people, knew how deceptive *that* appearance could be.

Laurent had lost a dear friend when he lost Jean-Luc—the closest thing to a father he'd ever known. And like Danielle, going on without Jean-Luc was often a struggle. Just thinking of Jean-Luc with his wool tweed cap set jauntily on the back of his head, his blue eyes twinkling and the delight he took in playing *Papère* to Jemmy and Mila brought tears to Maggie's eyes.

"How are your dear parents, *chérie*?" Danielle asked as she accepted the glass of brandy from Laurent.

Assuming Danielle had mistaken her emotion for worry over her parents, Maggie smiled reassuringly at her.

"They're good," Maggie said. "I talk to my mother nearly every day. And my dad is doing fine."

After six months of living at Domaine St-Buvard with

Maggie's increasingly deteriorating father, Elspeth Newberry gave in to Maggie's brother Ben who insisted they return to Atlanta where he could be more involved.

Naturally, Maggie thought, her back stiffening with resentment, Ben had been largely unavailable to her parents once they moved back—as she knew he would be—but her mother wouldn't hear any criticism of her brother. With Ben's marginal help they'd eventually sold the family house in Buckhead—long past time Maggie had to admit—and moved her mother and Maggie's niece Nicole to a condo near Nicole's high school. Maggie's father moved into a nearby memory care facility.

All neat and tidy.

Maggie's heart sank every time she thought of them all.

"I'm sure you miss them very much," Danielle said.

Maggie smiled. "I do, of course."

And that was true. Except for the times when she felt a wave of relief not to have to be the one to try to solve her parents' problems at any time of the day or night.

It had been easier for Maggie when her parents came to live at Domaine St-Buvard last year. Laurent had a good relationship with her father. Foggy-headed or not—her dad tended to respond with more lucidity when Laurent was around directing things.

Maggie smiled as she watched her husband as he frowned at the color of the brandy in his goblet.

Directing things was by and large the very definition of Laurent. Whether in his kitchen, his vineyard, with his children, or at the nearby monastery *l'Abbaye de Sainte-Trinité* where he had created temporary housing for transient vineyard workers, Laurent was always a leader.

He didn't defer easily or often.

Or ever.

"And *les enfants*?" Danielle said relaxing into her chair with her brandy, her eyes closing contentedly.

Maggie watched Laurent gather up dishes and disappear into

the kitchen. It was hard for him to sit still. There was always something to do, something to arrange, people to sort out. When Laurent entered the house, she heard Jemmy's voice in the kitchen as if in protest and she imagined Laurent had come upon the child doing something he shouldn't.

"They're good," Maggie said. "Mila's goat is turning into a pain but I suppose that's all part of raising kids. Hey, I made a joke! Might not translate, though."

"I understood it, *chérie*. Very amusing."

Ever since Danielle had moved to *Dormir* with Grace and Grace's teenage daughter Zouzou, Maggie and Laurent had seen much less of her than when she had lived closer. But the extra work was good for Danielle and kept her occupied. As happy as Danielle had been with Jean-Luc, being productive and feeling useful wasn't something that had been a big part of her life until now.

Danielle had seamlessly integrated into the little family at *Dormir* and provided a level of stability and maturity that Grace desperately needed. Even Grace often remarked that she had no idea how she'd managed before Danielle came to live with them.

Although the door to the house had closed, Jemmy's voice was louder now and more insistent. That was surprising since Laurent rarely brooked disagreement with his various edicts.

"Jemmy is growing up," Danielle noted.

She sees it too.

"I feel like he's a little ahead of schedule," Maggie said, glancing through the French doors. She could see Laurent's shadow—big and imposing—as he stood with his hands on hips looking down at his first-born who just as clearly was standing up to him.

"How so?" Danielle asked.

"He doesn't seem as compliant as he was a few months ago. He argues with me now."

"Ah."

"And Laurent too."

Danielle glanced toward the house and sipped her drink.

"He is his father's son."

Maggie laughed. "I'll tell Laurent you said so. I'm sure that'll make him feel loads better."

"Grace tells me that Jemmy's school wants to advance him an extra grade next year?"

Maggie sighed. It certainly wasn't a secret but she was sorry to be reminded of the issue on an evening when she'd nearly managed to ignore the stress and strains of the week.

"We all knew he was smart," Danielle said.

"Too smart," Maggie said. "I'm not sure putting him in classes with kids a whole year older is a good idea."

"Why not? Zouzou tells me Jemmy only plays with the older children as it is."

"That's just what I'm talking about. I want him playing with kids his own age."

"Jemmy is the best judge of that, surely?"

"He's ten years old, Danielle. He's not the best judge of what socks to put on in the morning. And yesterday he took the dogs to the village—and forgot them there!"

"So what is the answer?"

"I don't know. I want to homeschool him. Laurent wants him advanced."

"What does Jemmy want?"

"Danielle, I'm surprised to hear you even ask! I thought the French thought we Americans were too indulgent with our children. Would *your* parents have asked your vote on how you were schooled?"

"I was not as clever as Jemmy."

"Again, I'm not convinced that's a good thing."

That night as Maggie and Laurent were turning in for the night, Maggie leaned over in bed and touched his shoulder.

"What was all that between you and Jemmy tonight?" she asked.

"It was nothing. The light, *chérie*?"

"It didn't sound like nothing. Was he being disobedient?"

"*Non*. He just had a ...question."

"What was the question?"

Laurent sighed heavily and turned to Maggie and pulled her toward him with one arm while with the other hand he reached over and turned out the bedside lamp.

"It was just a question between fathers and sons," he said enigmatically, kissing her on the forehead.

Maggie knew she wouldn't get anything more definitive out of him. And perhaps that was for the best.

"It was a nice night," Maggie said as she settled in his arms.

Through the brief fluttering of the curtains at the window she could see the moon and imagined how it must be illuminating their vineyard below. She shivered for some reason.

"Danielle seems happy," Laurent said.

"I really think she is."

The fact that Laurent hadn't turned over to settle into sleep told Maggie that he was still thinking about something. She watched the moon and waited, enjoying the security of his arms.

"You are worried about your papa?" he asked quietly.

Maggie smiled in the darkness, feeling her heart fill with love for her husband. He had so much to do, so many people to worry about and care for.

"Him and everyone else," she said.

"That is a lot of worrying," Laurent said giving her a final kiss before turning away and falling almost immediately asleep.

It always amazed Maggie that a man who'd lived so many years on the edge—barely out of the reach of the police at any given moment, hardly able to trust even his own compatriots and partners in crime, who constantly measured and weighed the odds of catastrophe against the risks necessary for possible gain, not to mention the nefarious things he'd done in his life that Maggie *didn't* know about—that he could fall asleep so easily and sleep so soundly.

She continued to watch the moon until a veil of dark clouds stole across its face, easing her and her world into darkness.

3

Grace watched the leaves scuttle across the back patio. She pulled her cashmere scarf tighter around her throat and set her mug of coffee down on the stone wall that separated the patio terrace from the flower garden.

She made a mental note to make sure that Gabriel her handy man had put the manure in the proper places yesterday but decided she had a moment to indulge in a quick moment of peace and reflection.

Danielle had texted the night before to say she would spend the night at Domaine St-Buvard, as Grace had assumed she would. It was the first time in nearly nine months since Danielle had come to live with them that she'd not spent the night at *Dormir*. Grace was surprised to realize how much she missed waking up to the older woman's presence in the kitchen.

Over the months they'd quickly gotten into the habit of enjoying their morning coffee together at the big farmhouse table in the kitchen, going over the things that needed to be done that day—who would run into Aix to pick up Zouzou after school—what groceries needed to be shopped for, what extra-special meals needed to be planned.

Because make no mistake, people coming to a bed and breakfast in France expect amazing food.

Ironically the one thing Grace hadn't taken into account when she deliriously threw her arms around Laurent's neck eighteen months ago when he'd told her about his idea for creating

Dormir was that cooking sumptuous meals would reasonably be a part of the plan.

Not a cook herself (she'd had maids and cooks her whole life until recently), Grace had simply focused on making *Dormir* the quintessential luxury vacation stay exemplifying the best of the south of France. She filled the *gîte* with original local artwork, six-hundred thread count sheets, fresh flowers in every room, aromatherapy of rosemary, roses, lavender and eucalyptus, and plate after handpainted plate of fresh pastries from Bedard's Patisserie in Aix.

For the first three months she'd managed by buying takeout in Aix and arranging the meals on colorful faience and casseroles or badgering Laurent to make triple his usual amounts when he cooked at Domaine St-Buvard.

But when Danielle moved in after Jean-Luc's death, *Dormir* became what Grace had always envisioned it to be.

Perfectly French in every perfect way.

Grace left her coffee cup on the stone wall and moved to the end of the terrace walkway to get a better view of the vineyard that surrounded the property.

Dormir had once been a fine *mas* rising among a field of vineyards, the stately home for generations of *vignerons* that only a few in St-Buvard even remembered now. After the last world war the owner of the house never returned from the German prisoner of war camp where he'd spent the war. His wife and two children moved to Paris where she had family. Eventually the son sold the house to Eduard Marceau from Dijon who envisioned becoming a major winegrower in the area.

Thirty years after moving to the *mas* with Danielle, Eduard was childless and bitter about the fact. Never fully accepted by the villagers who viewed him as an outsider, Eduard decided that the answer to his problems might be the expansion of his grape empire. This had been a reasonable assumption since there were two large tracts of vineyard that abutted his own.

One was seventy-five hectares and owned by Jean-Luc Alexandre, a bachelor and brother of the notorious Resistance hero Patrick Alexandre. Jean-Luc's land had been owned by the Alexandre family for generations.

The other piece of land was owned by Nicolas Dernier of Paris. Monsieur Dernier was unmarried and when he died, his land passed to his nephew Laurent Dernier.

Unfortunately it was this event that would be the undoing of Eduard.

Since there were no children from their union, when Eduard died last year his land passed to Danielle who had by then married Jean-Luc. Danielle promptly sold both the house and land to Laurent.

The property was renovated to include two small mini-cottages, updated plumping, a new kitchen and a small swimming pool under the plane trees that at one time shaded the empty terrace of an unhappy woman and her vitriolic husband.

Sometimes when Grace was doing some endlessly tedious chore, like polishing the door knobs or beating bedroom rugs on the clothesline, she would catch sight of Danielle weeding the flower garden or raking the front gravel driveway and she would marvel at the fact that Danielle lived in this very house as its mistress for over thirty years.

There was no doubt that they were thirty miserable years.

Grace sometimes caught Danielle working in the kitchen—a kitchen that had been her own just a decade ago—making *pâte à choux* with Zouzou and Mila, their laughter spiraling up and throughout the house.

During those years when Danielle had been virtually imprisoned in the house by Eduard's pride and spite, had it been beyond imagining that someday she might create a life surrounded by people who loved her?

Grace smiled as she remembered the day Laurent made the offer to her: *Come back to France with Zouzou and work the gîte.* He would own it but she would run it. It would allow her to support herself and Zouzou and to remain in the country where she'd discovered she was happiest.

It was the saving of her. No doubt about it.

Amongst the amalgamated scents of wood smoke and the crisp autumn air, Grace could smell the overripe scent of fallen apples from the two ancient trees in the southern corner of the flower garden. Danielle and Zouzou had collected those apples for weeks at the start of the season and made *tartes Tatin*, apple tarts, apple fritters, and apple chutney. From now on until the day she died, Grace was pretty sure autumn would always smell to her like the kitchen of *Dormir* in October with the scent of baking or caramelizing apples and cinnamon wafting through the house.

More importantly, Grace thought with a smile, she had given the gift of that memory to Zouzou too,

The wind whistled gently overhead and Grace looked up in time to see a squadron of geese making its way south. She watched for a moment and wondered when in her entire life she'd taken so much pleasure just from looking up at the sky.

Her reverie was broken by the approaching purr of a motorbike. She glanced at her watch.

They'd said goodbye to their last guests of the season last week and Grace was looking forward to months to retool, regroup, and refresh. So far, the few bookings Grace had managed were just enough to support the next bookings. Grace hated the fact that she had yet to break even on *Dormir* but Laurent wasn't worried and so she tried not to be.

The motorbike's engine shut off abruptly at the front of the house. Brad was earlier than he'd said he'd come over but he'd been coming earlier and earlier. Grace knew he wanted to move in with her and God knows they had plenty of room, especially in the winter with six hand-curated, artfully designed and fastidiously furnished bedrooms among three cottages and only she, Zouzou and Danielle living there.

She picked up her coffee mug and made her way across the terrace to the gate that led to the front of the house, hurrying to get to the front before he knocked on the door and woke Zouzou. It was Saturday and one of the few days Grace didn't have to drag the child moaning and protesting from her bed to go to school.

Grace shut the gate behind her and walked quickly around the house in time to see Brad pulling off his helmet and running his hands through his hair. He had thick auburn hair and a close-cut ginger beard that served to showcase his cheekbones and full lips.

He was handsome of course. Grace hadn't yet graduated to a point of maturity where she could date a homely man no matter how charming or witty. And as Maggie had once teased her: *you know what you have to put up with to get a good-looking guy, right?*

All joking aside, there was some truth to that. A balding, pudgy man would not be as comfortable nagging her to let him move in. He'd be more inclined to be content.

"Good morning!" Brad called to her, his face crinkling into a smile as she walked toward him.

American, living in Aix at the Hotel Cezanne, he was supposedly writing a murder mystery although Grace had yet to see any evidence of any actual writing. She had not raised the question of *where* he got the money to allow him to live in Aix although Laurent had asked her about it no fewer than three times already.

She knew Laurent was protective of her and he knew her track record—with the possible exception of Windsor—was less than reassuring. She still cringed at the memory of Laurent carrying her screaming over his shoulder out of a Paris bistro three years ago in order to prevent her from making a further fool of herself over a man she never should have trusted in the first place.

She went to give Brad a quick kiss and then turned to let them in through the front door.

"You're early," she said.

"Well, I'm excited to see Arles. I've only been there once on a bus tour."

They were to pick up Maggie and Jemmy later that morning in order to attend a massive *brocante* taking place within the city's famed amphitheater. Danielle would bring Mila home later this morning where they would spend the day baking with Zouzou—something both girls and Danielle loved to do.

"You've probably already seen the best bits," Grace said as they entered the house. She worked to tamp down a flash of annoyance. She'd been hoping to have time to dress and relax before her day began.

"There's coffee in the kitchen," she said.

"Are you cross with me, darling?" Brad asked, stopping in the foyer and affecting a small pout.

Grace turned to him. "No, of course not." She smiled and gave him another kiss. "I can make some eggs if you like?"

He grinned. "That'd be great. I'm starving."

Grace went into the kitchen and pulled out the eggs from the refrigerator.

Zouzou would probably love it if Brad moved in, Grace thought. He always made her laugh. And she was sure Danielle wouldn't care. Ever since Jean-Luc died Danielle pretty much tended toward the philosophy of the more the merrier.

So why was Grace hesitating?

4

Unlike anyone else's family that Maggie had ever heard of, Saturday mornings tended to be even more chaotic than weekdays at Domaine St-Buvard. She wasn't sure why that was, since the kids were usually glued in front of cartoons on the TV set on Saturday mornings.

Now that she thought of it, maybe it was the cartoon soundtrack that seemed to give most Saturdays their feeling of barely controlled frenzy.

Laurent always went to the food markets on Saturday—the one in Aix was a given but he had a few others that were special to him in different ways. This one always had the best asparagus, that one had the best tomatoes, another could always be counted on for the first truffles of the season.

Food was important to Laurent and while Maggie had to admit that that focus had succeeded in adding a ten-pound weight gain to her frame since she'd married him, the joy and satisfaction that cooking gave her husband was well worth the price of a slightly larger pants size.

"How long will you be in Arles today?" Laurent asked as he stood in the kitchen glancing at the front page of the local newspaper. Maggie knew Laurent intended to cook something specific for tonight's meal, but he never went out shopping with a list.

"However long it takes Grace to find the perfect washstand for an antique pitcher and bowl she has."

Laurent frowned.

"I'm joking. Sort of," Maggie said. "I really don't know what she's looking for. Probably she doesn't either until she sees it."

"Good morning, *mes infants*," Danielle said as she stepped into the kitchen. Laurent turned to pour her coffee.

"Did you sleep well, Danielle?" Maggie asked.

Before Danielle could answer Mila ran into the room and hugged Danielle around the waist.

"Good morning, *Mamère!*" she said. "What are we making today?"

Mila loved spending her Saturdays baking with Zouzou and Danielle. Zouzou, who had had a weight problem two years ago was now—with Laurent's counsel—not only at a normal weight for her age but had developed a passion for baking. At fourteen, she was already determined to go to the French culinary academy in Paris after high school.

"I don't know, *chérie*," Danielle said, her eyes dancing with pleasure. "How about *macarons*? They are hard to make but I think we are up to the task."

Mila clapped her hands gleefully.

"Well, we all know how our Mila loves *macarons*," Maggie said, giving her daughter a kiss.

A horn sounded out front. Maggie glanced out the kitchen window to see that Grace and Brad had arrived.

Laurent kissed Maggie. "No candy for Jemmy. Or Cokes."

Maggie snorted. "Of course not. I am his mother after all."

"Which is why you spoil him," Laurent said as he gathered up his cloth grocery bags for his day of shopping.

The horn honked again and Jemmy appeared in the doorway of the kitchen.

"Mom, let's go," he said.

"Behave," Laurent said to him, raising an eyebrow to underscore to his son that he meant it.

Maggie kissed Mila and Danielle goodbye.

"Everyone have a fun day," she said as she grabbed her purse from the foyer sideboard.

Jemmy hurried out the front door to the waiting car.

The drive to Arles from St-Buvard was less than an hour and on a beautiful fall day like today felt even shorter. Since Laurent had set Grace up at *Dormir* Maggie and Grace had spent many Saturdays combing the roadside *brocantes* and village flea markets for just the right fabrics, pillow cushions, bed linens, artwork and *faience* to give any visitor to the *gîte* the most iconic South of France experience possible.

Maggie had never been much interested in second-hand items or antiques, but Grace had managed to arouse in her a passion for the hunt. Every afternoon that they'd spent looking for something unique or beautiful to enhance one of the *Dormir* cottages had been one that had aided in further bonding the two of them after their rough patch a few years earlier.

It helped that the scenes of the village *brocantes* were usually beautiful in themselves, typically medieval villages or cobblestone towns, often on the verge of golden sunflower or lavender fields.

Since Brad was driving Grace's car this morning, Maggie let Jemmy sit up front with him. Maggie had only seen Brad a few times since Grace had met him at an ex-pat party a few weeks back but she'd liked him instantly. He was easy going—something Maggie was convinced Grace needed. And he was American—again, something Maggie thought suited Grace better than a French lover, although she couldn't put her finger on why.

Laurent on the other hand was reserving judgment on the man.

As they entered Arles from the north, Maggie noticed there seemed to be more pay lots for parking than she remembered before. She was sure that half the lots they'd passed had previously been free parking.

"Just goes to show you how popular Arles is as a tourist destination," she said as she directed Brad in his second circling of the main square in their search to find an available spot.

"There must be a reason people love Arles so much," Brad said cheerfully. He turned to Jemmy. "Right, Sport?"

Jemmy was too interested in the scenery outside his window to answer and just as Maggie was about to reprimand him for not responding, Jemmy shouted and pointed.

"Look! There it is!"

The amphitheater rose around them like an ancient alien spaceship, its two-tiered stone walls a dramatic and pronounced hallmark of the ancient Roman city.

Maggie shivered as she always did when she saw the amphitheater. The fact that it could last so long and be the site of so much misery and death always took her breath away every time she saw it.

"Can we go in, Mom?" Jemmy turned in his seat to look excitedly at Maggie.

"We're meeting some people for lunch first," Maggie reminded him. "Be patient. The amphitheater has been here a long time. It isn't going anywhere."

"Wow," Brad said as he drove toward the imposing structure. "It's really something."

"Oh, there's one!" Grace called out. "Grab it, Brad!"

As Brad maneuvered the car into the spot, Grace and Maggie gathered up their shopping bags and baskets, optimistic that they would find treasures at the amphitheater *brocante* for *Dormir* and Domaine St-Buvard alike.

After paying for the parking spot, the four of them hurried through the narrow stone streets in the general direction of the amphitheater. Grace had arranged for them to meet the event planner for today's *brocante* at a restaurant across the street from the arena.

For a special mention in Maggie's popular Provençal newsletter, the event organizer had agreed to allow them into the *brocante* a full half hour before the rest of the public. It wasn't an unusual arrangement—not since Maggie's newsletter and blog had risen so high in subscription numbers to rate the kind of attention it now commanded.

"Who is this guy we're meeting?" Maggie asked Grace as they walked toward the restaurant.

"His name is Claude Bouquille," Grace said. "He does the organizing for all the main attractions and promotions not just in Arles but Aix and even some in Marseille. He's really excited about being in your newsletter."

Maggie's newsletter had been steadily growing from a simple blog about the ex-pat life in Provence to something that now had its own Etsy store and connections to vendors that covered the entire south of France with products from soaps and candles to handmade linens and faience. Her twenty thousand subscribers, although largely British, were growing to include a growing US audience too.

"Oh, did I tell you, that Fiona Bellemont-Surrey agreed to an interview in my next newsletter?" Maggie said to Grace.

Fiona Bellemont-Surrey was a British ex-pat who'd moved to Provence twenty years earlier and written a string of romance books that catapulted her to fame and prominence in the UK. She lived in the village of Saint-Rémy, about two hours from St-Buvard and Maggie had been trying to get her to talk to her for nearly a year.

Unfortunately, Belmont-Surrey had a reputation for being a bit of a bitch.

"I never heard of her," Brad said over his shoulder. "Should I?"

Maggie felt a sliver of annoyance.

"Well, you're probably not my audience, Brad," she said. "Fiona Bellemont-Surrey is kind of a big deal for ex-pat Brits living the Provençal lifestyle. I figure her name alone will boost my subscribers by a thousand or more. Plus, she's got her own blog of nearly seventy thousand subscribers she's agreed to let me send my newsletter to."

"How much does that translate to money-wise?" Grace asked.

"It could be a game changer."

"Like you need the money, darling."

"Well, everyone likes money," Maggie said. "But money isn't the point."

"What is?"

"Never mind, Grace. You sound like Laurent. This is what I *do*. I want to create a newsletter that's relevant. One that grows and evolves."

"Well, if it's important to you, it's important."

"Do you have any idea how condescending that sounds?"

Grace laughed. "And I wasn't even trying!"

Maggie watched Jemmy step in front of Brad where she could no longer see him.

"Jemmy, slow down," Maggie said. "I told you, we're going to the restaurant first."

"I heard you," he called back, a hint of petulance in his voice.

"He's fine," Brad said. "I've got him in sight."

Grace slipped her arm through Maggie's.

"Come on, darling," she said cajolingly. "It's going to be a fun day. Relax!"

5

After Danielle and Mila left for *Dormir* to spend the day with Zouzou, Laurent drove to the *l'Abbaye de Sainte-Trinité* and parked in the gravel parking lot.

He'd been working at the monastery with Frère Jean for over three years to help find local work and housing for the area's transients and assorted refugees.

Between *l'Abbaye de Sainte-Trinité* dormitories and the mini-houses Laurent had constructed on his vineyard property, all the harvest workers had comfortable housing for the duration of the work.

Laurent had a dozen people working his harvest this year. Most of them had moved on after the grapes were picked. It was as yet too early for the pruning and general field maintenance that would keep Laurent and his crew of young people busy in the spring.

Three of Laurent's houses had issues that currently made them uninhabitable. The other three workers who had yet to move on. A young couple with a baby had decided to stay and help with the garden at the monastery and do any work Laurent might have for them.

There were also three teenage boys still living at the monastery after the harvest although Frère Jean had confided to Laurent that without work to engage them they were becoming a problem.

As Laurent strode toward the main building of the monastery, an ancient stone structure, the wind blew in sharp angry gusts and the late morning sun already seemed to be fading with the steadily falling temperatures.

He entered the main hall and nodded at an elderly couple seated at one of the back tables, mugs of hot soup in their hands. Frère Jean was standing at the front of the room before an audience of around thirty people.

Laurent frowned as he watched the ex-monk—defrocked but still respected in every manner that mattered—attempt to get the attention and silence of the younger members of the audience. Laurent spotted several people who'd worked on his recent harvest including the three boys who'd together tended to cause more problems than any of the other workers combined.

André Charpentier, eighteen years old, was the son of an out-of-work car mechanic who'd worked in St-Buvard through last winter and then left, leaving André at the monastery saying he would return.

Jabal Berger sat next to André, his face slack but his eyes focused on André as if to emulate his friend's banter, sarcasm, and insolence.

Laurent knew the type—inclined toward trouble but without the originality to do it on his own—Jabal latched onto a leader and followed in his footsteps.

Usually all the way to prison.

Luc Thayer was the third boy. An orphan and a loner, he was rarely with the other boys and was surprised to see him with them now. His arms crossed and a mulish look on his handsome but scowling face, Luc was trouble in all the ways a wrongheaded sixteen-year-old kid could be trouble.

Unlike the other two who seemed to act up for accolades from the girls in the group or for their own amusement, Luc's behavior didn't appear motivated by praise or money or by the idea of doing the right thing.

Laurent moved deeper into the audience and saw Frère Jean look up and give him a look of relief. Laurent moved a narrow metal table holding a tray of dirty dishes out of his way. The sound of its legs scraping loudly on the stone floor echoed throughout the bare-walled dining hall. All the heads of the audience members turned to look at him.

Laurent caught André's eye first and detected—seconds before the mask of arrogance and contempt was donned—a moment of doubt and insecurity.

That would do. He'd made his point.

André elbowed Jabar in the ribs and snickered something to him which made the boy giggle but that was the extent of André's rebellion. Laurent was sure Frère Jean would have no more trouble out of them.

Luc did not turn around.

6

Maggie had been at Café Terrace before. Situated directly across from the Arles amphitheater, it was really more of a tourist café than a proper bistro, but the food was good and the service not too rude. And *that*, she figured, was about the best one could hope for in any French restaurant.

When they arrived at the café, lunch service had just begun. Before they'd even taken their seats Maggie had already had to have two heart-to-heart talks with Jemmy to keep him from dashing across the street and attempting to vault the stone parking stanchions put there to prevent people from parking or driving too close to the amphitheater.

"Lunch *first*, Jemmy," Maggie had said firmly to him. "I know you can be patient and I need you to do that now. How about a Coke with lunch?"

Already she could hear Laurent's admonishment in her ear. He didn't like either of the children to have too many sweets and he downright forbade snacking between meals.

But Maggie rationalized that since she was from Atlanta, the home of Coca-Cola, having a Coke now and then was practically Jemmy's birthright.

Still, she knew bribing him to behave was not good.

As soon as they entered the café, Grace led the way to a table where two men sat. The taller of the two, Claude Bouquille, jumped up and immediately exchanged kisses with Grace and introductions were made all around.

Claude's companion was a small ferret-looking man named Jacky. He had an odor to him and an ugly look in his eye. Maggie made a point to sit as far away from him as possible and parked Jemmy beside her.

"I am delighted to meet you, Madame Dernier," Claude said enthusiastically. "And even more delighted to be a part of your newsletter. My wife loves your interviews with area artisans. She harbors hopes of being interviewed herself."

"Oh? What does your wife make?"

Maggie had had hundreds of conversations like this over the last few years. It was seriously astonishing to her that there could be so many artists and creative vendors in Provence.

"Lavender infused soaps," Claude said. "I see you already have many advertisers for those kinds of products."

"Yes, well. This is Provence, right? One thing we have is lavender—but my newsletter subscribers love it."

"Of course. It is *la belle France, non?*"

The waiter, dour but at least sufficiently attentive, came and they ordered. Maggie was very aware that Jemmy was fidgety. She was sorry she hadn't brought him an electronic tablet to distract him but, again, Laurent wasn't a fan of using artificial devices to make the children behave and so she hadn't.

She was tempted to hand Jemmy her phone like she would if he were five but the very image of it prevented her. Jemmy had always been such an easy-going boy. What had changed? Why did he seem so impatient with everything now?

"Maggie?"

Maggie looked up just as the waiter handed her the glass of rosé she'd ordered.

"*Merci*," she said to the waiter who made eye contact with her. In fact, now that she thought of it, the man seemed fascinated by their conversation. She glanced at her group and had to admit they stood out a bit.

First there was Grace who was nothing short of gorgeous. Blonde with classic features, perfect alabaster complexion and crystal blue eyes, Grace would always turn heads no matter where she went. She was a goddess in human form. Normally, she alone would be enough to distract even the most cynical French waiter.

But then there was Brad who was movie-star handsome in his own right.

What a strange grouping we must appear!

Claude was tall and balding with an infectious grin. And his friend, Jacky...well, with his unshaven jawline and rumpled clothes he just looked homeless.

Maggie stole a quick look at Jacky and was startled to find him staring at her. She quickly turned her attention back to Claude who was speaking with the waiter.

"Thomas, you must have seen every manner of tourist over the years," Claude said. "They are all fascinated with the amphitheater, are they not?"

The waiter, a tall Ichabod Crane sort of fellow with straight, very white teeth, smiled and nodded at the looming wall of the Roman ruin.

"It is as beautiful as it is fascinating to all who see it," he murmured. "Especially the first time." Then he blushed as if he'd said too much and retreated back to the kitchen.

Claude grinned. "I know everyone in this town on a first-name basis. From the mayor to the waiters. In my business, it is essential. You'd be surprised how helpful even the little men can be."

"So tell me how you got involved in all these special events you put on," Maggie said.

"Well, my background is music and theatrical promotions. And honestly it was my wife that made me become more interested in doing events." He waved a hand to encompass the amphitheater.

"Have you been doing it awhile?"

"About five years. It's fairly lucrative and I get to meet a wide variety of people."

Maggie couldn't help but wonder if Jacky was who Claude was referring to when he said *a wide variety of people*. She wondered what possible function Jacky served for Claude.

"Claude said we can flag any item we like to be held back for later," Grace said, looking up from a small spiral notebook which Maggie guessed was her wish list for *Dormir*. "He said there is an antique water basin and some vintage bed linens that I'm thinking will look perfect in Plum cottage."

Grace had named the three guest cottages after fruit to keep them straight—and to help her handy man—who tended to struggle with understanding her French—to better sort out which cottage she needed him to work on.

"It is of course no problem," Claude said glancing at his watch. "Shall we go in a quarter of an hour?"

Already Maggie could see a line begin to form at the entrance to the amphitheater directly across from the café.

"That's impressive," she said, nodding at the growing crowd of people. "How did you advertise this?"

As Maggie watched the crowd her eye was caught by the sight of a young man dressed all in black. He wore a dark slouch hat and a half cape around his shoulders. His odd clothing wasn't what drew her eye however.

It was the unmistakable hate-filled glare that he was shooting at her table

"My advertising was not nearly as effective as it would have been," Claude said, "if I had been able to make the announcement in your newsletter." Although he was still smiling for some reason Maggie felt it was somehow less authentic than before.

"Well, my newsletter doesn't go out to the locals," she said. "You'd only have told people living in the UK."

"People in the UK have much disposable income," Claude said. "I would be happy to advertise my events to them."

"Well, next time you will," Maggie said, watching Jemmy push his French fries around on his plate, his eyes glued to the amphitheater entrance. She turned her attention back to Claude. "Did you have a display ad you wanted me to publish or...?"

"*Mais non*," Claude said, looking from Maggie to Grace and back again. "Grace said you might write about today's event. Is that not possible? Jacky is here to photograph anything you need."

Maggie was surprised. Most people opted for an ad. But she knew a small article—penned by her—would carry more clout to her subscribers.

Except what if the brocante is lame? Or worse, a rip-off?

She'd built up a bank of trust with her subscribers. If she told them the October Amphitheater *Brocante* was an annual sales experience not to be missed, they'd believe her. Not to mention the fact that her subscribers were mostly offshore. If they booked their flights for their next trip to Provence based on an event that Maggie said was worth experiencing—and it turned out not to be —then where would she be?

"Instead of a piece," she said, "since I already have one for next month's newsletter..." And that was true now that she had the Bellemont-Surrey interview nearly lined up. "...how would you feel about a display ad for your wife's lavender soaps? I can place it right up front so nobody misses it."

"You would do that?" Claude asked happily, his authentic smile back with a little something extra. "That would be *superbe!*"

Maggie and Claude shook hands and Maggie couldn't help but think that the best part of the deal—aside from not having to write copy she potentially didn't believe in—was not having to spend the afternoon with Jacky dogging her every step.

7

The impressive two-tiered amphitheater could seat over twenty thousand people and featured more than one hundred and twenty dramatic arches, several sets of viewing galleries and staircases, and a warren of catacomb subterranean tunnels and pathways.

As Maggie stared up at the amphitheater the thought came to her as it always did that this imposing structure—still such a vibrant, integral part of life in Arles—was built only ninety years after the birth of Christ.

Even more astonishing was the fact that this benign tourist attraction had also been the scene of countless bloody gladiatorial battles.

Maggie shivered at the thought of the brave and terrified men who were thrown to hungry bears and lions for the amusement of people who sat in these stone seats cheering them on before heading off to lunch somewhere in Arles.

"Darling?" Grace said turning to Maggie. "Are you all right? You look positively pale."

"This place always creeps me out a little," Maggie said with a weak smile.

Grace laughed her little bell of a laugh and slipped her arm into Maggie's.

"Okay, so let's stay focused. We're looking for antique lace and possibly an antique washstand today. Not heads on spikes. *D'accord?*"

Cued by thoughts of blood and mayhem Maggie turned to look for Jemmy. She spotted him walking next to Brad who was pointing out something at the top tier of the stadium seating.

Maggie turned back to Grace and the job at hand.

Even though today's event was supposed to be only antiques there were still the ubiquitous tables of *socca, pissaladier,* and pizza slices along with homemade jams from the nearby nunnery and table after table of spices, the scent of which could be detected the moment one emerged from any of the several tunnels that spilled out onto the arena's interior arena.

Maggie looked in amazement at the kiosk presentations of the colorful spices—most of which she'd never heard of before—as well as the mountains of dried rosebuds and sacks of semolina that looked like sandbags waiting for a storm.

Since October was fully into mushroom season in this part of France, Maggie wasn't surprised to see one table groaning under mounds of every possible variety of mushroom.

Grace charged ahead to the tables that appeared to be loaded down with linens as Maggie wandered over to the tables groaning with vintage dinnerware and crystal. She touched a finger to the rim of a delicate Spode ewer with rose buds painted on it and her throat felt thick and scratchy.

Instantly she recalled the three weeks she'd spent in Atlanta last summer helping her mother clear out the family home so that Elspeth and Maggie's niece Nicole could move into their new smaller place.

The whole process had been gut-wrenching but Maggie knew she'd had it easier than most people since she wasn't doing the job *and* grieving the loss of a loved one at the same time as so many people were forced to do.

All of the Newberry family china—every piece that had glistened on multiple table settings over the years through holiday after holiday—was as familiar to Maggie as her own face. She remembered all the years of family get-togethers and the happy days when her sister was still alive and her father still remembered who they all were. She remembered the whole family gathered around the family heirloom china for festival Christmas toddies and later singing carols around the baby grand piano.

The thirty-thousand dollar piano was eventually donated to the local women's shelter when Maggie's brother Ben finally gave up trying to find a buyer for it. Nobody wanted their family treasures.

Nobody in the family and nobody outside it.

Ben was divorced and living in a one-bedroom condo. Elise was dead. Maggie lived across the ocean.

That summer Maggie spent downsizing her parents' home marked the official end of family dinners, festive holiday meals, Thanksgiving and football weekends. All of it was gone in the time it took to cart the dishes and linens and crystal out the door where it went for pennies on the dollar to the Buckhead junkman or straight to the curb to be picked up by any vaguely interested neighbor before the garbage truck came.

Blinking tears away, Maggie turned from the vintage dishes before her and hoped very much that whoever had eaten off these dishes and celebrated graduations and weddings and Christmases with these champagne glasses had relinquished them because they were ready to pack up and tour the world with their lover.

But she seriously doubted that was the case.

"Darling! Did you see the Brussels lace?" Grace hurried over to Maggie, her face flushed with excitement. A long swath of

Swiss tatted lace lay in her arms. "It's exquisite. The notecard at the table said it was made in Zurich *by nuns.*"

"That's cool," Maggie said, forcing the image out of her head of her family's heirlooms sitting on the street curb.

"And did you see the furniture? There's a Savannah tufted chaise lounge in the most divine blush silk you've ever seen. They're asking six hundred for it. I think I'll offer three."

Maggie followed Grace over to the furniture which sat on wooden platforms in front of a lower section of Roman stone seats. She couldn't help looking up and wondering what the prisoners slated for execution had thought from this very same viewpoint. Were the spectators laughing? Encouraging?

"What do you think, darling?" Grace asked as she stood in front of a stack of quilted padded headboards.

"Is this a chaise lounge?" Maggie asked.

"No, silly. We haven't gotten there yet. What do you think about the headboards?"

"Don't all your beds already have headboards?"

Maggie knew Laurent had given Grace money for this shopping trip. She also knew that Grace had yet to pay a single month's rent on *Dormir*. She certainly didn't have the money to buy headboards she didn't need. But Maggie bit her tongue. This was Laurent's project. One of many.

Grace laughed. "Oh, you're hopeless. Where is Brad? It's often good to get a man's point of view."

It wasn't until that moment that Maggie realized she hadn't seen Jemmy for at least the last quarter of an hour. The moment they walked into the amphitheater she'd reassured herself that there was no mischief or harm he could possibly come to in here.

After all, except for Claude, Jacky, Grace and Brad, and the twenty or so vendors standing at their tables and booths straightening their wares and getting ready for the public to be let in there was nobody else in the place.

"I'm going to tell Claude to hold this back for me," Grace said, waving to Claude where he stood with Jacky by a long table of incense and North African spices.

"Where's Jemmy?" Maggie said as she turned full circle, scanning the arena interior, looking for the quick movements of a ten-year-old boy.

But Grace only had eyes for the antiques and treasures she'd come to find.

"I'm sure he's here some place," Grace said absently as she knelt to examine the fabric on a floral vanity chair.

Maggie turned and hurried toward the entrance they'd come through. All the other entrances were blocked. She climbed the nearest stairs which took her to the first tier of stone seats but high enough to get a good view of the entire interior of the Roman ruin.

Jemmy was nowhere to be seen.

To continue reading, order *Murder in Arles, Book 13 of the Maggie Newberry Mysteries.*

ABOUT THE AUTHOR

USA TODAY Bestselling Author Susan Kiernan-Lewis is the author of *The Maggie Newberry Mysteries,* the post-apocalyptic thriller series *The Irish End Games, The Mia Kazmaroff Mysteries, The Stranded in Provence Mysteries, The Claire Baskerville Mysteries,* and *The Savannah Time Travel Mysteries.*
Visit www.susankiernanlewis.com or follow Author Susan Kiernan-Lewis on Facebook.

Books by Susan Kiernan-Lewis
The Maggie Newberry Mysteries
Murder in the South of France
Murder à la Carte
Murder in Provence
Murder in Paris
Murder in Aix
Murder in Nice
Murder in the Latin Quarter
Murder in the Abbey
Murder in the Bistro
Murder in Cannes

Murder in Grenoble
Murder in the Vineyard
Murder in Arles
Murder in Marseille
Murder in St-Rémy
Murder à la Mode
Murder in Avignon
Murder in the Lavender
Murder in Mont St-Michel
Murder in the Village
Murder in St-Tropez
Murder in Grasse
Murder in Monaco
Murder in Montmartre
Murder in the Villa
A Provençal Christmas: A Short Story
A Thanksgiving in Provence
Laurent's Kitchen

About the Author

The Claire Baskerville Mysteries
Déjà Dead
Death by Cliché
Dying to be French
Ménage à Murder
Killing it in Paris
Murder Flambé
Deadly Faux Pas
Toujours Dead
Murder in the Christmas Market
Deadly Adieu
Murdering Madeleine
Murder Carte Blanche
Death à la Drumstick
Murder Mon Amour

The Savannah Time Travel Mysteries
Killing Time in Georgia
Scarlett Must Die

The Stranded in Provence Mysteries
Parlez-Vous Murder?
Crime and Croissants
Accent on Murder
A Bad Éclair Day
Croak, Monsieur!
Death du Jour
Murder Très Gauche
Wined and Died
Murder, Voila!
A French Country Christmas
Fromage to Eternity

The Irish End Games

Free Falling
Going Gone
Heading Home
Blind Sided
Rising Tides
Cold Comfort
Never Never
Wit's End
Dead On
White Out
Black Out
End Game

The Mia Kazmaroff Mysteries
Reckless
Shameless
Breathless
Heartless
Clueless
Ruthless

Ella Out of Time
Swept Away
Carried Away
Stolen Away

Made in the USA
Columbia, SC
15 December 2024